Born in Ice

by

Linda LaRoque

Born in Ice

COPYRIGHT © 2011 by Linda LaRoque

Published by *L.G. Smith Books*
Cover Art by *Diana Carlile*
http://www.designingdiana.blogspot.com

Publishing History
First Edition, 2011
Digital ISBN 978-0-9893792-6-7
Print ISBN 978-0-9893792-7-4

Published in the United States of America

Acknowledgements

This story wouldn't have been possible without the help of several individuals. First, my son Brad, a submariner, whose knowledge on the undersea environment and nautical information proved invaluable. Second, Terran, a sci-fic author, skilled in the construction of alternate worlds, for helping to bring the undersea city of Abyss to life. Third, my critique partners and fellow authors, Ciara Gold, Rebecca Giallongo, and Autumn Shelley for making this story the best it could be. And last but not least, my husband Larry for his timeless dedication to reading, editing, and offering encouragement.

Though I used a variety of references, please note that the actual effects of global warming described in this book are fictional and strictly the result of my imagination.

References: Golden Poison Frog
http://en.wikipedia.org/wiki/Golden_Poison_Frog
Global Warming May Alter Atlantic Currents Study Says
http://news.nationalgeographic.com/news/2005/06/0627_050
627_oceancurre nt.html
Amazon Rainforest
http://en.wikipedia.org/wiki/Amazon_Rainforest Brazil map
and map of Brazil and information page
http://www.worldatlas.com/webimage/countrys/samerica/brl
arge.htm
5 Deadliest Effects of Global Warming
http://www.environmentalgraffiti.com/sciencetech/5-
deadliest-effects-of- global-warming/276

Linda LaRoque

Prologue

2080 A.D., St. John's, Newfoundland

"You don't love me else you'd take me too. Nana can watch Jonathan. You just love him more."

"That's not true, honey. You know that." Zana tried to cuddle the girl, but she'd have none of it.

Her daughter shoved away and screamed, "I hate you."

Zana looked up and pleaded with the heavens for help. As she stood, she heard Gran's soothing voice from the other room. "Child, you know you don't mean that. You've got to be big and help Mama. She's doing all she can to provide for us all by herself." What would she do without the older woman?

"But…Jonathan always gets to go."

"I know honey, and that's my fault. I can't keep up with the little bugger. You're my big girl. You can help old Gran get around when Mama's not here."

Leaving Katy at home always made Zana feel guilty, and today was no different. But no way could she manage both kids at the store. At six years old, Katy wasn't a problem for Nana to watch. Jonathan was a different story. He was too active and wore the older woman out.

She worried the child might suffer from serious emotional problems. Not that she blamed her. After losing her father to an avalanche, having every moment of her life dictated by the elements had to be hard on an energetic child.

How had they come to such a sad state and would it continue to get worse before it got better? Since the 1990's, alerts had been issued about global warming. Suddenly, in 2045 warnings became fact. One of the sea's conveyer belts stopped working, causing a chain reaction, affecting others and throwing the Earth's weather patterns out of balance. Would nature be able to reset the ocean currents back on a normal course or were they in for even worse conditions?

Not knowing what was in store for them terrified her. It was all she could do to keep the four of them fed. Fortunately she worked from home as a computer programmer, but if she were to lose her job... She shuddered. *Don't buy trouble, Zana.*

Lifting Jonathan, she passed through the automatic sealing dead-air space to the garage. Though she'd turned on the exhaust system earlier and started the Polar Excursion to let it warm, the moisture from her breath formed ice crystals in the air. Even in the garage, the thermometer read minus twenty-nine degrees Celsius.

A squirming Jonathan babbled, "Go bye-bye," as she locked him in his car seat. The baby was fully dressed under his protective outerwear designed for particularly low temperatures. His clunky gloves kept him from removing the knitted facemask that covered his sensitive skin. She probably looked as strange as he did in her suit, the hood trimmed with silver fake fur to match her face covering.

With her remote control, she turned off the exhaust and pushed the door opener. She backed out and turned down the hill. The big tires on the powerful all-terrain vehicle designed especially for extremely cold weather, traversed over the snow and ice like an Aspen skier on snow skies. The darkened windows cut the stunning glare from the sun on snow and ice. Just before his accident, David bought the truck for her. He didn't want her and the kids out in something unreliable. It had been a Godsend since his death. It could and would continue to operate in all kinds of conditions, giving her independence she valued in getting the supplies they needed. Other families weren't as lucky, and she helped them when she could.

It had been two years since David died, buried under a mountain of snow while trying to rescue a family whose home was covered under an avalanche. The hill behind the house literally slid down on top burying them all. Twenty men perished that day as well as the six-member family inside. Zana feared the cold, ice, and snow would be the death of them all before long.

The trip into town never ceased to make her nervous. It was always a relief to get supplies and return home. Today was no different. Her dread eased as they neared the four-lane bridge that crossed a small waterway. The road wove close to the drop-off into the bay, and the snow-covered hills on the opposite side rose majestically toward the sky. In five minutes they'd have left this eerie pass behind.

Her heart stopped at the rumble in the distance and then pounded in her chest when the carpet of white moved. *No, no, no!* She stomped the accelerator in an attempt to outrun the avalanche. *Oh, God, please let me make it.* The vehicle rushed forward, and snow hit the road behind her. A nervous giggle escaped her lips. *She'd made it.* A gigantic wave of white moved under and over them blocking everything from view. They were thrust forward as if from a cannon. The last words she heard were Jonathan's terrified scream, "Mamaaa!" And her last thought was, *Oh Katy. I'm so sorry, sweetheart.*

One

2155 A.D. Atlantic Ocean

"Hey, Skipper, check out that small berg east ninety degrees. I see something red."

In the early morning light, Brock Callahan steered his salvage craft, *Retriever*, on a southerly course forty miles east of the coast of Barbados. They were over a thousand miles from their home base in Brazil and were in desperate need of a find—anything useable the sea coughed up from the melting ice flows. He had other means of income, but his crew depended on what they pulled from the sea for much of their livelihood.

Brock squinted in the direction Pepe, his junior crewmember, indicated. A mild mist hovered over the ocean's calm surface obstructing his view, plus his eyes weren't as keen as the kid's. Brock bellowed into the intercom circuit, "All stop."

He flipped his infrared eye down from his headset. He trained it off the port side and focused by blinking his eye as he searched the icebergs floating in the distance. The boy had sharp eyes. That's why he paid him more than the rest of the crew. The kid could find a diamond in a solid block of ice.

A hundred years ago ice would've been an oddity in this area. Now it was a common occurrence. Global warming had poured fresh water into the sea diluting the salt balance and disrupting the conveyer belts of the ocean's floor. This action upset the equilibrium of the north and south poles and brought about numerous environmental changes on Earth. Sheets of ice covered the northern most part of North America, deserts formed where previously vegetation thrived, water mass increased, and land mass decreased.

The slight breeze dissipated the mist for a moment; light glanced off something red beneath the frost's surface. Damned if Pepe wasn't right on again. It could be anything, but if they were lucky, it'd be some type of all-terrain vehicle. The bright red color was a good sign. For years, due to the sheet of ice and snow covering so much land, all vehicles sported vivid colored paint—primarily red. Though technology had improved over the past one hundred years of lethal weather, vehicles were scarce. Due to the small number of factories able to produce them, they were far too expensive for the average Joe. He'd be able to sell such a find for a nice sum.

Adrenaline shot through his system. His heart rate increased in anticipation of a valuable item for retrieval. Hopefully they wouldn't be disappointed. In this line of work it happened all too often.

Pepe, a gangly teenager with a slim build and feet too big for his body, fidgeted, struggled to contain his excitement as he waited for Brock's confirmation. Brock wanted to laugh out loud at the boy's eagerness but had difficulty not rubbing his hands in anticipation himself. He was as excited as the kid. He clapped Pepe on the shoulder. "Looks like you've done it again. Let's move in for a closer look."

Pepe grinned, pride stretching his young face. Brock hid his smile. Damn, he was attached to the boy and proud as all get out of his skills. He was a fine crewmember and the younger brother Brock had always wanted.

He flipped the eyepiece back behind his ear. "Luke, take the helm. Give me a fifteen-degree right rudder, steer course zero-nine-zero. Pull in fast, but ease back at one-hundred-eighty yards."

"Aye, on it."

The durable craft, fashioned after a Coast Guard Cutter designed for speed on the surface, raced across the water hardly leaving a wake.

Eighty feet long, the craft housed twenty-two crewmembers comfortably, more if necessary. The Command Deck stood three stories, with a kitchen, infirmary, and sleeping quarters on the bottom two. Below decks, the large hold stowed cargo. Aft on the poop deck, a small submersible sat ready for undersea exploration if the need arose.

In less than ten minutes, they stopped close enough for Brock to use the laser chipper. Brock jogged down to the poop deck. Several of the crew had the ice chipper ready. The targeted berg was small compared to the others. Careful not to damage their find, he aimed the chipper at the outer edges of the ice floe and fired. Ice and snow flew in all directions as if an explosive had been activated.

All hands waited, attention riveted on the hopeful prize, as he worked. The loud click-click-click of the chipper disappeared as it dissipated over the calm water.

Ten minutes later, the sun glared off what appeared to be a chrome bumper. When the ice fell away to fully reveal the nose of the ATV, a roar of approval went up from the crew and drowned out the noise of the boat's engines.

Brock grinned like a fool at the high fiving and back slapping of his men. It was about time they had something to celebrate about. He returned to revealing their prize. With short rapid bursts, he cleared as much ice as possible from around the vehicle and the front bumper so tow chains could be attached. He left enough ice for the vehicle to remain buoyant, so it would float—hopefully—all the way home. Without bringing it aboard, they'd pull it home behind the Retriever.

Luke urged the craft closer to the target. Pepe appeared at Brock's side, fully dressed in an insulated wet suit. Brock secured a line around the kid's waist. Pepe stepped to the rail and jumped the few feet to the piece of ice. He steadied himself and bent to study the exposed portion of the vehicle.

"Hot damn, Skipper. It's an early model Polar Excursion." Pepe threw back his head and howled. "We've struck gold."

Cheers rose from the craft. They'd party tonight. Metal and engine parts of any kind were at a premium in Abyss, but a usable vehicle made to traverse ice and snow was too nice to break down. It would sell in one of the regions to the north for more than it would bring disassembled.

It had been months since they'd found anything of value, and his crew had grown nervous. They needed products to sell or barter for necessities. With winter not far away and the failure of the ocean's conveyer current systems to work properly, Earth's inhabitants needed to stock up in preparation for whatever freak weather occurred. Trade with the undersea city of

Abyss provided citizens of their home base, Refuge, with medical supplies and manufactured goods they sorely needed. They'd become accustomed to modern conveniences—solar panels, appliances, and soft goods—things not produced in their community.

The shrill scream of the alarm split the air, its pulsing blast a constant reminder of danger. Luke's voice sounded over the intercom. "Contact. Pirate vessel off the port bow, bearing three-four-seven. Closing rapidly at twenty knots."

"Shit," growled Brock. Probably that damned rogue Rafael. Not that the Cuban was the only pirate to roam these waters, but this particular one took excessive joy in stealing from him. Brock didn't doubt for a minute that Rafael would shoot him in the back without an ounce of remorse. Rafael's hatred, a festering sore, grew worse each time they met on the water. The man blamed him for taking Marta from him and for her death.

One day Brock would have to kill his nemesis. Today might be the day.

His well-seasoned crew scrambled to their battle stations. Arms were manned, ready for word from him. Pepe had one tow chain attached and dragged the additional one Brock tossed over to add extra security.

Brock yelled into the intercom. "Prepare to cast off."

Shots zinged overhead sending shards of ice into the air. Brock's men returned fire as Pepe dodged, stumbled, and went down to his knees. Brock's heart jumped into his throat. *Damn, not the boy.*

He jumped across the small expanse of water. The berg wobbled threatening to toss him into the icy sea.

He braced to maintain his footing, and then grabbed Pepe by the seat of his suit and the scruff of his neck. Two crewmen stood at the rail ready to catch the nearly unconscious young man. With a heave, he tossed him to the waiting crewmembers.

An explosion burst on the port side sending water thirty feet into the air, rocking the craft and the ice floe. He almost pitched head first into the water. Damn, that was too close. Pushing off from the ice, he made the jump across to the craft. "Put a hole in the motherfucker, Digger."

Thirty seconds later, the shell hit the pirate vessel. It burst into a ball of fire. Brock didn't find pleasure in killing, but if *Retriever* was overtaken, he doubted Rafael or any other buccaneer would spare their lives. Hell, pirating was a dangerous profession.

Brock picked up the intercom mike. "All speed ahead, Luke. Get us out of here."

"Aye-aye, sir," boomed from the exterior speakers.

The engines roared to life as Luke accelerated. Brock gripped the rail to brace himself as they shot forward. Three crafts were in pursuit.

Within seconds, *Retriever* had pulled ahead and was out of the line of fire of the pirates. His superior craft had no difficulty out distancing their attackers. The buccaneer's outdated weapons couldn't compare to what his craft carried, but he wasn't taking any chances. *Retriever* was his pride and joy. He thanked his lucky stars his father had the foresight to purchase the salvage ship with his grandfather's ill-gotten gains. The Callahans had once been pirates, but no more.

Brock returned to the control deck and stood at a viewing console watching the ice encrusted red vehicle move with them on the ocean's surface. The tow chains remained flexed so he knew their prize was safe. Yet, it slowed them. As soon as possible, he'd haul it aboard.

Except for the occasional click and ding of equipment, an uneasy silence settled on the deck. The crew remained at their battle stations until he gave the order to stand down. He'd keep them on alert awhile longer. When it came to his men and craft, he didn't take chances.

He stared at the Excursion as, encased in the berg, it dragged and dipped in and out of the water much like a weighted inner tube behind a ski boat. Would they find bodies inside? It had happened before, more times than he could count. A shiver ran up his spine. A premonition of dread chilled him. Why this time was different, he didn't know, but he knew without a doubt his life was about to change.

Hell, ruminating wasn't accomplishing a thing. He needed to check on Pepe, not stand around and ponder. He strode downstairs to sickbay to find Digger bent over the boy. Brock knelt at Digger's side and together they searched for tears in Pepe's suit to locate his injury. The protective gear fit like a glove, thus preventing excessive bleeding. Finding his wound before removing the suit would avoid causing more pain and damage to the area. It was difficult to locate so must be small. Pepe stirred and groaned. "What happened? Am I shot, Digger?"

"We're checking, kid. Doubt it though. Not a big enough hole in you."

At the mention of a hole, Pepe's eyes rolled up into his head. Good. That'd make their job easier. The two of them unzipped the rubber outfit, tugged, and peeled it down to expose Pepe's chest. Damn, the insulated garment fit like a second skin making it tough to remove.

Digger rolled Pepe to his side and examined his back. "Here it is, Cal."

Sure enough, a small hole below his left shoulder blade oozed blood. Digger gently probed the wound. A shard of ice protruded, a common injury in their business when uncovering salvage encased in ice. This one was larger, the size of a small dagger.

Digger reached over and popped Brock on the shoulder with the flat of his hand. "He'll be just fine, Cal."

Brock nodded. Relief washed over him. He'd never forgive himself if the boy were seriously hurt. "At least his suit gave him some protection." Ice could be sharper than any knife, and without the protective suit, Pepe might have been dead.

"I'll take good care of him while you get into dry clothes."

Brock looked at the scarred face of one of his top men. Digger had been wounded more times than Brock could count, yet mended quickly. The crew nicknamed him Digger, as it seemed every move he made got him closer to his grave. He was the only crewmember to call him Cal, his shortened last name. They had a long history together and the title Skipper or Captain didn't roll off Digger's lips comfortably. He was a good friend, one Brock trusted. If the others resented the familiarity, they didn't let on.

Brock nodded and stood.

Digger lifted Pepe and stretched him out on a fold-down berth. Jonas, one of the finest snipers Brock had ever seen, joined Digger. They quickly, but painstakingly removed Pepe's suit. Later it would be repaired. Valuable, it would be restored many times before being discarded.

When they had him naked and wrapped in wool blankets, Brock turned to tend to his own needs. As he changed, he watched them clean the wound and apply a dressing. The wound was deep and the boy would need antibiotics. Though the ice was clean, he didn't cut corners when it came to his men's health. They were his crew, their loyalty and skills important, but they were also extended family, like brothers.

Once dry and warm again, he returned to the con deck and approached Luke at the helm. "Set our course for home."

Luke frowned. "Pepe will get better care in Abyss."

"Yeah, I know, but the wound isn't serious, and our pirate friends have more than one craft. They might try to screw with us." No one knew the whereabouts of their undersea berth near their home. They'd be able to safely unload their patient and their cargo.

They had a small hospital in their modest community of Refuge, one that could take care of the bulk of situations. When their technology wasn't enough, patients were transported to Abyss where expertise and equipment had no limits.

"What's our status, Luke?"

"We lost our pursuers ten minutes ago, Captain."

"Good. Let's stop and pull the vehicle aboard. We'll make better time that way."

"Aye, sir."

Thirty minutes later the vehicle was aboard and

secured to the deck alongside their submersible. Brock jogged back up top and stopped beside Luke. "Keep several men on the lookout for at least another hour."

"Roger, sir."

Hopefully the pirates had given up and turned back. Just in case, they'd remain on alert. The results could spell disaster if outsiders, especially Rafael and his bunch, located their secured dock.

After checking the controls, Brock left the deck and trotted toward sick bay. Before he reached the open door, he heard Pepe grousing. "This is stupid. I'm fine. Let me up from here."

Digger, jaw rigid, stormed from the room. Brock held out his arms to avoid a collision.

"If the kid doesn't shut up," Luke muttered, "I'm gonna pop him in the jaw."

Brock grinned, turned and headed back in the direction he'd come. The kid would be fine. Brock had other issues to worry about.

~ * ~

Eight hours later, *Retriever* entered the heavily guarded cove near Refuge. Powered doors, camouflaged with dense foliage, swung open. Brock eased his boat into the well-lit passageway. The tunnel was hidden from view. His men and a few citizens of Refuge knew of its existence. The bay door closed, and lights lit their way, winking off behind them as they traveled forward a half mile to reach their dock and well-sealed workshop. Located under a rock encrusted mountain, a freight lift carried crew and cargo up into a garage in Refuge. The grotto was the dock's only access.

A vehicle waited to transport a now asleep Pepe to

the hospital. He'd succumbed to the pain and asked for more pain medicine.

While their docking crew secured the craft, Brock, Digger, Luke, and Jonas used a winch to lift and move the vehicle onto the platform. With a high pressure water hose, they knocked away the chunks of ice that had kept the Excursion afloat. Silent, each with his own thoughts, they stood and studied the vehicle they'd salvaged. What would they find inside?

The vehicle was a self-sealing model, one that upon impact sealed the interior from water and gases, including oxygen. The purpose was to preserve any life-form inside. On occasion, individuals found in bergs were thawed, and life resuscitated.

In 2065 when widespread temperatures dropped to dangerous levels, a drug was developed to help protect body tissues, under certain conditions, from freezing. Individuals five years and older took a monthly dose of the preparation. The medication gave cells the ability to be frozen and thawed with minimal damage. Of course, there were exceptions, cases where the procedure failed, but the success rate was over fifty percent.

Lost in thought, Brock started at Luke's question.

"Do you know the location of the deactivation switch, Skipper?"

"Yeah." Brock walked around, peering inside the darkened windows. He couldn't see much, but a shadow in front gave him pause. "Call the hospital, and have them send a hermetic pod in case we find a body." The container would help preserve life if it was present. He was nervous as hell. Always was when they pulled one of these babies out of the water. It was a constant shock to see a human, frozen and resembling a figure in a wax museum display, but finding bodies without hope for survival haunted him.

"They've got one on the way."

He reached under the driver's side fender well. The small box was easy to locate. He twisted the lever, opened the container, and pushed the button. A flurry of clicks sounded around the car.

Brock opened the door. A blast of cold air whooshed out. The faint smell of death washed over him filling him with dread. He staggered back for a moment. The first thing he noticed was the child's seat in the back. Empty. He drew near again and saw the driver's seat was reclined. A body lay curled on its side holding a bundle close.

His voice gruff, he called, "Bring us a light. Luke, open the doors on the other side."

Digger held the light as Brock leaned in to look at the bowed figure on the seat. From the person's figure and profile, there was no denying the delicate features beneath the mask belonged to a woman. She was dressed from head to toe in a silvery grey snowsuit with fur-trimmed matching boots. Fur as soft and as gray as a dove's wing edged her parka making her appear even more ethereal. Dark lashes brushed her face covering, similar to a ski mask, made with cut-outs for her eyes, nose, and mouth.

He carefully pulled the blanket away from the bundle and groaned at the mummified features of what had once been a child. *Oh, God, no. Not a baby.*

Two

The men were quiet, the scene taking some of the joy from their find. Each appeared grateful when the pod arrived to take their minds off the two bodies. Without talking, the medical team moved the pod closer. Brock carefully lifted the shrunken infant now lying loose in its mother's arms and handed it to a medical attendant. Then he picked up the woman and placed her stiff body in the container. The medic returned the baby to her arms, and the technicians closed the lid and set the controls.

An hour later, after making contact with Abyss's hospital for instructions, the baby was taken from its mother by Refuge's medical team and placed in an airtight coffin. The woman's clothes had been cut away, and she lay naked under a thermal blanket, the pod controlling the slow increase in oxygen level and temperature. The hospital at Refuge wasn't equipped to handle a rebirth. Retriever had been refueled and supplies brought aboard for the trip to Abyss, the closest underwater city, and home of one of the most technologically advanced medical centers.

They were ten hours away from the underwater city and every man and woman aboard the craft was anxious, waiting for a response from their passenger—any sign to indicate she would live. When on break, they found excuses to stop by.

Brock moved to peer down at her, watching for a small flare of a nostril, a twitch of an eye. She lay curled on her side and would remain that way until her muscles eased enough for her to turn on her own. He couldn't help but wonder how long she'd been in the ice. His heart ached for her and her loss of her baby. It would be hard for her to deal with if she lived. As a parent himself, he could empathize with her loss. He couldn't bear it if something happened to Shelia.

Luke appeared at his side. "She's a beauty, isn't she?"

There was no denying that fact. "Yes, she is. I've never seen such unusual coloring." Her dark hair was now liberally streaked with white, whether due to her experience or a hereditary trait, he didn't know, but he bet she wasn't a day over forty. With her light olive skin tone, he suspected her eyes were brown, but he'd yet to see them. For all he knew, her coloring could have to do with being frozen. This was Brock's first time with a rebirth. Usually he sent Luke and several others to accompany the doctor with the person to Abyss, but for some reason he refused to examine, he'd insisted on going along. It may have been the presence of the child. Or was it something about this particular woman that fascinated him?

An hour later, he was back by her side, listening as the doctor explained to his nurse, evidently a new recruit, what the woman's awakening would be like, if she lived. "As her body temperature changes, she'll suffer severe pain. Narcotics will help a great deal but they must be used carefully or they could kill her." The short, skinny doctor shook his shaggy mop of gray hair. "I'm glad I won't be around to watch her recovery. One rebirth was enough for me."

Well, hell. Damned discouraging words to hear coming from the mouth of a medicine man. What a horrible fate for such a pretty woman—shit, for anyone—human or animal. Hands clenched, he growled, "Dr. Boone, are you saying this woman is going to be in constant pain?" For some reason, he wanted to pound the man on his head.

"That's exactly what I'm saying. But it will ease in time. It's possible too, Abyss has some new drug that will ease her rebirth, or perhaps they've advanced their use of nanotechnology to include cryo-therapy." The doctor propped his hands on his hips and tilted his head back to look him in the eye. Since Brock was six-foot-four, it was a good distance. "And don't glare at me. You know we'll do all we can for her."

Brock nodded, turned and stalked to the controls to relieve the man on duty. He gripped the edge of the control panel and blew out his pent-up breath. What had prompted him to come along on this trip? He should be home with Shelia. The nine-year-old minx would be driving his housekeeper, Darlene, crazy by now. The child was too smart, too precocious for her own good. She needed a more challenging school, but he wouldn't send her away from Refuge to some place like Abyss. He'd not have his child exposed to the life-style there. When she became an adult, he'd have no say, but for now, Shelia stayed with him. She needed someone other than Darlene with her when he was away, a smart person capable of broadening Shelia's learning. Maybe he could find a tutor.

A whimper echoed through the microphone inside the pod.

Dr. Boone called, "I need some help over here."

Brock tapped the shoulder of one of the crew and nodded toward the controls. The man jumped up and quickly took over.

Brock stood behind Dr. Boone and peered over his shoulder. "What can I do?"

The moan turned to a wail as the woman twitched, trying to move.

"Place your hands on her shoulder and hip and hold her still if you can."

Brock hesitated for just a second, fearing he'd hurt her. Taking a deep breath to calm himself, he inserted his hands inside the tubing which, ending in gloves, were designed for just this purpose. "Okay, Boone."

"Be careful. Don't apply much pressure. Her tissues and organs are very sensitive."

Her wail turned into a deep keening that sent chills up Brock's spine. The cabin was quiet but for Doctor Boone's instructions and the woman's cries of pain—the peripheral silence deafening in contrast.

Brock nodded and curved his large hands gently over the woman's shoulder and hip. She screamed and he jerked back.

"Hold her still. The pain can't be helped. She's fragile. Won't be but a moment now." Dr. Boone had shaved a small space at the top of her skull earlier. The pod was just below the doctor's eye level making it easier for him to view his patient. Through a small compartment, he could reach far enough inside to give her an injection. Five minutes later, she was still, but continued to moan.

"Where the hell is your staff, Doctor?"

"Calm yourself, Captain. Even we medical folks

have to eat and relieve ourselves on occasion." He shrugged and shook his head. "I didn't expect the pain killer to wear off so fast or I'd have kept one of them here."

"Sorry. I'm not usually so caustic. This is my first rebirth."

"Haven't attended that many myself so I understand your discomfort." He closed the medical cabinet and turned to Brock. "Keep your hands on her awhile longer, Brock. Human touch might offer her comfort. The records found with her indicate her name is Zana Forrester of Newfoundland. Talk to her. I'm sure she can hear what's going on around her but I doubt she understands what's being said. Her reality is likely similar to experiencing a bad dream, one accompanied by agony."

Brock looked over to the smaller container at her feet where they'd placed her baby. Lord, what did you say to someone who'd lost so much? Her baby and who knows what else. What if she left a husband behind, other children?

He cleared his throat. "Uh, Zana, this is your Captain speaking." Chuckles and guffaws sounded around the room. He tossed his crew a dirty look and they shut up. Unable to resist, a chortle rumbled from his chest. "Well, now, in truth, I am the captain of this boat, the *Retriever*. You've been rescued from an iceberg and we're rushing you to one of the finest hospitals for care."

Her eyes flew open, beautiful hazel, more green than brown, her expression one of stark terror. He leaned closer. Her gaze probed his face for answers, and then she struggled to loosen her invisible restraints.

"Boone, I've upset her. Get over here."

From his elbow, Boone whispered, "What'd you say, man?"

"Just that she's been rescued and we're taking her in for care."

"Ah, she wants to know about her babe." Boone elbowed him in the rib and lowered his voice. "Tell her the child is being cared for while I put some drops in her eyes."

Brock looked at the older man as if he were nuts. He couldn't lie to the woman about something so vital to her.

"Do it, man. It's the only humane thing to do."

Finally Brock nodded and turned his gaze back to the woman's. He patted her hip awkwardly. "Not to worry, Zana. Your child is being treated, too. You're in a medical pod undergoing the beginnings of re...uh...careful monitoring. We're rushing you to Abyss where you'll both receive the finest medical care available."

She stopped struggling, blinked several times as the medicinal drops splashed across her irises, and then closed her eyes. Fat droplets slid from beneath her lids. Mesmerized, he watched as the one from her left eye ran toward her nose, then down her cheek to drop onto the bedding. She lay quietly, still curled on her side. He released a sigh of relief that she'd relaxed. Unable to resist, he let his now cold hand slide back and forth on her hip. The caress wasn't sexual, merely a comforting touch meant to sooth. As he carefully removed his hands from the pod, he glanced down to find her watching him. Her striking hazel gaze stared into the depths of his soul.

He froze. For a minute he feared she could read his mind. Did she believe him or think he lied? Poor woman, he doubted his words were absorbed by her consciousness, but if they were and it gave her any peace, he hoped she believed him.

His older sister's suffering at the loss of her child had been terrible to watch. Distraught, unable to move forward with life, she'd taken her own a month later. She'd called to tell him goodbye. By the time he reached her, he was too late. She'd slit her wrists. Deidre didn't have a strong constitution and losing her child pushed her over the edge. Delia, his baby sister believed she could whip the world single-handed but an accident had taken her life. An ache closed around his heart and he shoved the memory of Deidra and Delia from his mind. He hoped Zana Forrester could hold up to the hardships life handed out.

When her lids dropped, he sighed with relief and though he went back to work, his gaze often strayed to the woman and the team that hovered nearby.

They were still two hours out of Abyss and though Dr. Boone gave their patient two more injections, she moaned softly the entire trip with several bouts of hysterical keening. Her body had relaxed some and she'd been eased onto her back. Her knees were still slightly raised. The doctor had applied restraints to keep her from thrashing about. Every hour, Boone added lubrication drops to her eyes...

Brock was a nervous wreck, out of his element. He'd rather face gunfire, danger of any kind, than watch someone suffer, especially a woman. This would definitely be his last rebirth delivery. Why he'd felt so compelled to take part in this one he didn't know. Yet, he did. This woman intrigued him. He was attracted to her. He snorted. *Get over it, old man. She's not for you.* His track record with women ran from bad to worse. A terrible marriage and now he'd stupidly become involved with his housekeeper. Nope. Love wasn't in the books for him. Women he loved ended up dead. Guilt nagged at him more often than not. Disgusted with his thoughts, he turned his attention to their destination.

Abyss from above was a wonderful site. Each time Retriever approached the colony, it was difficult to take his eyes off the evolving site. To think an undersea city could actually be built was astonishing, to see it—mind-boggling. A large, round agricultural pod provided an umbrella for the smaller pods. Closer to the ocean's surface, solar panels soaked up and stored energy from the sun for plant and animal growth. There, fields of crops grew, and other fields spread out where dairy cows and cattle could graze. Close by were meat packing plants and factories to prepare foods for transport.

Below it was a central circular pod of living quarters, with shopping areas, restaurants, and parks. Arms branched off to smaller pods that housed entertainment areas, educational facilities, medical services, manufacturing plants, banking and governmental departments.

Theirs was a no-currency system. Citizens lived by a point arrangement, all managed by small handheld computers. The chits they earned paid for their basic needs and any extra could be saved for pleasure. Apartments were allotted on job status and a person's position in the community. The Governor and other dignitaries had plush, big apartments; lowly workers a mere cubicle.

In Brock's opinion, it was a disgusting way to live. No way would he allow someone else to have that much control over his life. In Refuge, some points were used, but they also had the old American dollar and his people could pay or barter for their needs. Residents could live in one of the caves or adobes left by the previous residents or collect wood to build their own.

Most importantly, they could love and mate with whom they chose, not some pre-selected individual. Due to space limits and to prevent problems typical during the teen years, children in Abyss were paired at an early age. In adolescence, small amounts of pheromones kept the pair interested until they were old enough to marry. Larger doses were administered regularly for the remainder of their lives. This practice eliminated dating rituals, thus preventing conflicts common among societies that have love- marriages. It also kept couples faithful and happy in their relationships.

Their lives in Refuge weren't perfect, but they were their own. He'd never subject himself to Abyss's barbaric customs and he held little respect for those who did.

Retriever sailed into the emergency bay at the hospital. A medical team, led by Dr. Jonas Bartholomew, waited for them. Shoving his way aboard, Bartholomew gave the patient a quick examination and transferred her to a more technologically advanced pod. Nurses inserted an IV into her scalp. Why the hell hadn't Boone done so rather than having to inject her so many times?

Boone handed over Zana Forrester's medical charts to one of the techs and briefly talked with Bartholomew. This would be Brock's last chance to see their passenger. He stood beside the pod listening to the wheeze and click as oxygen was measured and released.

Goodbye, Zana Forrester. May you find happiness in your new home. Most do, just us oddballs who are looking for something else, who don't. Brock grinned. He and his group from Refuge were a mishmash of people, most with nothing in common except a desire for freedom. Wishing he could reach out and stroke the soft skin of her cheek, he looked one last time and turned his attention to Luke. Time to go, before he got sentimental and made a fool out of himself.

~ * ~

Zana's eyes opened and she blinked several times. She tried to focus through the drug-induced haze on the source of the voices near her speaking in soft tones.

"Are we going to stay overnight, Cal, or head home? The crew is dog tired."

"If they'll let us stay in one of the hotels, I'll cover the costs. We've had a harrowing twenty-four hours. Of course, the men will have to sleep in four-hour shifts. I want half of the crew onboard *Retriever* in case of trouble."

Something was horribly wrong. She needed to move but couldn't. Her memory was blank except for waking in terrible pain, people working over her, and the man mentioning an iceberg. Why couldn't she remember? Pain crept through her limbs making her back bow to help ease the ache. The moan that escaped her throat turned into a shrill shriek as the pressure rose in intensity.

The two men hurried to her side. Their large shadows loomed over her. Gray eyes frowned down at her in concern as their owner, the man who'd stayed by her the most, shouted at someone. She felt a cool stinging sensation at the crown of her head. Lethargy slid over her limbs. Her eyes on the man, she smiled. His scowl disappeared and the full lips above his stubble-covered chin tipped to grin in return.

She remembered. He's the one who said her baby was being cared for, but she had a daughter, too. Oh, God, what about her daughter? Where was she?

The lights went out. Dreams haunted her.

In the reclined seat, she snuggled Jonathan close in her arms. Creaks and groans sounded around them. She held her breath as the vehicle shifted and dropped further down into the ravine. Suspended in time in their solid white grave—the snow around them quickly solidified into ice. A small amount of light reflected off the mass around her, but she couldn't see clearly. She stroked Jonathan's cold cheek and held her hand over his nose. No vapor. He was gone. His little body didn't have a chance against the elements. Her eyes drifted closed. Blessed sleep and then coma would soon rescue her from this living nightmare.

Time had no meaning. Her existence was constant pain, horrific screams, soothing voices, liquid being splashed into her eyes, and numbing relief racing through her veins.

She cried out, "Jonathan! My baby, I want to see my baby."

Muted voices whispered, "We're sorry Mrs. Forrester, but he didn't make it."

"Noooo, please God, no." Screams of pain and rage left her hoarse. Thrashing about, she tried to leave her cocoon, but restraints held her in place and drugs took her to the land of nothing—no pain, no feeling, no Zana. Dreams of her daughter, the sweet child she'd last seen looking through the window, face contorted with resentment, as she and Jonathan left, haunted her. And those hurtful words, *"You don't love me, else you'd take me too,"* echoed in her head.

The look of accusation on Katy's face wrenched at her heart. At least she was safe. Zana had that one consolation.

When someone neared, voice raspy, she called out, "My daughter and grandmother, do they know where I am?"

A kind, plump face looked down at her, soft blue eyes filled with compassion. "We're trying to locate them, Mrs. Forrester, but we're not having much luck."

Gentle hands bathed her, rubbed lotion onto her skin, and massaged her muscles until she cried with pain. Then she was left to rest. At some point, she'd been catheterized and had an IV tube inserted in a port in her chest. Each new day was like all the others.

It appeared she would live.

But did she want to?

Three

Brock heard Shelia's squeal of welcome before he made it up the incline to the cave his parents had made into a home thirty years ago. The sight of the entrance, mostly hidden by foliage, never failed to fill him with warmth. It was much nicer than the small dwelling his grandparents had occupied below in the compound. Of course, Refuge, then a young community, lacked the advances available today.

In those early years, buildings were scarce and most citizens were grateful to have a roof over their heads. He could afford to build in town, but after his parents' death, he'd moved into the cavern and worked on it to make it even more hospitable. It suited his needs and with Marta's help, they'd made it into a comfortable home.

His child ran out the entrance, red ponytail flopping behind her head, down the carved stairway to the roadway below. He held his breath fearing she'd fall, but agile as a gazelle, she traversed the rock steps and from the last one jumped into his arms.

He staggered back, pretending he might drop her. "Ugh, you're going to break my old back, girl."

She giggled and clung to his neck. "Oh, Daddy, am not. What took you so long? Pepe wouldn't tell me anything, even after I visited him every day and even took him flowers."

"You took Pepe flowers?" Brock chuckled and set her on her feet. "Bet he liked that."

She rolled her eyes. "They made him sneeze."

Brock swallowed his laughter. Most likely, Shelia picked her *flowers* on the hill around the house. Though they were pretty, they were weeds and Pepe was allergic.

"Is it true you fished someone from the sea? Will the person be okay?"

"Yes, we did indeed. A woman and her little boy." He laid a hand on her shoulder. "I think the woman will survive, but the child was already dead."

"Ah, that's sad. How come he died?"

"I'm not sure, but it's possible they'd been in the water a long time. He may have been too young to take the medicine to allow him to survive the freezing."

He laid his hand on top of Shelia's head, thankful his child was safe and healthy. "What'd you and Darlene do while I was gone? She hasn't done any redecorating, has she?"

The last time he'd been gone for several days, Darlene had rearranged the furniture in his bedroom and the living area. The woman was becoming a little over-confident as to his affections. He enjoyed her company but had no intention of marrying her.

"One night she took me with her to the Pirate Bar so she could dance."

"She *what*?"

"She took me'

"I heard you the first time. You know I don't want you in that place. What was Darlene thinking?" That was the last straw. Exposing a nine-year-old to the seamier side of life wasn't his idea of being a good caregiver.

Shelia's brow puckered. "Ah, Daddy, we didn't stay long. She just danced a couple of times and only had three beers."

He pulled some money from his pocket and handed it to her. "Go buy yourself a soda or something, and then drop by and tell Pepe to come see me in the morning."

The cheeky brat had the gall to grin. "You just wanna kiss Darlene and don't want me around." She skipped away, and yelled back, "But, that's okay 'cause I like her."

His faced heated. *I just bet you do and that's what she's counting on.* "Kiss, my foot," he bellowed. "I'm going to ream her hide for taking you to the Pirate Bar." Hell, he needed to kick his own ass. How much did Shelia know about him and Darlene? Hopefully she didn't know it went beyond kissing.

As to the Pirate Bar, the place wasn't dangerous, but he didn't want Shelia exposed to the language and groping couples that frequented the place. Why the hell they didn't take themselves someplace private, he didn't know. The more he thought about it, the madder he got.

He took the steps two at a time. At the entrance, he keyed in a code and the massive wooden door that fit perfectly flush inside the cave's entryway whooshed open. "Darlene, where the hell are you?"

"Well, hello to you, too, master of the house." She appeared from the laundry room looking seductive as usual. "So, the little miss spilled the beans, huh?"

"Dammed right. What were you thinking, woman?"

She pursed her red lips into a pout. "I was bored." She pressed her generous curves up against him, wrapped her arms around his neck, and tried to pull his head down for her kiss. The smell of freshly applied strawberry lip-gloss reached his nostrils. It blended with her heady perfume. She was definitely in seduction mode. He resisted the tug and his body's response.

"We were there an hour, that's all." Her blue eyes told him a different story. She was lying again.

Like a cat, she rubbed against him. Any other day, he'd have led her to the bedroom where they'd often enjoyed a sexual romp. But not today. Hazel eyes popped into his mind further hardening his resolve, and his body.

Unfortunately Darlene thought the response was for her and thrust her body against him. Disgust washed over him. Hands on her shoulders, he shoved her back. Darlene was a user. She didn't love him and he probably wasn't the only man enjoying her sexual favors. It was time to move on. Thank God he'd not let her move in with them when she'd pleaded with the excuse it would be so much easier when he was away.

"Darlene, you've gone against my wishes where Shelia is concerned one too many times. You're fired."

She gaped at him. "You and Shelia need me." Her lip trembled. "I'm fond of the girl and she cares for me. Who'll take care of her and the house?"

He raked his hand through his hair. "You've been a good housekeeper, Darlene and Shelia loves you, but you're not a good role model." He squeezed her shoulders. "We've enjoyed each other's company, but it's over, time to move on. I don't want you to come here again."

"You can't mean that, Brock."

"That's where you're wrong, Darlene."

~ * ~

Trembling with excitement, the visitor peered down into the pod. Ah, yes, it is you. Open your eyes for me. Look up and see the face of your assassin, the person to release you from this pain.

Breathing fast with anticipation, joy, and dread, the visitor jumped when the woman inside the pod moaned. Her eyes popped open and she blinked to clear them.

Yes. Dry eyes were a condition associated with rebirth.

Zana's hazel eyes, wide with interest, looked up.

"Hello, there. Had any other visitors?" The visitor looked around to see if they were watched. No. They'd not been seen. The only nurse on duty had entered the supply room just off the high-tech area. There'd been a flu outbreak in Abyss and the ward next door was full. Medical personnel, according to the news, worked double shifts to keep the virus from spreading. Probably one of those freaks from the outside world brought it in. That's what the citizens got for allowing traders to come and go in Abyss.

Alone, unwatched, it wasn't hard to find the IV switch on the pod. The little light blinked green. One little push and it went solid red. It would take a minute or two for the pain to set in. What a shame to miss hearing Zana's screams. On impulse, the visitor shut off the oxygen.

"Sweet dreams, bitch."

The visitor had just entered the transportation pod outside the medical complex when the alarms sounded. Doors whooshed open and closed up and down the hallway as people rushed to the intensive care area.

Have fun, folks.

~ * ~

One day Zana woke and knew she would live. She accepted the fact with wariness and apathy. Her visitor never returned. She asked the nurses but no one had seen the person. Not sure if it'd been a man or a woman because of the way they were dressed, Zana decided it had only been a dream, one induced by the drugs she took. A bad one, as she'd been in excruciating pain for hours afterward. Evidently there had been a power outage and her pod equipment hadn't worked. The staff had been particularly diligent afterwards and rarely left her alone.

As if instinctively knowing she was ready to face life, Helen, her favorite nurse, beamed down at her from above. "It's time for you to get up, dear." She started flipping dials, pushing buttons, and unplugging equipment. When she opened the pod, a whoosh sounded at the release of air pressure.

Panic welled in Zana's chest. She couldn't breathe. She gasped in an effort to suck in air. Her eyes must have begged for help as Helen clasped her hand. "It's okay, dear. Take it slow. What you're experiencing is natural. Though you didn't realize it, your lungs have been functioning for several weeks. They're fine. It's you that has to adjust. Calm down and let your brain do its job."

Zana closed her eyes and willed herself to relax. A few minutes later, she squeezed Helen's hand and smiled.

"All right then, here we go." She lifted Zana's shoulders with one arm and slid her legs around off the bed with the other. The sheet that covered her nakedness dropped exposing her shrunken breasts and emaciated body. Zana gasped.

Helen held her steady and crooned. "Now don't you worry about your figure. After a few months of exercise and good food we'll have you looking good as new." She slipped a soft blue gown over her head and helped Zana insert her arms into the long sleeves. The material felt heavenly against her skin. Slippers to match were tugged onto her feet and Helen eased her off the bed smoothing the gown down over her hips. "This is a lovely color for you." Zana stood for thirty seconds. Her legs trembled with the strain and she gratefully dropped into the chair with wheels.

"Here we go." Helen shoved the curtains aside and pushed her toward a curved floor-to-ceiling window that went half way around the room. The panoramic view of the ocean filled the white room with a tint of blue. How had she missed this? Evidently the pod and her cubicle had blocked the sight. She'd seen only medical equipment, medical personnel, and opaque white curtains.

"Now then, this view ought to cheer you. There is so much to see out there and it's never the same." Hands on her hips, Helen gazed at the scene. "I've been here my entire life and I'm still amazed."

"Where am I?" Zana looked at the window. "Is that a big aquarium?"

The short, plump woman patted her hand. "Don't you worry about that right now. Dr. Bartholomew is on his way. He'll explain everything."

Zana caught the woman's hand before she could leave. "Thank you, Helen. You've all been very kind to me. I'm grateful."

"Oh, honey, I can't tell you what a pleasure it's been to watch over your recovery. We weren't sure you'd make it at first. Seeing you up today is rather a treat for us."

Zana looked around the room, and indeed, several other medical staff watched her, big smiles on their faces. Tears pooled in her eyes at their kindness. She smiled and nodded to them.

Her smile wilted on her face. She wanted to be happy, but her heart weighed heavy in her chest. Her precious baby boy was dead and Katy… Zana had no idea where her daughter was, whether she was alive or dead. She had nothing to be cheerful about. She fought to keep the moisture in her eyes from spilling over. Crying would serve no purpose and once she started it'd be hard to stop.

Looking for a distraction, she turned to the undersea panorama outside the glass wall. Fish and other sea life moved gracefully in the blue vastness. Colors from every stripe in the rainbow danced outside the window. The walls danced with their reflections. She focused on the calm beauty of the underwater scene, letting its rhythm replace the anxiety in her mind.

Big double doors swung open and a tall, thin, bald man rushed through. Everyone turned and went back to their business. He looked at her pod, frowned and surveyed the room until he found her. Big smile on his face, he loped her way.

"Hello, my love," his big voice boomed.

Zana cringed. *My love?* He bent down and kissed her nurse full on the lips. She hoped her shock wasn't evident on her face. The doctor's behavior was unprofessional, in her opinion.

"Hi, pumpkin. How's our patient?"

"She's fine, Jonas, doing very well and anxious for some answers." She pinched her lips. "And would you please call me by my name while we're on duty."

He cleared his throat, ignored his nurse, and looked down at Zana. "Hmm, is that right, Mrs. Forrester? Are you doing better?"

She nodded and glanced at Helen, who hadn't moved, waiting to see what would happen next between the doctor and Helen—or was it "pumpkin"? She restrained a smirk.

"Mrs. Forrester, Helen is my wife and I can't resist teasing her."

Helen snorted. "Jonas, Mrs. Forrester has waited long enough. Don't keep her in suspense any longer."

He pulled a chair around to face her and sat down. "Yes, yes. You've been with us two months now. I can't fault you for wanting some answers." He turned to his wife. "Helen, would you bring me a tranquilizer patch in case we need it?"

Zana stiffened. *Two months?* It felt more like two weeks.

Dr. Bartholomew patted her knee. "Now, don't tense up. We may not need it at all. Everyone reacts to news differently and I just want to be prepared. You've come a long way, young woman, and I don't want us to lose ground."

Helen returned and placed a small box in his hand. He dropped it into his coat pocket. From the same pocket, he removed a small computer.

Zana watched as he used a little pointer to whiz

through data. Finished, he put it away and directed his dark brown eyes on her.

"From your purse and the identification in your vehicle we've learned you are Zana Forrester from St. John's, Newfoundland."

She nodded.

"You were born in 2050."

"What happened to me? Did I have a car crash?"

"Yes. Evidently you were caught in a heavy snow slide. We believe your Polar Excursion was buried in a ravine and sometime in the past seventy-five years, snow pushed it out to sea. Buried in an iceberg, you were caught in the ocean's currents and carried from Newfoundland, past Ireland, down around Barbados, and back up again. There's no telling how long you'd been in the water or how many revolutions you made. Many of the Caribbean Islands, including Barbados and Cuba, are now under water else you might have been spotted sooner. Fortunately for you, your extreme-weather vehicle's interior sealed on impact."

Zana couldn't breathe. *Seventy-five years. So much land mass gone.* She gasped and tried to talk but no words would come from her mouth. Locked in a mental time warp, Zana watched as the doctor, in slow motion removed the patch from his pocket and applied it to the inside of her wrist.

"Try to take small breaths. It will only take the patch a moment to calm you. I know this is a lot for you to take in." He held her hand palm up and rubbed the patch. Almost immediately the effects of the drug rushed through her system calming her, easing her tense muscles. "We'll do everything in our power to make connection with your family."

She was rolled to a bed and carefully placed on it. Helen fluffed her pillow and tucked the sheet beneath her arms. "Sleep now," said Helen. "You've plenty of time to learn the rest."

Four

Zana lay on her bed in the small hospital room staring up at the ceiling trying to make sense of what she'd just learned. It was August of 2155 and she'd been at Abyss, a city under the sea, for almost two months. She'd been born one-hundred-five years ago, but in real years, she approached thirty-one. The entire idea was crazy.

According to Jonas, her Polar Excursion had created the perfect environment for her to lie safely in her frozen state. However, it was the medication she'd taken since she was fifteen that received credit for maintaining the health of her body's tissues until she could be revived.

She wasn't the first person to be scooped from the sea and returned to life, nor would she be the last. A lump settled in her throat and she fought back tears. If only Jonathan had been old enough to take the 'miracle pills' as they'd been called when developed in 2065, if only there had been some hope his little body would survive. Then she might find some joy in her existence.

Her thinking was ridiculous. Facts were facts. The minute the snow washed them into the ravine her son didn't have a chance in the elements.

Their last moments together were now fresh in her mind. She'd unbuckled him from his child's seat, cuddled him in her arms and sang him to sleep all the while praying he wouldn't suffer when the cold took him. Sobs tore through her, shaking her frame. Her muscles, still sore from rebirth and therapy, cried out in rebellion. Unable to stop despite the pain, she wrapped her arms around her waist and curled into a ball on the bed. Exhausted, she swiped at her tears. *The only thing I have to keep me going is finding out what happened to Katy and Gran.* She closed her eyes and fell into sleep.

"It's time for your therapy." Helen popped into her room startling her awake. Her voice cheerful, she added, "We mustn't be late."

Zana groaned at the intrusion. Sleep was her only escape, her only way to forget. She burrowed back into her pillow and tried to ignore the nurse, but Helen shook her shoulder and wouldn't take no for an answer. "Come along now, you don't want to fall behind. A consistent routine is essential to your recovery." The medical staff kept to their schedules and no excuse would make them alter the routine. She had to give them credit, things ran smoothly at Abyss.

"Okay, okay, I'm coming." Zana rolled over and sat up on the side of the bed. "Give me a minute to freshen up." Helen helped her up and to the bathroom. Every day at ten o'clock, Zana reported to the gym for an hour of therapy. After a thirty-minute massage, she poured her tired body into the hot tub. When she pulled herself up and out, she dropped into the manual wheelchair Helen held steady for her. Though managed to walk to the gym, Zana didn't have the strength to make it back to her room under her own steam. She wondered with all the high tech stuff around Abyss why they didn't have some type of powered wheel chair. Her only conclusion was the staff wanted to have full control over their patients' mobility until they were stronger.

Helen rolled her back to her room for a three-hour nap. Before she left, she announced, "And don't forget, we're meeting someone new for dinner tonight at seven o'clock sharp. Wear something pretty."

Zana sighed with resignation. Her evening meals were taken in a lush dining hall where Dr. Bartholomew and Helen introduced her to a different man each evening. The first night, on their way out, she'd informed them, "If you're matchmaking, I appreciate it but I'm really not interested."

Helen's eyebrows rose a notch. "But dear, surely you want the companionship of a man. No woman wants to be on her own."

Jonas put his arm around his wife's shoulders. "Now, pumpkin, don't press her on the issue." He turned to Zana. "We want you to learn what our culture is like and feel it will be less boring if you hear about it from others."

Well, that was fine, but the men appeared to be interested in her only as a prospective spouse. It appeared couples didn't socialize for just friendship sake, or singles for that matter. At least that's the notion she got from Helen. All the couples in the dining hall were married and she hadn't seen any couples that appeared to be dating. "Don't you have some women I could learn from?"

"Sure we do. We'll have some stop by and take you to lunch."

They were true to their word, but they continued to parade men past her. The men were attractive enough, but she didn't have a thing in common with any of them.

Zana grew stronger each day. She explored the city via an electric-powered conveyance. Today, on the way to her lunch date, she entered large doors at the passageway into something like an elongated elevator car. Automatically, clasps latched onto her vehicle keeping it locked in place. On the dash was a button that read, "Go." She pushed the button and shot through the tunnel at what felt like warp speed to exit in another area. On her first trip with Greta, a lovely blonde close to her age who'd taken her under her wing when she'd been learning how things worked, she'd screamed the entire sixty-second trip. She and Greta laughed for five minutes after the transport stopped. Zana's legs wobbled for an eternity as if she'd been on the sea.

She'd bought a few clothes and the clerks had been thrilled with the real money found in her purse. Her mood of melancholy lifted somewhat. Maybe she would be able to move on with life as Helen and Jonas suggested.

Greta now waited for her at a small cafe in the shopping district. She'd found them a table and waved as Zana approached. Zana sat down across from Greta. "Have you been waiting long?"

"No, I just arrived and fortunately this table was unoccupied. I grabbed it so we wouldn't have to wait." She handed Zana a menu. "Let's hurry and order. For some reason I'm starved today."

They chatted while waiting for their food. Greta had been born in Abyss and though she'd been to other undersea worlds, she only been on land once. "I couldn't wait to get back home. There were so many pollens in the air, I sneezed the entire week." She laughed. "My nose was red and blinking when I returned. You know, like the reindeer in that old children's Christmas story."

The temperature in Abyss was kept at a year round constant of seventy-eight degrees. Hot water from undersea geothermal vents traveled through pipes to add heat when it was needed. Cold water provided air conditioning. No doubt all allergens and pollutants were removed from the air before it entered the community areas. She wondered what it'd be like to never feel the sun or fresh air on your face. What was she thinking? If a person had never experienced these common sensations they'd never miss them. Much of her own life had been spent indoors. As with everyone in the area, people shopped as infrequently as possible. Many businesses operated online. The frigid weather in St. Johns was dangerous and only those trained for hazardous temperatures ventured very far from their homes.

Their meals arrived and while she ate, Zana looked around. Certainly, in Newfoundland, she'd had nothing like the freedom of movement here in Abyss. People bustled in and out of the shops. Their carefree laughter and chattered caused a low racket. It was unusually crowded today. "What's going on? Why are so many people eating out?"

"It's the first of the month—payday and the lottery." Before Zana could ask about the lottery, Greta's husband, Arturo, who ran the restaurant, stopped by their table to say hello. He kissed his wife before shaking Zana's hand.

His smile showed off a beautiful set of teeth in his attractive, tanned face. Arturo's darkness complimented

Greta's fair skin and hair. They were an attractive couple.

"It is a pleasure to meet you, Zana. Greta talks about you often." His expression turned serious. "It is very sad about the loss of your child. You have our condolences."

Her happiness faded and, voice thick, she said. "Thank you." She worked to push her emotions aside, but it didn't work.

"Oh dear, I'm so sorry, I've upset you," said Arturo. "I should have kept my mouth shut." He smiled apologetically at his wife. "Greta tells me I have no tact."

"No, no, that's all right. I have to learn to accept the loss of my son and move on." *And now that I'm stronger I've got to look for Katy.*

An employee called for Arturo and he left to attend to business. Greta patted her hand. "We want you to be happy, Zana, and find your place here. I understand you are a computer programmer. There should be plenty of jobs open for someone with your training."

"Possibly, but technology has come so far in the past seventy-five years. I can't imagine anything is like it was back then."

"Someone will be willing to train you. I'm sure of that." She pushed her plate to the side and drew doodles in the condensation on her water glass. "Have you gotten close to choosing a mate?"

A mate? What the hell did she mean? "I don't know what you're talking about. I'm not ready to marry."

Greta's open expression closed. "Oh, I'm speaking out of turn here. Forgive me."

"What do you mean?"

Greta looked at her watch and stood abruptly. "Oh dear, I've got five minutes to return to work. I'll be in touch." With that she was gone.

Zana sat in a stupor, contemplating Greta's words. Jonas and Helen had been parading men in front of her in hopes she'd find one attractive enough to marry? Not bloody likely. For one thing, a pair of gray eyes haunted her. Secondly, she wasn't in the market for a husband, not right now, anyway.

None of them had gray eyes like the ones she'd seen when she'd first woken. Had she been searching for their owner? She didn't like to think so, but couldn't deny the sound of his deep voice and his steady gaze had given her comfort. Would she ever see him again? She doubted it. An ache of loss filled her. She brushed it aside. Here she sat mooning over a man whose name she didn't even know.

~ * ~

"What do you think of our city, Zana?"

Zana's gaze moved from the beautiful underwater view outside the restaurant to meet that of Abyss's governor, Samuel Whiteside, his dark eyebrow cocked in question. With his near black hair and blue eyes, he was a good-looking man. Oddly enough, he seemed familiar to her, but she couldn't for the life of her figure out why. Something about his smile and the dimple in his left cheek reminded her of someone. Maybe it would come to her in time.

She found it amazing the tall, well-built man was still a bachelor. Actually, Helen said he'd been married, but several years ago his young wife died shortly after their son was born. Helen would only say it was a tragic accident.

"It's amazing. Of course you know it's nothing like what I'm familiar with. In some ways I find it intimidating."

"Really, how so?"

She shrugged. "Oh, I don't know exactly. I guess it just all seems so perfect."

"And there is something wrong with that?" He lifted his wine glass and swirled the ruby red around in the stemware before taking a sip. The wine, she learned, was produced at a vineyard in Brazil. If Abyss or one of the neighboring underwater colonies didn't have something they wanted, they traded with one of the settlements on land.

"Nothing in nature is perfect." She didn't trust anything that gave the appearance it was.

Eyes narrowed, he started to respond but Helen quickly asked, "Have you had any luck locating Zana's family in Newfoundland, Samuel?"

He turned his attention to Helen, and Zana breathed a sigh of relief. This man was nice enough and good looking, but too polished for her taste. No, that wasn't true. She just wasn't interested in becoming involved in a relationship.

"No, and it's strange." To Zana, he said, "We've not been able to find any record of you or your family in all the data bases we've checked into. It's as though you never existed."

"But, you have my driver's license as proof. Surely that's some help."

"You'd think so. We'll continue to search. I'm sure we'll come up with the data you need to contact them. It's just taking longer than we expected." He patted her hand. "I promise you, we'll find some answers.

She knew the Bartholomews wanted her to be attracted to this man. He was the governor, for heaven's sake, a man of prestige and power and would be a good catch for her. He was good looking, charming, and though she liked him, the chemistry was not there.

Dinner over, Samuel held her chair as she stood. He took her arm and led their group to the lobby area outside the dining room. The Bartholomews withdrew to give them privacy.

"It was a pleasure meeting you, Zana, but I can see we're not suited for each other. I hope you find the right man."

She sighed with relief, grateful he shared her feelings and wouldn't pursue another dinner as some of the other men had. "I'd be grateful if you'd be my friend, Samuel. I'm truly not interested in beginning a serious relationship right now. I must find my daughter before I can go on with my life."

One of his eyebrows rose a notch and he turned and nodded to Jonas. The couple rushed over. "Well, good luck then." He shook Jonas's hand and nodded to Helen. "It's been a pleasure. Goodnight."

Jonas and Helen exchanged looks and turned to her. Helen took Zana's arm. "Come by our apartment for a while, Zana."

A few minutes later Zana sat on the sofa in Jonas and Helen's living room. Helen sat beside her and Jonas lowered himself into a recliner. With chrome arms and legs, the fabric was a see-through plastic-like substance, yet it didn't squeak and creak when he moved around.

He steepled his fingers and stared at her. "Zana, it was our hope you'd find one of the men you've met attractive so we could see that your mating agreement took place. We're very fond of you and want to see you settled and happy."

"But why? I have no desire to get married. At least not right now."

"My dear, I'm afraid that's not an option in Abyss."

An odd sensation of distrust crawled up her spine. "Why not? I can get a job and support myself."

"Of course you can," said Helen, "but that's just not the way it's done here. The only singles we have are widows and widowers and they remarry as soon as a mate can be found."

"You've been here five months now, Zana," said Jonas. "For two of those, you've been out in our society here under the sea."

She nodded.

"Have you seen any fighting among the teenagers when they go out, heard any arguments between men over women, or visa versa?"

As a matter of fact, she hadn't. She'd seen teens in a group but they appeared to be in pairs. Nothing like the unattached groups she'd gone out with before the temperature dropped to dangerous levels in Newfoundland. Actually, the married couples she'd seen together appeared too mushy gushy for her tastes. "No."

Jonas beamed. "That's because we have a controlled society. There is no dating. That ritual, which many times causes dissension among adolescents and adults alike, is not allowed here. Everyone happily mated at an early age. Young children are watched to see which individual of the opposite sex they tend to favor, and then pheromones are used in adolescence to ensure their joint attraction. At different stages of their lives, the hormones are increased to trigger sexual desire and fidelity."

Zana could only gape at them in incredulity. What they suggested went against all of her values. It sounded like something an author would make up when writing a science fiction novel.

"I know you find this shocking, but in the enclosed confines of a society such as ours, it is necessary. Surely you can see that."

Maybe she could understand their thinking but she couldn't condone it. Surely there was a better way. She shook her head. Drugging people went against her ethics.

Jonas cleared his throat. "The men you've met are all interested in you. Their wives are dead and we need you to make a choice soon before problems arise among them. They've been without a sexual partner for some time."

She couldn't believe her ears. Standing, she shook her head. "I'm sorry. I can't take part in this ritual. I'm not in the least attracted to any of those men and have no intention of being hyped up on drugs to get that way."

Doctor Bartholomew frowned. "I'm afraid you don't have a choice, Zana. We cannot allow you to live here in Abyss as a single."

Five

Retriever pulled into the traders' bay at Abyss. Brock had a load of silver he'd acquired from Mexico in trade for the Polar Excursion. Abyss's governor had promised a monthly delivery of meat and medical supplies for the next six months in payment—a nice exchange for them both. Though Brock disliked Governor Samuel Whiteside for personal and political reasons, in business matters he respected the man's honesty and knew their contract would be honored.

Stepping from his craft, he looked up to see the governor himself walk through the door. Brock's hackles immediately rose. He'd never forgive the man, his sister Delia's husband, for the accident that took her life. Hell, he'd never forgive himself for the accident that still hadn't been explained to Brock's satisfaction.

Brock knew his reaction was mirrored by Samuel. His brother-in-law nodded, facial expression reserved. They skirted each other like two boxers.

If only on that fateful day Delia turned eighteen he'd not brought her to Abyss to celebrate her birthday at one of the resorts, she'd never have met Samuel Whiteside. She'd fallen hard for the man. Within a week, Samuel and Delia were married. Now she was dead.

Samuel, posture guarded, walked up and offered his hand. "Callahan."

Brock shook the man's outstretched hand and muttered, "Whiteside."

Samuel's grip was strong, but his hands were smooth, not those of a manual laborer. Brock asked, "Did you come all the way down here to make sure I didn't cheat you?"

"No, but since I'm here, I'd like to take a look."

"All right. Come aboard." They went below. The silver was stacked in waterproof containers, each bar wrapped in soft cloth. Brock opened a box, lifted a block, and handed it to Whiteside.

Samuel carefully unwrapped the wedge and whistled. "Very nice. I'm pleased."

Brock turned to Digger who stood by waiting for orders. "Go ahead and get this unloaded. I'll be signing the invoices."

"Will do, Cal."

Brock and Samuel moved to the poop deck and got off the boat. In the shipping office, the paperwork was ready for signatures and in five minutes they were signed and Brock's copy safely tucked in his shirt pocket.

He signed for two packages for Dr. Boone— medical journals and supplies. As they left the office, the governor stopped Brock.

"We have a passenger for you, Callahan."

"What? No one said anything about a passenger when I called in for a delivery date."

"I know, but this just came up."

"What just came up?"

Whiteside looked toward the corner of the area where several chairs were arranged. Back ramrod straight sat the woman whose hazel eyes had haunted

Brock's dreams. Her silver hair had been cut. It swayed against her shoulders when she tilted her head to meet his gaze. Chin thrust forward, her expression relayed her determination. His respect for her grew. Smart woman, and, God, she was beautiful. Oh yeah, he'd be glad to take her away from Abyss. He spat on the floor in disgust and glared at Samuel. "Found someone else who didn't like your societal rules?"

"As a matter of fact, yes. She refused selective mating. So, will you take her?"

Brock growled, "Hell yes, I'll take her. I wouldn't leave my dog at the mercy of your demented social system."

Whiteside sneered. "It's better than living like a dog in a cave or hovel."

Brock grabbed the front of Samuel's business suit, fist raised, ready to loosen a few perfect teeth. "Better than to die at your mercy in a freak, unexplained accident in this God forsaken place."

Before he could swing, three men were on him. One applied a low voltage control device to his neck. He stiffened and jerked as the electric current passed through his body.

His crew jumped in to pull the guards off him. Fists flew and more of the governor's men joined the fracas.

Samuel hollered. "That's enough, you imbeciles. You want to kill him?"

Both groups of men fell back. Curses bantered back and forth, but finally they settled down. Digger stood at one elbow, holding Brock steady, Luke at the other. They plunked him in a chair. Now Brock despised the son of a bitch more. Brock had lost his sister to the man. Today, by Samuel's men attacking him, he'd added insult to injury.

~ * ~

Zana cringed as she watched the ruckus from her chair in the corner. Both big and brawny, they'd be fairly matched in a fight, but the governor, for all his size, didn't have the stringy toughness of the trader, Brock Callahan. When she'd refused to select a mate, she'd been given a choice. She could join the rebels who'd found her or live in confinement until they could find another society to take her. She'd chosen the rebels.

Now she wasn't so sure. The governor and citizens of Abyss didn't appear cruel. Isolation might not be so bad until a place could be found for her.

The captain rested only a moment. On unsteady feet, he approached her. She stood to meet him. Her breath hitched at the intense grey eyes looking down at her. He was the one—the man whose touch and voice had soothed her while she struggled with pain. No, she'd not misunderstood the kindness she'd seen in Captain Callahan's eyes and heard in his voice when she'd been in that medical pod before arriving at Abyss. Though now his face was hard with anger, she didn't fear him.

"Mrs. Forrester. I'm Brock Callahan. If you're ready, we'll board and get underway."

She hesitated. Was Refuge a violent place? Samuel called them rebels. She wasn't afraid of this man, but what about the people of Refuge? What were they like? And she'd not seen this man other than when she was drugged, her perception warped. Had she not seen his true temperament? Was this his true character—a man with an explosive temper? Evidently Samuel had a temper too.

"Make up your mind, lady. I haven't got all day. It's me or this place." He sneered and threw a glance at the governor. "Me and my poor little community or here with a drug induced romance." He turned on his heel and walked toward his craft.

The sound of his voice, despite its belligerent tone, and the memory of his compassion made her move. That, and the fact she agreed wholeheartedly with his opinion of Abyss and their practices.

"Yes, yes, I'm ready." She picked up the blanket in which she'd wrapped her belongings—the blanket she'd tucked around Jonathan in the Polar Excursion. That and her handbag were all she had of her former life. The few clothes she'd bought in Abyss didn't amount to much and easily fit into her makeshift rucksack.

He stopped, turned on his heal, and returned to her side. His expression softened. "Good. Let me help you, then." He took her bundle and with his other hand cupped her elbow to escort her to his craft. Her first trip on the *Retriever* was a blur. Now she looked it over carefully. Large, probably one hundred fifty feet in length, its lines sleek, the bridge large and three stories high. The hull and decks were painted blue, the color of the water for camouflage she suspected.

Before they boarded, a city guard approached.

"Mrs. Forrester, this is for you."

He handed her a prettily wrapped small blue box with a silver and white bow.

Zana was stunned. "Are you sure it's for me? I can't imagine who'd be giving me a gift." She took the prettily wrapped box and admired the lovely paper and bow.

Mr. Callahan snorted. "Probably from one of those rejected suitors of yours. I'd be careful with it if I were you."

She wanted to laugh at his disgruntled response, but out of courtesy to the governor, who'd been kind to her, decided she'd keep her opinion to herself until another time.

Governor Whiteside threw him a dirty look. "That remark is quite unnecessary, Callahan. Mrs. Forrester made many friends while here."

Yes, Zana had made friends, but after she'd rejected their ultimatum, they'd avoided her like the plague. Everyone, that is but Jonas and Helen. She'd seen them often and suffered through their pleas to change her mind about the mating. Leaving them had been difficult. They had been her lifeline during her recovery.

Governor Whiteside, smile rueful, took her hand in his and squeezed. "I wish you happiness, Mrs. Forrester. If you change your mind about our policies, sent a message and a transport will come for you."

"Thank you, Governor, but I'm content with my decision."

He nodded and stepped back.

"I'll be expecting my delivery on time, Governor," muttered Callahan as he helped her board.

"We honor our contracts, Callahan, and you know it."

"See that you continue that good record."

Once aboard, she was led up the two flights onto the control deck to a small lounge area. The area was neat and clean. It appeared Captain Callahan took pride in his vessel and saw to it that his crew did likewise. She'd just gotten comfortable when the engines hummed to life. Within minutes they were exiting the bay. Panic gripped her. Her stomach dropped to her toes. Was she doing the right thing? Yes. She sighed with relief. There was no way she could live with the societal laws in Abyss.

There was nothing fancy about the interior of the *Retriever.* Of course, it wasn't a pleasure boat, but one for work. She looked down at the package in her hands. Carefully she untied the ribbon, tore off the paper, and removed the lid of the box. She withdrew a small card. It read.

We'll miss you, dear, and hope you'll be happy.
Jonas and Helen.

Emotion caused an ache in her throat. She'd miss them too. They'd been very kind to her and were the only friends she had. With no links to the past, her history was a blank slate. Sadness crept to the surface and she fought to push the emotion down. She blinked back a tear and turned her attention to the gift. Inside was a gold foil box. She opened it to reveal a selection of twelve pieces of chocolate.

Oh my. She had a weakness for sweets. She picked up a piece and popped it between her lips. The chocolate dissolved in her mouth. Mmm. Delicious. She wanted another but they were so rich, she'd be ill if she ate more.

A young man watched her, longing written all over his face. She held the box out. "Would you like a piece? I'll never be able to eat all these. They're so sweet they're almost sickening."

He looked toward his boss. Callahan nodded. "Go

ahead, Pepe."

"Well, if you're sure, Mrs. Forrester," said Pepe.

"Of course I'm sure." He selected a piece and swallowed it whole. "Have another." Eyes alight with excitement, the boy chose another piece. "Would anyone else like some of these? I really don't want to eat them all."

No one else was interested so she closed the box and placed it on the table.

~ * ~

Brock sat in the chair facing the attractive woman, elbows on the armrests and hands clasped under his chin. *God, she's lovely.* Her skin was free of powder, her lips and cheeks lightly tinted. Probably permanent dye. "Are you comfortable? Would you like something to drink?"

Her lips tilted in a half smile. "No, I'm fine. Thank you for taking me aboard."

"You're welcome." He studied his hands a minute before looking up. "Selective mating is an abominable custom. I wouldn't wish that on my worst enemy."

"I guess if you grew up knowing your life would follow that path, it wouldn't be so bad. You wouldn't realize why you needed a booster shot." She shivered. "But having full knowledge you needed an injection to maintain your love for someone is disgusting."

Face grim, he nodded. "Even worse is the fact that very few people living in Abyss know they're being doped. Citizens are required to keep appointments with the doctors every six months for a check-up and *inoculations* which are in fact their booster pheromone shots."

Her eyes widened. "That's terrible." She leaned

forward in her chair, her brow furrowed in thought. "Why did they tell me about the drug then? Dr. Bartholomew was upfront with me before my decision to leave."

"Because you resisted." He shrugged. "I suspect few people do, especially men if they have a long line of women paraded before them to choose from." He wondered why she had. Did she not want to marry, start another family? Maybe there weren't many eligible men or they'd been unsuitable. "Why did you resist? Were none of the men to your liking?"

"Before I can move on with my life, I must find my daughter."

A stab of jealousy sliced through him. He'd wanted to hear her say she wasn't drawn to any of the men. *You're a fool, Brock Callahan. Here you are mooning over a woman you don't even know.* In her situation, he'd react the same way. Finding his family would be foremost in his mind.

She studied his face. "How did you find out about the deception of Abyss's medical community?"

"We have a doctor from Abyss now living and practicing in Refuge. Like you, he was a rebirth but fell in love with a young woman and they married so he decided to stay in Abyss and practice medicine. When he figured out his wife's affection was drug induced, his loyalty to his new community turned to disgust. He left Abyss under the pretense of testing vaccines on some of the unsuspecting souls in the land colonies." He couldn't help the snort of derision that flew from his mouth. "You see, though the undersea community is advanced medically, they don't mind using us unfortunates as guinea pigs."

She raised a slender hand to her mouth. Her nails were clipped short and buffed to a healthy shine with no artificial color. "That's horrible."

"Yes, it is."

They sat quietly for a few minutes, each with their own thoughts. Brock was about to excuse himself and move back to the con deck when he felt her touch on his hand. She folded it in both of hers. Stunned, Brock stiffened and almost groaned at the wave of warmth that radiated up his arm.

"I know you, don't I?"

He nodded.

"Your grey eyes, I looked for them during my recovery. I thought I had dreamed them, that you weren't real."

Before he could react, she drew his hand to her cheek. "Thank you for being there for me. I remember your eyes. I remember your voice. They were a comfort to me."

Brock heard a chuckle and saw Luke's back shaking with mirth. No doubt Luke was remembering the, "This is your captain speaking," comment. He pulled his hand free. "No thanks are necessary. We were glad to help."

He sat back, making sure he was out of her reach. Not that he thought she was coming onto him. She wasn't. It was just in her nature, he thought, to be touchy. He'd heard that about some people from the past. In Abyss, couples showed a great deal of affection, kissing in public, hugging. People in Refuge were a bit more restrained. At least their feelings were genuine and not drug induced.

It'd been a long time since he'd been with a caring

woman, one as tender as Zana. Of course there was Darlene, but their relationship had been about sex, nothing else. He mentally shook himself. Though he craved Zana's touch, it was one of gratitude. He wanted more than thanks from this woman but he'd not go there. She was the type of woman, one he could love, that he avoided. Plus, his men were present. It was time to move this conversation to another subject.

"We need to talk about what you can do when we reach Refuge. What are your skills?"

"Seventy-five years ago, I programmed schematics for weather satellites. I'm sure technology has advanced so much my skills are obsolete."

"Don't be too sure. Yes, we've advanced a great deal, but places like Refuge don't have the tools Abyss has. I bet our people can train and catch you up in a short period of time."

She nodded, her smile wilting on her face. Her skin turned pale. "Can I have a drink of water?"

"Sure." He walked to a refrigerator built into the wall, pushed a button, and a bag of water popped out. Before handing it to her, he twisted the tube protruding from the top to break the seal.

She took several sips. Her color improved a little, but she laid her head back on the cushion with her eyes closed. Great, that's all he needed, for her to get sick.

A shout sounded from below decks. "Cal. Get down here."

He ran to the stairs and used the handrails to slide down. His feet never touched the steps. On his knees, Digger bent over Pepe as the boy twitched and jerked on the steel deck floor while clutching his belly. Foam oozed from the corners of his mouth.

"Holy Hell, what happened?"

"I don't know. I just found him like this.

The two of them picked Pepe up and carried him to sick bay. "Make him as comfortable as you can, Digger."

"Will do, Cal. I'll check the medical database and see what meds we can give him."

Ten minutes later, Brock climbed the stairs and found the control deck empty. "Luke. Where the hell are you? Who is driving this craft?"

"Here, Cal. I've got her on autopilot." Luke stood over Zana, wiping her face with a damp rag as her body twitched in pain. The box of chocolates lay spilled at her feet.

Fear knifed through his gut. What the hell was going on? Poison! Someone had tried to kill Mrs. Forrester, and poor Pepe had been caught by his love of sweets.

He lifted the woman in his arms and headed for the stairs leading to sick bay. She weighed little more than Shelia, light as a feather. She snuggled against his chest and moaned. He held her closer wishing he could keep her safe. Worry gnawed at his gut. Were she and Pepe going to die?

He quickly placed Mrs. Forester on a fold-down cot.

"Luke, see if you can do anything for them while I go back to the bridge and contact Abyss for help."

Two minutes later, an emergency medical doctor answered his message. "Explain their symptoms."

Brock explained quickly.

"I'm sorry, it sounds like a virus. We can't allow you to dock and endanger Abyss' citizens."

"What? Now you listen to me. One of the sick is Zana Forrester who we picked up from your fair city today. If she got a virus, she got it there, but one of my crew is sick, too. Their symptoms began almost simultaneously. They've been poisoned by chocolates your Dr. Jonas Bartholomew and his wife Helen gave as a gift to Mrs. Forrester. That's attempted murder. Now I'm turning this craft around and you better let me enter the medical bay."

"Hold another minute, Captain Callahan. Let me notify Governor Whiteside of the situation and get clearance."

"You do that."

Whiteside's voice boomed from the microphone. "We'll be ready for you, Brock. It won't take long for the medical team to analyze the chocolates and determine what poison was used."

Brock heaved a sigh of relief. "Thanks. We'll be there in one hour." He clicked off the receiver and switched the controls from automatic to manual. Within seconds, he'd keyed in the coordinates and set the speed as fast as *Retriever* could travel. Luke wore a headset taking instructions from a doctor. His face grim, he shook his head at Brock. Damn, an hour might be too long.

Six

Brock clenched his fists in frustration as he strode up and down the carpeted floor of the small waiting room just outside the doors to the medical pod. They'd arrived at Abyss's above sea platform and pulled into the emergency-docking bay. Years ago, it'd had been an oilrig but had been converted for use as a landing dock. There were three different stations—one for cargo, one for emergencies, and one for visitors. Each had an elevator that led to different locations in Abyss. The elevator trip below took less than five minutes. Now they waited in the holding area. Where the hell was the emergency team? If they didn't open that friggin' door in the next two minutes, he'd blast his way in.

They'd transferred their two patients to hand-carry gurneys for quick transport. Quick...hell? Would they die while Abyss's doctors twiddled their thumbs?

Pepe lay unconscious on his cot, his skin a deathly pale green. He'd lost control of his bladder. They'd stripped him of his soiled clothes and wrapped him in thermal sheets. Brock feared it was too late for Pepe and wanted to weep. The boy was his responsibility and he'd failed to keep him safe. If Pepe didn't live, how would he face his mother? Worse yet, how could he live with himself?

Still awake, Mrs. Forrester lay, legs drawn up to

her chest, twitching, mewling cries her only sound. Brock was ready to commit murder. Her pain was terrifying. He was powerless to do anything to help. Though he didn't believe the boy would recover, there might still be time for her.

The bay door opened to admit the medical crew decked out in full virus protection gear. Brock grabbed the first man in and shoved him toward the two victims. "It's about damn time. They're dying while you screw around here."

The young man ignored his aggressiveness and calmly said, "I'm Dr. Raymond. If you want our help, keep your hands to yourself. We have procedures that must be followed."

Grabbing his hair in frustration, Brock nodded. It took the doctor thirty seconds to assess the situation and set his people to work. Both patients were immediately transferred to wheeled pods. Men grabbed each corner, flipped a switch, and the legs folded up.

"Show these men to your medical bay, Captain Brock."

"What the hell… Why aren't you taking them to the hospital?"

"The Governor's orders. He's afraid the citizens of Abyss will panic."

Brock threw his hands in the air. Cursing under his breath, he led the men into the elevator and retraced his steps to the deck aboard *Retriever* housing their sick bay. Dr. Raymond followed on his heels with more of his medical team carrying equipment behind him.

As his personnel hooked up the pods, Dr. Raymond picked up the box near Zana's feet and looked inside. "Is this the suspicious candy?"

Brock swallowed a retort. "Yes."

He turned to a blonde man holding a glass box and dropped the package of chocolates inside. "Get these to the lab. We need an answer in five minutes."

"Yes, sir." The young man took off at a lope his footsteps pounding on the metal stairs as he raced up to the poop deck.

Beeps sounded and lights flashed on and off as the medical crew worked over their patients. Brock reached inside the open pod to touch Pepe's hand. Cold, it felt clammy under the heat of his tanned skin. The boy's color had worsened. A deep sense of despair settled in his belly. This kid he was so fond of wasn't going to make it. All of Pepe's joy of life snuffed out in such an agonizing manner.

He turned anguished eyes on the doctor. *Please tell me I'm wrong.*

Doctor Raymond sadly shook his head. "I'm sorry, Mr. Callahan. I'm afraid it's too late for him. We'll be lucky if we save the woman."

Fear clutched Brock's heart. Loosing Pepe was bad enough, but to hear they may lose Mrs. Forrester, too....

He stumbled to the chair against the wall and sagged into the metal contraption. Luke placed a cup of coffee in his hand and then squeezed his shoulder.

Brock wanted to weep. He'd watched Pepe grow up. It seemed only yesterday he'd been a toddler, then a young lad they'd had to constantly chase away from Retriever for fear he'd get hurt. Finally Brock found him a job just to keep him safe.

Samuel Whiteside came in and pulled a chair closer to his. "Do they know anything yet?"

Brock coughed to dispel the knot in his throat. "If they do, they haven't told me." He snorted. "I'm surprised you're here. Aren't you afraid you'll catch something?" Samuel didn't wear the protective suit like the medical team.

Samuel sighed. "I knew you wouldn't let that go. People in an enclosed area can panic quickly. Even though I believe Mrs. Forrester and the boy were poisoned, convincing our citizens of the fact would be difficult."

Brock didn't want to be understanding, but he'd seen panic among a group of people and it could get ugly. He didn't blame the governor.

"Plus, the council banished Mrs. Forrester from the community when she refused selective mating. She can't return unless she decides to accept our societal structure."

"Even for medical care?"

"For any reason. I know that may seem harsh, but it's our law."

Brock shook his head. Now wasn't the time to argue societal structures.

"Have you arrested the Bartholomews?"

"They didn't send the chocolates, Brock."

Brock bristled but waited for Samuel to finish speaking.

"We've got investigators on it. They found the candy shop where the sweets were made, but Jonas and Helen have never been in the store."

"Someone else could have bought the stuff for them."

"That's true, but I don't think so. The Bartholomews are devastated. Ever since we got the word, Helen's been in a state of hysteria and has been sedated."

Brock finished off his coffee. "She could be a good actress." His voice hoarse, he raged, "Dammit, the boy isn't going to make it. Someone will pay for this if I have to commit murder myself."

Samuel's face froze. "Don't be rash. Give the doctors time to determine what kind of poison was used and we'll have more clues as to who did this."

"What about the messenger? Can't he tell you something?"

"The candy was handed to him by the owner this morning. Unfortunately, our inspector discovered the proprietor's body in his shop shortly after you called."

Brock jerked his gaze to meet Samuel's.

The other man nodded. "It looks like the same toxin."

Brock jumped up as the blonde doctor came through the door and rushed to the cubicle where Dr. Raymond worked over Zana. He started to follow, but Samuel held him back.

"Let them do their job."

They watched as the two doctors talked. Raymond appeared to be issuing orders. People ran from the room and disappeared. The doctor looked up and saw them watching. He turned and said something to the remaining individuals in the room, and then approached them.

Brock held his breath and waited. Dr. Raymond nodded to the governor and then turned to Brock. "It's a rare, but deadly poison from the Phyllobates terribilis, better known as the Golden Dart Frog. One found only in the rainforests on the Pacific coast of Columbia."

A frog? A damn frog? He knew there were many dangerous ones in the rainforests, but who would go about collecting them and extracting their toxin?

"I think we can have an antidote in time to save Mrs. Forrester's life and with the use of nanotechnology, we can speed up her recovery. I'm afraid it's too late for the boy. He's gone, Mr. Callahan."

Brock nodded and dropped back into his chair. *Oh, Pepe, I'm sorry, son. I tried so hard to protect you and then something stupid like this happens.* Now he had three deaths on his hands—Deidra's, Marta's and Pepe's. Hell, not three, but four. He felt responsible for Delia's death also. If he'd not brought her to Abyss, she'd be alive today.

Samuel and Dr. Raymond had their heads together deep in conversation. Actually, the doctor spoke and the governor listened, his face an ashen mask.

What the hell was that all about? Hopefully it didn't concern him. He raked a hand through his hair and rose. Voice gruff, he asked, "Can I see him?"

The doctor nodded. "Come this way."

"I'll wait for you in the hall, Brock. I'd like for you to come to my apartment. We have matters to discuss."

~ * ~

Zana woke to the sound of voices—one the doctor who'd been in and out during her brief periods of consciousness. "She's improving slowly, Mr. Callahan, but it will be a week before you'll want to leave Abyss."

"Thank you, Doctor." The deep rumble of the captain's voice closed around her. She sighed with relief. He hadn't left her here to fend for herself.

She wasn't alone.

He took her hand. "The doctor says you're going to live. It was poison in the candy. Can you think of anyone who'd want to kill you?"

Kill me? She shook her head. No one would want to kill her. She didn't know anyone other than the Bartholomews, Greta, and the few friends she'd made.

"Samuel doesn't think Helen and Jonas could have done it. Helen is beside herself with worry. Plus, they found the sweet shop's proprietor dead."

Terror rose in her throat and she stifled the scream she longed to release. Who would want to kill her? Oh, dear, Lord. The boy. What about him?

"Pepe?" Her lips trembled and she bit the bottom one to still them.

His features contorted. He didn't speak but shook his head and turned aside to block her view of the pain in his eyes.

She couldn't stop her tears. Her body shook with sobs. The movement hurt. She cried out and clutched her stomach.

He was instantly solicitous and hands on top of hers, ordered, "You must be still. Dr. Raymond said you're lucky to be alive. Just rest and get well."

She clutched his hand and squeezed. "I'm so sorry about the boy. I know you were fond of him."

He nodded. "Yes, I was. He was the little brother I'd always wanted."

Samuel waited for Brock when he left sickbay. A guard sat in a chair in the hall next to the doorway. Someone would watch her at all times. He and his crew would remain on the *Retriever*. Even at Abyss's medical platform, his ship was vulnerable to pirates.

They couldn't afford to take chances. He'd join them there shortly if his visit with Samuel didn't keep him late. Brock couldn't imagine what they needed to discuss, but it would give him a chance to see where Delia lived while a citizen of Abyss.

The governor's digs were not elegant and fussy as Brock had expected. The place was warm, comfortable, and homey. A brown plush sofa with a pair of matching chairs sported tan, turquoise, and red Aztec print pillows. Colorful prints with large splatters of turquoise hung on the wall. The room screamed of Delia's taste. Thoughts of his vibrant sister brought a lump to his throat.

A small child, probably two years old ran laughing into the room. "Daddy, Daddy."

Brock watched in amazement as Samuel's face lit with joy as he scooped the toddler up into his arms, tossing him into the air. Squeals of delight rang through the room and Brock found himself smiling. He and Shelia had frolicked in much the same way when she'd been a tot.

Samuel put the boy on his feet. "That's enough play for now. We have a guest I want you to meet. This is Captain Callahan, son. He's your uncle."

Dark headed like his father, the child half hid behind Samuel and turned big gray eyes up to Brock— Delia's eyes. He felt the breath leave his body in a whoosh. Stars floated before his eyes and for a minute he feared he'd collapse to the floor in a faint. He dropped into a chair before he fell.

"Brock, this is my son, Daniel. Your nephew."

~ * ~

"What's an unka?"

Samuel chuckled, lifted Daniel, and plopped him in Brock's lap. "Here, Callahan, explain it to him while I get us some coffee."

Brock turned the boy in his lap so he faced him, his little legs crossed at the ankles. He wanted to hug him tightly but feared he'd scare him. Best to take things slowly. Daniel studied him carefully. As if giving his approval, he grinned exposing a set of beautiful baby teeth. Brock's heart twisted and he wanted to cry with joy and rage. He wanted to kill Samuel for keeping Delia's child from him. The fact that he'd done so enhanced his suspicions that he'd had something to do with Delia's death. He wasn't leaving this time until he had answers.

A small hand rubbed his jaw. "You scratchy. Need to shave."

"Yep, I guess I do."

"My daddy gots to shave, too."

"Is that right?"

"Uh huh. What's an unka?"

"Well, let's see." He scratched his beard, making a rasping sound for effect. "It means your mama was my sister."

"Oh." He arched a brow in thought. "My mama's gone to Heaven."

Brock coughed to cover the sound of tears in his voice. "I know. I miss her very much."

Daniel patted his cheek. "Don't cry, Unka Bock. You need a hug?"

Laughing, Brock lifted him against his chest. Little arms went around his neck. "What I need is a tight hug. How about it, little man?"

Daniel squashed his neck tight. Brock savored

every squeeze as he rubbed the child's back, drawing comfort even from that small pleasure. This was his baby sister's child.

"I see you've gotten acquainted," said Samuel as he entered the room with a tray loaded with sandwich makings, a coffee pot, and two mugs.

Daniel jumped from his arms. "Be back."

"He's a wonderful boy, Samuel. Why the hell have you kept his existence from me? I could kill'

"Shsss. Not now."

Bare feet slapped against the polished floor as Daniel ran back into the room, a picture in his hand. He crawled into Brock's lap, eliciting a grunt of pain as a knee hit him in the groin.

Daniel shoved the picture in front of his face. "See. Mama, Daddy, and me."

Brock took the picture and held it away so he could focus. It was a formal color portrait. Delia, head resting against Samuel's chin, held her newborn baby, joy and pride glowing on her face. They appeared to be the perfect family. Was it a real portrayal?

"Your mama was very pretty." He tweaked Daniel's nose. "You were kinda cute, too."

"Yeah, that's what Daddy says. Daddy cries sometimes when he looks at it."

"Is that so?"

His little head bobbed up and down. "Uh huh. He misses her too."

Samuel lifted Daniel. "It's your bedtime, mister." He turned to Brock. "I'll be right back. Pour yourself some coffee and fill you a plate. Don't wait on me."

"Night, Unka Bock."

"Goodnight, Daniel. I'll see you again soon."

"'K."

Brock hadn't realized how hungry he was until he started eating. He'd inhaled two sandwiches when Samuel returned and sat on the sofa across from him. He heaped his plate.

"Sorry it took so long, but he had a thousand questions."

"Do you take care of him all by yourself?"

"No, he has a nanny, but I like to put him to bed myself. Plus, she goes home early as a rule, but stayed late tonight until I could get here."

Brock waited until Samuel finished eating. He didn't have to ask for answers. Samuel wiped his hands, leaned back against the sofa and fixed him with his gaze.

"Delia didn't die from just a freak accident. She was poisoned with the same poison used in the candy sent to Mrs. Forrester. Dr. Raymond confirmed my suspicions today."

Seven

"What are you talking about?" Brock asked. "She fell from one of those high-speed transports, didn't she?" Fell, hell, thrown was more like it. This, to his way of thinking, was next to impossible. The metal safety bars were strong enough to hold a five hundred pound man.

"Yes, she was."

Samuel's hand shook as he poured more coffee and for just a moment Brock's gut twisted with sympathy. How could he trust this man's actions? For all Brock knew, the man was a good actor. Maybe Samuel truly loved Delia. Perhaps Brock had played a part in her death, himself. What a shame his hard-headedness had kept him from being around to keep an eye on her. It's possible he could have prevented her death.

"Her safety bar malfunctioned, but Mother said she'd been ill, complaining of stomach cramps. They'd just finished lunch at one of the restaurants and were headed home." He drank from his cup and sat it on the sleek mahogany coffee table. "Concerned about food poisoning, I had her stomach contents examined. The lab could find no food-borne disease, but found an unusual toxin they couldn't identify. Today Dr. Raymond informed me the toxin that killed Delia was hard to isolate because they didn't suspect poisoning right away. When they performed an analysis, stomach acids weakened the toxin making it hard to identify."

Brock was stunned. Samuel's expression resembled a death mask; his mouth pinched tight, his eyes haunted with grief. Voice hoarse, he rasped out, "Someone killed my wife."

Pain gripped Brock's chest and he gasped for air. Though Samuel appeared distraught, Brock didn't trust him. Hands fisted, to keep them off the man, he raged, "Why didn't you tell me about your suspicions?"

"If you'd come back after her memorial service and talked to me, we could have discussed things then." Samuel couldn't keep the anger and disgust from his voice. "For that matter, why the hell couldn't you have forgiven your sister for choosing to live here instead of treating her with silence for two years?" Delia had suffered through her brother's neglect. Brock was her hero, the only family she had left. She'd wanted him to be a part of their child's life, to share their joy in her pregnancy. But, Brock never answered her letters or communicated in any way.

"She suffered, deeply." Samuel struggled to keep tears from gathering in his eyes. He'd wanted to kill Brock for the way he'd treated Delia.

"You're lying." His voice a low growl, Brock added, "I wrote her every week, but the mail all came back unopened. I even showed up at this door once and some old hag turned me away. She informed me you and Delia were vacationing at another colony."

Heat infused Samuel's face. "Watch how you talk about my mother."

"I've seen your mother, and this woman wasn't her. Mrs. Whitehall is white headed. This lady was old, skinny, and wrinkled, but her hair was black as tar, very little gray in it."

"The woman sounds like our housekeeper, Leona Juarez. When were you here?"

"In June, a little over a year after your wedding."

Samuel nodded, a slight smile twisting his lips. "Delia hadn't been feeling well and we suspected she was pregnant. With the excuse of taking a short vacation, we visited a gynecologist in Labyrinth." As far as he knew, Leona hadn't mentioned Brock's visit. If she'd told Delia, she'd have been beside herself with joy.

Brock rubbed the back of his neck. "I admit to being pigheaded, but six months after your wedding, I started trying to get in touch with Delia."

"You were more than pigheaded, you were cruel. Delia cried for hours every day."

Samuel enjoyed the expression of pain etched on Brock's face. *Serves you right, you bastard.* He'd never thought to love someone. For some reason, pheromone matching hadn't worked on him. Experiments and tests proved his body was resistant. The minute he saw Delia, he knew why. She was his mate—chosen not by chemicals, but by his heart, mind, and body. Though he believed their society's method of mate selection was viable, necessary for a trouble-free environment, he was pleased he was different. When Delia had returned his affection, he'd been elated.

His father had been governor before him, but it was his mother, called Governor Matriarch by many, who'd actually run things. Father spent his time in his medical lab with his research projects and he was grateful for her intervention. She was furious at Samuel's news and forbade the marriage. He was thirty years old at the time and Abyss had no law to prevent their union. Mother had not spoken to either of them until she learned Delia was pregnant.

Brock bellowed and hit the coffee table sending knick-knacks dancing across the surface. "You still should have told me you suspected she'd been murdered."

"Keep your voice down." Samuel waited a second to listen for Daniel's call and breathed a sigh of relief when it remained quiet. "Hell, I didn't know for sure until today."

"But, why? Why would anyone want to harm Delia?"

Samuel wondered the same thing. He'd find out if it was the last thing he did and the person would pay. He leaned back and closed his eyes. "For the life of me, I can't come up with a reason that makes sense. Everyone here liked her." And they did. She'd been popular and made friends easily. Oh, his mother had been livid when they'd married, but her attitude changed at the news of a grandchild. She'd mothered Delia, and when Daniel arrived she'd spent a lot of time at their place—too much in his opinion. But, knowing how important the child was to her, they'd put up with her constant presence. Her attitude toward Delia turned from one of acceptance to real affection. Tears stung his eyes. How had something so wonderful turned so wrong?

"Samuel. Samuel."

His eyes popped open as he pushed away from the cushioned back. "I'm sorry, what'd you say?"

"What can be the connection between Delia's death and the attempt on Mrs. Forrester's life?"

"I don't know. It doesn't make any sense. I barely knew the woman. Our mating interview didn't go well."

Brock tensed. Mating interview? "What the hell are you talking about?" He lurched out of the club chair. "You were trying to dope her?" He knew she'd been exposed to selective mating, but not with Samuel. The idea raised his hackles.

"Give it a rest, Brock. You know how things work here. Zana needed a mate and if she and I'd enjoyed each other's company, I'd have pursued a joining." He shrugged. "We didn't suit. Plus, I'm not a good candidate for pheromone selection anyway. I'd given up on having a family until Delia came along. Now that she's gone, I'm destined to be alone."

Brock dropped back against his chair. Samuel and Zana? When had she become Zana in his mind? The picture of the two of them in marital pheromone bliss didn't please him one whit. He shuddered inwardly. The idea irritated the hell out of him. Not that he had any designs on the woman. Yes, he was drawn to her, but he'd been attracted to loads of women. The relationship never progressed beyond a few romps in the hay.

Samuel sat in silence, his eyes fixed on an image in his mind. A sad smile tilted the corners of his mouth and he leaned forward to retrieve the picture Daniel had left on the coffee table. His fingers caressed the frame as he studied the likeness. Brock felt sorry for the man. How ironic the governor of Abyss couldn't abide by his society's guidelines. "Have you ever thought about leaving this place?"

Samuel's laugh was harsh. "Leave everything I've ever known? No, my life is here. I have Daniel. He's enough to keep me happy."

"By the way, how is it you and Delia were allowed to have a baby so early in your marriage?" Most couples in Abyss waited years before having a baby. Permission to procreate was given using a lottery type system. Every new year, those wanting to have a child, entered their names into a drawing. Each month, on the first day, a name was drawn. The lucky winner would visit the clinic where her method of birth control would be reversed so she could conceive.

As with their method of selective mating, Brock considered it to be a barbaric practice, but, he could understand the need for limiting population growth. Their reproduction policy was similar to the law implemented in China in 1979 where couples were limited to having one child. There were some exceptions but they were few in number and rigidly controlled. In Abyss, there was only so much space available. Controls were necessary.

Samuel placed the picture he'd been studying back on the table, his expression resigned. "Delia had difficulty tolerating her birth control method. The doctors changed it several times but they either caused stomach cramps or nausea. When they removed her internal device, we were supposed to wait to have relations until they found something else for her." He grinned. "I must say, we couldn't keep our hands off each other."

Brock snorted. "I get the picture."

"Anyway, when she suspected she'd conceived, we decided to leave Abyss for confirmation she was pregnant. On her next visit to the clinic they pressured us into terminating the pregnancy but Delia refused.

The council tried to coerce her, making matters worse. You know how stubborn she could be. Hell, I couldn't see killing our child, either. I told them to give their permission or I'd resign and we'd leave Abyss."

Brock restrained a shudder of disgust. "Thank God for that." The thought of destroying that sweet child raised his hackles.

Samuel nodded. "They reluctantly agreed."

"Didn't that cause hard feelings with the citizens of Abyss?" Brock would have been royally pissed if he'd waited years to have a baby and just because Samuel was governor, he didn't have to follow the rules of their society. It really wasn't fair but Brock was grateful Daniel had been born.

"Yes, some. To help disperse some of the hard feelings, I paid a large fine, money that was divided among those waiting in the lottery pool."

Brock wondered how pacified they actually were. Some might have enjoyed the money. Others might have still harbored resentment. "Is it possible some disgruntled citizen could have tried to kill Delia, tampered with her food and the transporter?"

"Anything is possible, but I don't think so. If they'd wanted to eliminate Delia because of the baby, they'd have tried to take her life before Daniel was born."

His reasoning sounded logical to Brock. If not because of the pregnancy, why would someone want to hurt his sister? Someone had to have the answer. Poor little Daniel. He'd just met the boy but loved him as if he'd held him immediately after birth. He hated that the child lived here in Abyss and would be exposed to the despicable lifestyle.

"What if Daniel has inherited your resistance to pheromone treatment? Would you subject him to a life without the type of love you and Delia experienced?" Though he'd never love again, he couldn't bear to think of anything sadder than Daniel never experiencing love and family. Yes, his marriage hadn't been happy, but at least he had Shelia as a result. He'd like to have had more children, but it wasn't meant to be.

"I don't think that will be an issue. Daniel and a girl in his playgroup have formed a strong bond already. I'm sure she's the one who'll be his mate. He has several close girl friends. If not this one, there will be another."

Brock snorted. "That's disgusting, Samuel. I know it, and in your heart, you know it, too. How can you subject that precious child to something so barbaric and sterile?"

"I'll say it again, Brock. It's how things work here. Just because I'm not happy, doesn't mean he can't be."

"Why don't you and Daniel move to Refuge? You'd have no problem finding work. Hell, you could start a business of some kind. Daniel would have his cousin Shelia and lots of other children to run and play with outdoors like children are supposed to."

Samuel raked his hands through his dark hair. "Leave it alone, will you?" He stood and started stacking their dirty dishes on the tray. "We need to get some rest. I'd offer you the guest room but would prefer to not be killed in my sleep."

"Smart thinking. I'll either return to the ship or stay at the hotel."

"Will you be leaving for Refuge in the morning?"

"No. We'll wait until the doctor releases Mrs.

Forrester. Plus, I want some answers about Delia before I leave. I want to see the accident report and understand how the hell a seatbelt can malfunction."

"Yeah, I'd like to look at it again too. And I'd like to find out what happened to all those letters between you and Delia that never got delivered."

Brock released the breath he'd been holding. "You believe me?"

"Of course I do. I never doubted your devotion to your sister, just your pigheadedness." Brow furrowed, he cocked his head. "Something stinks to high heaven here, and I plan to get to the bottom of it. Whoever did this is going to pay, preferably with their life."

"I agree, and I'll take great pleasure in carrying out the sentence. Even if it's you, Samuel." Though his opinion of Samuel had risen during their discussion, he didn't fully trust the man. He'd yet to prove himself.

Eight

It was five minutes past eight in the morning. Lights simulated sunshine, making the entertainment pod glow like the sunny outdoors. Last evening, it had been dark. Walkways were lit with strategically placed lampposts throughout making the area resemble an eighteenth-century town. Architects designed the lighting to help establish normal sleep patterns, provide the vitamin D individuals needed for good health, and for some people, prevent depression.

Brock had called Samuel earlier to let him know where he'd spent the night. He'd just finished breakfast in the hotel's coffee shop when Samuel, dressed casually in slacks and shirt, came by to meet him. Samuel looked better without the prissy suit.

"Let me stop by the desk and pay my bill before we leave. Retriever will be pulling out of the docking bay no later than one this afternoon, and I won't have time later."

Brock and Samuel had no trouble getting copies of the accident report and they stopped at a small café for coffee to read the details. Officials investigating the crash couldn't find any concrete evidence indicating the safety bar failed. They'd performed test after test with the same findings—nothing was wrong with the safety device. They concluded Delia hadn't locked the safety bar.

He tapped the page where Samuel was reading. "How can this be?"

"It doesn't make any sense," said Samuel. "Delia was very careful to always lock herself in, to make sure the hasp caught. She'd not had the belt tight enough her first time out alone, and the car jerked forward and stopped. Her head hit the shield, and she had a nasty bump. She wouldn't have forgotten again."

"Could she have been so incapacitated by the poison she wasn't thinking clearly? Is it possible she or someone else hit the emergency release switch?" From Brock's understanding, the button wouldn't work unless the craft slowed down to a crawl.

"I don't see how as she'd never have been thrown like that."

Everything they learned pointed more and more to foul play, and only one person was with her when she crashed. "We need to talk to your mother. She's the only one with her in the vehicle that day and who knows what happened."

Samuel lurched from his chair, bumping the table. Their coffee sloshed onto the shiny surface making a mess. "My mother did not kill my wife. Get that out of your head right now."

Brock stood and grabbed Samuel's arm. "Keep your voice down, man." He dropped money on the table and ushered him out of the café. "No one is accusing your mother, but she's the only witness we have, right?"

Samuel shook off his grip. "Yes, she is but I don't know what more she can tell us. She went through questioning numerous times right after the accident."

"Look, man, what could it hurt?"

"It could upset her, that's what it could hurt."

They stood at the rail looking down on the activity thirty floors below. The people looked like ants as they walked amid the potted trees and plants that dotted the shopping mall courtyard. In one area, a playground exploded with activity as kids slid down the slides and kicked to fly higher in their swings. His pleasure in their fun soured at the thought of what the future held for them and his nephew.

Brock turned back to Samuel. "I don't intend to go in her home and accuse her of murder. I would like to understand what happened that day, hear it from her. You've talked to her and had your questions answered. Let me have mine answered."

The level where Mrs. Whiteside's apartment was located echoed the site of Samuel's, only it was less grand and smaller. Still, it was considerably larger than housing of the average citizen, couple even. He could tell the size as false facades separated the dwellings, setting them apart from each other. Two Grecian pillars stood guard beside the ornate door decorated with acanthus leaves, Greek gods, and goddesses. Brock stood to the side as Samuel rang the doorbell.

Samuel was surprised his former housekeeper answered his mother's door. He didn't know the two women were acquainted.

She appeared taken aback to see them. "Sir... Governor Whiteside, Mr. Callahan, come in, come in. Your mother will be pleased to have company, sir."

"Mrs. Juarez, I didn't know you knew my mother."

"Why yes, we've know each other since childhood. Well, actually, I was eleven years old when your mother came into our family."

Now why hadn't he known that? Probably because his mother didn't talk about her life before she married his father. He'd gotten the impression her childhood hadn't been a happy one.

"How do you know Mr. Callahan? I don't remember him ever visiting Delia." If so, he'd have heard about it. Delia would have been thrilled.

She paled. "I, uh—"

"Who is it, Leona?"

"It's me, Mother. I've brought you a visitor."

"Answer my question, Mrs. Juarez."

"Your wife had his picture. She showed it to me often."

Samuel nodded. "Yes, I see." He walked from the hallway into the living area, Brock following behind him. Mother sat in her favorite chair, an ugly wingchair covered in maroon velvet. Her tiny feet were propped on a footstool of the same fabric. Her black pantsuit made her white hair appear silver. The jade shawl across her shoulders brought out the green tint in her eyes.

She raised her arms to him. "My boy, how good of you to come see me."

He bent down and kissed her cheek. "Hello, Mother. Where's Edith? I was surprised to see Mrs. Juarez here. I didn't know you even knew her."

"Of course I know her, have all my life. Edith is out for a few days, not feeling well, so Leona came by to help me out."

"All the time she worked for me and Delia, you never mentioned knowing her."

"I thought you knew. Delia knew we'd grown up together." She patted his cheek. "Who'd you bring to see me? Is it that sweet grandson of mine?"

Samuel straightened and motioned Brock forward. "No, Mother. It's Brock Callahan, Delia's brother."

Katherine Whiteside straightened in her chair, the pleasant expression dropping from her face to be replaced by one of haughty arrogance. Brock thought it impossible for the small woman to look down her nose at him from her position below him, but she did. He offered his hand. Mouth pinched, she looked at it, and then turned to her son.

"What is this man doing here, in my home? Explain yourself, Samuel."

"Mother'

"How could you even speak to him after the way he treated our sweet Delia?" She turned on Brock and sneered. "Get out of my home."

"That'll be enough, Mother." Samuel motioned Brock to the sofa and sat in the chair beside his mother.

"You overstep your bounds, young man. This is my home, and I want him out." She pointed at Brock, shakily gripped the arm of her chair, and stood. "Get out," she screeched.

"Sit down, Mother. He's not leaving. We need your help. A man died yesterday, poisoned, and Zana Forrester almost lost her life as well."

Her eyes widened. "She's still alive?"

"Yes, thank God."

She dropped back into her chair and sniffed as if a bad smell permeated the room. "What does this have to do with me? With you or Brock Callahan for that matter?"

Katherine exchanged a silent message with Mrs Juarez. The woman turned to leave the room. Brock stood. "Ma'am, please stay. We need to ask you a few questions, too."

She gasped. "Me?" Her eyes darted between the three of them. "I…I can't imagine how I can help."

Brock took her elbow and led her to the sofa where she sat down and ran her hands over the knees of her silk clad legs.

"I'd like to know why you didn't tell Delia and Samuel I'd been by to see them."

Hand over her heart, she stammered, "Why, I…I…" Her face scrunched up as she struggled not to cry.

"Oh leave her alone. She did what I told her to do. And yes, I had Leona throw away her letters to you, and those you sent."

Brock's despair at Mrs. Whiteside's lack of concern at how she'd cheated Samuel, Delia, and him turned to anger. He wanted to throttle the old woman, but at the expression of shock and pain on Samuel's face, he tamped down the desire to commit murder.

Samuel fell against the chair back, shoulders slumped. His face was ashen. "Why on Earth would you do that, Mother? You knew how much Delia wanted to hear from Brock, how happy she'd be." Samuel gasped for breath as if talking took extreme effort. Brock worried Samuel might be having a stroke or heart attack.

"Are you okay, man? You need some water or something?" He stood up. "Where's the kitchen?"

Mrs. Juarez moved. "I'll get him something."

Samuel's head dropped back against the chair cushion, eyes closed. Katherine watched her son closely, concern etching her brow, but Brock suspected it was only for her son, not remorse at what she'd done. He couldn't believe the gall of the old broad. Who'd she think she was anyway? God? He wanted to say more but out of concern for Samuel, kept his mouth shut.

Mrs. Juarez rushed back into the room with a glass of water. "Here, Mr. Whiteside. I hope this will help."

Brock snorted. "I think a glass of brandy would be more helpful."

Samuel took the glass and emptied it. He handed it back to Leona, nodded, and then turned to his mother. A tinge of color crept up his face replacing his paleness of before. Brock exhaled a sigh of relief that Samuel had recovered from the shock of his mother's admission.

Lips pursed, she muttered, "Son, I thought it best for both you and Delia if she cut ties with Refuge and the heathen people she sprung from."

He stared, Brock assumed, waiting for something sensible to come from her mouth. The color on his face deepened.

"She might have wanted to go home, tried to talk you into leaving here, take my grandchild."

"You had no right, Mother. No right at all to play around with our lives. Who the hell do you think you are?"

"You'll not talk to me that way. I'm your mother and deserve your respect."

"My mother! Mothers don't hurt their children like you've done me." He dropped his head into his hands. "God, the torment Delia experienced, all because of you!"

"Now, son—"

He held up a hand. "I don't want to hear it, probably just more lies anyway. What I do want to hear is your account of what happened the day Delia died."

"I've told you and the police a thousand times what occurred. Why again?"

"Brock needs to hear your account. We've looked at the police records, and they could find no reason for the safety bar to have malfunctioned. So, tell me again, Mother. What happened that day?"

"This is ridiculous." She waved her hand at him. "If Brock Callahan had been concerned about his sister, he'd have been here before now looking for answers to that terrible accident." With an exaggerated sniff, she pulled a handkerchief from the pocket of her long dress and touched it to her nose. "It was horrible, something I'll never forget. That poor girl, the mother of my precious grandson, broken into a thousand pieces right in front of my eyes."

She covered her face with the white cloth and wailed, "I can't talk about it anymore. Don't ask me to, son. Have pity."

Brock had never seen such a display of drama. He wouldn't be surprised if she broke into an operatic aria and waved the napkin for effect.

For a minute Brock thought Samuel would waver and give into the old woman's theatrics. "That'll be enough, Mother. I'm onto you now and your machinations."

She turned on Brock with a snarl. "Why now? Why dredge it up all over again?"

"Because we've discovered Delia didn't die in an accident. She was murdered," said Brock.

Mrs. Whiteside paled and sputtered, "Why,

why…that's…ludicrous."

"No, Mother, it's not. The reason Delia was sick, is because someone poisoned her while you were at lunch that day. The same toxin was used yesterday to try to kill Zana Forrester. It killed one of Brock's crew members, a young man barely twenty years old."

"Poisoned? Who would want to harm Delia, or for that matter, this Zana person?" She sniffed. "I hear she refused selective mating. What a shame about the boy. Do the police have any idea how the poison was administered?"

"In chocolate candy. As a matter-of-fact, the candy shop owner was also found dead, so it will be difficult to figure out who sent her the chocolates."

"I'm so sorry. I had no idea. I thought Delia had developed a virus." Brock watched her. She didn't act sorry. He'd never observed a person more egocentric than this woman. It was as if she wasn't capable of caring about anyone other than herself. Maybe she loved Samuel and Daniel, but in his opinion, it was a scary attachment.

"Mrs. Whiteside, who did you and Delia have lunch with that day?"

She pursed her lips. "Edith met us there with a friend. I can't remember the woman's name. They'd been shopping as it was Edith's day off."

"Would any of the women there have had a reason to kill Delia?"

The old woman stiffened her back, chin in the air. "Of course not. What a ridiculous question."

Brock shrugged. "Maybe. Maybe not." Could the poison have been administered before they left Mrs. Whiteside's apartment? It was possible. He tried to remember how long after eating the candy before Zana had taken ill.

"Who drove the transport on the return trip that day?"

"I did, of course. Delia was sick, shaking, moaning, and clutching her stomach. Why, she could barely walk. Edith helped me get her in the vehicle."

His gut churned. "Why wasn't emergency medical care called in?"

"Why would we? We thought she had a virus. Until today that's what we've all thought." She sent Samuel an accusing look. "You should have told me she was poisoned, son."

"Knowing would have served no purpose, Mother, only cause you to worry."

"Did you see Delia lock the safety bar that day?"

"Of course I did. As sick as she was, think I didn't check?"

Brock had no choice but to believe her. In truth, she had no reason to cause Delia harm. She was a self-centered old woman, but that didn't make her a killer. He wondered if Samuel's lab reports indicated if the dose of poison Delia ingested was lethal. Without a doubt, the accident had killed her, but was it just an accident or a backup plan?

He stood. Samuel rose too. "Thank you for answering my questions, Mrs. Whiteside. I hate bringing this all up again, but had to hear the details for myself."

"I hope you find out who did this terrible thing."

"Oh, you can count on it, Mrs. Whiteside. We'll find out, and when we do, we'll know who is trying to kill Mrs. Forrester. If I don't kill that person first, whoever is responsible will be convicted and given the death sentence." He turned to Samuel. "That is the penalty in Abyss for murder, is it not?"

"Yes, death by lethal injection."

Nine

Upon returning to *Retriever*, Brock went immediately to sickbay to check on Mrs. Forrester. The guard opened the door to let him pass. Dr. Raymond and several members of his medical team stood around the pod working with equipment. He turned when Brock entered and motioned him forward. "Would you like to see what we're doing?"

Hell yes, he would, as the patient was pale as death. "Please tell me you're not removing all the blood from her body."

Dr. Raymond laughed. "I'd be lying if I did."

His horror must have shown on his face as the doctor quickly squeezed his shoulder and added, "Don't worry, we're cleaning it and then sending it back into her body. Mrs. Forrester is making good progress."

Brock released the breath he'd been holding and nodded as he gazed down at the woman who'd captured his interest. Hell, more than his interest. She was quickly becoming an obsession, a dangerous one. He mentally shook himself and returned his attention to Dr. Raymond.

They'd attached a device to the side of the pod. Blood moved through it, traveling through a multitude of tiny compartments. As it did so, a greenish-yellow substance leaked into a separate small partition beside the larger one.

The doctor pointed to the disgusting color liquid. "Poison from the Phyllobates terribilis. We're using nanotechnology to remove the toxin from her body and organs."

Brock moved closer to better see the machine in action. Not that he could see anything in particular, just blood moving.

"The robots are too tiny to see with the human eye but they're doing a wonderful job at cleaning Mrs. Forrester's system. They release the poison and return to her body to continue their job."

Brock knew about nanotechnology but hadn't seen it in operation before. Even in their small hospital in Refuge, they had nano capability but it was used for severe wounds where tissues were damaged almost beyond repair. If only they'd had the technology aboard *Retriever,* Pepe might be alive today.

"How long will this take?"

"One more treatment should have her system clean. Then the healing of her tissues will begin. We'll use nanobots programmed to repair cells."

He patted Brock on the back. "She's going to be fine, Mr. Callahan."

"Who would I talk to about obtaining this technology to keep aboard my boat?" He'd be damned if he had another crewmember die because they didn't have the tools to keep them alive until they could get help.

"You can talk to me or a salesman in the hospital equipment division."

"I'd prefer you." He'd seen the doctor in action and trusted him more than he would a salesman.

The following morning Brock, along with Digger

and Luke, watched as Dr. Raymond attached a one-inch size cube to a computer. "Let's suppose you have a man whose leg has been mauled by a shark. I can program these one million bots to repair all the tissues—some to muscles, others ligaments, bone, nerves, and rebuild blood."

As the doctor talked on, Brock decided. They had to have the technology. Yes, Dr. Boone had nanobots in the hospital, but what if they had a crisis of some kind and they needed to care for more than one person at a time?

"Would it take that many bots to mend the damage?"

Dr. Raymond smiled. "No. Actually, one-fourth that amount is more than enough." He picked up the square and broke it into four parts. "You could leave two of these in your community and carry the other two with you on voyages."

They spent the remainder of the morning learning how to program and administer the nanobots into a patient's system. As they gathered to leave the lab, Dr. Raymond clapped Brock on the shoulder.

"Would you like for me to have a system readied for you to take with you, Captain Callahan?"

"I'm tempted but need to check with our Dr. Boone first. I'll get with you in the morning." They couldn't afford to buy indiscriminately without being aware of medical funds available and an inventory of equipment. The doctor nodded and offered his hand. "I look forward to your decision."

~ * ~

Brock entered sickbay to see that Zana had been moved from the medical pod and lay on a bed with pristine white linens. A nurse sat beside her and stood so he could sit down. Curled on her side facing the door, Zana had both hands under her left cheek. From the expression on her face, she didn't appear to be in pain. He looked up at the nurse standing beside him.

"She's better, Mr. Callahan, but still in some pain. We are administering a new drug that lasts twelve hours, yet doesn't put the patient fully to sleep. She needs every bit of rest she can get, but we can better evaluate her recovery during her wakeful periods."

"Her color is better." Her cheeks weren't as pale; her lips carried a tinge of pink.

"Much improved, sir."

"If you'd like to take a break, I'll sit with her."

"Thank you. A couple of turns around the deck to stretch my legs will be welcome." She stopped at the door. "I'll only be gone ten minutes."

Brock watched Zana sleep, the soft flutter of her lips as she inhaled and exhaled. He couldn't resist a chuckle when a snuffle slipped from her mouth. No doubt she'd have a fit if she knew he'd caught her snoring, no matter how soft and cute it was.

He wiped the grin from his face and leaned back in the chair, unable to take his eyes from the woman who'd captured his attention from the moment he'd unsealed the Polar Excursion. After leaving her in Abyss, he'd not expected to see her again. Yet life had other plans. He didn't believe in fate. He believed you created your own destiny. It would be easy to care for her, but he'd sworn to not love another woman. Not because he believed all of them were fickle in their affections, because they weren't. No, the women he loved died. Did his love make them more susceptible to death? He snorted in disgust. Ridiculous. He didn't believe in jinxes and such, but he didn't want to take that chance, and he wouldn't.

What were he and his crew going to do for four more days while Mrs. Forrester recovered? The citizens of Abyss didn't want his men mingling with them so Brock would have to find ways to keep them busy onboard *Retriever*. Maintenance chores were never finished on a water craft. He'd have to come up with something else to fill up the hours.

~ * ~

Zana woke to find Captain Callahan sitting by her bed reading on a handheld computer. "Cap…" The word came out as a croak. He looked up and smiled. She coughed to clear her throat. "Captain. Are you reading a novel?"

He waved the computer. "This? No. I'm shopping for weapons." He laid the device on the medical tray by her bed. "How're you feeling?"

"Like I'll live." Weird. She remembered thinking the same thing several months ago while going through rebirth. At the time, she wasn't sure she wanted to, now she knew she did. Refuge would offer a new start, a chance to build a new life and recover from the losses she'd experienced. Hopefully, in the building she'd be able to find information about her daughter.

"Good. How about some fresh air? Mrs. Cray is on duty today and said we could take you up on deck when you woke."

"I'd love to." Her hand went to her hair. She must look awful. And she'd love to clean her teeth. "I need a comb or brush."

"No need to worry about your hair. It's windy out

and brushing would be a waste of effort."

"But, doing so will make me feel better and I do need to brush my teeth." She pointed behind her.

He handed her the items and anxious to breathe fresh air, she quickly brushed her teeth, washed her face, and removed the tangles from her hair.

He stood and bent over the bed. Before she could try to get up, he'd pulled all the cover lose from the bed and wrapped her up like a baby.

"Wait a minute. I can walk."

"No, you can't. Nurse Cray's orders." She gasped as he lifted her in his arms. "She has a chaise all ready for you."

With no difficulty bearing her weight, he cradled her against his chest and followed the man she assumed was her guard up the stairs. The bright sunlight stabbed at her eyes. She squeezed them shut to give them time to adjust to the glare. The sun warmed her face; the wind lifted her hair from her neck and stirred it around her face. She tilted her face back to enjoy nature's kiss.

Brock laid her on the reclining chair and Mrs. Cray tucked another blanket around her. Zana's eyes adjusted to the glare and she looked up at the cloudless sky, blue and endless. She dropped them to the wide expanse of blue beyond the guardrail. The swells of the Atlantic rocked the boat and she relaxed enjoying the rhythm. She breathed in the clean fragrance of sea air mixed with the acrid odor of fresh paint. Sounds from the hull of the boat indicated some of Brock's men scraped away peeling paint while others followed to apply fresh.

Her trip aboard Retriever several days ago had been rushed. She'd not had time to enjoy her first view of Earth since her plummet into the ice. The view, the breeze, and the sunlight—how could anyone live without them?

The hum of voices lulled her. She closed her eyes and let sleep envelope her.

Two days later, with Brock's arm around her waist, she walked once around the poop deck. When they reached her chaise, she sagged into it and leaned back sideways, too weak to raise her feet off the beautifully shellacked wood beneath her.

Brock chuckled, lifted her legs to the lounge chair, and helped her shift to her back. Eyes narrowed, she shot him a dirty look before closing her eyes. "Not funny, Brock Callahan."

He patted her leg. "I know. Been there myself." He settled in a chair. "Do you want to sleep awhile?"

"No. Just need to catch my breath." She allowed her breathing to return to normal. "I've been thinking."

"Hmm, about what?"

"How I can support myself in Refuge." Lying in bed, she'd had loads of time to contemplate her future. She'd settle in the community and determine what the people didn't have and would enjoy—maybe a restaurant or clothing shop. "I've decided to sell my Polar Excursion and use the proceeds to start a business."

He gaped at her as if she'd grown an extra head. Surely her idea wasn't that bad. "What do you think?"

"I think let's worry about you getting well. You'll have time to dwell on making a living later."

~ * ~

Brock jogged down the inner stairs from the command deck to check in on their patient. Tomorrow they'd cast off for home and he wanted to make sure Dr. Raymond had released her as fit for travel. The guard by her door snored softly, his head propped against the wall. Brock snorted and kicked the chair leg. The man jumped up and went for the laser gun at his hip.

"Stand down, soldier." Brock looked into Zana's room to find it empty. "Where is she?"

"Above deck, sir."

"You let her go alone?" Brock wanted to deck the man—first for being asleep on duty and second for allowing Zana to step out on her own."

The man stiffened. "Of course not. I assure you Captain Callahan, I take my responsibility seriously. One of your men is escorting Mrs. Forrester. I believe his name is Digger."

Brock nodded and strode down the hall toward the stairs leading to the poop deck. At the top, on her way down, stood Zana—alone. Hand on the rail she took a couple of steps.

His heart jumped into his throat. "What the hell are you doing?"

She froze and eyes wide, looked down and then around. "Why, what does it look like? I'm about to come down these stairs to my room."

"You shouldn't be by yourself. You could fall." He held up a hand. "Wait right there. I'm coming up."

"Don't be ridiculous." She took another step.

Brock bellowed. "I said to stay." He ran up, taking two steps at a time and took her arm.

She yanked from his grasp. "I am not a dog to be ordered about, Brock Callahan, nor a child. Don't you think I have sense enough to know when I need help and when I don't?"

"You're my responsibility while you're on the boat. I won't have you falling and getting hurt." He had enough on his conscience to deal with. Adding a preventable accident was unacceptable.

"Where's Digger? I was told he escorted you above deck."

She propped a hand on her hip and rolled her eyes. "Someone called him to the bridge."

"He should've accompanied you below." Brock would give him a piece of his mind at the first opportunity.

Mouth pinched, she huffed. "Digger is probably standing above listening to this stupid conversation right now."

Brock glanced up the stairs. "You up there, Digger?"

"Sure am, Cal." Brock bristled as Digger choked to cover his laugh. "Since you're with Mrs. Forrester, I'm headed for the engine room."

What was so damn funny? Brock didn't see a lick of humor in the situation. He'd not have this woman hurt on his ship and on his watch.

Expression smug, Zana cocked a brow. "See, I told you."

He took her arm again. "Let's get you off your feet. Don't want you overdoing it. I assume Dr. Raymond will be by in the morning."

"Yes, he said he'd like to see me one last time, but he didn't expect to find anything to keep us here. I know you're ready to get home."

He was. He longed to see Shelia and the men were ready to be with their families. Though they'd stayed out for longer periods, they'd not had the free time they'd experienced on this trip. Idleness made the time pass slowly. The men were bored.

"Yes, I am but I don't want to leave if you're not fully recovered."

"I'm grateful for the care you and your crew have given me. I know I've thrown a wrench in your schedule and probably caused you to lose income by being stuck here."

"You're not to worry about that. As a citizen of Refuge, you have our protection at all times."

"I appreciate that, Captain Callahan, I really do." Her expression turned mutinous. She raised her chin a fraction. "But please remember I am an adult. I won't be treated like a child and ordered about."

He shrugged. "Whatever."

~ * ~

How many lives did the woman have? The visitor laughed. It turned into a strangled cough. A sip of water from the glass on the table helped.

Never had a victim been so elusive. It just made the game more seductive. I'll see you dead, yet, Zana Forrester.

Ten

Retriever pulled into the harbor at Refuge. The cove was well protected. A small fortress stood on each side of the inlet, allowing guards to monitor anyone nearing Refuge. Overhead, white fluffy clouds dotted the blue sky. Only in the high seventies, the sun warmed their skin without being oppressive. It couldn't be a more beautiful day, perfect for showing Zana around Refuge.

He'd chosen to dock here rather than in the grotto. He wanted Zana to see Refuge from the sea. Plus, their cavern was secret. Not everyone was privy to its location. He believed Zana trustworthy but needed to know her better before revealing their secrets.

A grin stretched his face. Shelia jumped up and down on the dock, waving, Lola at her side.

Zana joined him on the deck. "Whose little girl?"

"Mine."

"She's a doll. Your wife is pretty too."

Yeah, she is. "My what? No, that's Lola, Digger's wife. Shelia stayed with her while we were out this trip."

"Where is her mother?"

"My wife passed away several years ago."

"Oh, I'm very sorry."

He nodded and returned his attention to his daughter. Marta's death wasn't a subject Brock wanted to revisit.

They docked. He took Zana's arm as they crossed the gangway to dry land. He waited for Shelia's attack, but her launch didn't come. Instead she approached quietly, eyes on Zana.

Swallowing his chuckle, he said, "Lola, this is Zana Forrester. She's joining our community."

"Welcome to Refuge, Mrs. Forrester."

"Thank you. May I call you Lola? And please, call me Zana."

"I'd like that." Lola took her hand, pain radiated from her eyes. "I'm so glad you're recovering nicely. We've been praying for you."

"Thank you." Zana's voice cracked. "I'm so sorry about the boy."

Lola's lower lip trembled. She hugged Zana. "We are, too, but it wasn't your fault. You mustn't blame yourself."

"How's his mother?"

Lola pulled back, her brow furrowed with concern. "She's having a hard time of it, but we're keeping a close eye on her." She squeezed Zana's hand. "I'm sure she'd like to meet you when you're up to it."

"I'd like that."

Shelia looked up at him, eyes full of questions. "What boy? What're they talkin' about, Daddy?" He dreaded having to tell her about Pepe. She'd been crazy about the boy and would take his death hard.

Brock touched Shelia's shoulder and eased her forward. His heart broke at the thought of her reaction to Pepe's death. How on Earth had they been able to keep the news from her? They were a close knit community and shared in each other's grief. They must have taken great pains to keep it from Shelia so he could be there.

"I'll tell you all about it later. Come say hello to Mrs. Forrester. She may need you to help her get settled here in Refuge."

"Hi." She stood, hands stuffed in the pockets of her overalls. "Are you the lady Daddy fished from the sea?"

Zana's choked laugh elicited a grin from his daughter. Zana extended her hand and Shelia took it. "I am indeed. Please call me Zana."

"Cool."

"Now, brat, how about a hug for your old man?"

She launched herself at him. Arms around his waist she squeezed. "I missed you, Daddy."

Brock held her close and bent down to kiss the top of her red head. He breathed in her little girl aroma. His nose twitched. She'd been playing hard again and needed a shower. "I missed you too, squirt. Were you good for Lola?"

She crossed her arms and cocked a hip. "Of course, Daddy. I'm always good."

Yes, she usually was, but her inquisitive nature sometimes got her in trouble.

He turned to Lola. "I'm glad to see you brought the transport. I'm not sure Zana is strong enough to walk all the way up the path to the fortress."

Brock picked up Zana's bag, took her elbow, and started toward the transport. "She's going to stay with me and Shelia until we can find a permanent place for her."

Zana stopped walking. "I can't impose on you."

He shuffled her forward. "It's not any trouble. I have the space, and it will give us some time to find a lodging that will work best for you. Most of our houses are full and though a few villagers wouldn't mind making room for you, I figure you'd probably prefer to have your own place. I have a small bungalow some men are working to make livable. It should be ready in a week or so."

A frown wrinkled Zana's brow. "Oh, is that necessary? I'm not sure I can afford rent plus renovations." Zana's silver streaked hair brushed against her face as they walked. She pushed it behind her ears, allowing him to view her exquisite profile. Her high cheekbones were slightly colored, but whether from permanent cosmetics or excitement, he wasn't sure. If he brushed his fingers across her cheek, would it be as soft as it appeared? He intended to find out, but not today.

"Don't worry about the costs. It's my property so I'm paying for the repairs. We'll talk about rent later."

Zana enjoyed watching Shelia. Sunlight bounced off her hair with almost as much energy as the child had as she skipped to the vehicle. "Can I drive?"

"No." Brock and Lola answered in unison.

Zana swallowed her sigh of relief. The child, a handful for sure, appeared well adjusted and happy. Her opinion of Brock Callahan rose another notch. Being a single parent wasn't easy, she knew from personal experience.

"Shoot." When they reached the transporter, Shelia sat in the back, arms crossed over her chest, her expression mutinous. Lola slid in beside her and Brock helped Zana into the front before getting behind the wheel. He'd been over solicitous, staying close to make sure she didn't over do. The attention was beginning to wear on her nerves.

The trip didn't take long, the village nothing like she'd expected. Located on the coast of Brazil, the shoreline had moved several miles inland due to global warming, the influx of fresh water into the ocean. Mountains formed by nature millions of years before stood watch in the distance over the small community. Behind them, glimpses of the rainforest stood out against the blue sky. White washed adobe houses and apartment buildings, in a variety of stages of habitation, lined several dirt streets. Farther behind and up trails leading to the mountains, a few dwellings could be seen, but most were confined to the inner area surrounded by a tall wall which appeared to be adobe.

They stopped at the base of a mountain, across from the entrance to the adobe enclosure. Lola moved up to the driver's seat. "If I can help you get settled, Zana, let me know."

"I'll do that. Thank you." Zana liked the woman. It'd be nice having a new friend to help her adjust.

Brock took her elbow. "Are you ready to go up to my house and get comfortable?"

"Sure, but where is your house?" She looked around. Why didn't they go with Lola inside the compound? "I don't see anything out here other than rock and greenery."

"My house is in a cave." He pointed. "See that piece of copper reflecting light?"

She saw several shards of light hit something shiny that appeared to move. She covered her eyes to shade the sun and squinted. "I see something glimmering."

"That's the wind chime beside my front door."

Zana was fascinated. She'd heard of cave homes

but never seen one. It took them five minutes to make their way up the path. Brock didn't complain when she stopped to rest, but Shelia ran ahead and stood waiting for them at the top. She set the chimes in motion. The rich bong of the long cylinders echoing a welcome.

As Zana caught her breath, she took in her surroundings. A wrought iron gate covered in ivy hid the front door of solid steel. Brock placed his hand against one panel and the doors slid open. They stepped into a spacious room cool in comparison to the heat outside. The thick rock walls were perfect for energy retention, keeping the home at a comfortable temperature. Zana expected rough rock floors but they were smooth and shone like glass. Cement, she thought. He'd used it to level the floor and polished it.

A fireplace was cut into one wall. A large brown leather sofa faced it, and a woven rug covered the space between the two. Brock carried her bag to the last of three doors, entered and sat it on a queen-sized bed covered in a bright turquoise and brown patterned spread.

He laid a hand on Shelia's head. "Let's let Zana rest. She's been sick and might be tired."

"Oh, I feel fine. I'd really like to explore your home if you don't mind." She was intrigued with what she'd seen so far. The guest room had a small window. Actually, it was more like a skylight. A cavity narrowed as it branched up to the outer cave wall where glass or something transparent allowed light to enter. The room wasn't large, the bed, a storage cabinet, and dresser its only furniture. Bright rugs covered the floor on each side of the bed. No doubt the cement was cold, especially in the winter, and the visitor's toes enjoyed the warm fabric.

"Sure, go ahead. I need to return to *Retriever* for a while and will take Shelia with me. Will you feel comfortable here alone?"

Why wouldn't she? "Is there any reason I shouldn't?"

"No, but if you need us, there is a communicator in the kitchen on the bar. If you key in number one you'll reach the guard tower at the compound, and number two will reach me. If you push the button on the alarm system on the wall in the living area, it alerts the entire community and is only for dire emergencies—like the cave is under attack."

Zana shuddered. "How likely is that to happen?"

"Not very. The only reason I mentioned it is so you'll know the procedures."

Her moment of panic subsided. "I'm sure I'll be fine."

Zana explored the kitchen with its stainless steel countertops, sink, and mismatched cooking and cooling devices. The appliances were more advanced than the ones she'd owned but not as high teach as those at Abyss. Of course, the only appliances she'd seen were in the Bartholomew's apartment and those were rarely used as they often ate in the dining rooms. Most likely Brock had found them while salvaging. A wooden chopping block stood against the far wall of the galley shaped kitchen with an open bar on one side. Pots and pans hung from a rack suspended from the ceiling. Brock must like to cook.

Shelia's bedroom was a carbon copy of the guest room, but a tad larger with a double size bed, and decorated in reds. As she approached Brock's room, a sense of anticipation besieged her. Why? She didn't know other than he intrigued her. She wanted to know more about this man with the gray eyes that had offered comfort in her misery.

She peeked into the room. As with the rest of the dwelling, the floor was polished, and a large woven rug covered the majority of the space. A king size bed occupied the far wall, the tall frame and headboard made of roughhewn lumber. The spread was plain serviceable, and brown in color.

A tall chest occupied the adjacent wall. She stepped closer and studied the objects sitting on top—a hair brush, a small nautical clock, a collection of sea shells, and a wooden box she assumed held a few pieces of jewelry. No way would the man own cuff links. He wasn't the suit or tuxedo type, but she wouldn't be surprised to find an earring or two. She smiled and caught her reflection in the small mirror attached to the rock wall.

The room held no feminine presence. Zana searched to find one small hint that a woman once occupied this masculine space, but found none. Could Brock Callahan not bear to have reminders of his late wife around him? Did he still love her? The idea didn't set well with Zana nor did she like the hint of jealousy that grabbed her when she'd seen Lola on the dock with Brock's daughter. She had no right to be jealous. Yes, the man had been kind to her, but he was probably kind to everyone. Plus she didn't want the emotion messing up her plans to find her daughter.

Sunlight winked at her from the glass, and she followed the source to a small opening in the wall. A window—whereas Shelia's room had a skylight,

Brock's room had a window. She rushed over to peer out and saw an area that resembled a courtyard. Was there a door somewhere leading outside? She'd remember to ask later.

Back in the guest room, she stared down at the bed. A little nap sounded good. She flipped back the cover, kicked off her shoes, and crawled into the bed fully dressed. Maybe if she lay still her pantsuit wouldn't wrinkle too much.

Tonight she'd approach Brock and ask for her Expedition. Evidently it was worth some money, and with it she could make a new start. With that issue settled in her mind, she drifted to sleep.

Eleven

Several days after *Retriever* returned to Refuge from the undersea city, Abyss's transport pulled into the harbor at Refuge. Brock could see Dr. Boone standing on the dock waiting to take possession of the nano technology package Dr. Raymond put together for them. When Brock approached Boone about the funds to purchase an upgrade, the man had jumped at the possibility and had squirreled away enough money in funds to cover the cost. Tough negotiator that the doctor was, he'd charged Brock a handsome price for the hospital's old nano system. The deal was fair. Both he and Dr. Boone were happy with the outcome.

As he walked toward the dock to welcome their visitors, Zana and Shelia not far behind, Brock watched as those on deck milled around enjoying the fresh air. While happy to have the new nano technology, he was happier still to welcome his two personal visitors. How long had it been since Samuel had breathed natural air or walked on land? This was probably a first for Daniel.

After the crew moored the craft, Samuel stepped onto the ramp. Brock was pleased to see the man he'd hated with a passion. Kinship had replaced hostility. Delia would have been delighted to know they'd made peace and he'd become acquainted with his nephew. Samuel had called the day before to let him know when to expect them. Shelia couldn't wait to meet her uncle and cousin.

Samuel reached out and took Daniel from someone's arms still on the vessel. Brock's heart jumped at the opportunity to see the boy again. He grinned as Daniel twisted, slinging himself from side-to-side to see everything around him.

Shelia caught up to him and danced at Brock's side as they made their way down the dirt road worn between the encroaching jungle plants. The citizens of Refuge strived to keep the wild vegetation as far from the path as possible as snakes were often a problem.

Shelia squealed. "Isn't he cute, Daddy? Do you think he'll let me pick him up? Boy, Uncle Samuel's a hunk. Darlene will flip when she sees him. She told me she's got a thing for dark-headed men."

Heaven forbid Darlene would get her claws into the man. He couldn't think of anything worse. Samuel sat Daniel on his feet and took his hand.

It was good to see Shelia laugh again. She'd taken Pepe's death hard and for several days burst into tears at odd times during the day. Zana had been a world of help, knowing exactly what to say to ease his child's pain. He tugged on Shelia's ponytail. "He's a little boy, brat. I doubt he'll be still long enough for you to carry him for long."

"Oh pooh," she said and kicked at the dirt.

He chuckled. "He's not a doll, you know."

"I know, Daddy. I'm not a baby, you know."

Yeah, and he hated the thought she'd be a teenager in five years. She was growing up entirely too fast to suit him. Each day she looked more like her mother. She'd be a beauty and would no doubt have boys flocking around her in a few years. Hopefully she'd be too busy to pay them any mind.

A shriek split the air. Daniel had seen him. His precious face lit with glee, and he yelled, "Unka Bock, Daddy it's my Unka Bock!" He took off at a run, and Samuel scrambled to catch the toddler before he got far.

A keen sense of love pierced his heart. Delia's child, a miracle, a child he'd not known existed until just over a week ago.

Shelia grabbed his hand. "Come on, let's run."

"Hold on, squirt. Zana's not up to jogging."

"Oh yeah, I forgot."

Zana grabbed her hand. "But we can walk faster, can't we?"

Shelia grinned. "Yeah."

Laughing, the two broke out into a fast walk. Brock shook his head and hoped Zana didn't relapse. He jogged to catch up with them.

As they neared, Samuel released the boy, and Daniel ran into Brock's arms. He swung him around, and then hugged him to his chest. "Hey, little man. I'm so glad to see you."

Daniel patted his cheeks and kissed his face. "My Unka Bock!" He turned to his father. "Right, Daddy?"

"That's right, son." Samuel shook hands with Brock, nodded to Zana, and then looked down at Shelia. "And who is this young lady?"

Not known for shyness, she spoke up. "My name is, Shelia, and I'm your niece. Daniel is my cousin."

Samuel squatted to Shelia's eye level. "I know and I've wanted to meet you for a long time. Your Aunt Delia talked about you all the time. She thought you were the cutest and sweetest little girl on Earth."

"She did? Why didn't she come see me then?"

"I'm sure your daddy will explain everything soon." He stood up. "Okay?"

"Okay." Shelia turned to Daniel. "Hey, Daniel, I'm your cousin. Can I carry you?"

Daniel reached for her and fell into her arms. She staggered under his weight for a minute, but regained her balance. He studied her for a second then patted her cheeks. "You Shedia, my cuzin."

"That's right. I've always wanted a cousin."

Zana's gaze stayed on the children, a sad smile titling the corners of her mouth. Shelia was just a couple of years older than Zana's daughter had been; Daniel near her son's age. What a poignant reminder they must be for her.

Though still thin, she looked much better than she had when they'd arrived. The fact that she'd been able to walk this morning was a testament to her improvement.

Brock watched Samuel as he studied her. "Zana? How are you?"

She looked up at him and smiled. "Still a little weak, but better each day."

Daniel ordered, "Down." He wiggled out of Shelia's arms and started running down the path.

Samuel darted forward and lifted the toddler into his arms. Brock could hear him scolding the child softly. He didn't doubt Samuel knew the dangers of this area. Shelia danced along beside them, with her arms waving, no doubt extolling the virtues of Refuge.

Zana stumbled and Brock caught her before she fell. Her mouth was pinched, pale face set with determination. Fear gripped him and he stopped. He'd not have her overdoing and make herself ill. "You're worn out. This is too much for you."

"No, I'm fine. Just let me rest a minute, catch my breath."

Her breathing was rapid; sweat beaded her forehead and upper lip. Neither were good signs. "Take as long as you need." He pulled her back against his chest. "Lean on me and relax."

"Thank you."

Her rump nestled against him. Warmth shot through his system. He gritted his teeth in hopes his body wouldn't give away his attraction to this woman. When his arm circled her waist, she stiffened for a minute, but then relaxed and closed her eyes. Her dark lashes lay against her ashen cheeks as she allowed her breathing return to normal.

Damn, he should've brought the transport so she'd not have to walk, but she'd insisted the walk would be good for her. From now on he'd follow his gut instincts. The woman didn't realize her limits.

Five minutes later, she patted his arm and straightened. "I'm better now. Let's move on."

Hands on her shoulders, he turned her to face him. He scanned her features. Her color had returned to normal and she was no longer sweating. "Okay, but let's take it slow."

When they reached the market located just inside the compound, the crowd opened to allow them to join Samuel, Shelia, and Daniel. Shelia held the floor.

Face animated, her red ponytail bounced as she talked using her arms for emphasis. "This is my Uncle Samuel and my cousin Daniel. Isn't he cute?"

Darlene, dressed provocatively in an off-the-shoulder purple blouse and tight red shorts, sidled forward and reached for Daniel. But her eyes were on Samuel. "He sure is." Daniel leaned back against his father to evade her. She tickled his belly. He shoved her hand away. "Ah, a little shy, are you?"

Daniel spotted him and Zana approaching and crawled up Samuel's shoulder, arms outstretched. "Ana, my Ana." Samuel had brought the boy to visit Zana and play on the poop deck while she recovered on *Retriever.* She'd enjoyed the child and cuddled him close while reading stories. Once they'd both fallen asleep. Samuel had to return to work. Brock sat watching them, a deep longing eating away at his heart, until they woke. Furious with the direction his mind had taken, he'd been short with Zana and hurt her feelings. His rudeness infuriated him more. He'd muttered an apology, scooped Daniel up and strode off the boat to return him to his father. As he'd passed Digger, the man looked at him as if he'd grown an extra head. He shoved the memory away and focused on the scene before him.

Chuckling, Zana lifted the boy, and he curled little arms around her neck before turning a smug expression on Darlene. For some reason, Daniel didn't like Darlene. Leave it to a child to put a person in their place. It took all Brock's strength to keep from laughing out loud and making his redheaded housekeeper, make that ex-housekeeper, angrier than she was already. His men and some of the villagers didn't bother to smother their humor.

He stepped up behind Shelia and placed his hands on her shoulders. "I can see Shelia has introduced you to my brother-in-law and nephew, Delia's husband and son." All eyes were on Samuel, the man he'd hated with a passion for taking his sister from them. A lump formed in his throat making speech difficult. His people waited quietly.

Voice hoarse, he continued, "We've made peace between us. I hope you'll all make them welcome here and watch over this little scamp." He reached over and tweaked Daniel's nose. With the confidence of a child secure in being protected, the boy leaped from Zana's arms. The crowd laughed at the child's antics as Brock caught him and hugged him close. "You all know how dangerous this area can be, so, if he should escape his caregivers, I charge you with returning him to his father."

Digger stood close to the front, a broad grin stretching his scarred face. He saluted. "Aye, aye, Captain." He threw his free arm around his beaming wife's shoulders.

"We'd be pleased to help keep an eye on him, Brock." Lola was as pretty as Digger was ugly. They made an interesting couple. Their devotion to each other was admirable to observe. What a shame they'd had no children as both would have been good parents.

"Thanks, Lola. We appreciate the offer, but Samuel and Daniel are only visiting until tomorrow."

He turned his attention back to the group. "Now, Zana Forrester is here to join our family at Refuge. She's been staying with Shelia and me until we get her cottage ready, but has been recovering from an illness. Soon she'll be looking for work." He led Zana forward. "Please make her welcome and help her get settled."

Digger and Lola were the first to step up. They shook hands with Samuel, and then moved to Zana. "We're so pleased to see you well, ma'am," said

Digger.

Darlene shoved her way forward. "Hello, Zana. I'm Darlene, Brock's house—ah, friend," she simpered, then flashed Brock a sly wink. Brock wanted to throttle her.

Before Zana could respond, Luke and other crewmembers greeted her and moved on to make room for the others

Zana was amazed at the friendliness of the people. She felt welcome and was grateful she'd made the decision to leave Abyss. While recovering, she'd been shocked to learn Samuel and Brock were brothers-in-law. Their attitude toward each other, especially after their confrontation the day she'd boarded *Retriever*, had been refreshing to see. She didn't know what had occurred between them to ease the strain, but without a doubt, Daniel was a catalyst.

Lola approached with a woman, probably in her early forties, her face, furrowed with lines of grief. "Zana, this is Constance, Pepe's mother. She wanted to meet you."

Tears welled in Zana's eyes. She took Constance's hands and squeezed. "I'm so sorry about your son."

The woman nodded as tears rolled down her cheeks. "Thank…you. He was a good boy."

Zana pulled Constance into an embrace and patted her back as she cried. Zana's sobs mingled with the grieving mother's. After all, they'd both lost children.

Constance pulled back and squeezed Zana's hands. "Thank you. Welcome to Refuge."

As people began to disburse, Brock led her aside. "I think you need to go up and rest."

About to drop where she stood, Zana nodded.

"I'll walk you up."

"That's not necessary. I can make it fine."

"Maybe you can, but you're not familiar with the dangers around Refuge and I'll worry if I don't see you up those stairs."

Yeah, she'd hate to poop out half way up. "Dangers? What dangers?" She didn't know much about her new home. She'd spent most of her days sleeping and taking short walks with Brock or Shelia. They'd not mentioned anything to be afraid of.

"I'll tell you all about those soon. Don't worry about it now."

"Okay. I hate to take you away from Samuel and Daniel though."

"They'll be there when I get back."

When they reached the foot of the steps, he scooped her up in his arms.

"Wait. I can walk."

"I know, but this is easier on you and faster. You want to feel up to having dinner with us tonight, right?"

She relaxed against his chest. *Enjoy being pampered, Zana.* "Of course. I wouldn't miss it for the world." She leaned against his wide torso, slipped her arms around his neck, and tried not to get caught breathing in his aftershave. The fragrance was heady and masculine, fast becoming her favorite scent. *Distract yourself, Zana. A man isn't in your forecast.* She glanced at the surrounding foliage but her gaze returned to his profile. His nose had a crook. He must have broken it at one time. Not hard to imagine with his temper. No doubt he'd engaged in a scrap or two in his line of work. The fault only added to his magnetism, his rugged cheekbones, strong jaw, and stubborn chin.

At the door, he turned his head. His gray eyes bored into hers and for a minute she couldn't breathe. Had he realized she'd been studying his features? Lordy, she hoped not. His gaze dropped to her lips. She held her breathe in anticipation. Was he going to kiss her? Did she want him to?

He cleared his throat, sat her on her feet, and then opened the door. "I'll lock up as I leave. Call if you need us."

Twelve

When they returned home, Brock noticed Zana's door was closed. He opened it a crack and saw her curled up in the bed. He turned to the two children. "Shhhh, Zana is asleep. Let's be quiet and let her rest a while longer."

Shelia brought out colored pencils and paper, and Daniel drew pictures of what'd he'd seen today.

The boy announced, "I'm gonna draw a pawot." He'd been fascinated with the talking parrot, and Brock wouldn't be surprised if Samuel ended up taking one home with him.

As they played, Samuel joined him in the kitchen while he prepared dinner. He'd bought vegetables and meat in the village and now started a beef stew. A loaf of whole grain bread would round it out, and they'd have fresh fruit for dessert. It was something they grew readily at Refuge.

Samuel took a sip of his wine and set his glass on the counter separating the kitchen from the dining area. Perched on a tall stool, he studied Brock. "So, you like to cook?"

"Yeah, I do." Cooking relaxed him. Plus he liked to eat.

"What about the redhead, Darlene, your housekeeper? Does she do much cooking?"

Brock didn't miss the expression of condemnation

on his brother-in-law's face. "She cooked for Shelia when I wasn't here, but mostly she kept house." He chopped away at the potatoes on the cutting board. "You can wipe that disapproving look off your face, too. She's not helping out around here anymore. I found out she took Shelia to the Pirate's Bar one night while I was gone." He mumbled under his breath. "Among other things."

"Not exactly a good role model for a young impressionable girl, I'd think."

"You got that right." What had he been thinking having her around his daughter? In his defense, Darlene seemed harmless when she'd first started working for him. Then she'd laid on the charm. Yeah, right, like he'd resisted. They'd been discreet, or so he thought. Shelia's remark the other day about him wanting to kiss Darlene had been an eye opener. Darlene had wormed her way into Shelia's affections in hopes their relationship would become something permanent. Hell, that wasn't exactly true. Darlene did take good care of Shelia while he was gone, cooked her favorite foods, and played games with her. She genuinely appeared to enjoy his daughter's company, but she wasn't wife material, not for him, anyway.

Samuel grinned. "Well, the way she rubbed up against me, she doesn't appear to be the monogamous type. Daniel didn't take to her, that's the best recommendation I know to stay clear of the woman."

"Yeah, she's a barracuda," said Brock. "She told Shelia she liked dark men. Watch your step, man."

The click of sandals on the hard floor announced Zana's arrival before he saw her. Her soft voice blended with the excited chatter of the kids as she admired their artwork. She glanced up and smiled at him in amusement. Hazel eyes glittered with delight. His breath caught in this throat. He'd known she was lovely, but fresh from sleep, pleasure transforming her features, she was stunning.

"Close your mouth, old man." Samuel tried without success to wipe the grin from his face, but coughed instead. "Looks like you're smitten."

Brock cleared his throat. "Appreciation has nothing to do with being besotted." *Yeah, keep telling yourself that, old man.*

Zana entered the kitchen. "Something smells good. I'm starved."

Brock motioned her to a barstool beside Samuel. "Would you like a glass of wine?"

"Sure. That sounds heavenly." She settled on the stool and wiggled to get comfortable. He poured a glass and passed it over to her. She took a sip. "Mmm, this is good."

"Made at our own winery here in Refuge."

She glanced at Samuel. "I believe this is even better than the wine I tasted at Abyss."

"Yeah, they're stingy with their best vintage."

"Now, that's not true, Governor Whiteside. We'll sell you some—for a price."

Samuel snorted and raised his glass to Zana. "And there is the catch—a price we can't afford."

Brock could only grin. Yes, it was expensive but worth every penny.

Zana propped her elbows on the bar. "I'm curious about something. Samuel said Refuge was on the east coast of Brazil. Why is there is so much dry land mass? I thought Brazil was more rainforest than anything."

Brock topped off his and Samuel's glasses with the dark ruby red wine. "In your time, it was, but it was already beginning to change. What you see here is a small glimpse of what has taken place the world over.

"With global warming, the equator shifted. Some areas that were once frozen are now arid. Same goes for the area here. Much of the rainforest has given way to desert-like terrain." He walked to the bookshelf in the den and returned with the latest World Almanac. "This should explain much of what's occurred the past hundred years." He opened the book to a map of South America. "Note the amount of land mass that's disappeared in the last fifty years. You can flip to the back for maps to use for comparison."

He and Samuel carried bowls of stew to the table. Short glasses of soymilk sat beside the kids' bowls.

With his wine in one hand and the plate of bread in the other, Brock led the way to the table. "You two kids run wash your hands. We'll wait for you."

Samuel bent to lift Daniel from the floor. Shelia piped up, "I'll take him for you."

From the bathroom, noises of splashing water and giggles echoed down the hallway. "I can do it myself," squealed Daniel.

"Okay, already, do it then." Face like a thundercloud, Shelia stomped to the table and slid into her chair, disgust on her face. "He got water all over the floor, Daddy."

Samuel moved to rise. Brock motioned him to stay put. "Sit down. He can't hurt these floors or walls. Shelia got them plenty wet herself once upon a time."

Shelia grinned. "Yeah, but Darlene puts up an awful fuss when I do now. She said it makes extra work for her."

A smile tickled Zana's lips. Spoon held in midair, she turned to Shelia. "You're getting old enough to help her now. I bet you could be a big help."

The squirt snorted. "I don't like cleaning house, cooking and stuff. I'd rather help Daddy work on the boats, or help out in the winery." She shrugged. "Anyway, Daddy fired Darlene for taking me to the Pirates Bar."

Daniel came to the table pleased with his efforts. "See, I did it."

Samuel winced at the boy's wet shirt. "Yes, I see. Good job, son."

An idea popped into Brock's head. It might just work, for both of them. His house would be clean, and he bet Zana was a good cook. Shelia would be exposed to the right kind of woman for once. Now, how did he know Zana would be a good influence? He didn't, but instinct told him to trust her with his most precious cargo, his child. The girl needed a woman's influence. One who wouldn't have her wearing paint by thirteen and frequenting unsavory places. Samuel nudged him in the ribs interrupting his train of thought.

"What?" He glanced around the table to see all eyes move from him to Zana.

Zana's mouth was pinched, her chin in the air. "I said how could you expose your child to such an unsavory person?"

His face heated. "Now, just a minute. Darlene overstepped the boundaries my last trip out, but she's taken good care of Shelia and this house for several years."

Shelia piped up. "What does unsavory mean?"

Brock took a bite of his stew to bide for time. He chewed, swallowed, and laid his spoon down. "It means unpleasant." He lowered his voice and spoke to his bowl. "Among other things."

"She's not unpleasant," said Shelia. "Darlene is my friend." His daughter shot Zana a dirty look. "And Daddy's, too. He kisses her sometimes."

"That's enough, Shelia." He glared at Zana and growled, "I assure you, Mrs. Forrester, my daughter's welfare is of the utmost importance to me, and I do not need you or anyone else questioning my methods of parenting."

Zana didn't flinch and wasn't convinced. She'd opened her mouth to say more when Daniel's sob drew their attention. Oh, dear, they're bickering upset the boy.

She hopped up, rushed around the table, and lifted Daniel in her arms. "Hey now, what's wrong? Did we get too loud?" Children didn't like conflict. They didn't understand the concept of arguing to voice opinions and that it didn't necessarily mean the two people were angry with each other. How could they understand? Their little minds focused on what they could see and hear at the moment. Zana cuddled the boy close enjoying his scent and soft skin. After an afternoon of running around in the heat, he didn't smell sweet but rather tangy, like a little boy. It reminded her of Jonathan.

He nodded and shook his finger at Brock. "No fuss, Unka Bock." The child was so cute. Her heart twisted with longing for her own children.

Zana swallowed the lump in her throat and patted Daniel's back. "We're not fussing, sweetheart, and it's not Uncle Brock's fault. I said something to make him mad." She nodded to Brock, then to Shelia. "I am sorry for interfering."

She'd give Brock Callahan a piece of her mind when they were alone. No doubt he loved his child and she appeared to be well adjusted and happy, but the thought of that brassy woman caring for Shelia made Zana's blood boil. The very idea of taking the child to a bar.

It was hard for a single parent, especially one away from home on occasion. Surely with all the citizens of Refuge he could have chosen a better role model. She bit her lip. Maybe he'd learned his lesson and would choose better next time. She dearly hoped so.

~ * ~

The next day, just before noon, Zana stood with Brock and Shelia as Samuel carried Daniel aboard the vessel that would take them home. The boy waved, a grin stretching his face, and shouted for at least the tenth time, "Thank you for the pawot, Unka Bock."

She couldn't keep from grinning at the expression of resignation on Samuel's face as the child clutched the cage tightly in his little arms. The wire coop was almost bigger than the boy, but he wouldn't turn it loose and let someone else carry the bird. The parrot squawked its displeasure at being jostled by the unsteady journey across the gangway. It's a miracle they made it aboard without all three being tossed into the cove.

Quick to forgive, Shelia hadn't mentioned Darlene again, but things were strained between Zana and Brock. Oh well, it couldn't be helped. Zana was right; he was wrong. The woman wasn't fit to care for a child, much less one as sharp as Shelia. Kissed sometimes indeed. Thank goodness kissing is all Shelia thought they did. Not that she knew for sure Brock was more involved with Darlene, but, his reaction to his daughter's comment made one suspect.

As they walked back toward the village, she fumed at the jealousy niggling at her mind. It was an emotion foreign to her and she didn't like it one bit. The stab of regret she'd experienced on her arrival when she'd assumed Lola was Brock's wife had startled her. She wasn't looking for a relationship, locating her daughter took precedence over everything else, but sometimes the heart didn't cooperate. Brock Callahan was a dauntingly handsome man. With his tall and muscular build, silver streaked dark hair, and gray eyes, he was the epitome of a pirate. If he wore an eye patch, she'd know so. She chuckled silently. Nothing like stereotyping an individual. It'd be easy to fall captive to Brock Callahan's charm, but she didn't think he was a one-woman man. And she wasn't into sharing.

Anyway, if he cared for Darlene, then Zana definitely wasn't his type. The woman was brash and exotic in her attractiveness. In comparison, Zana was plain and ordinary.

She stumbled, and Brock's hand shot out and caught her elbow. "Careful. We can't have you getting skinned up."

She lifted her arm from his grasp. "That's what I get for daydreaming. I'll keep my mind on the path from here on." His touch unnerved her.

Shelia led the way, flitting from one side of the road to the other, picking a flower or lifting a stone from the dirt. Like yesterday, she was dressed in overalls with a short-sleeved t-shirt underneath. The lime green enhanced her red hair pulled back into a ponytail. She dropped a stone into her left pocked. What did the girl have in her right pocket that made the denim bulge so?

They'd reached the path that led up to Brock's house and stopped. She looked from the trail toward the village stockade. There were no other homes outside the compound. "Why the walls? Is it dangerous to live here?"

"It can be at times. Once, since I've been grown, a band of pirates attacked, and we fended them off from behind the barricade. Several times we've had to drive off animals coming down from the jungles in search of food."

Zana was stunned and stumbled back a step. Wild animals? Pirates? "Why don't *you* live inside then? How can you let Shelia roam about by herself?"

"There you go with the fifth-degree again, treating me like I'm an unfit parent." He pulled Shelia to his side. "Show Zana your weapon."

Shelia removed a silver object, about the size of her hand, from her right pocket. Ah-ha, so that's what caused the bulge. She stepped closer to get a better look. It had a handgrip with a trigger-like device but no barrel.

Brock took the gun. "It's a high-powered laser pistol, one capable of killing a raging bull elephant if necessary. Just a figure of speech, as we don't have pachyderm in Brazil. Shelia's been trained from a small child to protect herself. This little gun makes a loud zinging noise, so if it's fired, someone will hear and come to her aid immediately."

He turned and pointed to the watch stations on the fortress walls. "Guards are on duty at all times. We don't take any chances with the safety of our citizens, especially our children. You are safe here with us, Zana. This evening I'll furnish you with your own pistol. Later you'll receive training in other weapons for your own protection."

Carrying a pistol was a foreign concept for Zana. It seemed she'd traded one danger for another. Ice and sub-zero temperatures in Newfoundland, selective mating in Abyss, and now wild animals and pirate attacks in Refuge. Though Abyss's mating practice wasn't dangerous, it went against her personal beliefs. She'd rather carry a weapon and face pirates than be subjected to an artificial relationship. Yes, she'd made the right choice.

~ * ~

Brock sat in his favorite chair, feet on the coffee table, with a mystery novel open in his lap. He'd reread the same passage three times without a word registering. He wanted to talk to Zana but hated to interrupt her. Ever since they'd finished dinner and the dishes, Zana had her nose stuck in the book he'd suggested she read to catch up on the effects of global warming. Shelia was in bed. Zana had kicked off her shoes and curled up on the sofa. Comfortable, soft, and too darn attractive for his comfort, she looked like she belonged in his home. He should be sitting beside her, arm around her shoulders, stroking her long silky hair as she read.

He snorted in disgust and she glanced up for a minute. When he didn't speak, she returned to her book. He breathed a sigh of relief and mentally shook the image from his mind. *Get a grip, old man.* The woman wasn't through grieving; she wasn't ready for a relationship. And hell, neither was he. He liked bachelorhood just fine, but he did want to do right by Shelia. She needed a woman's influence, a positive one. He'd been foolish to allow Darlene to become more than just a housekeeper, to wiggle her way so deeply into Shelia's affections. More important, he'd been stupid to sleep with the woman.

From his chair, he watched Zana. She'd read awhile, and then stare off into space as if digesting the information. What did she make of all the Earth's changes? He couldn't imagine what it would be like to be hit with seventy-five years of history all at once.

He had a plan, one he'd worked on all day. In his mind, he'd kicked around the right way to introduce his proposition to her. None sounded right. Hell, he might as well spit it out.

He jumped when she spoke, having no idea what she'd just said. "What? I'm sorry my mind was elsewhere."

"I asked how many undersea cities besides Abyss are there now. I mean, this book lists fifteen, but it's several years old and I assumed there are more today."

He closed the book he'd been reading and sat it on the table beside his chair. "There are a total of seventeen now—seven in the Atlantic, seven in the Pacific, and three in the Indian Ocean."

She thought for a minute. "So, is Abyss the closest? Is that why you took me there for medical treatment?"

"Yes, it's the closest with an advanced medical center. Plus, we do a lot of business with them and though I don't approve of their social system, I do trust them. I can't say the same about all of the cities." Some were downright unethical in their trading practices, as he'd learned through experience.

"Ah, I see. What about the selective mating thing? Do they all have the same practice?"

"Many do, but those that don't have some other type method in place to limit their population. Some are almost as offensive as Abyss's selective mating. In my opinion, a few are actually fair. They have a waiting list for families. When a space becomes available, if the family is too large, they're pushed back on the list." He sighed. "It's tough to keep waiting but at least it is a fair system."

"Yes, much better than the ones like Abyss." She smiled and nodded toward his book. "Thank you for answering my questions. Sorry to interrupt your reading."

Head bent over the large history tome, she flipped through a few pages and must have found what she looked for as she stopped and followed a passage with her finger.

If he planned to broach the subject he'd been contemplating, he better get started. "Zana, I want to ask you something."

She looked up. "What is it?" Closing the book, she adjusted her position on the sofa to be more comfortable. Her feet must have been cold because she pulled her long skirt down over them.

"Your cottage will be ready day after tomorrow. I know you'll be looking for work and you'd prefer to be in your field of technology."

"Yes, if I can find a job where I can use my

training, that'll be ideal, but I'm beginning to think my skills are too far out of date."

He feared that also, but he didn't want to come right out and say so. "Well, I'm wondering if, until you find something better, mind you, if you'd be my housekeeper?" The expression of disbelief on her face didn't encourage him. "Shelia and I don't make too much of a mess, and I can cook breakfast if you fix dinner before you leave each day."

She stood up. "I don't think so."

He rose and faced her. "Why not? It's honest work. I'll pay you a good salary or by the hour if you'd prefer."

Her face a frozen mask, she glared up at him. "I assure you, Mr. Callahan, I'll not have people here think I am another Darlene…your floozy." Brock was too stunned to speak. Before he could blurt out a retort, she continued. "I didn't leave Abyss and their disgusting selective mating ritual to whore myself here in Refuge."

Brock shook with unreleased anger. How dare she believe his offer less than honorable? His eyes raked her from her bare feet, up her body, to the crown of her head. He grabbed her chin and tilted it so her eyes would meet his. His voice was a growl, gruff even to his ears, when he muttered. "I assure you, sweetheart, you are not my type. Your body is safe." He dropped his hand. "Give me your answer in the morning."

Thirteen

Brock could have cut his tongue out at the expression of pain that flickered in Zana's eyes. He erased that thought when, hands on her hips, she spat out, "I can give you my answer now."

"Let's hear it then."

"I will work for you until I've been reimbursed for my Polar Expedition." She waved a hand in front of his face. "Then, you'll be rid of me. With the money from my vehicle I'll start a business of my own. I won't need your help."

"What the hell are you talking about? That vehicle has been sold, and you *have* no share in the proceeds."

She jabbed her finger at the air in front of him. "I beg to differ with *you*. It belonged to me. The title in the glove box had my name on it. I was in it when you pulled it out of the water. Undoubtedly it was mine. You knew it and sold it. Now you owe me." She shrugged and inclined her head. "I'm willing to give you a portion of the profits. After all, you did pull me from the sea, and I guess if you hadn't, I might never have been found."

"Woman, you are nuts. Your car was salvaged. The *Retriever* is a rescue vessel. That's what my men and I do—recover garbage and lost items, then sell it for profit."

Her mouth fell open. She sputtered, emphasizing

each gasp with her finger on his chest. "Are...are...you calling me and my child garbage?" Her face contorted with rage and despair. Tears pooled in her eyes.

A fist closed around his heart and squeezed. He choked out, "No. Hell no. I'd never refer to a human life as garbage."

God, the woman twisted his meaning. He raked his hands through his hair and struggled for the right words. "What I'm trying to say is, my men and I scour the sea and land for items not being used. We bring them in, repair them if possible, and sell them. Some things are repairable like your Expedition. Others aren't, but there is always a need for parts, metals, artifacts, and other items we find."

She wiped at the tears, fisted her hands, and faced him. "That's all fine and good, but in those instances you don't know who the property belongs to. This time you do. *Me*." She shook a fist at him. "And did you hear what you just said? You said, '*Your* Expedition.' You admitted it belonged to me."

He was beating his head against a brick wall. "You're twisting my words, woman. Items found during a salvage operation become the property of the craft that recovers them. Nowhere does it say to look for the original owner. In your case, it wasn't known if you'd live or not. Of course, we hoped you would and provided medical care as quickly as we could. But, whether you lived or not would not alter our ownership of the find." He threw up his hands. "It may not be fair, but that's the way it is."

"I'll take you to court if I have to."

He couldn't help his reaction. The mutinous expression on her face did him in. Falling back into his chair, he struggled to keep from laughing. A few snickers escaped.

"Laugh, you big ape. We'll see how funny this all is when I'm collecting my money." She turned on her heel and marched toward the hallway.

"Wait." Brock felt sorry for her. She didn't have a clue how much society had changed in the time she'd been asleep, frozen in time. "I'm sorry. That was rude of me." He motioned to the sofa. "Please sit down and let me explain a few things."

~ * ~

Zana slept fitfully, tossing and turning, reliving her conversation with Brock. She didn't believe for a minute the laws on scavenging were as airtight as he implied. If he thought he was dealing with a weak little woman, he had another thought coming. She'd fight for what was rightfully hers.

She rose to the smell of food cooking. Her reflection in the looking glass mirrored her exhaustion. Finding the bathroom she shared with Shelia empty, she quickly showered, dressed, and headed for the kitchen. Somewhat refreshed, she found Brock and Shelia at the table eating.

Shelia flashed a smile. "Good morning, Zana. Daddy saved you some breakfast." She turned to her father. "See, I told you she'd be up before we left." Gracing Zana with a knowing grin, the child proceeded. "Daddy was afraid you might be one of those people who liked to sleep late."

"Shelia, you know that's not what I said."

Zana joined them at the table with a plate of eggs, bacon, and toast. Brock poured her a cup of coffee from the pot on the table. She waited for him to continue, to explain his comment.

"I said, Zana stayed up late last night and might want to sleep in a little longer this morning."

"Hmmm, well, as you can see, I'm up and ready to start my new job."

He studied her. "You seem a bit peaked. No need to start today. Go out and get a little exercise, see what all you're going to need for your cottage, and get acquainted with the village."

Zana examined his face for motive. Was he trying to soften her up so she'd give up her idea of getting her share of the Expedition? He appeared sincere but who knew. She didn't know how to judge the man's reactions.

"Shelia will take you around today."

"I can get the house cleaned and still have time to explore." She'd not give him the opportunity to accuse her of shirking her duties.

"Ah, Daddy, I'd planned to work in the vineyard today."

"Not today. You'll stay here and help Zana clean house, then show her around."

Shelia, brows furrowed, studied Zana. Zana wanted to squirm under the child's perusal, but instead she smiled reassuringly and bent her head to her breakfast.

"So, you're our new housekeeper?" From the tone of Shelia's voice, she wasn't excited about Zana taking Darlene's place.

What on Earth was going through her head? Surely she didn't think Zana would be on kissing terms with her father. "For a short while. Just long enough for me to find a job in my field and collect on a debt."

"Oh, okay." The child visibly relaxed as if she'd

been protecting Darlene's turf. Zana swallowed a snide comment. The woman was welcome to him.

Zana didn't fail to notice Brock's scowl above the rim of his coffee cup. A lock of dark hair half hid the eyebrow arched at a dangerously high level. *Cock that thing at me all you want, mister. I'm not backing down.* As if reading her thoughts, he smiled. Her heart lodged in her throat.

It wasn't fair for a man to be so good looking and make her breathless with a twitch of his lips. She returned the gesture, and then his words of last night echoed in her head causing an ache in her chest. Heat rose in her face, and she raised her cup to cover her frozen smile.

He pushed his chair back and stood. "Shelia, I want you to help out and learn. After Zana leaves, you may need to take over some of the household chores."

"Daddy, you know I hate doing stuff around here. Please, let me go to work with you. You know I'm a hard worker."

He rounded the table and bent to press a kiss to the top of her head. "Yes, you are, one of the best, but you need to learn other things. Someday you'll marry and need to know how to keep house."

"Pooh, I'll never marry."

Zana couldn't restrain her chuckle. "Shelia, I said the same thing once. Believe me, it's best to be prepared."

Shelia shrugged. "Whatever."

By noon, the house, or she should say cave, gleamed. Shelia had helped, albeit reluctantly. Once Zana got her started, the girl worked hard, and Zana couldn't fault the results. They ate a light lunch and started for the village.

At the front door, Shelia quizzed her like a pro to make sure she knew the code and how to sound the alarm. She checked Zana's pistol and insisted Zana practice releasing it from its holster several times. Shelia preferred keeping hers in a pocket but nervous, Zana wanted easier access. And, most of her clothes had no pockets.

"You've got to be prepared. No time for thinking."

Zana couldn't help but admire the child's knowledge and maturity where security was concerned. Shelia, satisfied her student was ready, led the way down the path.

"Have you ever had to use your weapon?" The thought of this child, any child for that matter, having to defend herself gave her the shivers.

Shelia stopped on the step below her. "A couple of times. Once when a snake wouldn't move off the path. That wasn't a big deal, but then a wild pig charged me from one of the bushes." She chuckled. "About gave Daddy a heart attack. He kept patting my back and telling me how good I'd done but it was hours before he quit shaking."

Zana was appalled. "Well, I expect so. I can't imagine." And she couldn't. "I'm surprised he lets you go out alone." Katy and Jonathan had the usual childhood accidents but nothing compared to a feral animal attack. She shuddered. "I hope we don't meet any dangerous animals while we're out and about." Her head swiveled from side to side searching the foliage and boulders on either side of the path.

"Probably not." She giggled. "Relax, Zana, we're okay. Come on."

Zana followed, Shelia chattering as they descended the steep path. "Didn't you have to teach your children to protect themselves?"

Zana stopped, and Shelia turned, a frown etching her little brow. "I'm sorry about your children. Does it hurt to talk about them?"

Throat clogged, Zana coughed and rasped out, "Thank you. I miss them terribly." She blinked back tears. "But, you know, it's probably good for me to talk about them." She walked down and laid a hand on Shelia's shoulder. "I had to teach my daughter how to be safe in the freezing weather. That was our greatest hazard during that time. She rarely was allowed to go outside and then only for short periods of time. My son, Jonathan, wasn't old enough yet."

Shelia took her hand, and they walked the last few steps down together. "What was your daughter's name?"

"Katherine. We called her Katy."

"That's a nice name. I wish I could have a nickname, but Shelia is already short."

"I bet your daddy has some pet names for you."

Shelia giggled. "Well, he does call me 'brat' a lot."

"Yes, I've heard him call you that, very affectionately, though." Brock obviously adored his child. It pleased Zana to observe his interaction with Shelia. She was lucky to have such a dedicated parent. Yes, he'd make some unwise choices, but hopefully he wouldn't repeat them. She couldn't help but wonder if he cared for Darlene, if he still saw her on occasion. The idea didn't sit well with Zana. Not because she was jealous. Heck, she didn't have anything to be jealous about, but if he became serious, it should be with someone who'd be a good mother for Shelia.

"Yeah, I think he likes me a lot."

Zana put her arm around Shelia's shoulders and squeezed gently. "I know he does."

"What was Katy like?"

"She was a minx just like you. Only she had dark hair."

"What's a minx?"

"Well, in the dictionary it says something about being an impudent young lady. To me it means a mischievous, fun loving little girl who I enjoy being around."

Shelia appeared to like Zana's definition and smiled giving Zana a glimpse of the beauty the child would become. Brock would have his hands full one day.

They passed through the compound gates and turned left at the first street inside. Actually, it was more like a path than a road as it wasn't wide enough to allow more than one small vehicle to pass through at a time. Little houses lined up on each side, one looking very much like the other.

Shelia pointed. "There it is. It's the one with all those people working." She took Zana's hand and Zana broke into a trot to keep up with her.

Men and women bustled around the cottage painting the exterior. Inside two women painted in the living room. Smiling, they nodded while an older gentleman approached, his hand outstretched. Shelia hurried into the kitchen. She heard her excited chatter and a woman's laugh.

"Mrs. Forrester, welcome to Refuge. We're delighted you've joined our small community. I'm Paul

Hansen."

"Thank you." She shook his hand and then looked around the room, delighted with what she saw. "This is wonderful."

"Let me show you through the rest of the house. If you see anything you want changed, you just say so."

It was perfect. A short hallway off the living area led to two small bedrooms, each just large enough to hold a double bed and a chest. Between them was a small bathroom. Zana couldn't see a thing she'd change. She even liked the wall colors.

"Ma'am, Brock said if you came by to send you over to the furniture supply house to pick out some furniture. It's nothing fancy, mind you, but it will work until you can locate something better."

Well, the man thought of everything. "Thank you, Mr. Hansen. Can you tell me how to get there?"

From the kitchen, Shelia piped up, "I know where it is. I'll take you over there." She waved at the workers and skipped out the door. "Bye, guys."

Zana picked out the bare necessities for the cottage. She didn't want to be too indebted to Brock. There'd be time later, when she had a regular job, to buy additional items and decorate. After they left the furniture store, she quizzed Shelia on the city government. Shelia waved toward the next block. "Well, over there's the courthouse. The Refuge Police have a small office and jail there." She grimaced. "Mostly for guys who get drunk and disorderly. We don't have much crime. The post office is across the street from there."

"You have a courthouse?"

"Of course. Don't all towns have one?"

"Well, yeah, but being so far into the future, I

wasn't sure what to expect." And the fact that pirating and salvaging were apparently legal...or so she'd been led to believe. Lord knows what else had changed while she'd been floating around in an iceberg. "Let's walk over there."

"What for?"

"I just want to see it, okay?"

"Okay, but it's a boring place."

Shelia knew everyone in town, and her happy chatter echoed up and down the long hallway. Zana visited with the police chief, the mayor, and several other dignitaries. They were all kind and welcoming, but they all had the same answer. Salvaging was protected under some regulation. Possession was nine-tenths of the law.

~ * ~

The woman didn't waste any time. By four o'clock, Brock had received calls from half of city hall informing him of Zana's questions. She meant business. He couldn't help but admire her tenacity, but he wasn't giving in to her demand. The money from her vehicle had helped the people of this community. Yes, they could gather enough money to pay her back, but it was the principle of it all. She lived here now and needed to adapt to their ways.

Delicious smells of spicy food and Shelia's prattle combined with Zana's muted replies greeted him as he entered his home. For a minute, he watched them, enjoying their interaction and thinking how nice it would be to come home to this domestic scene every night. Shelia sat at the bar. Her ponytail bobbed with each movement of her head. Zana moved gracefully around the kitchen, stirring a pot on the stove before returning to the bread she sliced on the cutting board. Tonight she had her hair pulled up and clipped on top of her head emphasizing her graceful neck. Instead of her pantsuit, she wore a long skirt that called attention to the sway of her hips. He could get used to having this sexy woman around.

Zana laughed at something Shelia said. Her eyes sparkled, those full red lips opening to show a row of fine teeth. She saw him, and the smile froze as it had that morning. Regret washed over him. He'd hurt her feelings last night, and she hadn't forgotten. If he could take the words back, he would, but she wouldn't believe he'd not meant them. He'd have to find a way to prove they weren't true.

"Hey, ladies. What smells so good?"

"Daddy." Shelia jumped down and rushed into his arms. "Why are you so late?"

"Got caught up at city hall."

"Zana and I went there today, too."

He grinned down at her. "So I heard."

Zana stopped what she was doing, lifted her chin, and announced, "Dinner will be on the table in fifteen minutes."

Brock wanted to laugh at the steady chatter Zana kept up at the dinner table. Each time he mentioned their visiting the courthouse, she brushed off his question and continued her discourse on her cottage. Or descriptions of interesting items at the furniture store.

The minute Shelia headed for bed, Zana jumped up. "I believe I'll turn in, too. We had a busy day."

Brock's gut churned with tension. "If you don't mind, I'd like to talk to you about something."

Shoulders stiff, she sat back down on the sofa and

waited for him to speak.

"Did you receive answers for all your questions while at the courthouse?"

"Yes, but I'm not dropping the issue. I plan to petition the governor."

He released the breath he didn't realize he'd been holding. Just as he thought, the woman wouldn't give up. "Zana, I am the governor. Any complaint you have will come to me, and my answer will not change."

She opened and closed her mouth. "I don't...you're lying. That can't be."

"I assure you, it's the truth, and before you say it, I did not invent this law. It was on the books before I was born."

She dropped her head. For a minute, he feared she was crying, but when she glanced back up, the eyes that met his were tearless, clear, and determined. "There has to be a way, and I'll find it." She scooted forward on the sofa and stood.

He rose to meet her. "There is a way. You'll get half the proceeds from the vehicle, half of all I own, and be my partner in all my businesses."

She snorted. "Sure, there is, and you're going to tell me what it is, right?"

"Yes, I am." He laid his hands on her shoulders. "All you have to do is marry me."

Fourteen

The color faded from Zana's face. She dropped back onto the sofa. In mere seconds, the color returned—crimson. Hell, he'd shocked her this time. "You're out of your mind."

"Maybe, but it solves both our problems."

"What problems do you have?" She waved her arms and spat out, "You've got this house, an adorable child, all the money you need, and run this community. I can't see how I can help you with a thing."

Ha, he wished that was the truth, that he was immune to her, didn't want her. But he did. She was his number one problem. If he could convince her to marry him, would she accept the fact that he didn't, couldn't, and wouldn't ever love her? "You could be a mother to Shelia. She needs a woman's influence, a good role model."

"I can do that without marrying you." She smiled. "She's a delightful child. I enjoy being with her." She looked at him and her smile faded. Was he that transparent? "But we have nothing in common. I'd never marry to secure what rightfully belongs to me."

He sighed. "I can appreciate your stand and frustration on the subject of the vehicle. I realize you can provide for Shelia's needs, but what about mine? I want a wife, a mate." He cleared his throat. "I want babies."

She snorted. "Last night I'm not your type, and now you're proposing marriage, children?"

Hell, he should've known that remark would come back to bite him on the butt. "Yeah, I said that, but I was mad. Your remark comparing my relationship to Darlene and your job here got to me."

"Yeah, I can see why. After all, I'm not your type."

He cleared his throat. "I lied and I apologize for my despicable comment. You're more my type than Darlene could ever be. I find you very attractive, desirable. Darlene means nothing to me, never did other than being reliable help at the house and friendly diversion. She didn't show her true colors until the last few months. If I'd known Shelia was aware of our relationship, I'd have fired her much sooner." The attraction he'd had to Darlene didn't compare to what this woman did to him. He stood up, and turned his back so she couldn't see the proof of his arousal. He paced and refused to look at her. "Hell, I want you, woman. I'm not saying I love you, because I don't and don't plan to. Love is a complication. I don't know you, and you don't know me. I think we'd get along well together, and Shelia needs a woman in her life."

Zana sat up. "You're something else, mister. If you think you can get out of paying me what you owe this easily, you're wrong." The sofa let out a sigh as she stood, and he turned to gape at her. She didn't mince words, did she? "Why should I marry when I can get along on my own?" She stuck her face inches from his. He could feel her warm breath on his chin and smell her clean scent. Her slim finger jabbed him in the chest. "Anyway, I don't even like you."

At the glint of anger in his eyes, she dropped her

hand and stepped back.

"Is that so? You don't like me, or feel even the least amount of attraction to me." It was a lie. She did like him. He knew it and would make sure she knew it too. Brock had seen it in her eyes when she was ill. Desire was another story. He'd have to test that theory.

"Yes, you do."

Her mouth fell open. She sputtered. "No, I do not, and I find this conversation demeaning. I'm going to bed."

Before she could move an inch, he wrapped one arm around her waist and pulled her flush with his body. With his free hand, he captured her head, his long fingers catching in her silky hair. He pushed against her hips, so she'd feel his arousal. Her eyes widened in shock and he couldn't restrain his grin. "I think you're wrong. You're not immune to me. Your pulse has quickened, and I'm sure as hell not immune to you." Dropping his head, he kissed her temple, pleased by her gasp of surprise. "Shall we test my theory?"

She shoved against his chest. "No. My answer is no. I'll not marry you, I don't like you, and I sure as hell don't desire you." She struggled against him. "Let me go."

He chuckled against her ear, enjoying her hiss of anger. "Come on, one little kiss. If there is nothing between us, what could it hurt?"

"Oh, all right, but hurry up and get it over with. I'm tired."

We'll see how tired you are, sweetheart. "When I'm loving a woman, I don't rush. I take my time."

"Hah! You better get busy. The clock is ticking."

Damn, she knew how to dampen a man's ardor.

She was a hard case, for sure, but he was determined. He didn't expect anyone else would come into his life or that he'd have another chance at acquiring such a fine mate. She got along well with Shelia, and she loved Daniel, that was obvious. They might have more children and she'd be a good mother. He smiled at the idea. He'd like a larger family. If they married, his daughter might kick up a fuss and give her a hard time, but Brock didn't doubt for a minute this woman could handle his little redheaded minx.

Zana watched the parade of emotions cross Brock's face. What was going through his thick head? She didn't have all day, but her curiosity was piqued. His length pressed against her softness unnerved her, stirring feelings she'd rather not admit. He better get on with the kissing if he wanted to prove his point. She slapped him on the chest. "Times up. I'm outta—"

Warm lips covered hers, their heat, softness and moisture moving over her mouth, giving, and drawing a response from her. Her lips softened to conform to his as he played upon hers. A low humming started in her veins and heated to a steady thrum. Her knees trembled, and she locked her arms around his neck. He groaned, and his hand on her hip pulled her even closer against his hardness. He'd not lied about his desire for her—the evidence a heady awareness.

He broke the kiss and bent her head back to trail kisses along the column of her neck. Was her mewl one of protest or desire? She didn't know. She was drowning. He whispered against her neck, "I knew there'd be magic between us."

She jerked from his embrace. Her skirt wadded in his fist kept her from going far. With as much dignity as she could muster, she yanked it from his hand. "That may be so, but it's not enough to base a marriage on. Anyway, Mr. Callahan, what about your relationship with the lovely Darlene?" She smirked and threw up a hand. "I know, I know. You say she means nothing to you, but how do I know you're not seeing her. She might not agree or approve, and when I marry I don't intend to share."

He bristled. "That's insulting. I've not seen her, except in public, since I fired her. I'd never marry Darlene and she had no disillusions about our relationship."

"So you say. I wonder if she knew that."

"If she didn't, she was kidding herself. I never implied our involvement was anything more than friendship." He exhaled and shook his head. "Look, I know I let things get out of hand with Darlene, but that's over. She'll not set foot in this house again. I trusted Shelia to her care and Darlene betrayed that trust." His face reddened. "It embarrasses the hell out of me that Shelia saw Darlene and me kissing."

Zana didn't doubt his sincerity, but it didn't alter her feelings. She couldn't marry him. A successful marriage needed love and commitment.

"My energies must concentrate on locating my daughter right now. Nothing else."

"Have you considered she may no longer be alive?"

Her heart leapt to her throat. She nodded. "A thousand times a day. But, I need closure, regardless of the answers I get."

"I respect your desire for information and will do all I can to help you locate her whether we marry or not."

"Thank you." His offer of help touched her.

He frowned down at her. "Does your silence mean your answer to marriage is no?"

"It does. I intend to try to make it on my own." And she did, though she was sorely tempted by his kiss. *Don't be a fool, Zana. One great kiss doesn't mean the next one won't be a flop.* Which wasn't likely as this man probably didn't fail at anything he put his mind to. Still, just because there were sparks between them didn't mean they'd have a good marriage. He could be a wife beater for all she knew.

One of his long fingers stroked her bottom lip. She struggled to remain in place, to not turn around and run. "I'm extremely disappointed, but…if you change your mind, let me know."

~ * ~

Two days later, to her relief, Zana moved into her cottage. Brock's closeness made her a nervous wreck. He took every opportunity to brush against her or pat her hand or arm. His small touches filled her with longing, not just for sex but for companionship and closeness. She couldn't let herself care for him. He'd delay her goal of finding Katy. Plus, it was too soon after her ordeal to become involved in a relationship. Her emotions were too raw.

The store delivered her furniture, and her neighbors, Betty and Helga, helped her settle in. Brock had sent bedding, including a beautiful yellow-green bedspread the women insisted matched her eyes. Betty, hands on her hips, announced, "I think he's sweet on you, Zana."

Shelia, intent on stacking Zana's few dishes, gifts

from the neighbors and citizens of Refuge, in the kitchen cabinets, retorted, "Who is sweet on Zana?"

"Why your daddy, sugar. Haven't you seen the way his eyes follow her around?" Helga, the older of the two women, grinned down at the child. "Maybe you'll have a new mama soon."

Hands fisted, Shelia looked from Helga to Betty. "My mama is dead. I don't want a new one." She flashed a look of pure hatred at Zana. "And if he marries anyone, it'll be Darlene. He used to kiss her when he thought I wasn't looking." She pointed an accusing finger at Zana and spat out, "And he hasn't kissed you once."

Zana reached out. "Shelia…"

Shelia whirled away and ran out. Zana lunged for the door trying to catch her, but Helga caught her arm. "Let her go, dear. She needs time to get used to the idea."

"There is nothing between me and Brock. Nothing. And I need to catch Shelia and reassure her." She stepped out onto the small porch. "She doesn't need to be running wild out here by herself. She might get hurt."

Betty laughed. "That child? She knows how to take care of herself, and when she doesn't, someone always has an eye on her. We take care of our children. She'll be back before you head up the hill for dinner."

Sure enough, an hour later, a silent, sullen Shelia sat on her stoop. It was time to head up the steep incline, clean the house, and cook dinner.

Before she could lock the front door to her new home, Shelia set off down the street. Zana wasn't about to give her the pleasure of rushing to catch up. As she passed people on the road, Zana waved and chatted. Shelia stopped to talk to several children. When Zana approached, they eyed her with speculation. Rather than interrupt them, she nodded and continued on her way. It wasn't long until she heard Shelia scuffling along behind her.

Zana waited for Shelia to catch up. "Shelia, there is nothing going on between me and your father."

Shelia didn't respond and wouldn't look at her. She continued to walk with her head down.

"And even if your daddy remarries someday, his wife will never replace your mother."

"You don't like my daddy?"

"Why, I like him fine, but I'm not interested in getting married right now. I must concentrate on finding my daughter."

Her answer satisfied Shelia. She nodded and ran ahead.

With Shelia's help, albeit begrudging, the house was neat as a pin, and Zana prowled in the refrigerator for something to cook for dinner. "Shelia, have you any idea what you'd like for dinner? Your father hasn't mentioned his food likes and dislikes, so tonight its ladies' choice."

Though Shelia appeared to have accepted Zana's earlier explanation, she'd been quieter than usual while they cleaned.

"Do you know how to make pizza?" Anger forgotten for the moment, Shelia's eyes lit with hope.

"I sure do."

"All right! Can I help?"

"You bet. First, find the pan, and then I'll let you start mixing the dough."

An hour later, Shelia, with several gobs of sticky dough stuck in her hair, beamed her satisfaction as she spread tomato sauce over the oddly shaped piece of unbaked crust. Zana had vegetables chopped, meat sliced, and cheese grated for her to top it with. A salad would round out their dinner.

As soon as the meal was prepared, she made a sandwich to take with her for supper. She'd leave as soon as Brock arrived. Tomorrow she'd buy groceries for her kitchen.

She met Brock at the door. "Dinner is ready to pop in the oven. I'll be here in time to clean and cook tomorrow afternoon."

"Wait. Aren't you going to eat with us?"

"No, I need to leave now, so I won't be walking home in the dark." Home, the word sounded strange on her tongue and in her head.

"Stay and eat your evening meal with us. Shelia and I can walk you down after dinner each night. You need to eat with us, not all by yourself."

"That's nice of you, but I don't think it's a good idea. I need to settle in and get used to my home and surroundings. Thank you for all you've done to help me get settled." It'd be too easy to get hurt here, both by this man and the child. Even with her childish temper, Shelia was a delight. She was already getting attached to the minx and as much as Brock irritated her, she admired him, and yes, desired him. It'd be too easy to fall in love with him and Shelia.

Brock stood at the door and watched as Zana started down the hill. She could feel his eyes on her back. Swinging her bag as she walked, she strove to appear nonchalant. As she walked, her eyes scanned the area to each side of the path. No need to be careless. Her weapon was within easy reach. If she looked back, would Brock be standing watch, waiting until she reached the compound before turning to go inside? Though his proposal had irked her, no, it had been an insult; he did care for her safety. She snorted to herself. Marry him for half of all he owned. He'd said he liked her, but he didn't love her. A lifetime was a long time without love.

Lights were coming on in the village spread out below her. It was lovely, peaceful. Though there were no skyscrapers or fancy buildings, the structures were neat and cozy. It was so different from what she'd come from.

Loneliness overwhelmed her and she struggled with the desire to cry. If only she could find Katy, she'd have something to live for, look forward to. Not knowing her daughter's fate was a dark cloud over her head. Jonathan was gone, but there was hope for finding Katy—her child, her sweet, insecure little girl. If she lived, she would be eighty-four years old.

Fifteen

Her heart stopped at the rumble in the distance and then pounded in her chest when the carpet of white moved. No, no, no!

Zana woke in a cold sweat, the sheets drenched. Sobs shook the bed and turning, she buried her face in her pillow. Would she ever get past her guilt for leaving Katy at home, or the horror she'd felt when carried into the ravine by rapidly moving snow and being covered by the powdery white substance? She didn't think so. In the enveloping darkness, she'd held her son as he took his last breath and felt his body grow cold. As she waited for her own life to slip away, she'd revisited her regrets, mostly those concerning Katy. Yet, Katy was alive and would have a future. That was her only solace. She didn't know which dream was worse—the ones of the snow slide or those of Brock Callahan. His lips kissed her senseless. His large hands stoked a fire in her body that left her weak with wanting. *Damn the man.*

Brock had a friend who specialized in locating missing persons, and he promised the man would use every resource to gain information about Katy. If she still lived, Zana would do everything possible to locate her. If her child was dead, she'd search for the strength to move on with her life.

~ * ~

Brock had a plan. He'd bide his time, court Zana, and with any luck, win her over. She'd make a good wife and mother for Shelia. Yes, she'd be an excellent bedmate, too, and with her quick wit and intelligence, his life wouldn't be boring.

He smiled into his morning coffee. His body heated at the memory of their kiss. She could deny the attraction all she wanted, but she'd been as into that embrace as he had.

Dressed in her favorite short overalls and lime green knit shirt, Shelia appeared at his elbow. She'd fussed when he'd tried to braid her hair so he'd pulled it back into a ponytail. He doubted he'd ever become adept at fixing the minx's tresses. "Daddy, what are you grinning' about?"

He took another swig of coffee and swallowed the grin along with the brew. "I'm just in a good mood." Hell, why was he acting this way? He didn't want to love the woman, just marry her, and get a mother for Shelia, more children. *Watch yourself, old man.*

"Can I go to work with you this morning?"

"I'm not in that good a mood, brat. You're going to school where you belong."

"Ah, rats!"

With cup in hand, he walked from the breakfast bar to the kitchen sink and rinsed the dish. He draped his arm around Shelia's shoulders and ushered her toward the front door. "Come on. You don't want to be late."

As the door closed behind them, Shelia skipped ahead down the steps.

The sun peeked over the mountains to the east casting its rays on the village below. The walls and adobe houses glowed like gold. He took a deep breath enjoying the fresh scent of fall approaching. Soon it'd be cooler. Hopefully winter would be mild, not like some they'd experienced. A hundred years ago, he'd have been looking forward to spring, but global warming and the resulting little ice age had altered their seasons. He loved this place. It was the only home he'd ever known and he had no desire to live elsewhere.

He hollered down at Shelia. "Why haven't you begged to spend the night with Janie lately?"

She stopped and turned back. "Cause the last fifty times I asked, you said no." She waited for him to reach her.

He chuckled. "Might be because her mother had a new baby."

Shelia grabbed his hand and looked up at him, eyes wide with hope.

"I spoke to Janie's mom yesterday, and she asked if you could sleep over tonight." Of course he'd put himself in her path and ask about Janie and the baby in hopes she'd invite Shelia over.

Shelia jumped into the air, ponytail flying and bouncing around her head. "Yipee!" She squeezed him around the waist. "Can I go?"

He hugged her close and dropped a kiss to her flaming hair. "Yeah, you can. Just remember to be quiet around the baby and help clean up after yourself."

"I will. Zana's taught me heaps of stuff. I can help with the dishes and everything."

Indeed she could. She'd learned a lot from Zana. Zana bragged on her often.

"Can I go right after school?"

"No, ma'am. Zana will drop you off on her way home this afternoon. You have her call me on the transmitter after lunch and I'll settle arrangements."

Things couldn't have worked out better for his plan.

~ * ~

Zana loved her morning job. Working with Digger's wife Lola at the winery kept her busy, and the money allowed her to be independent. She was out-of-touch, but learning was intriguing and kept her mind occupied. Of course, it was part time while she trained, and the changes that had taken place in the past seventy-five years were phenomenal. This was a completely new field for her. There'd been no wineries in Saint John's. Though Lola mentioned the methods they used in monitoring the vines had been used since the 1990s, the entire setup was novel to Zana.

A small computer was attached to each grape vine in the field. From the computer station they could monitor soil temperature, moisture, humidity, and so much more. With just a few adjustments on the computer the plants; environment could be changed to accommodate its needs. It was a large operation, a huge investment. Zana wondered how Brock and the other part owners had been able to afford the technology required to maintain the vineyard. Were they wealthy or had they borrowed the money? Whichever, it was none of her business.

Refuge's vineyard was small compared to many. She knew some grapes were brought from other countries, but their very best and expensive wines were produced from local varieties. Probably the vintage Governor Whiteside drank while she was at dinner with him in Abyss.

Katy's fate filled Zana's mind every waking

moment, but working forestalled dwelling on her worries during the day. At night, she played a dozen scenarios over in her head—finding Katy and making a life with her—caring for her daughter in her old age. Her child was probably a grandmother, maybe a great-grandmother. There'd be children to love and nourish.

~ * ~

At noon, Zana met Shelia at the school. The large building housed all twelve grades. Built of adobe, it had a wide portico that ran the full length of the three story structure. It was one of the few taller buildings in the small community.

Shelia waited, chatting excitedly with her friend Janie. A grin stretched her face, and her hands emphasized her words, setting her body in motion. Her ponytail, stray curls loose around her face, bounced around her head. When she saw Zana, she squealed and ran to meet her.

Shelia grabbed Zana's hand. "Guess what?"

Zana laughed. "I can't imagine. Oh, I know, you have a boyfriend."

Janie giggled at Shelia's grimace. Zana restrained her rising laughter at the child's expression of distaste. Whatever she wanted to share, it had her wound up.

"Gross, no way," said Shelia. She flashed Zana a smile. "I'm spending the night at Janie's tonight."

Zana looked at Janie for confirmation. The pale blonde nodded vigorously. "It's the first time since Mama had Peter."

"Yeah," added Shelia, "He's three months old now."

Zana's heart lurched. He'd be smiling, interacting with his family. Memories of Katy and Jonathan at that age flashed before her eyes. *No, Zana, you can't dwell on the past.* She put an arm around each girl. "So, what's the plan? I need to talk to your father."

"You gotta call him soon as we finish lunch." Shelia grabbed her hand and pulled her toward the path home. "Let's hurry." She turned and waved at Janie. "See you later."

Holding Zana's hand, Shelia almost dragged Zana down the street. She had to trot to keep up. "Slow down. I'll be worn out by the time we get to the house if we continue at this speed."

Shelia slowed down. "Oh, okay, but can you walk a little faster than usual?"

Zana increased her pace to a brisk walk. She smiled at the child's enthusiasm. Sleepovers were important to girls. She'd enjoyed many as a child. "What will you girls do tonight?"

"Sometimes Janie's mom lets us help bake cookies. We listen to music and play games."

"That sounds like the same things we did when I was a girl."

Shelia eyed her with curiosity. "Did you get to go often?"

"Yes, as we weren't able to get out and do a lot of things because of the weather. The cold kept us from playing outside. Our parents preferred it when we were at one another's home. They knew we were safe."

"Gee, that's awful you couldn't play outside."

"It wasn't so bad. We still had fun." Kids managed to have fun regardless of their environment and she and her friends had been no exception. They'd reached the front door. "Whew. We made it."

They stepped inside. "Run start your chores while I

fix lunch."

Later, Zana punched in Brock's code and he picked up immediately.

"Callahan, here."

"Brock, Shelia said I was to call. She said she's spending the night with Janie."

His deep voice rumbled into the phone sending a tremor up her spine. "That's right. I'd like you to walk her to Janie's house on your way home, if you would. And, take off early so she can get there about five. She's invited to dinner, too."

"Sure, I'll do that. I'll see you tomorrow—" She was anxious to break the connection. The man made her nervous, especially with his ideas about marriage and other things.

"Wait." He cleared his throat. "I'd like to stop by your house about six this evening and take you to dinner."

She tensed. "Whatever for?"

He guffawed. "For your lovely company, of course."

"No. I'll be eating at home—alone, but thank you for the invitation." She'd seen a couple of restaurants in town and smelled their heavenly fare, but sitting close to Brock over candles and wine was too tempting.

His voice deepened. "Why ever not? You're not afraid of me are you? Maybe I make you nervous."

Her face heated. Grateful he couldn't see her, she blurted, "Of course not."

He chuckled. "Hmm, I think you're lying. You've been mighty skittish around me lately. If you don't go, I'll think—"

"Oh, all right. Something quick so I can get home

at a reasonable time."

If she could see his face, she knew he'd be wearing a smug expression. "See you at six." He clicked off before she could respond.

~ * ~

Zana peeked out the window in the living room. Brock stood on her small porch with a large bouquet of flowers in his hand looking every bit like a man on a mission. *Darn his hide.* It wasn't near dark, and her neighbors had found an excuse to mill around outside. She wanted to sink through the ground. The damn man wanted everyone in Refuge to know he was courting her. And she didn't doubt for one minute that he thought he could wear her down until she accepted his proposal. Well, he could think again. *If* she ever married again, it would be to someone who loved her, not a man who wanted a mother for his children. The idea was archaic.

She opened the door and stepped back. "Get in here. You're making a spectacle. The entire neighborhood will be talking about us in five minutes."

He breezed inside leaving a light waft of spicy cologne in his wake. Dressed in khaki pants, a sky blue shirt worn out, and heavy sandals, he looked entirely too handsome. He'd shaved and his dark silver streaked hair had been cut so that it just brushed the bottom of his collar.

All innocence, he asked, "What do you mean? I just brought you some flowers." He poked his head back out the door as if to look.

She hissed and grabbed his arm. "You know what I mean. My neighbors are already speculating about us." Disgusted with him, she propped her hands on her hips.

"Did you have to bring the bouquet?"

His brow wrinkled. "You don't like flowers?" He looked her up and down, and smiled. "You look lovely." She'd put on her only nice outfit, a lavender sleeveless sundress with rounded neck and skirt that dropped to mid-calf. Her sandals were soft natural leather.

"I love flowers. And thank you, but I don't want people to think we're a couple, or dating, because we're not." She took the flowers and stomped into the kitchen for something to put them in. A pitcher was all she could find. Filling it with water, she dropped the long stemmed peach roses and sprigs of baby's breath in the container and settled them at a more attractive angle. They were beautiful. She couldn't resist one little sniff before turning back to him. "We're just having a friendly dinner together. If it's anything more to you, I'm not going."

Arms folded across his chest, he rocked back on his heels. His gray eyes twinkled with amusement. "Whatever you say." He took the flower filled pitcher from her and placed it in the middle of her kitchen table. "They look very nice in here. Add some cheer."

She had to admit, her place did need some decorative touches, and the color softened the starkness of her little kitchen. "Yes, they do."

He took her arm. "Shall we go?"

Zana didn't like the expression of satisfaction on his face. It didn't bode well for her.

Sixteen

"Where are we going?" Zana asked as they walked along the dirt street.

"Do you like Italian food?" Lasagna was one of Brock's favorite dishes. Spicy enchiladas rated second. "Or, if you'd rather, we can have Mexican."

"I like both, so you choose."

"Italian it is, then." A few people were out and nodded or spoke to them as they passed. Some grinned. Even in the dim light Brock could see the blush rise from her neck to her face. His satisfaction was sweet. Zana had been correct in thinking the citizens of Refuge would know he courted her, but he wanted more than that. He needed them to know he'd marked her for his own, sending a message to the other single men to back off.

For August, the night was mild, pleasant. He wondered if Zana was cool and resisted the urge to put his arm around her shoulders. From the embarrassment radiating from her she'd probably jab him in the ribs.

Refuge didn't have many restaurants, but the few they had were excellent. Eating out was a real treat for citizens, not a common occurrence like in the twenty-first century. Fast food restaurants were obsolete. History books detailed the eating habits of their predecessors. It also highlighted their health issues—obesity, high cholesterol, diabetes, and other concerns of their time. Brock guessed there were some advantages to the catastrophe resulting from global warming and the Earth's changes. In many areas of life, doing without had led to a healthier lifestyle.

Tony's outdoor terrace was dimly lit with colored lanterns. Tablecloths of red and white checks covered each table. They were early and only six customers sat chatting and drinking wine. Several couples looked up, smiled and nodded, but then returned to their beverages.

"Are you warm enough to sit outside?" He liked her smile of appreciation at the cozy atmosphere.

"Yes, it's lovely out here."

As they stepped through the arched doorway, Tony appeared with a flurry in his big, white apron, surrounded by a flood of spicy aromas. "Governor! What a surprise to see you here."

Brock cringed at the title. Rarely did citizens of Refuge call him Governor. It was usually Captain Callahan or Cal.

Tony's grin of glee was proof the man wanted Zana to be impressed with her date. The matchmaking fool might ruin Brock's plans if he got too enthusiastic. He tried to gage her reaction, but her expression was unreadable.

"And who is your guest?"

"Tony, this is Zana Forrester, our newest resident in Refuge." As if the man didn't already know.

He took her hand and kissed the back. "Ah, lovely lady, welcome."

Eyes crinkled with humor, she retrieved her hand. "Thank you."

"Zana, Tony is the owner of this establishment and prepares the best Italian food I've ever eaten."

Tony clapped him on the back. "Ah, you are full of flattery, but I love it." He stepped ahead of them. "Come, let me seat you."

Taking Zana's arm, Brock guided her along behind Tony to a table that looked out on the garden. Lush green plants filled the area, creating the effect of a tropical paradise. Zana turned in her chair to study the rock waterfall and the goldfish in the small pond at its base.

She turned back to him. "This is lovely. I haven't seen many gardens here in Refuge."

"Many people fear they'll draw snakes or other creatures, but Tony's wife, Lucia, insists on some greenery in her life."

She shot a cautious glance at the plants.

"Don't worry. Lucia has several pets she turns loose in there each night. They keep it pest free."

Brock handed her a menu. "Let's order. I'm starved."

He ordered a bottle of wine. They sipped at the red beverage while enjoying the soft music coming through the sound system. The atmosphere or perhaps it was the wine, appeared to relax Zana. With elbows on the table, she folded her hands and propped her chin on them. Her eyes, filled with questions, fixed him in his chair. He resisted the urge to squirm and waited for her to fire away.

She picked up her wine glass and twirled the rich red in the rounded bowl before taking a sip. "This is very nice." She sat her glass down and studied her hands.

"Our winery produces some of the best wines in the area. We're quite proud of them."

"Yes, I've heard. Remember, I do work at the winery in the mornings. Lola has been trying to educate me on the types. Is this one of the wines from your local grapes?"

"I hadn't forgotten, and yes this red is produced from Refuge grapes, our best. We sell some of it, but a number of bottles stay here for us to enjoy."

She looked back up. "Brock, I'd like to know about Shelia's mother. Since I'm around her so much, it might be good for me to know what happened to her."

It was Brock's turn to study his hands. His marriage to Marta had been a dreadful mistake. She'd made his life miserable, yet he'd not wish on his worst enemy the death she'd experienced. And she'd given him Shelia. Marta had loved their child as much as he did. She'd been a good mother. One day he hoped to find a way to atone for his part in her premature demise.

He downed the last of his wine, picked up the bottle to top off her glass and refilled his. "It's a fair question." Especially since he wanted her to marry him. "She died from a poisonous snake bite." It was his fault. If he'd tempered his anger…

"We'd had an argument, which wasn't uncommon for us, but this one was worse than the others. She ran out of the house, wasn't careful, and startled a snake in the foliage behind the house." His gut clenched with guilt. "I was mad and didn't immediately go after her. She'd been gone for an hour or so before I got worried. By the time I found her, it was too late to save her."

She reached across the table to lay her hand on his arm. The soft touch heated his already warm skin. Before she could withdraw, he twined his fingers with hers.

Zana wanted to retrieve her hand, but the expression of pain etched on Brock's face stilled her, as did the sensations his thumb created as he stroked hers. She quickly looked up to see if he was aware of what he was doing. No, his thoughts were in the past, with his wife.

"I'm so sorry, Brock." Death from snakebite was a horrible way to go. She hoped they were able to spare her much of the pain. "It must have been dreadful seeing someone you love die so terribly."

"Yes, it was. When the doctors realized they couldn't save her, they kept her fully sedated, yet she still suffered. Watching her, compounded by my guilt for not going after her sooner, ate at me for years. It still eats at me."

"You didn't know she'd been hurt."

"No, but if I hadn't been so angry…" He released her hand and leaned back in his chair with a thud. "She didn't love me, never had. In her heart, she denied the love she had for another man, because she wanted the life I could give her here in Refuge."

Zana's heart pounded. People could make such messes of their lives. Even though her marriage ended tragically, she'd been lucky. She harbored no regrets, only wished she and her husband had more time together.

He shook his head. "We met, fell madly in love, or so I thought, and we got married. By the time Marta realized she'd made a mistake, she was pregnant." Zana watched as his jaw tightened in determination. "After Shelia was born, she wanted to divorce and return to her village with our child. No way would I agree to give Shelia up. So, we suffered through, trying to make the best of our situation."

Zana released the breath she didn't realize she was holding. She ached for them both. Being tied to a loveless marriage was tragic. A divorce would have been best, but she understood neither wanting to miss out on their child's life.

"Despite our differences, Marta was a wonderful mother. Shelia adored her and was just three at the time of Marta's death. It was terrible for her. She couldn't understand why her mother didn't come home."

Pain clutched Zana's heart, her own loss rising to the surface. Tears gathered in her eyes and she struggled to keep her voice steady, but failed. "You've done a wonderful job with her."

His eyes flew to her face. His face, tan from work in the sun, was lined by exposure to the elements. His age was indiscernible to her. He didn't look very old, yet with the streaks of silver in his dark hair, it was hard to tell. Loss and hardships could do that to a person. She was a prime example. Before being frozen in ice, her hair lacked any gray at all. Now her shoulder length tresses bore a multitude of silver strands.

The crinkles around Brock's gray eyes, deepened with concern. He squeezed her left hand. "I'm sorry. I've upset you."

She coughed into her free hand and shook her head trying to dissolve the knot in her throat, but her words came out in a croak. "No…no…I'm fine. I needed to know about Shelia's mother." But, in truth, she wasn't fine and might never be again. Would the pain at losing Jonathan ease and the desire to find Katy lessen as time moved on? Right now, she didn't think so.

"What about you? Did you have a happy

marriage?"

The pain eased somewhat and she smiled. "Yes. Very happy." She laughed. "Not to say we didn't have our disputes, but our anger never lasted long."

"I envy you."

"We were fortunate." If only David's life hadn't been cut short, maybe she'd not be in her present situation. Of course, she wouldn't be alive, but hopefully she'd have had a full life with her husband and children. She mentally shook herself. It didn't do to dwell on the past. "We never know what direction our life will take."

"That's a fact." He studied her for a moment as if trying to make up his mind about something. Finally he spoke. "You probably don't want to hear this, but—"

She held up her hand. "If this is about marriage, no, I don't."

"Please, hear me out. I won't press you. I promise."

She might as well listen, as he'd make sure he got his two cents in one way or another. "All right, get it said."

"We've both suffered loss. The only difference is you had more to lose. Yes, I lost a wife, but unfortunately our relationship wasn't a good one as yours was. Your husband's tragic death was terrible, but you had wonderful memories to sustain you. Your accident and the loss of your children is incomprehensible, and I know you'll never give up on finding your daughter. My respect for you would be less if you did, but life is fleeting. It's not often we get a second chance at being part of a family. I think you could be mine. Maybe I can be yours."

Stunned at his declaration, Zana wanted to respond

but he rushed forward.

"I know we hardly know each other, but I need a mother for Shelia and I want a wife. I'm tired of being alone. None of the women in Refuge interest me. You do. I think I made that clear before you moved out of my home and into your cottage.

"I like you, enjoy your company, and I think you feel the same way. Like can grow into a comfortable happiness, you know."

"You've not mentioned love, Brock." She'd never marry without it. "A major requirement of marriage."

His face flushed. He shook his head. "Love is a fool's emotion, it's fleeting, doesn't last. Plus, the women I love die. I don't ever intend to invest in that sentiment again."

Zana couldn't believe the man. "That's the most ridiculous thing I've ever heard." Surely he wasn't serious. The expression on his face said otherwise. He didn't flinch under her perusal. She shrugged. "No problem, as I don't love you either. At least we're even in that department."

His smile was forced. "There, see, we could have a marriage based on mutual respect. We'd both benefit from the relationship."

"I've made my feelings clear on the matter, Brock. Marriage is not something I want to think about right now, especially one without love. I have a mission, and I won't be deterred."

"You don't have to search alone. I'll do everything in my power to help you find your daughter whether we marry or not."

Zana knew his offer to help her was sincere, but as to marriage, she didn't think she could commit without love being present. Yes, like and respect was important, but would commitment be present without love? Maybe. His wanting a mother for his child and a wife, yeah right, a sex partner, weren't reason enough to enter into a permanent relationship.

"What if we married, had children, but weren't happy? Would you want to be tied to an unhappy marriage as you were before?"

"Happiness is a state of mind. There are all forms. I don't expect to be happy. I'll take being content."

She could only shake her head at his reasoning.

"This isn't a spur of the moment proposal. I've given it a lot of thought. This relationship would be built on respect rather than heightened and misguided sentiments."

"I'll think about it, but don't get your hopes up." Her answer would still be no. She wanted the heightened emotions and mature love, not just comfort.

The remainder of the evening they spent talking about Refuge. At her front door, Brock bent to kiss her. She placed a hand on his chest. "Uh-uh. No kissing."

He grinned and arms propped on the doorframe leaned in, surrounding her with his warmth and heady masculinity. Her breath hitched and heat pooled in her belly. She squeezed back against the door in a near panic. She didn't need or want to become involved with this man. A relationship would just be another complication in her life.

"Why ever not? Just a kiss between friends. What can it hurt?"

His lips were dangerously close to hers. She shoved against her chest. "Stop it. I'm not going to kiss you."

He backed up giving her more room. "Okay. Maybe next time."

"Don't count on it." She turned and hit the keypad with her palm. The door clicked open. "Thank you for the dinner. I did have a good time."

"You're welcome. I hope we can do it again sometime."

"Maybe. But, forget the flowers."

~ * ~

Shelia chattered away while they cleaned house. Topics ranged from baking cookies to changing Janie's baby brother's diaper. "The smell was gross, Zana. I thought I'd puke."

Zana chuckled at her sounds of disgust.

"I'm not ever gonna get married and have kids. They're too messy."

"You'll change your mind one day. And when that sweet little baby is yours, the smells and messes won't seem so bad."

Shelia snorted, and then said. "Well, he *was* cute when he fell asleep."

The front door opened, and they both looked over to see Brock in the entryway. Zana immediately felt a chill run up her spine. Brock never came home early, but there he was walking toward them.

His eyes on Zana, he said, "Shelia, can you go to your room for a while. I need to talk to Zana privately." Suddenly Zana couldn't breathe. She gasped for air. This was it. He had news, and it wasn't good.

"Ah, can't I stay? Is it about her daughter? You don't care if I stay, do you, Zana?"

Voice stern, he said, "I care, Shelia. Do as I say."

Shelia huffed in disgust but did as her father asked.

Zana's legs threatened to give out from under her. She grabbed the wall for support, eased her way to one of the chairs, and plopped down. "It's not good, is it?"

He moved to the chair facing hers, leaned forward, and took both her hands in his. "No, it's not, but it could be worse."

"Tell me."

"Your house, with Katy inside was buried under an avalanche. It took rescuers four weeks to get to her and your grandmother."

A wail echoed through the room. Zana was shocked to discover the sound came from her. She pulled her hands from his and covered her mouth to stifle the howl only to have the noise replaced by sobs. Her child had suffered, oh God how she'd suffered.

Brock moved to sit on the coffee table, their knees touching. His hands moved up and down her arms warming her icy skin. "They believe your grandmother died right away, but it took Katy possibly a week to freeze. She'd foraged in the house for food. When they found her she was buried under what appeared to be every blanket in the house."

"She's dead, my precious child is dead."

He squeezed her shoulders. "No, Zana, she went through rebirth."

Hope clutched at her heart. "She's alive?"

"She was at that time. According to what my source discovered, health and rescue records indicate she was put up for adoption. She was adopted by a family and moved from the area. There's the problem. When the temperature continued to drop in St. John's, computers froze and records were destroyed."

His expression of sympathy sealed her daughter's

fate. "I'm sorry, Zana. She could be alive and well somewhere, but there is no trail for us to follow and find out more. Every possible avenue has been investigated with no leads to your daughter's adopted name or where she moved."

Her dreams were dashed. She'd never find her child unless God intervened and made their paths cross. All she could do was pray. Her sobs increased in force. Her body shook. Brock moved to the sofa and gathered her in his arms. He held her as her misery flowed from her soul in rivulets of tears.

At some point, exhaustion claimed her. Brock carried her to the guest room and put her to bed. She remembered Shelia helping him remove her shoes and pull the cover over her. The child kissed her cheek and whispered, "I'm sorry, Zana."

Her sweet compassion caused more tears to trail from her eyes, but fatigue won and sleep claimed her. *She'd never see Katy again. Not in this life anyway.*

Seventeen

Zana woke to the smell of coffee and frying bacon. Warm breath ruffled the hair on her face. She stiffened. If that pirate Brock Callahan was in bed with her she'd commit murder. She opened her eyes to see Shelia, head propped on her hand, stretched out on the bed facing her.

She yelled, "She's awake, Daddy."

Zana cringed and covered her ears. "Goodness, child, not so loud."

"Oh, sorry." Shelia's grin melted into a serious frown. "I'm sorry about your little girl. Daddy told me he couldn't find her."

Zana reached out and clasped Shelia's free hand. "Me, too, sweetheart, but it's something I have to accept."

"But, you're not gonna give up, are you?"

She released Shelia's hand and sat up. Her clothes were a wrinkled mess. With her fingers, she combed her hair into some semblance of order. "No, I'll never stop looking, but it will be a miracle if our paths cross. I probably wouldn't recognize her after all these years."

"Why not, she's your daughter. How could you not recognize her?"

"It's been seventy-five years since I've seen her. If she's still alive, she'll be eighty-two years old now."

Shelia's eyes grew wide. "Golly gee, Zana. That's

older than you are."

Zana grinned. "Yeah, just a little." How old did Shelia believe her to be anyway?

Brock stuck his head in the door. "Come on, Shelia. Let Zana get ready for breakfast. Go set the table." She hopped off the bed and scampered out of the room. He smiled at Zana. "You feel better this morning?"

She nodded. "Thank you for last night."

"You're welcome. Hurry now before the eggs get cold."

As the week passed, Zana replayed in her mind different scenarios—Katy hearing about Zana's rebirth and finding her, bumping into Katy while visiting Abyss, or Katy seeing her mother's name in a newspaper article about survivors recently fished from the sea. Her daughter would rush to find her and move to Refuge to live with her mother. While she'd been in Abyss, Zana had placed advertisements in as many online papers she could find. Day after day she waited with the hope she'd get a response, but received none. She'd been terribly disappointed but refused to cancel the notice in hopes that one day someone would get in touch with her.

What would it be like to care for your aging daughter? Probably not any different than it was caring for Nana, David's grandmother. The older woman had been a joy to have in their home. The children enjoyed stories of the 'old days' and Nana had kept Katy occupied by playing board games with her. She could hear the echo of Katy's giggle when she beat Nana, which didn't happen often. Zana suspected the older woman let the child win on purpose.

One week turned into two. Zana accepted the fact that finding Katy would be a miracle, but she remained firm in her resolve to not give up. Miracles did happen. Her hourly wage at the communication center increased. Lola apologized for not being able to hire her on full time. Zana was thankful for the raise. It wasn't enough to live on, but, if she were honest with herself, she didn't want to give up her time with Shelia. She grew more attached to the child every day.

The day was hot. The sun beat down on Zana's bare shoulders, the light breeze making the heat bearable. She was grateful for the sundress she wore. The skirt didn't cling, and swished against her legs as she walked. As she approached the school, Shelia spotted her, waved bye to her friends, and ran to meet her.

Zana couldn't resist a laugh as Shelia joined her. "If I didn't know better, I'd think you looked forward to our homemaking chores every day."

"Ha, no way." She skipped along beside Zana. "I'm just glad to be out of class."

"Don't you like school?"

"Yeah, it's okay, but I'm not learnin' anything useful. All that math and stuff." She snorted. "It won't help me be a vintner. That's all I want to do is work in the vineyards and make wine."

Zana chuckled. She'd not been crazy about math herself, but a teacher in middle school found a way to change her way of thinking. "If you don't know your math, how will you read recipes, calculate ingredients, adjust temperatures, and any number of other facts necessary to make good wine."

"Well…I'll let my workers do that."

"Shelia, a good boss knows everything about her business. It's her responsibility to make sure the employees know what they're doing and not make mistakes. That's why people with advanced degrees many times start at the bottom in a business and work their way up to the top." Zana put her arm around the girl's shoulder and squeezed. "Plus, if you can't read and understand the accounting books, someone could cheat you out of all your money."

"Golly gee, I never thought of that." She kicked at a rock on the path and shuffled her feet as they walked. "Darn. Guess I better start paying attention."

She looked up at Zana. "What about all that history and stuff? I can see why reading is important, but diagramming sentences and grammar is for the birds."

Zana sighed. "Learning history keeps society from repeating past mistakes. At least it's supposed to." Not that people were always smart enough to learn from their errors in judgment. "As far as grammar is concerned, you don't want to sound ignorant when you correspond with people who buy your wines. Who knows, someday you may want to write a book about producing wine."

Shelia thought for a minute and then grinned. "Yeah, that'd be cool."

They walked on in silence for a while. As they marched up the stone steps toward Brock's house, Darlene appeared on the hillside about one hundred yards to the right of the front door. Her arms were loaded with flowers. What on Earth was Brock's former housekeeper doing on the hill around the cave? Maybe Brock didn't care who gathered flowers around his home.

When Darlene saw them, she hollered, "Shelia. Come see what's in bloom."

Shelia dropped her book bag on the steps and broke into a run.

Zana called out, "Hey, wait a minute."

Barely breaking her stride, Shelia turned and waved. "Come see the flowers."

Zana took off after her, her walk turning into a jog. Something didn't feel right here. Darlene hadn't been to see Shelia in several months and now she was here picking flowers? Zana didn't trust the flamboyant woman and she didn't think it was jealousy. No, she didn't like the fact that Brock had been involved with Darlene, but Zana's internal radar implied there was more to worry about.

It didn't take Shelia long to reach the hilltop and she and Darlene disappeared over the knoll. Fear clutched Zana's heart. Not being able to see the child further panicked her and she broke into a fast run. As Zana reached the top, horror gripped her. She opened her mouth to scream but no words escaped. Flowers scattered on the ground, Shelia struggled to free herself from Darlene's clutches as she pulled the child toward two approaching men.

Zana screamed, "Help, help, pirates," as loud as she could in hopes she'd attract the lookout's attention. Drawing her ray gun from her dress pocket, she hit the button for a quick charge and fired on the two men approaching. Her shots missed but sent the men scurrying for cover. Afraid to shoot at Darlene for fear of hitting Shelia, she tossed the gun to the ground and at a run jumped on Darlene's back. With one hand she latched onto a handful of the fake red hair and pulled while swinging the other, getting in licks wherever she could.

Taken by surprise, Darlene loosened her grip and Shelia broke free.

"Run, Shelia. Run to the compound," Zana screamed.

Shelia ran a few yards, and then hesitated and went for her weapon.

Darlene shook Zana off. Zana landed on her butt. Darlene lunged for the child, and Zana scrambled to reach the woman's foot, caught her heel and she hit the ground.

"No, Shelia. Go!" She listened this time and threw herself into a run. The men took off after her but as soon she crested the hill, shots rang out from the watchtower driving them back. Zana sagged with relief.

"You bitch." Darlene's foot connected with Zana's chin. Her head snapped back and connected with a rock. Her vision blurred and then went dark.

~ * ~

Trembling like a tree in the wind, Brock held his daughter against his chest. What the hell was going on? Luke had been on lookout, heard the shots, and saw Shelia running down the hill screaming. According to Luke's account, a man's head had appeared above the hillside and Luke had ordered the other two guards to open fire. He'd run down to meet the child, lifted her into his arms, and brought her inside the fortress. The alarm sounded. When everyone outside the compound was inside, he'd locked the huge doors. Luke had handled procedure by the book. All citizens were accounted for except Zana.

"Daddy, you're squeezing the breath out of me."

He flopped back onto one of the stiff back chairs in the tower and sat Shelia on his lap. His trembling had lessened some, but his heart thundered in his chest. "Sorry, pumpkin. Now, tell me again what happened."

Most kids would be crying, but not his child. She was agitated, but not because she'd narrowly escaped abduction. Zana was on her mind.

Shelia jumped off his lap and used her arms for emphasis as she told the story again. "You shouldda seen Zana, Daddy. She jumped on Darlene pulling her hair and hitting her with her fist. That's how I got loose. Zana yelled, 'Run.'" Shelia bit her lip. "I wanted to help her, went for my gun, but Zana screamed, 'No. Go.' So I decided I better do like she said."

Thank God Shelia had listened or she'd be in their hands too. Were they mistreating Zana? She better not have a mark on her or her captor would not just die, but die horribly.

Tears gathered in Shelia's eyes. "Daddy, we gotta save her. They'd a took me if it hadn't been for her. I love her, Daddy."

Brock pulled her back into his arms and patted her back. "It'll be okay. We'll find her." And he would. No one invaded his domain and took what belonged to him. And Zana may not be his yet, but she would be. They'd wanted to hurt him by taking his child. For what purpose, he didn't know. Thank God Zana had saved her.

"Brock. A man is on the cliff holding Zana with a knife at her throat."

Brock grabbed a set of binoculars and rushed to the window where Luke stood and peered through the lenses.

"Damn, it's Rafael Santigo." He turned to face the others. "Digger, take Shelia to Lola, and then arm a crew of six men."

"Aye, aye, Captain." Brock watched as Digger took Shelia's hand and they sprinted down the stairs.

Brock turned his attention back to the hill. A man with a white cloth attached to a stick walked down the hill. *So, Rafael wanted to parley.* "Luke, call Juan. Tell him to bring his best weapon."

"On it, Captain."

Rafael's man stopped at the bottom of the hill, waiting. Well, he wouldn't have to wait much longer. "I'm going down, Luke. Have Digger and the men at the gate."

~ * ~

His head came into view first, dark hair brushed his shoulders, and several days' growth of beard covered his chin. Expression grim, his eyes locked on the tree where she'd been tied. Her breath caught in her throat. Brock's chest was bare, sunlight playing across his rippling muscles. She swallowed. He was an amazing specimen of manhood. Her admiration died. Fury gripped her. She struggled against her bindings. Why was he coming in alone? Where were his men? He should come in armed with guns blasting. Or, a sneak attack.

He didn't break stride as he continued forward. His pants hugged his long legs and were tucked into his boots. She didn't doubt for a minute the monster knife he carried was hidden on his person somewhere. Lot of good it would do him against all four people. What was the man thinking? There were probably more hidden out there.

~ * ~

Satisfaction surged through Rafael Santiago's veins as Brock Callahan topped the hill coming into full view, and strode toward Rafael. Callahan stopped eight feet in from him. His gaze flicked to Mrs. Forrester and then back to Rafael.

"Are you unhurt, Zana?"

"I'm fine." She sniffed. "He plans to kill you, Brock. Why are you here unarmed, without your men?"

Brock's face twisted into a rueful smile, and Rafael wanted to wipe the smirk off his face. His pompousness further enraged Rafael. He couldn't wait to sink his knife into the object of his hatred.

"You don't trust my prowess, Zana?"

"Of course I trust you, but you're outnumbered. You're a fool, Brock Callahan." She turned her attention to Rafael. Tears, illuminated by the light, pooled in her hazel eyes. "Please, Rafael. It's not too late to change your mind, to work something out with Brock," she wailed. "He's a good man. Whatever is between you, surely it's not worth killing over."

Ignoring her, he asked Brock. "Are you prepared?"

"To the death." Brock nodded toward the woman tied to a tree. "First, promise me, if I lose, you'll release Mrs. Forrester to my crew, and you and your men will pose no threat to them. If you lose, I promise your men and your scheming sister can leave with your body."

"Fair enough. You have my word…on Marta's departed soul." He had nothing against the woman, Brock's men, or his people. Yes, he'd received a sum of money from a wizened old man who wouldn't tell where he hailed from, with a promise of more after he'd killed Zana Forrester. The messenger would not give the client's name or explain why Mrs. Forrester needed to die. Rafael had taken the money, but he had no intention of adding cold-blooded murder to his crimes. He'd killed out of necessity, and would again if he had to, but he wasn't a contract killer. Nor would he kill an innocent woman, especially one Marta's child was so fond of. To his way of thinking, it was free money.

His oath was easy to give. He shrugged his head toward the tree. "You've got one minute to say your good-byes."

In four long strides, the big man reached Mrs. Forrester. Rafael watched with growing interest. Was it true Callahan was interested in the woman? She was attractive enough and from Darlene's description would be a good mother for Marta's child. His heart twisted at the thought of Shelia being without either parent. He shrugged the pain away. Someone in Refuge would give her good care.

He couldn't hear all of their conversation, but made out a few words. *Please Brock…Shelia…Shelia…* He shook his head and encircled her in his arms. She dropped her head to his chest and sobbed.

"Time's up, Callahan."

Brock pulled away. He removed the communicator from his bicep and clipped it on her arm. Face stern, he pulled her head forward and kissed her full on the lips. Then, without another word, he turned and walked toward the circle.

She struggled against her bonds. "Wait, Brock. Please!" Brock's steps didn't falter. He appeared to be immune to Mrs. Forrester's pleas. "Don't trust him. He's lying."

Brock halted and swiveled to face her. "That's

enough, Zana. Calm yourself. This is between me and Rafael." When he turned back, the smile he'd had for the woman vanished, the expression replaced with one of calm determinations. "Can't you take her out of here? She doesn't need to watch."

Rafael was tempted, but stiffened his resolve. "Forget it. She stays."

Brock's face turned deadly and for a minute, fear rippled through Rafael. Maybe he underestimated the man. He mentally shook the apprehension off. His hate for this man would see him through; allow him to be the victor tonight. He sized up his enemy. Brock's size was impressive. Tall, his solid build was imposing, but Rafael had trained for this night for months. He'd beat every man in their village, even Pedro, a massive rock of a man feared by people for miles around. Yes, he was prepared, he'd win. Rafael walked away from the tree holding his hostage to an area with flatter ground. "Are you ready to die, Callahan?" He pulled his shirt over his head and tossed it to the side.

"Die?" Brock spat on the ground and stared at Rafael, the fool who dared to attempt to take his daughter and now held Zana captive. Yes, he might die tonight, but so would Rafael. His men would see to it and get Zana out unharmed. She had his communicator and would signal Digger if he died. Not that Digger would need the alert. He and his team were moving around behind Rafael's men at this very moment. Brock wasn't afraid to die, but he'd prefer to live to see his grandchildren, have a life with Zana. He wouldn't go down quietly. "You're mighty sure of yourself, pirate."

Rafael grinned and withdrew his knife from his belt. "That I am, old man." His smirk vanished. Hate filled his eyes and he growled, "Let's do it."

Before, Brock could pull his knife, Rafael charged, knocking him on his back. Dust flew up around him. The pirate's men roared their approval. Brock's left hand shot up and caught Rafael's wrist just before the man's knife plunged into his chest; his right clouted the pirate up side his head, slamming him aside. Brock unsheathed his blade and jumped to his feet.

Rafael was fast recovering and charged again. Brock sidestepped and tripped Rafael, sending him sprawling. He dove to pin him, but Rafael rolled. Brock missed, a collective sigh escaped from Rafael's crew, and Brock leapt up before being pinned himself.

The bystanders were quiet as he and Rafael stalked each other. They were well matched and for the first time Brock accepted the fact defeating Rafael might not be as easy as he'd expected. He stiffened his resolve. Losing wasn't an option. He believed Rafael would honor his promise and let Zana go free, but he wasn't ready to die. Shelia needed him. He had plans for his future. They included Shelia, Zana and a family.

They circled, weighing their opponent and chances for attack. Brock lunged, Rafael deflected throwing Brock off. He jumped back but too late. Rafael's knife sliced across his abdomen. Pain speared him. Zana's shriek echoed through the air. Rafael threw up his hands and jumped into the air, a bellow of triumph issued from his throat.

Brock swallowed the burning in his gut, charged, and caught Rafael in the chest with his head. The man flew backwards and skidded on his butt. Before he could recover, Brock dove, Rafael twisted and they rolled a few feet down the hill. Pointed rocks and thick brush bit into their bare skin. Brock landed on top and had Rafael pinned, his knife at his throat for the deathblow. Blood oozed from his wound wetting them both. The smell made his stomach roil. He shook away the sensation and concentrated on holding Rafael down. One slip and the slick blood could cause him to lose his grip. Rafael glared. He spat in Brock's face. Brock didn't flinch.

Face twisted with hate, Rafael snarled, "What are you waiting for? You're a coward, Callahan? Don't have the balls to kill me with my eyes open, huh?"

Brock pushed the blade into Rafael's neck. Blood oozed from the wound and trickled down each side leaving a red trail before it dripped onto the dirt.

"Why did you try to kidnap my daughter?"

"Why do you think? I wanted you here to exact my revenge." Rafael struggled and Brock pushed the knife in a little deeper.

"Be still or I will torture you in front of these people before I kill you."

Rafael stilled.

"And Mrs. Forrester? Did you kidnap her with the intention of killing her?"

The other man's surprise was genuine. "Whatever for? I'd never heard of her until Darlene told me who she was, that you wanted to marry her. When Mrs. Forrester made it possible for your child to flee, I figured she'd serve my purpose as well as the child. I'd never harm Marta's daughter. Never."

Brock believed him. "I have no desire to kill you, pirate, but you've caused me considerable trouble on the sea and after this stunt, I can't let you live." Images of Marta on her deathbed, her screams of agony blending with the cries of their terrified daughter, filled his head. Allowing Rafael to live would ease Brock's conscience, allow him to atone somewhat for his part in Marta's death, but he couldn't do it. The man had invaded his territory, tried to lay hands on his child, and taken Zana hostage. He'd appear weak before his people and others who might try to invade their territory.

Rafael bucked trying to toss him off. His face twisted with pain and Brock recoiled at the glitter of tears in his nemesis's his eyes. "Kill me you bastard. I want to die. You took Marta, destroyed my life. I have nothing else to live for."

Brock's heart twisted a little. Rafael's love had been deep and lasting. Whether the man was deranged by his loss, Brock didn't know. He didn't want to kill him, but couldn't afford to let him live. At least he could send him to his death with a small crumb of happiness.

"Marta loved you, man, and would have returned to Rio Ara if she'd not been pregnant with Shelia."

"You bastard, you're lying."

"No. Her last words before she died were to tell you she loved you. That she was sorry she'd screwed up both your lives."

Rafael's face contorted and he closed his eyes. "Thank you."

Brock drew back his arm.

"Wait. I must tell you something."

"Make it quick." He wanted to get this over with. Dizzy from his wound and blood loss, he struggled to maintain focus, to keep his eyes from drifting shut.

"An old man gave me money to kill Mrs. Forrester.

I took it because my people needed it, but I would never kill an innocent woman."

Brock froze. Adrenalin rushed through his veins providing him additional energy. Who could want this woman dead? He shook Rafael. "Did he give a name, where he was from?"

"No, he told me nothing. I swear."

Rafael didn't flinch from Brock's gaze. Brock nodded and then plunged the knife into Rafael's heart.

Eighteen

My God, Brock killed the man. He'd won the fight, why did he have to kill him?

Brock's men stormed from the trees. One of them cut her bonds. She rubbed her wrists to restore circulation.

The sound of Darlene's cries of grief filled the air as she sobbed against her brother's chest. One of Rafael's men pulled her up while the other two lifted the fallen man and carried him into the trees.

Zana still shook whether from fury, fear, or pure illness, she didn't know. Her head ached and her stomach rolled with nausea. She stumbled to where Brock had collapsed to a sitting position on the ground.

Covering his hands with hers to hold the cloths Digger slapped into place, she moaned, "Oh, God. Don't you die on us, you big oaf."

He'd grinned up at her. "It's not as bad as it looks. Hurts like hell, though."

With a man Zana didn't know, Digger had Brock wrapped within seconds. They got him to his feet. "We have a transport to take you to the hospital, Captain. You think you can make it down the hill or should we get a stretcher?"

"Hell no to both. I'm not going to the hospital and I don't need a stretcher." With a man supporting each arm, he stumbled forward.

Zana was near tears. The stupid man. "Damn you, Brock Callahan. You scared us half to death. You are going to the hospital. You've lost too much blood."

He stopped and growled down at her. "You're not my boss, woman. I'm going home."

The dam she'd been holding in broke and she burst into tears. Stomping toward the house, she yelled back, "You're a damn fool, Brock Callahan"

Thirty minutes later, Brock laid spread eagle on the dining room table, out like a light from the pain medicine Dr. Boone had given him. He and a nurse worked at stitching Brock's abdomen closed. He'd refused use of the nanobots insisting it should be saved for serious injuries. It's not like they could be used up. Zana considered it to be just another show of his stubbornness.

Wrapped in bandages from under his arms to his waist, Brock was lifted onto a stretcher and rolled into his room to his bed. Zana couldn't resist following. There wasn't a thing she could do, but she needed to be near him. Her concern and what it indicated scared her. She cared too much about this man.

Digger placed a hand on her shoulder. "He will be fine, Zana. He's had worse wounds and pulled through. Tomorrow he'll be growling like a bear."

Throat tight with tears, she could only nod. She didn't want to care so much about this man, especially after his rudeness on the hill. Plus he'd killed the pirate. Without flinching he'd driven his huge knife into Rafael's heart. She shuddered. How could he be so cold? It didn't sit well with her.

Though he wanted to marry her, he didn't love her. Yet he'd come to rescue her and was willing to give his life in doing so. She didn't understand the man and what motivated him.

With his hand at her back, Digger nudged her toward the door. "Come, let him sleep. We'll check on him again in a few minutes."

Dr. Boone stood at the now cleaned off table. "Mrs. Forrester, come over here and let me check that head of yours."

She reached up and touched the knot and winced. "I'm fine, Dr. Boone. It's just a little sore."

"I'll be the judge of that. Now, sit down."

Rather than argue, she sat.

"Do you have a headache, nausea?"

She nodded.

He flashed a light in her eyes and took her vitals. She winced when he touched the knot on the back of her head.

"You have a mild concussion. I want you to stay here where my nurse, Carol, can keep an eye on you while tending to Brock."

"But I want to go home to my cottage."

"You can go tomorrow. Tonight you must be watched." He lifted a small envelope from his pocket and removed a small square of what appeared to be translucent paper. "Open your mouth." He laid the square on her tongue. It dissolved instantly. "Now, to bed with you."

"Thank you, Dr. Boone."

"You're welcome. If you don't feel better in the morning, I want to see you in my office."

Digger took her elbow and let her to the kitchen bar. "You must eat something before you fall."

Her stomach rebelled. She didn't think she could

choke down a bite of food. "I don't think I can eat, but thank you."

"You need to have something in your stomach," said Carol. She sat a bowl of stew on the counter. "Your body needs it."

Zana slid onto one of the bar stools. She took a small spoonful to see how it went down. It settled in her stomach so she tried more.

Carol smiled. "Good?"

"Yes." Zana had to admit, either the food or medicine worked wonders. Her head no longer pounded.

"Digger found you something to sleep in. I'll put it in the guest room. After a hot shower you'll sleep like a baby."

"Thank you. I'm more than ready for one."

She met Digger coming from Brock's room. "How is he?"

"Sleeping soundly." He patted her shoulder. "You get some rest too. Luke will be relieving me shortly. I'm going home to Lola and Shelia. The child will be full of questions."

"Poor little tyke. Give her a hug for me."

Dressed in Brock's soft long-sleeved shirt and a pair of boxer shorts cinched up as tight as the drawstring would allow, she stepped from the bathroom into the hall. Carol and Luke sat on the couch talking.

~ * ~

The bed felt heavenly. She settled under the covers and tried to relax. Panic gripped her. Today's events flashed across her mind—Darlene with her arms around Shelia, the child running down the hill, shots... She struggled to drive the thoughts from her head. Instead her body shook.

"Zana?" The door opened and Carol came into the room. "I need to check on you before you go to sleep." Zana's teeth chattered. Carol flipped on the bedside lamp and studied her. "Ah, Dr. Boone was afraid you might suffer anxiety." She withdrew a patch and placed it on her wrist. "It's not uncommon after situations like you experienced today. It didn't hit your body until you relaxed."

Zana could only nod and wait for the medicine to travel through her blood stream. When the trembling stopped, Carol patted her shoulder. "I'll check in on you again later. Call if you need me."

~ * ~

A crash sounded from the bedroom down the hall woke Zana.

Luke yelled, "What the hell?" Footsteps sounded on the concrete floors. Zana ran down the hall to Brock's room.

Luke held Brock's shoulders as he sat on the side of the bed gripping his abdomen.

"What are you doing, Captain? You're gonna bust those stitches wide open."

"I want to get up. Help me."

"No. You've lost too much blood."

"I need the bathroom."

Carol took Brock's other shoulder. "Let's get him on his feet and we'll walk slowly."

Luke grumbled but did as the nurse told him. Carol stepped out of the bathroom to give Brock some privacy. When he shuffled out his face resembled a death mask. He gasped with pain as they eased him back down onto the bed. Carol left the room and came back with a syringe.

Brock saw the needle. "I don't need any shots. You're...not going to...fill me with drugs."

Zana squeezed Luke aside and sat beside Brock. "You're in no shape to do anything. Now be still so you can heal."

He arched a brow, or tried. The expression turned into a grimace. "You've been mighty bossy today, woman."

She flushed and stood. "Well, you've been an ass, so we're even. You need to rest and let your body heal. Without the pain medicine you won't sleep and might be stuck in your bed for days. Is that what you want?"

"Shit!" He eased back down on the bed. "All right."

"Roll to your side, Mr. Callahan."

He rolled toward the wall, a groan rumbling from his chest. Carol tugged his boxers down a fraction exposing a taut buttock and swapped a generous area with alcohol.

"Hurry the hell up."

She jabbed.

"Yeow!"

Luke snickered. Zana bit her lip to keep from giggling. She wondered why Brock needed an injection yet Dr. Boone had given her a dissolving paper-like wafer for her pain. Maybe it had to do with the strength of the medication or the type. She'd ask Dr. Boone or the nurse as soon as she got a chance.

"You two are enjoying this a bit too much." He eased on to his back, sweating and gasping for air.

Luke and Carol turned to leave and Zana followed. Brock grabbed her hand. "Stay with me a minute. I need to talk to you."

What could it hurt? He'd be out like a light shortly. She'd wait until he fell asleep.

He tugged until she sat on the bed beside him. "Lie down beside me so I don't have to look up at you."

"I don't think so. I could accidently hurt you." Actually, the close proximity to his naked torso made her uncomfortable. He oozed masculinity despite his incapacitation, her attraction to him scared her. His near death earlier had thrown her for a loop. She didn't want to care for the man. Caring meant getting hurt, responsibility, but it meant receiving in return. Was she ready?

What was she worrying about? The man just wanted to talk. He wasn't professing undying love. He'd come after her because he felt responsible for her, and Rafael was the foe. Brock wouldn't leave anyone in enemy territory. His ethic was too strong. But, he'd killed the man when he could have let him go. Surely Rafael would be too embarrassed to show his face again. Could she see past the sin of killing another person?

"Zana?"

She lay down beside him, his arm behind her head. He raised his hand and stroked her hair. "Are you okay?"

Anger rose to the surface to be replaced by a choking in her chest. Voice hoarse, she sobbed, "No, I'm not. Why did you do something so stupid as to come up there unarmed? You could have been killed. Who would have taken care of Shelia? And why did you have to kill him?"

"Hush now, don't cry." His lips touched her hair

and she struggled not to turn and weep against his chest. "I knew Rafael wanted a fight to the death. He said so in his note. It would have been dishonorable to him to let him live."

"That's ridiculous."

"To you maybe, but he knew the consequence of seeking revenge by taking innocents hostage. Any man would have done the same thing. A man has the right to protect his family and his people. If I hadn't killed him, he'd be back to try again."

Though she didn't like his answer, it made sense.

"You could have died."

"Yes, sweetheart, but Shelia would have been cared for. Digger or any number of people in Refuge would have raised her as their own."

She shuddered with unrestrained sobs. "No one can replace her father. And I'm not your sweetheart so quit using terms of endearment on me."

He laughed, the movement eliciting a groan. "Stop your weeping. I'm fine, Shelia's fine, and you're fine." He sighed. "I harbor no guilt in killing the man, no regrets. The deaths that haunt me are those of my sisters, Marta, and Pepe. Seems everyone I love dies."

"Brock, you can't continue to blame yourself."

"But I do. I can't and won't put it behind me. It's my burden to carry 'til the day I die. 'Ss why I won't ever love you." The medicine kicked in. His voice softened as sleep threatened.

His declaration hurt, but at least he was honest.

"Tomorrow all will return to normal." His fingers trailed up and down her bare arm eliciting tingles in their wake and a longing deep inside her. "With one exception."

She stiffened. Now what? "And what exception is that?"

"I'm going to pursue you with a passion. You'll be my wife within a month."

In your dreams, mister. Yes, she was tempted, by everything about him. He stirred her heart and her soul. Her body longed to be held close, wrapped in his arms, but she wasn't ready. Anyway, she couldn't marry a man unless she loved him. And the brute hadn't said he loved her, had actually said he couldn't and wouldn't love her, more than once. She wanted to poke him in the ribs to make her point. If he thought she'd marry him without a commitment of love, he had another thought coming.

She snorted. "Dream on, big man."

A loud snore answered her.

Nineteen

Zana exhaled a sigh of disgust and made to ease away from him. His hand dropped to clasp her waist, pinning her to him. It was either wake him or remain on the bed. The cheeky man. She twisted her neck to see if he really slept. He wasn't beyond playing possum, of that she was sure. His chest rose and fell in a steady rhythm. With each breath, his lips fluttered emitting a soft snore. The sound tickled her and she struggled not to laugh, but sobered. She closed her eyes and mouthed a brief prayer for his recovery. She'd give him a few minutes and try again.

"Good morning, darlin'."

Zana jerked to a sitting position and glanced over at the grinning rogue beside her. She jumped off the bed and peered down at him. "How do you feel?"

"I hurt, but Carol and Luke came in a couple of times while you were sleeping and gave me another shot, so the pain's not too bad."

She blushed to the roots of her hair and swallowed a silent groan. The nurse and Luke had seen her sleeping beside him. What must they think? That she slept in his bed often?

He grabbed her hand. "Hey, don't be embarrassed. You were exhausted so we just let you sleep."

The door opened and she yanked free. Luke walked in. "Ah, Zana, I see you're up. You were sleeping soundly when we tended Brock's wound so we tried not to disturb you. Do you feel rested?"

She flashed a half smile. "Yes, I do. Thank you for letting me sleep."

"You've been through a lot. Your body took what it needed most—deep, mind-numbing sleep."

It made sense. She wouldn't dwell on it anymore. So, she'd slept beside Brock. Nothing happened between them. If he felt some satisfaction at her being in the same bed with him all night, he didn't let on. His attention was now on Luke and trying to sit up on the side of the bed. She eased from the room. Hopefully a shower would wash away the dregs of her headache.

~ * ~

"Daddy, Daddy!" Shelia's squeal of delight echoed through the house. Joy stretching her face, she ran into the bedroom to see her father. Digger caught her and laid her gently on the bed beside Brock, her head on his shoulder. Brock's arm circled her shoulders in a hug.

Tears glistened in the child's eyes as she touched her daddy's cheek.

Brock covered her hand with his free one. "I'm okay, sweetheart, just sore."

Shelia sniffed. "I was so scared you wouldn't come back."

Zana's throat closed. Her vision blurred. Poor little tyke. Zana had been afraid he wouldn't too.

Voice gruff, he said, "I'll always be back. Now you dry those tears and say hello to Zana."

Shelia's head popped up. She eased from the bed and threw herself at Zana, arms locked around her waist. Zana stumbled and chuckled as she wrapped her arms around the small frame. She grunted at the pressure of Shelia's tight squeeze. Her little arms were strong.

"You saved my life. I love you, Zana."

Emotion stuck in Zana's throat and for a minute she couldn't speak. She stroked Shelia's hair and managed to squeak out, "I love you too, child."

And, she did. There was no doubt in her mind. She wasn't a replacement for Katy, but a delightful addition to her empty life. Her heart twisted with yearning— longing for more. If only she could gain information about Katy. Even if her daughter was dead, closure would help her move on. If she were still alive, time with her would do much to heal her wounds.

Brock looked at her, satisfaction and hunger etched in his weary face. The intensity of his gaze startled her. Hand on Shelia's shoulder, Zana took a step backward breaking contact with Brock's stare.

Susan, the day nurse, came in and laid a plate of food on Brock's chest. It was heaped with fruit, bread, cheese and chunks of warm meat. All foods he could pick up with his fingers. "Eat this. Food will help you heal."

He smiled weakly. "Thank you, Susan."

Susan spread the bar with the same offerings she'd placed before Brock. According to the nurse, food came in waves from the women of Refuge. Zana filled a plate and savored the delicious food. Evidently her ordeal hadn't decreased her appetite. She chewed slowly, enjoying the juiciness of the fruit. Susan and Digger chatted as they ate. Shelia took her plate into the bedroom and sat on the end of the bed while she ate. Zana could hear the soft murmur of her sweet voice mixed with Brock's base.

Zana rinsed her plate and put it in the dishwasher. She walked into Brock's bedroom and reached for their dishes.

Shelia hopped off the bed. "I've got them, Zana."

"Thank you, pumpkin."

She flashed her daddy a smile. "Welcome, Daddy."

Dr. Boone arrived right after lunch to check on Brock. Zana stood in the doorway and listened.

"You're a stubborn man, Captain Callahan. If you were at the hospital I wouldn't have to traipse up and down all those steps." He removed the large bandage covering Brock's abdomen, checked the wound and the waved to Susan to put on a fresh dressing. "You'll be fine. I'd like for you to stay in bed three more days."

Brock snorted. "I can't—"

"I know, I know, you'll do what you want, so I'm not going to waste my breath. Just be careful. I'm leaving medicine to ease your pain. Take it."

Then he'd turned on Zana. "Let's go into the guest bedroom, Mrs. Forrester. I want to check on your progress." He spent several minutes checking her eyes and wound. "Now, about your episode last night. You understand it's a delayed reaction to what you experienced and witnessed on the hill. I'm leaving you a couple of patches in case it recurs. I doubt it will, but we want to be prepared." He patted her hand. "If you've not had a repeat of performance by this evening, and no nausea or headache, you may go home."

After the doctor left, Zana peeked in to Brock's room. He was asleep, his face so pale she wanted to stroke the pinch marks from around his mouth, eyes, and forehead.

She couldn't pretend indifference to this man. He

possessed a magnetism that drew her. Would his heat destroy her, burn her up, or would it make her life warmer, richer for its warmth? Brock was a good man, of that she had no doubt. He was well respected as a leader in this community, and he was an excellent father, but his soul was burdened with past pain. Would he ever be free from the effect of his losses?

Shelia still sat on the foot of his bed, her mouth tense with concern. Zana put an arm around her and hugged. The child relaxed against her. "Why don't you lie down? If he needs something you'll hear him and can come get us."

Shelia nodded and stretched out beside her father. Afraid to get too close but wanting to touch him, she placed her small hand on his where it lay on top of the sheet. Zana didn't doubt the child would be asleep in a few minutes. Her fear and worry had worn her out. A nap would do her good. Zana pulled the spread up over Shelia's legs and left the room.

Zana returned to the kitchen where Susan chopped ingredients for a rich stew. She glanced up and smiled as Zana joined her at the counter. Digger was gone.

"Can I help?" She washed her hands and grabbed a knife to cut vegetables.

Susan carefully took the knife from her hands. "No. You go lie down. You've been through much the past few days. Your body needs healing too. Head injuries need watching and rest. You never know how that might affect you if you don't take care of yourself. You don't want a repeat of what happened last night." She nodded toward the bedroom door. "I'll take care of Brock and the child. Tomorrow you can take over if necessary."

Her head on the pillow, Zana breathed in the scent of the clean sheets. She took a deep breath and closed her eyes and let her mind wander. The past few days seemed surreal. Had she really attacked Darlene? Zana had always known her protective instincts ran strong, but they'd never been tested. Thank God she'd reacted quickly to free Shelia. At least she now knew Rafael wouldn't have hurt the child, but regardless, she'd carry the scare always. They all would. She shuddered at the memory of Brock, face fierce in battle, muscles straining, plunging the knife into Rafael's heart. She now better understood his reason for not letting the pirate live, but doubted she'd ever be able to obliterate the picture of Rafael's sightless body and Brock covered in blood from her mind.

What would tomorrow bring? It would probably involve Brock's declared intention to pursue her in earnest. She better make up her mind whether she wanted to be caught or not.

~ * ~

Zana bristled. "What do you mean you need help getting into the shower? You had a shower last night."

Brock swallowed his grin and strove to keep his face void of emotion. "I've sweated since then." It wasn't a lie. He preferred to shower at night and then again in the morning. But, he wanted to get Zana alone with him in the bathroom and explore the attraction between them. He wasn't above a little mischief to get what he wanted.

Head tilted, she skewered him with those amazing hazel eyes narrowed as he struggled to keep from laughing. She looked him up and down. "Why'd you get dressed then?"

"Carol insisted she help me before she left. She was so tired I didn't want to bother her with a shower."

"No one is coming to relieve her? What about Luke and Digger?"

"I've dismissed everyone." He might regret his desire to get back to normal before the day was over.

Zana blew out her breath in an exaggerated sigh. "Oh, all right. I'll help you to the shower, but then you're on your own."

"Fair enough."

She stomped to the bedroom. He followed admiring the twitch of her butt in the snug fitting pants. While he sat on the bed, she removed his shoes. He froze when she started unbuttoning his shirt and his body lurched when her cool hands touched his bare flesh to smooth it off his shoulders. Maybe this wasn't such a good idea.

All business, she didn't act at all embarrassed as she went about undressing him. She fitted her hand under his elbow. "Stand up."

Standing was easier today but doing so still pulled on his stitches. He resisted a croak of pain. To cover he started unhooking his pants. They dropped, caught on his hips, and he wiggled so they'd slip down to his feet.

A giggle drew his gaze to Zana's laughing face. He grabbed her shoulder to steady himself to step out of the pants pooled on the floor, wobbling as he did so. She giggled harder and he growled, "Think that's funny, do you?"

"Well, your little dance is cute. I've never seen a man dance in his," she looked down, "uhum…boxer shorts."

He flushed and moved his hands to her waist.

"You're evil, woman. Laughing at a man in my wounded condition." She smelled sweet and he leaned closer for a better whiff. Coconut, she smelled like fresh coconut with maybe a hint of vanilla.

She leaned away from him, eyes narrowed and asked, "What are you doing?"

"I like how you smell."

"It's just shampoo. Nothing special." She tried to remove his hands from her waist, but he held on. "And certainly not for your benefit, you oaf."

He pulled her closer, close enough her breasts brushed his chest. His body shuddered at the contact, and he resisted crushing her against him. She eyed him, ready to bolt or to slap his face, whichever mood struck her first. He suspected the latter as she wasn't the running from a battle type.

"What do you think you're doing?"

"I'm going to kiss you, Zana Forrester."

She gripped his biceps to push him away. "No you're no—"

He covered her lips with his and took advantage of her open mouth. His tongue slipped inside and twined with hers tasting her sweetness. She struggled against him. He winced in pain. She stopped, carefully wrapped her arms around his waist, and allowed him to draw her closer.

"Oh, Zana, honey." He nuzzled her cheek. "You're so sweet." His hands traveled her back, cupping a buttock. Her hands burned a path around to his chest and circled his neck. Lifting her face to his, she offered her mouth and he kissed her again, moaning at the sensation of her pelvis pressed against his.

"Why are y'all kissing?"

At Shelia's voice, they jerked apart.

In shock, they stood frozen, struck dumb, and then Shelia squealed. "Does this mean you're getting married? Are you going to be my mama, Zana?

Zana shot him a heated glance. "No, honey, it doesn't. People kiss all the time. It's an expression of, of…" She looked at him for help.

He shrugged, at a loss for words.

"But, why, Zana. Don't you love us?"

"Shelia." Brock started forward then remembered he wasn't dressed. He yanked a sheet off the bed and ushered his daughter to the door. "You don't ask questions like that."

"But, Daddy, you're almost naked. Only married people get naked together."

Zana rushed past them out the door. "Let me know if you need some help when you get out of the shower." He didn't miss the look of amusement on her face. He read her message loud and clear. *Have fun explaining.*

He watched her go, and then turned to Shelia. "Yes, that's true, but Zana helped me undress so I can take a shower. I kissed her. End of story. Now get out of here and let me take a shower."

Her expression wilted. "But, you like her as a girlfriend, don't you?"

Brock gaped at his child. "Yes, I do, but she's not sure she likes me that way. Yet." He winked. "So, I'm going to kiss her every chance I get to convince her to marry me." He hugged her. "She already loves you, brat."

She grinned. "I know." She jumped up and down. "We'll make her love you, too, Daddy."

He hushed her. "Don't let Zana know we're

plotting to catch her. It's our secret."

Standing under the warm water, he remembered Shelia's comment. *We'll make her love you.* His jubilation dimmed. What if Zana fell in love with him? He wanted her affection, but he didn't want to see her hurt. If she fell in love, she'd want him to return the sentiment. And, he didn't intend to invest in the emotion. Why couldn't life be simple—marry, have a good sex life, raise a family, and not get all involved in emotions. Was that too much to ask? Probably, but that's the way it had to be for him.

With all the pain medicine he'd taken in the past few days, his worry about Zana's safety had fallen to the back burner. Now his concern rushed forward with a vengeance. He'd alerted Digger and Luke to the threat Rafael mentioned before his death. Had they been able to learn anything while he'd been laid up? Staying here, Zana had been safe. His men had been near and watched out for her. He had to get well and take over. She was his responsibility. He'd be damned if he'd let her come to harm.

~ * ~

Zana's legs shook as she made her way to the kitchen. Damn the man. He oozed male sexuality, and she couldn't deny she wanted a taste, to experience the fire that would explode between them. She took deep gulps of air and hand shaking, turned on the cold water and filled a glass. Some sloshed over the side as she lifted the tumbler to her lips and took a sip. She patted her cheeks and forehead with her wet palm, the coolness cooling the heat in her face.

Shelia's tennis shoes squeaked against the shiny cement floor as she exited Brock's room. Zana expected to be bombarded with questions but the child didn't join her. She went to her bedroom, whistling a tune Zana didn't know, and came out with her school bag. Shelia moved toward the front door.

"Bye, Zana."

"Do you have your ray gun?" Zana strode to the entrance and stood beside Shelia at the open door. Zana would probably never get used to the dangers of Brock living outside the compound. Though the men on watch knew when to expect Shelia to leave for school, and followed her progress, Zana couldn't relax until she entered the gates.

"Yep." She hugged Zana. "See you this afternoon."

Zana watched Shelia trot down the steps, ponytail flipping with her every move. When she reached the bottom, she turned and waved. Zana returned her gesture and went back into the house.

Grunts and groans came from Brock's room.

"You need some help?"

"Yeah." He sat on the side of the bed, his pants around his ankles, and sweat beading his brow. A shirt lay across the foot of the bed. She helped him into it, and then to stand so she could raise his trousers.

"Thanks."

"Do you have some shoes you can step into?"

"In the closet."

She located a pair of loafers and sat them on the floor at his feet. He stepped into them and shuffled to the living room. He eased down into his easy chair. "I think I'll rest just a minute before going out."

"That's a good idea. You don't want to overdo." He was pale. The shower and the effort of dressing had worn him out. She knew telling him he needed to rest another day would be useless. Within minutes he was sound asleep. She made the beds, cleaned the kitchen and bathrooms.

When Brock woke, she had a potato and ham soup made. He growled like a bear. "Hell, half the day is gone. Why didn't you wake me?"

"You didn't tell me to, so I let you sleep. Evidently, you needed the rest."

He snorted with disgust. "It's almost time to meet Shelia."

"Yes, but you need to eat before we leave."

He started to argue. She held up a hand. "It's ready and won't take you ten minutes. You have to eat."

As if in answer, his stomach growled. "Oh, all right. I am hungry."

He ate with relish and grinned. "It's good. Thank you."

"You're welcome."

Brock finished off two bowls of soup and a large chunk of bread lavishly buttered. Zana set their dishes in the sink and gave them a quick rinse. She'd put the bowls in the dishwasher later. Brock stood by the door waiting. Impatient to be off, she wouldn't be surprised if he growled for her to hurry.

She grabbed her handbag and started for the door. No need to make the big guy wait. He laid a hand on her arm to stop her before she walked through the door.

"I need to replace your weapon." He went to a wall safe, opened it, and removed a gun. Before handing it to her, he checked to make sure it was operational. "I want you to spend some time at the practice field to sharpen your aim."

Zana wanted to object, but knew he was right. If

her aim had been better, the fiasco on the hillside might have ended differently. Maybe Rafael and his bunch wouldn't have captured her. She'd have gotten away. She put the laser gun in her pocket. "All right. I'll do it as soon as I get some time."

She was anxious to leave. Being this close to Brock was weakening her defenses. His kisses had shaken her, made her want to say yes to his marriage proposal, but the man had said nothing about love.

"Good. I'll worry less about you." He turned her to face him. His gray eyes bored into hers. "I couldn't stand it if you were hurt. You mean a great deal to me, and to Shelia."

"But, you don't love me."

His gray eyes darkened. "No, I don't, and I'll not lie to you and say I do." He cupped her cheek and slid his fingers into her hair. "But, it would hurt me greatly if anything happened to you."

Zana searched his eyes and found sincerity flaring from them. His expression was pained. With a groan, he pulled her face up to meet his and kissed her. She melted into his embrace careful not to hurt his wound, and gave herself up to the magic of his kiss. Hands fisted in his hair, she hung on and allowed him to plunder her lips. Her tongue tangled with his and he drew hers into his mouth. One hand cupped her breast and stoked the nipple, teasing it into a hard nub. Her body screaming with sensation, she gasped against his lips, "Brock."

His lips moved to her ear and trailed kisses and nips with his teeth along the tendon of her neck. Heat formed in her belly and spiraled down to between her legs.

"Zana, honey, I want you so bad. I know you want me too. Let's don't fight this anymore."

She pulled away and worked to control her breathing. Yes, she wanted him, desperately. She thought she loved him, something she never expected to experience again. But she had standards. He'd asked her to marry him before, but is that still what he wanted? Maybe he just wanted a fling. "I'm not going to have an affair, be your mistress."

He raked a hand through his wild hair, the hair she'd messed up. "Who said anything about an affair? I want to get married. I want you in my bed every night, not just on occasion."

Zana turned her back. She didn't want him to see the tears that threatened. "But, you don't love me, will never give me your heart. You just want a mother for Shelia, a bedmate."

"Dammit, that's not entirely true. Yes, I want a mother for Shelia, a wife and partner. Not just any woman—I want you, Zana." He laid his hands on her shoulders. "I promise I'll make you happy."

Did he really mean it? She turned and searched his face. Could she trust him? He'd never lied to her about anything else.

He captured her hand and brought it to his lips. "Please marry me, Zana."

No words of love. Could she be content with what he offered? Heart in her throat, she croaked out, "Yes, I'll marry you, Brock."

Twenty

"Am I supposed to call you Mama, now?" Shelia looked so cute in her pink bridesmaid dress with a flounce around the hem. The little girl had been thrilled when Zana asked her to stand up with her during the service and had taken her role seriously, holding the bridal bouquet like a professional while Zana and Brock exchanged wedding bands. Whoever said redheads didn't look good in pink needed to see Shelia today. She would be a beauty someday. Right now her face was scrunched with lines wrinkling her forehead.

Zana cupped her chin. She wanted the child to be comfortable around her. "You can if you want, but calling me Zana is fine, too. Whatever makes you happy." She tweaked the child's nose and grinned. "As long it's something nice and not an ugly word."

Shelia giggled. "Okay, I'll call you Zana, then." Shelia hugged her, then turned and ran to meet her friends. They'd formed a group on the dirt street. Vehicles weren't a problem as there were few cars in Refuge. An occasional jeep or small open transport could be seen kicking up dust.

Zana watched her join the small group of happy children, a feeling of warmth surrounded her heart. Shelia was a precious child, one easy to love. A sudden sense of guilt infused her. A lump formed in her throat. Did she deserve this happiness? She shook the feeling away. She'd not let what she'd lost destroy this moment, the joy in her future.

Someone grabbed her around the waist from behind and squeezed. "Eek!" When warm lips nuzzled her neck, she relaxed against Brock's hold. "I wondered when you'd remember you had a new bride that needed your attention."

"Never fear, sweetheart. I'd not forgotten and assure you I'll tend to your every need." He loosened one arm and looked at his watch. "In about one hour."

"You wicked man." Butterflies danced in her stomach in anticipation of their wedding night. She wasn't afraid, but the thought of being intimate with Brock left her slightly nervous. It'd been so long since she'd been with a man. She wanted to please him, their first time together to be perfect. Knowing Brock, he'd see that it was wonderful, wouldn't settle for anything less.

"That's me." He turned her in his arms and pulled her face close to his. His lips met hers in a short, possessive kiss. "Mmmmmm, you taste good. Like punch and cake."

She leaned her head against his chest. "The wedding was beautiful, wasn't it?" The community had gone all out to provide them with a beautiful ceremony and party afterwards. From the flower filled chapel to the lavish spread at Tony's on the patio. Since it couldn't hold everyone, people wandered in and out of the restaurant.

"Yes, it was. And, if I may say so, I've never seen a lovelier bride." His eyes dropped down to the goodly amount of cleavage pressed against the pale golden green satin of her gown. He lifted one hand and allowed his fingers to trail across her bare skin leaving gooseflesh in their wake.

Flushing with heat, not all of it embarrassment, she shivered and grabbed the roaming appendage. "Stop that. There are children here."

He looked around and snorted. "If Digger hadn't insisted you stay with him and Lola all week, I wouldn't be in this constant state of arousal and could behave myself."

Zana swallowed a chuckle. "He was only trying to maintain my reputation, didn't want us to start the wedding night early." And the anticipation of waiting to have sex would intensify their enjoyment tonight.

"More like harass me, if you want my opinion." Though she wouldn't admit it, Zana thought so too. His men were thrilled to see him so happy but took great pleasure in ribbing and aggravating him at every turn. They thought him in love. If Zana didn't know differently, she'd think so too, but guessed love wasn't necessarily a requirement of happiness.

It'd been two weeks since Brock's proposal. Staying in her cottage and then with friends allowed Zana to clean out the little house and move her few things up the hill. Brock insisted she go shopping and buy more clothes. She'd done so but used her own money, tucking a little back for a rainy day. Her major purchase had been her dress with spike heels to match. The fabric enhanced the silver streaks in her hair and brought out the green in her hazel eyes. It fit like a glove from bust to knees. Long, the slits up each side the only feature that allowed her to maneuver. Strapless, a long, sheer matching scarf wrapped around her neck and flowed down her back to below her hips.

"You should've worn a sack for a wedding dress then instead of this sexy…" His eyes flicked up and down her. "Thing. Have I told you how beautiful and sexy you look today?"

"Probably ten times."

Samuel, with Daniel in his arms, clapped Brock on the back. "It's good to see you happy, old man." He leaned in and gave Zana a brief kiss on the cheek. Daniel launched into her arms.

He patted her on the cheeks. "You purty."

"Well, thank you. You look mighty fine in your suit."

"Scratches. Don't like it." He pulled on his collar.

Brock and Samuel laughed. Brock lifted Daniel from Zana's arms and patted him on the back. "We know how you feel, buddy, dressed up in these monkey suits."

Daniel twisted around and giggled. "We go see monkeys?"

"You're looking at them, son. Me, Brock," he tickled his son in the belly, "and you." Daniel squealed with delight and wiggled to get down.

"I better get this kiddo to bed so we can leave in the morning," said Samuel.

Brock shook Samuel's hand. "Thanks for coming to stand up with me. Having you and Daniel with us means a lot."

Samuel grinned. "I wouldn't have missed it for the world. It's great to see you both happy."

Samuel was well liked by the people in Refuge. As he wove through the crowd, people stopped him to offer a handshake and make Daniel laugh. From the sound of his excited laughter, he enjoyed the attention.

Brock whispered in here ear. "I think now is the time to make our escape." They worked their way toward the exit, bidding their guests goodbye as they passed. It was dusk with just enough light for them to maneuver. The night air was cooler. In a few months, the temperature would drop considerably. They might even have snow. Though the weather was quite warm in the summer months, the surrounding water remained cold. A few icebergs floated around taking their sweet time to melt.

Zana shivered and Brock released her hand, removed his coat, and slipped it over her shoulders. "Thank you." She didn't tell him part of her discomfort was due to nerves.

"You're welcome." Arm across one shoulder, his hand cupped her waist and they strolled up the steps. Lights illuminated the entrance set into the rock face. When they reached the top, Brock keyed in the code to open the door and swung her up into his arms.

"Brock! You're going to hurt yourself, break your incision open."

"Naw! Dr. Boone said I'm healed and can do anything." He waggled his eyebrows and set her on her feet in the living room. "If you know what I mean."

She laughed. "I know exactly what you mean and wasn't worried about that in the least."

Brock checked to make sure the door closed and locked securely. He turned, lifted his coat from her shoulders, and tossed it across the room to land on the sofa. His eyes never left her as he allowed them to caress her from head to toe. Zana's stomach tingled. She felt a moment of sheer panic and resisted the urge to run.

With his hand at her waist, he led her to the living room. He stopped and pulled her into his arms. "You're shaking. What's wrong? You're not afraid, are you?" He cupped her breast and stroked the underside. Heat blossomed in her core and shot up her body. "Of this, of having sex with me?"

She leaned into his hand. "No, never. It's just been a while, seventy-eight years to be exact." She had no doubts he'd please her, but would she please him?

He chuckled. "That's a long time." His face sobered. "We'll take it slow, one step at a time." He unwound the scarf from her neck and dropped it on top of his coat. One yank and his tie was loose and joined the pile. She reached up and unbuttoned the top two buttons on his shirt.

"Thank you."

"You're welcome."

His lips were inches from hers. "Would you like something to drink, a glass of wine, water?"

"No." She sealed her lips to his and poured her heart into the kiss. With a groan, he lifted her off her feet and held her body flush to his. When he lifted his head, she murmured against his neck, "All I want is you."

~ * ~

Brock showered in Shelia's bathroom while Zana freshened up in the master bathroom. He shrugged into a knee-length silk robe that he kept handy when he needed to traipse around the house and didn't want Shelia to catch him in his skivvies, or less. He'd wear the garment for modesty sake, but would be more comfortable without it.

Barefoot, he padded to the kitchen. He retrieved

the bottle of vintage champagne he'd saved for a special occasion, and set it in the ice bucket he'd chilled earlier. Brock opened the caviar Samuel had brought from Abyss and scooped some into a bowl. He set the dish on the tray with the champagne and two fluted glasses. He plunked a cluster of grapes on a small plate and added them to the bounty. *The crackers, where had he put them? Ah, yes, on the end of the counter.*

He'd just sat the tray holding their food on the dresser, when Zana came out of the bathroom. His breath caught in his throat at the woman standing before him waiting for his response. She wore a scrap of a short gown the color of her wedding dress. It had tiny straps that held the bodice barely covering her breasts. *Man, oh, man.* His gaze traveled from her face, down her pebbled breasts, small waist and flaring hips to long legs ending in bare feet.

"You are beautiful." He crossed the room, placed his hands on her shoulders, and looked his fill.

Zana moved closer and put her arms around his waist. She laid her forehead against his chest. "That's how you make me feel—beautiful and cherished."

His lips touched her hair and he breathed in the coconut scent of her shampoo. "Good, I hope I always do." He let his palms caress her bare back. "Satin, your skin is smooth as silk."

She stepped back and untied his robe. When she pushed it off his shoulders and let her eyes roam his form, he stopped breathing, waiting for her reaction. He was a large man and feared his size would scare her, but the smile that tilted her lips erased his doubt. "My, my, you're an impressive specimen, husband."

He exhaled. "I'm glad you approve." He pulled her

close, her soft curves molding against his hard frame, his erection captured between them, pulsing with a life of its own. "Zana, honey, you feel so good." He cared for this woman. Yes, he wanted sex with her, to join their bodies, but he also wanted the joy of holding her close afterwards, their hearts beating in unison. She splayed her hands across his chest and his flesh jumped at the thrill of her touch. On tip toe, she pressed her mouth to his. Heart pounding, he clasped her to him and without breaking their kiss, walked her to the bed and sat down with her standing between his legs. Sucking in a lung full of air, he gasped, "I think you're overdressed."

Hands shaking, he stroked the satiny flesh of her thighs. He raised his eyes to hers and watched them lower with passion as he found the hem of her gown, peeled it up her body, over her head. He tossed it to the foot of the bed.

His gaze dropped to her breasts. They were perfect, small but with a fullness that would fill his hands. With a groan, he leaned forward and pressed a kiss to one of her dusky nipples before drawing it into his mouth. She moaned and clasped his head with both hands, held him in place, and arched into his touch. He laved the peak with his tongue and suckled.

Pleasure coursed through his veins. Seeing Zana's body, touching her, was heaven. Hearing her cries of pleasure intensified his desire for her. Their coming together would be explosive, satisfying in more than just a sexual sense. He was a lucky man.

Brock marveled at his fortune at having this beautiful woman as his wife, to share his bed. He lifted her onto his lap and turned, laid her on the bed, and stretched out beside her. His hand splayed across her lower abdomen. *Would their child grow here?* Lord, he hoped so. Nothing would give him more joy than to have another child to love and dote on. He gathered Zana in his arms and poured his love, into his kiss. *Love? No, not love. Yes, he adored her but love was out of the question.*

Zana was drowning in the sensations Brock's touch evoked. He stroked her back, buttocks, and legs causing shivers to race up and down her body while his lips played on her mouth, sipping and tasting. He kissed her neck and moved lower to capture a nipple in his mouth. His hand massaged her stomach and dipped down to stroke the soft folds of her sex. He knew just how to touch her, to love her. *No, Zana, not love. He liked her, desired her.*

She arched into his hand, clutching his head to her breast. Heat and tension spiraled in her sex, and traveled up to her belly. Muscles tightened in anticipation. *Oh God, she would shatter before he entered her.*

"Brock…I…can't wait. Please, *now.*"

His body covered her. His gaze locked with hers as he slid inside, filling her fully. She gasped at the stretching sensation, every nerve ending alive, twitching, and anticipating his next move. He stilled and allowed her body to adjust. At last he withdrew and plunged pushing her up in the bed. His hands gripped her waist to keep her close. Zana lifted her knees to hug his hips and matched her movements to his strokes, reaching for the release her body craved.

The coil wound tighter and she shattered, her body quaking with wave after wave of release, wringing a keening howl of pleasure from her. As her shudders dwindled, Brock plunged one final time and roared in triumph as his large frame jerked again and again in climax. Shaking with aftershocks, he collapsed on top of her. She caressed his back and pressed kisses against his wet neck.

He rolled to his back taking her with him. His fingers trailed up and down her back. She shivered and he used his palms to caress her, warming her skin. "Lord, woman. Sex with you may be the death of me."

She smiled against his chest. "It was good, wasn't it?" And it was, more than she'd imagined. Her heart was invested in their relationship. The only thing that could have intensified her joy in their joining would have been his love. She'd never expected to be happy again, but she was. She could be satisfied with what she and Brock had. Finding information on Katy was still a priority, but she wouldn't let her goal interfere with her happiness. Not just for her own sake, but for Brock and Shelia also. They were a family now.

Brock squeezed her. "Good? I'm surprised we didn't burn the bed to a cinder." He pulled her up for his kiss. "Thank you for marrying me and making me so happy."

Lips just inches from his, she said, "Thank you, Brock, for giving me a second chance at happiness." Her throat tightened. "It's something I didn't expect." And she was happy. If he said he loved her, she'd be ecstatic. Finding Katy would make her life complete. She snuggled closer, enjoying the warmth of his skin touching hers. Maybe someday the unexpected would happen and her daughter would be part of their family. If not, she'd relish and be thankful for what she had.

He threaded his fingers through her hair. "Oh, honey, neither did I." He grinned and gave her butt a gentle pop. "But now that I have it, I expect to partake as often as possible." He growled and rolled pulling her under him.

"I'm ready when you are, husband."

He kissed her and then pulled back. "I need nourishment first." He jumped out of bed and walked to the dresser where he'd set the food. She admired his form, the sleek muscles and taut buttocks. He returned, placed the tray on the bed, and slipped under the sheet. He leaned back against the headboard and lifted the bottle of wine. "Champagne, madam?"

"By all means." She scooped caviar onto a cracker and stuffed it in his mouth. He chewed while he wrestled with the cork in the bubbly. It popped and foam ran over the sides. He tried to catch the overflow in the ice bucket but some splashed across the bed. She giggled. "Christening our bed?"

He leaned in for a kiss. "I think we already have."

~ * ~

Brock woke with a crick in his shoulder. He'd slept with his arm under Zana's head, her body molded to his. Though he ached, he didn't move for fear of waking her. He smiled with contentment as he studied her in slumber. Her dark lashes lay against her soft cheeks. A whisper of soft breath passed through her slightly tinted lips. He resisted the urge to lean closer and taste them. They'd made love twice more last night and finally fallen into exhausted sleep around three a.m. It was nearing seven. Samuel and Daniel would leave at eight. Shelia would meet them on the dock with Digger. She'd spent the night with them.

He hated to wake her, but they had to get ready. He leaned over and nuzzled Zana's neck. "Wake up, sweetheart. We've got an hour until Samuel's boat leaves."

Arms lifted over her head, she stretched, the sheet slipping to expose her lovely breasts. He bent to take one in his mouth. She arched into his touch and stroked his head. "Do we have time for this?"

"Not really, but I think they'll wait until we get there." They'd have to as his body wouldn't be denied with this sexual feast before him. He found her core and stroked. She gasped and squirmed under his hand.

Breathing raspy, she breathed, "If we're late, they'll know what we've been doing."

He grinned and rolled lifted her to straddle him. "Oh yeah, love, they will. Let's not disappoint them."

Thirty minutes later they approached the dock to find Digger holding Daniel while Samuel loaded their bags. The toddler wiggled and yelled, "My Unka Bock and Ana. Down Diga. Go see Unka Bock."

Digger was a natural with children. What a shame he and Lola didn't have any of their own. "If you'll hold Shelia's hand and go with her, I'll put you down."

He nodded. "'Kay."

Hands locked, the two children ran to meet them. Brock lifted Daniel and tossed him in the air. The boy squealed with delight, and then reached for Zana. "Whoa, buddy, you're going to land on your head." He handed him over to her and draped an arm across Shelia's shoulders as they walked toward the pier where Digger and Samuel waited. "Did you have a good time with Lola and Digger last night?"

"Sure did. Lola needed to go to the winery and let

me go with her. I got to help with the computers. She said I'm a natural."

"Is that right?" He didn't doubt it. The kid loved everything to do with the production of wine. Hopefully it wasn't a phase. If she continued to show interest in the years to come, he'd send her to the best Vintner school available. It'd be nice for her to take over the operation one day and allow him to concentrate on salvaging. He'd never developed the knack or interest in the vines that Shelia appeared to have. He'd taken over the winery from his father and the business had prospered. Maybe under Shelia's leadership Refuge wines would become world famous.

"Yep. After we left, we stopped by Janie's house so Lola could see the baby. Janie asked if I could spend the night with her tonight. Can I?"

Hot damn, how could he get so lucky? Another night alone with Zana would be wonderful. Night heck, they'd have all day. They reached the pier and Samuel lifted Daniel from Zana's arms.

"Does her mother know about this invitation?"

"Of course she does, Daddy."

"We'll see. I need to talk to her mother."

"Lola's already talked to her. Ask Digger. He'll tell you." She tugged on Digger's arm. "Isn't that right?"

"Sure is, Brock. If you say Shelia can go, I'm to walk her over there when we leave."

"Well, it is the weekend. I don't see what it could hurt." He tweaked a pigtail. "But you do need to stop by the house and get some clean clothes."

Shelia jumped into the air. "Yippee!"

Laughing at Shelia's antics, Samuel stepped forward and shook Brock's hand. "Come see us when you can."

"We will." Brock watched Zana, as arm around Shelia she talked with Digger. His wife seemed so at ease with his daughter. How lucky could a man get? He returned his attention to Samuel.

Samuel's eyes flicked to Zana and then back to him, his expression sober. "I'll be checking into that situation we talked about earlier. We'll find out what's going on, Brock, who's trying to kill Zana." He shook his head. "How could someone who's been as much as dead for seventy-five years have enemies?"

"I know. It doesn't make sense. I hope you find out something. For the life of me, I can't understand why someone would want to kill her." The woman didn't have a mean bone in her body and she hadn't been around long enough to make enemies. It infuriated him to feel so inept, unable to lay his hands on the culprit and strangle the life from him.

Zana joined them and slipped her arm around his waist. He hugged her to his side wishing he could keep her safely there until they caught the predator. Trying to keep his anger from his voice, he said, "Thanks, Samuel. I'll be anxious to hear—about the council meetings."

"I'll have everything ready." Samuel leaned in and kissed Zana's cheek. "Oh, by the way, my mother has invited us all to dinner during your next visit to Abyss. She's been curious about you, Zana." He turned and with Daniel in his arms, boarded the boat.

Brock chuckled. "Well, that's a surprise." They waved to Samuel and Daniel as their boat pulled away from the dock.

"Mrs. Whiteside's dinner invitation? Why?"

"Because the old bat doesn't like me, that's why." Brock snorted. "I guess because she wants to meet you, she'll tolerate me."

Zana giggled and gigged him in the side. "You must not have made a very good impression."

He snorted. "The woman is something else. I've never seen a more stuck-up individual. I don't know how Samuel managed to turn out normal with her raising him."

She slapped at his arm. "That's terrible. Just because she doesn't like you, doesn't mean she wasn't a good mother."

"Let's see what you think after you meet her. When she turns that haughty nose up at you, you'll feel differently."

That evening, they sat on the sofa enjoying a glass of wine in the living room. Rather than cook, they'd finished off the food Brock had stocked in the cooler. Zana was stuffed and content. Curled against Brock, enjoying his warmth and companionship, she counted her blessings. A few months ago, her future had appeared dim. Now, though she'd not found Katy, she could at least look to the future with optimism. She'd not given up on finding her daughter. The only other thing that could add to her happiness would be Brock's love. She didn't doubt he cared deeply for her, but she was falling in love with him and longed to have her feelings returned. Losing so many loved ones had to be hard, but everyone suffered tragedies. She was a living example. Losing her two children didn't keep her from loving Shelia. His fear might seem irrational to her, but it was his to own and deal with.

Brock's arms tightened around her. He leaned

down and kissed her forehead. "In some ways it's nice not having Shelia underfoot." Zana snuggled against him, feet pulled up under her on the sofa. They'd enjoyed their privacy, being able to make love freely throughout the day. "But I miss the brat."

She chuckled. "Yeah, it is quiet around here, isn't it?" Zana missed Shelia being around too. She looked forward to being a family and hoped they'd have a child. If they had more than one, what would they do for additional space? Could they bore deeper into this rock and make another room? She'd have to ask Brock.

Brock sighed deeply and Zana waited for him to continue. When he didn't, she pushed away from the crook of his arm and looked up. His jaw was rigid, a muscle twitched. What on Earth was bothering him? "What's wrong?"

He raised his hand to her hair and pulled her head back to his shoulder. "I need to tell you something and you're not going to like what I have to say."

Zana's heart dropped to her stomach. Was her happiness about to be destroyed? Had he learned something about Katy?

He released a loud sigh. "I guess the only way to do this is to just spit it out."

She waited. Finally, he spoke. "Just before Rafael died, I learned he was hired to kill you. I believe it's someone from Abyss."

Twenty-One

She'd spent hours trying to think of who might want her dead. Brock had quizzed her on who she'd met, what she'd done while in Abyss, had anyone expressed dislike or been rude. As to the poisoning incident, she'd always believed it an isolated occurrence, an accident in that the tainted candy hadn't been meant for her, but someone else. She'd not given it another thought until Brock informed her of Rafael's visitor. Now she knew the poisoned candy had been meant for her all along and the predator who wanted her dead didn't mind who else might be killed in the process.

Her belly clenched in panic. Not knowing her enemy's identity increased her fear. She was tempted to stay home and hide. She mentally shook herself and continued down the road to the winery, fully aware that whenever she was out, someone dogged her steps. If the culprit tried again, Brock intended to catch him in the act.

In a few days they'd travel to Abyss. Brock had business to take care of and would confer with Samuel on possible suspects. They planned to take Shelia, too, so she could spend time with Daniel. Of course, they'd have dinner with Mrs. Whiteside, Samuel's mother. Zana couldn't wait to meet the lady Brock called "the snooty old bat." She giggled at the image of the older woman looking down her nose at Brock.

~ * ~

Retriever had pulled out of the bay at Refuge late Sunday evening. Brock had shown Zana and Shelia to his quarters to get settled. He smiled remembering Zana's comments. She'd run a hand over the spread on the bed attached to the wall. "Wow, a queen sized bed." Yeah, he liked to sleep comfortably but it barely left enough room to walk around. She'd admired the compact clothes chest and locker built into the wall, but raised an eyebrow at the small bathroom and smirked. "I can't imagine you fitting in that cramped space, Brock." He'd merely grinned.

Now, Monday morning they were two hours from the oilrig elevator at Abyss. It'd been several months since Brock had been on the sea and he'd missed it. He'd risen early and let Zana and Shelia sleep a while longer. The sun glowed, muted by the mist, as it rose above the water line. This was his favorite time of the day. He stood on the deck enjoying the wind in his hair, the salt spray against his face. The air was cool but in his jacket and insulated pants, the temperature didn't hamper his pleasure in the beauty of the morning. He took another drink of coffee from his insulated mug and relished the heat as it trailed down into his stomach.

Shelia's chatter broke his reverie and he turned to greet her and Zana. "Good morning, girls."

"Morning, Daddy. Luke said breakfast is about ready."

He leaned down and placed a chaste kiss on Zana's lips. Heaven forbid he give her a heated kiss like he wanted to, in front of Shelia. His child thought kissing was disgusting. Zana squeezed his waist and asked.

"Did you sleep well?"

"Like a baby. Always do when at sea. If there are no problems, that is, like pirates or bad weather." Nothing was more relaxing than snoozing to the oceans gentle sway. He was a seaman at heart and would stay on the water all the time if he could.

A big grin on her face, Zana winked at Shelia. "We noticed, didn't we? That you slept like a baby, that is."

She giggled. "Yeah, Daddy, you snored something awful last night. It was so loud my cot rattled." Delighted with her last remark, the child burst out laughing.

Smug expression on his face, Brock gigged her in the side. "I did not. That must have been Zana."

Shelia sobered. "Uh-uh, because Zana and I couldn't sleep and got to laughing at all the funny noises you made."

"You laughed at me? I'm crushed." He shook in head in mock sorrow. "Let's go eat."

Brock caught Zana casting sideways glances at him as they made their way to the galley. His lips twitched as he struggled to keep a straight face. It was nice his wife and Shelia were bonding. As Shelia walked ahead, Zana's arm circled his waist and squeezed. He slipped his around her shoulders and grinned down at her. "Was it that bad?"

"No, not really, but it was entertaining to two wide awake girls."

After breakfast was over and the kitchen clean, they returned to the deck to find the oil rig in view. Shelia danced around with infectious excitement. Brock and Zana laughed at her antics. It was Shelia's first trip to Abyss. If not for Samuel, she wouldn't have joined them this trip. Samuel had offered the services of Daniel's nanny again, to keep an eye on Shelia and show her around while he and Zana were in meetings. He was glad Shelia would have more time with her cousin. She'd also be spending the night with them, and he and Zana would have the honeymoon suite he'd reserved to themselves.

Brock enjoyed Shelia's response to Abyss. Arm across her shoulder, he said, "It's an awesome sight, isn't it?" Shelia knew about Abyss, but after what happened to Delia, he'd kept her away from the undersea city. For some reason, with Zana caring for his daughter, he wasn't as afraid she'd be dazzled by what their community offered.

Shelia grinned. "Yeah."

"Just remember, their ways are different from ours. Things may look grand, but their customs are different."

"Okay, Daddy." Someday soon he'd have to explain those differences to her.

It didn't take the crew long to secure the craft to the rig and roll the gangplank across to the docking area. He kept a firm hand on Shelia until the sailor on the dock gave the okay to cross. Brock nodded and she scurried across and jumped from foot to foot until he and Zana joined her.

Shelia was glued to the glass walls of the elevator car as they dropped deeper into the oceans depths. Brock had to admit the view was fantastic. Though the water darkened as the car lowered, fish and other aquatic life were clearly visible and flashed past the glass.

Samuel stood waiting for them when they exited

the elevator. Shelia launched herself at him, hugging his waist. "This is so cool, Uncle Samuel. I can't wait to see everything."

He laughed and patted her back. "That's good, because Mrs. Joseph has scheduled numerous activities for you and Daniel. You're going to be a busy girl for the next couple of days."

He hugged Zana. "You're glowing. Marriage to this big galoot must be agreeing with you."

She laughed. "Yes."

Brock shook Samuel's hand. "Who're you calling a galoot?"

"Meant affectionately, I assure you."

Assuming the niceties were over, Shelia announced, "I'm ready to go, Uncle Samuel." She grabbed her powered suitcase on wheels with one hand, took Samuel's with the other, and started tugging. "See you guys later."

"Mind your manners, miss." It was one thing to be excited but her behavior bordered on rudeness.

"Yes sir." She looked at her shoes.

Samuel placed a hand on Shelia's neck. "Patience, kiddo." He turned to Brock. "You think you can find your way to the hotel? Need any help with your luggage?"

"No, we're fine. You go ahead. We'll get settled and meet you in the lobby thirty minutes before the meeting."

Brock placed their smaller bag on top of the large powered suitcase and with his free hand on her elbow, ushered Zana forward toward the transporters lined up ahead. He viewed them with apprehension. If it wasn't so far, he'd rather walk. But, walking wasn't an option.

He loaded their luggage in the back, settled Zana into the front seat and joined her on the other side. He started the vehicle and they entered the resort wing.

As they shot through the tunnel, icicles pricked the skin of Brock's neck. He couldn't prevent the horrific images of Delia flying through the air and colliding with an oncoming vehicle from invading his mind. Cold sweat broke out on his body. He drove the morbid memory from his mind, but was grateful when they arrived at the hotel and the bellman took their luggage. This was his honeymoon, albeit a working one. Thoughts of Delia's death didn't belong.

They signed in at the desk. Their hands were scanned for the entry panel into their room. After they rested for a while, they'd meet Samuel. Their trip wasn't entirely pleasure. It was time to renew Abyss's wine contract for the following year.

Brock smiled as Zana twirled around the room and then plopped back on the king-sized bed set on a platform. "This is beautiful, Brock. Though I'm thrilled with the suite, a regular room would have been just fine." The wall behind the bed was mirrored and reflected the undersea scene outside the wall to ceiling window. Brock stepped to the curved area and peeked from one side to the other making sure they couldn't be seen by the rooms adjacent to them. Obviously a block of rooms separated the honeymoon suites, so they'd have privacy. Good. It'd be a shame to close the drapes cutting off the view.

He joined Zana on the bed. "For our honeymoon? Never." She snuggled against him. "I missed making love to you last night." Shelia had shared his quarters with them on a fold down bunk above their bed.

"Then get busy and show me how much."

It didn't take long to strip them both of their clothes. Then he was inside her, stroking her warm, moist flesh. She held him close, matching her movements to his. Never had he been this happy, so in tune to another person. Their lovemaking was beyond anything he'd ever experienced.

She stiffened. He muffled her cries with his mouth, his sounds of pleasure mingling with hers, and poured his seed into her body. He rolled and carried her with him to lay sprawled half on and half off his chest. He stroked her back and kneaded the soft flesh of her buttocks.

"I love you, Brock."

Her whisper stopped him cold. His breath caught in his throat and for a minute he couldn't breathe. Fear knifed through him—fear of losing her if he didn't say the words back—fear of losing her to the demon who stalked her. He stifled a groan. More importantly, he feared he already loved her, and if something took her from him, he'd never be whole again.

A tear landed on his chest.

"Zana…sweetheart…I—"

She rolled turning her back to him. "Forget I said it."

He turned, slipped his arm under her head, and with the other pulled her back against him. She remained stiff in his arms and then her body shuddered. He dropped his forehead to her hair. Ah hell. Why did she have to say the words and ruin everything? His lips touched her shoulder and he nuzzled his way up to her ear.

"Did you mean it?" He didn't know what he'd

rather hear—yes or no. In his heart he knew the answer. She'd never lie.

"Do…you think I go around saying things…things I don't mean?"

"Sweetheart—"

She scooted from the bed before he could say more. A minute later he heard water running in the shower.

Brock flopped back on the bed, arm over his eyes. He'd ruined everything… No, she'd ruined everything. Dammit. They'd been happy. Now those three words hung between them like an iron curtain. Shit. He slammed a fist against the mattress.

He jumped up and strode to the glass wall. A small shark swam past upsetting a school of fish. As a group they changed direction, their movement so precise it appeared to be computer generated. The scene soothed his agitation and regret. Mood heavy, but not one to dwell on what couldn't be undone, he struggled to find a way to erase this memory from Zana's mind.

Determined to fix things with Zana, to restore the rapport they'd had, he turned from the window and walked to the bathroom to join his wife.

Zana heard Brock come in the room, still nude from their lovemaking minutes before. She held her breath, praying he'd turn around and leave the room. She didn't want to hurt him, but couldn't respond sexually or emotionally right now. If he touched her she'd either grit her teeth or scream in frustration.

He reached for the shower stall door. She cringed and backed further into the huge compartment designed for two people. "I'll be out in a minute, Brock."

It took him a moment to respond. His hand fell

from the door. "Take your time."

Even though the glass was steamy, she could see his face set with regret, as he turned and left the room. Oh, God, she'd made a mess of things. She dropped her head against the wall and let the tears flow. *You're a fool, Zana Callahan. He told you what to expect.* Taking deep breaths to calm herself, she shut off the water and stepped from the shower. She'd not let him know the extent of her pain.

~ * ~

Brock sat in a chair in Samuel's office and scanned the list Samuel handed him. Zana's rejection still stung and he had difficulty concentrating. He thrust his hurt aside. Keeping her safe was the best way he knew of to show he cared.

Samuel waved at the document. "This identifies every person leaving Abyss, and their destination, for the past three months. I've gone over the list multiple times and can't find one name I'd consider suspicious." He shrugged and moved around to stand behind his desk. "I have no idea who Zana met while she was here, but Dr. and Mrs. Bartholomew went over the list and didn't believe any of the individuals traveling knew her."

"I guess it'd be possible for someone here to contact an outsider by communicator or mail, get them to carry out their orders."

"In the case of phone transmissions, we can trace those; however, we can't trace computer transactions or outgoing mail. I'll get someone to check the phone records." Samuel shook his head. "This person is smart. I doubt they'd be so careless as to leave a trail."

"What about the Bartholomews? I know you never

believed they could have poisoned Zana, but what if you're wrong." For the life of him he couldn't imagine why anyone would want Zana dead, what they had to gain.

Samuel sighed. "Why would they want to kill her after spending so much time and energy helping her get well? It doesn't make sense."

"Because she wouldn't undergo selective mating."

"No, I don't think so. They're fond of Zana and wouldn't hurt her." He raised a hand before Brock could contradict him. "To be sure, I've got some of our finest specialty police working undercover, looking into the backgrounds of all those on the list." He raised a hand to silence Brock. "And they're checking the Bartholomews' backgrounds. I also called in Greta, one of the few friends Zana made here. The young woman turned into a blubbering mess in professing not to know anything. I believed her, her concern for Zana's safety evident, but to be safe we're scrutinizing her history too. Though it's doubtful she has the resources to come up with thousands of dollars."

Brock liked that idea and nodded but something else bothered him. "Is there any way a person could leave Abyss and not be detected or their departure covered up?"

"It'd be highly unusual, but not impossible. Even here we have corrupt society members, ones who can be bribed. We've begun to suspect a criminal element is growing here, one similar to the Mafia of the past." His eyes on the distant wall, Samuel thought for a minute. "It would require someone with a lot of influence and money. That fact would lower the number of suspects considerably." He scratched his chin. "I'll have my agents go through the financial records of everyone in Abyss and check for large deposits though I doubt anyone would be stupid enough to put the money in their account."

~ * ~

Katherine checked her appearance again in the living room mirror. She didn't look bad for her years. Plastic surgery and modern technology had taken care of that. But to children of two and nine, she'd look ancient. For their sake she'd worn something other than her usual black. The gold of the pantsuit brought out the gold in her hazel eyes. Even at her advanced age, she wasn't above a little vanity.

She turned and surveyed the room. It was neat as a pin. "Edith, do you have everything ready for the children?"

"Yes, Katherine. This is the third time you've asked and the third time I've said yes."

Katherine snorted. "Well, excuse me."

Edith came in with a tray and set it on the coffee table. "You're excused. I know you're all keyed up about this, but don't have a clue why. Daniel was just here a couple of days ago and why you'd be excited to see Brock Callahan's child I don't have a clue."

"Yes, well, I have my reasons." She was curious about the child and her new stepmother. Callahan and Mrs. Forrester's marriage came as a big surprise. Samuel had regaled her with details of the wedding when he'd returned from his trip to Refuge. Why he'd wanted to attend was beyond her. The place was nothing more than a village. Primitive, she doubted it had electricity and running water. It was probably like the one where she'd grown up—the origin of the nightmares that still plagued her on occasion.

Samuel had relayed the news of Zana's kidnapping by that Rafael fellow and Brock's heroic rescue. It seemed Zana Forrester Callahan, like a cat, had nine lives. She admired Brock for taking the pirate's life. If one of her loved ones was kidnapped, she'd see that their captor suffered before his death, and she'd not have let his team members live either.

The doorbell rang and Katherine hastened to her wing-backed chair, sat down, and smoothed her pants over her knees easing away any wrinkles. Acting fragile put her at an advantage. In truth, she got around quite well when she wanted to. Edith opened the door and Daniel barreled forward pulling a redheaded girl in his wake.

"Nana, Nana, I gots a cuzin."

Her precious little boy, dark headed, resembled his daddy, but he'd inherited Delia's gray eyes. Why couldn't they have been blue like Samuel's or even hazel like hers? "Slow down, Daniel. First things first. Where is my kiss?"

He dropped the girl's hand and toddled forward. Katherine leaned down for her grandson's peck on the cheek. She hugged him to her for a short moment enjoying his sweet smell. He was one of the few joys in her life.

"Now then, who is this young lady you've brought to meet me?"

"This is my cuzin, Sheda. Sheda, this is my guandmuver."

"Hello, Mrs. Whiteside." Uncertain, the child smiled and put an arm around Daniel's shoulder. Ah, she'd already formed an attachment to her cousin.

Katherine admired family devotion and considered it admirable when exhibited by a child.

Katherine held a hand out to her and Shelia placed hers in it. Katherine pulled the child closer and studied the pert nose, freckles, and red hair. The girl would be a beauty one day. "I'm pleased to meet you, Shelia. Thank you for coming to see me today. I get very lonely and having young people around is a nice diversion." She waved at the sofa. "You two have a seat and tell me what you've been doing."

Mrs. Joseph, Daniel's nanny, spoke from the entryway. "Mrs. Whiteside, if it's okay with you, I'll leave the children and come back for them in an hour."

"That'll be fine, Mrs. Joseph." She turned back to Shelia and Daniel. "Now, tell me what you've been doing."

Shelia gradually warmed up and between bites of cookies and finger sandwiches, gave a glowing review of Abyss and how different it was from Refuge. Katherine quizzed her on what her life was like in Refuge. Her answers surprised Katherine. Evidently they weren't nearly as backward as she'd thought. Brock Callahan must be a wealthy man to own a vineyard and his salvage business. His wines were popular in Abyss and sold for a good price.

"I want to be a vintner when I grow up," Shelia added.

"Is that right?"

"Yes, ma'am. I work at the winery every chance I get. Daddy won't let me skip school and work, but now I don't want to miss. Zana told me to be good at my job I needed an education so I wouldn't get cheated by people." Shelia sat up straighter. "I'm going to study hard so I'll be the best."

"Your step-mother sounds very smart. Does she have any children?"

Shelia's smile dissolved. "She did have, but her little boy died when they were frozen in her Polar Excursion." Eyes rounded with concern, she shook her head. "Zana has a daughter named Katy, but she can't find her. She's looked and looked. It makes her really sad and she cries sometimes. She has bad dreams, too. Daddy got a man he knows to help search but the man brought Zana bad news."

"Really." Katherine's heart thumped in anticipation. What kind of news had she gotten? Katherine thought she'd buried her life so no one could trace her. Had she not been as clever as she'd thought?

"Yeah. Daddy's friend learned Katy was adopted by a family that moved away from Saint Johns, but the records were lost so he couldn't find out Katy's adopted name or nothing." She shook her head. "I feel so sorry for Zana. When Daddy told her, she cried and cried. She couldn't stop. It was awful. Daddy fed her some of that strong alcohol he keeps and put her to bed in the guest room. The next morning she was better but said she'd never give up her search, not until she found her daughter or learned of her death."

She grinned. "This was before they got married, 'cause she sleeps in Daddy's room now."

"Is that right?" Hmmm, so, Mrs. Forrester didn't plan to give up on finding her Katy. Katherine had to admire her determination.

"Yep, sure is. Zana loves her daughter something awful." She looked out the window at the fish, her expression wistful. "I wonder if my mother loved me that much. She's dead, you know."

"Yes, child, I know. And I'm sure your mother loved you very much."

Her face brightened. "You think so? Daddy says she did."

"Of course she did. Why wouldn't she? You're a delightful little girl." Shelia intrigued Katherine. There was no guile in her expressions or the comments she made. Brock Callahan had done well so far in raising her. Katherine's thoughts turned to Shelia's description of Zana's distress. Was it possible that her mother truly loved her, wanted to find her? Maybe she'd been too harsh in judging her and should rethink her plan of action. But Katy was no more. She'd died long ago in the jungle of Columbia. Katherine had taken her place. Would Zana be pleased with the person her daughter had become? Probably not, but life experiences changed people, not always for the better.

Shelia's giggle broke her train of thought. "Did you know that Zana's daughter is around eighty-four years old now?"

Twenty-Two

Brock held Zana's hand as they walked through the hallway of Abyss's exclusive apartments. The tension from yesterday's disappointment had eased somewhat. Zana, determined to not let it ruin their time in Abyss, pushed her hurt to the back of her mind. Brock showered her with affection and kindness. She knew he tried to make up for what he couldn't give, but knowing he didn't love her still stung.

They stood just outside the door to Katherine Whiteside's apartment. For some reason, the prospect of meeting Samuel's mother filled her with trepidation. She shivered.

Brock's arm slid around her waist and he hugged her to his side. "Relax. She's a tough old broad, but harmless."

Earlier they'd stopped by Samuel's and visited with the kids. Shelia chatted about her visit with Daniel's nana. She described Mrs. Whiteside as a "neat old lady with a cool apartment." Of course, all the cookies the two children had feasted on might have influenced her opinion somewhat.

Daniel added, "Nana's got pets, too." His lower lip trembled and he shook a finger. "No touch."

Zana wondered what kind of pets, but they needed to leave to arrive on time.

The door opened. Samuel grinned and stepped

aside. "Come in. I'm the butler tonight." Dressed in black slacks and a black silk shirt, he looked nothing like a servant. He was a handsome man. He reminded her of someone but she couldn't figure out who.

Zana smoothed the skirt of her gold, knee-length dress and stepped inside. With his hand at her back, Samuel ushered her toward a maroon wingback chair occupied by a regal older woman swathed in a long black satin dress that covered her from neck to toe. Ropes of pearl strands hung around her neck and large baroque pearls dangled from her ears accenting the silver of her hair. Gold-flecked hazel eyes studied Zana with interest as she and Samuel approached and stopped before the chair. Brock stayed several steps behind them.

"Mother, this is Zana Callahan."

Zana extended her hand. Mrs. Whiteside didn't respond for a minute. Why, the snooty old woman was snubbing her as she'd done Brock. Struggling to keep her face respectful, she went to pull her hand back. Just before Zana did, Mrs. Whiteside took it in her cold, frail one. She clasped it weakly.

"Hello, dear. I'm so pleased to meet you. Samuel has been singing your praises for months." Her expression spoke volumes and said she thought her son's admiration misplaced.

Zana swallowed her chuckle and looked at Samuel in question. She had nothing to prove to this woman.

He shrugged. "What can I say? Since Brock fished you out of the sea, your exploits, or I should say the crises you've faced and overcome interest me, as well as many others in this community. We feel we've invested in you." He waved toward the sofa. "Come, sit down. You too, Brock."

Zana sat down beside Brock. He nodded to Mrs. Whiteside. "It's good to see you again, Mrs. Whiteside."

She sniffed. "I doubt that, but thank you anyway. I'm glad you and your bride could join me for dinner. It will be ready shortly. Would you like a glass of wine while you wait?"

Zana wondered why she disliked Brock so. Samuel had married his sister, Delia. He was Daniel's uncle. Maybe she disliked people from Refuge in general. The thought didn't bode well for Zana.

"Not for me," said Brock. "How about you, sweetheart?"

"No, I'm fine, thank you."

Samuel sat down in the chair opposite his mother.

Zana gazed around the room, her eyes lighting on the big window that brought the beauty of the undersea world inside. The antique furniture depicted life in the 1950s, a style Zana had seen often in home design magazines when she'd lived in Saint John's. Her home there had reflected some of the 1950s colors and a few collectables but nothing like the pieces on display in Mrs. Whiteside's living space. They were rare and expensive, something Zana and David would never have been able to afford.

"Your home is lovely, Mrs. Whiteside. I love the colors and styles of the mid twentieth century."

The older woman beamed. It seemed Zana had scored a point.

"Thank you. I love these old pieces." She patted the arm of her chair. "Of course this wing chair doesn't go with the rest of the furniture, but it's comfortable."

She touched the pearls that lay on the bodice of her dress. "And please, call me Katherine." She nodded at Brock but her smile didn't quite reach her eyes. "You, too, young man."

Brock looked surprised and glanced at Samuel who shrugged. Evidently the woman's behavior tonight was an enigma. Zana wondered what Samuel's childhood had been like being raised by this woman. Zana didn't know anything about his father except he was deceased. Katherine appeared to be in her seventies, but with modern medical science disguising the aging process, it was hard to tell. If her guess was accurate, Katherine must have been in her forties when Samuel was born.

"Zana, do you have children?" The question startled Zana. She must have looked frantic as Samuel spoke up.

"Mother, I don't think that's a subject Zana would want to discuss."

Katherine looked from one to the other. "Why ever not?"

He sputtered, "Because—"

"It's fine, Samuel. Talking about Katy and Jonathan is the only way I'll heal." She took a deep breath and exhaled. "I had two children, a girl and a boy. Katy, my precious little girl, was seven years old when the snow slide covered my Polar Excursion pushing it into a ravine." Grief welled up inside her and threatened to choke her. She felt Brock's arm caress her back and leaned into it. "My son, Jonathan, was only two. He was with me and died from the elements."

"I'm so sorry, dear. How awful for you."

Katherine studied Zana as she talked. She smiled when she talked about her daughter. Her face twisted with pain when she relayed her son's death.

"At least I was with him when he passed. I took him from his car seat and held him in my arms to keep him warm as long as possible, until we both fell asleep before freezing." Tears ran down Zana's cheeks. "I have no idea what happened to my daughter other than she survived the avalanche and was adopted. I've tried to locate her, but the adoption records have been lost." She covered her mouth with her hand as if to hold her sobs inside. "I have no idea if she's dead or alive." Zana turned to her husband and sobbed against his chest. He rubbed her back.

Katherine felt her own eyes mist. The woman truly loved her daughter. "I'm so very sorry. Not know must be heartbreaking for you." She coughed to clear the lump in her throat. No need to get too emotional here. "Thank you for telling me about them."

She thumped her cane against the floor. "I think dinner is ready. Come help me to the table, Samuel."

"Yes, Mother." Leaning on Samuel, she shuffled to the head of the Danish Modern table she'd spent a fortune for early in her marriage. A matching china cabinet against the one wall in the dining area held her collection of chartreuse Russell Wright dishes. She sat down and gently touched the smooth teak surface.

Two chairs down, she noticed Zana ran her hand lovingly over the beautiful piece of wood, a gesture similar to her own. Heredity was a funny thing. She'd not wanted to have anything in common with this woman, yet here they both exhibited an admiration of beautiful things. Their devotion certainly couldn't be attributed to environment. No, that wasn't true. Her mother had loved beautiful furniture and vintage styles.

She vaguely remembered the items her mother painstakingly collected.

"I hope you like shark. It's a plentiful commodity here at Abyss."

"Edith cooks for Mother and she prepares it in a variety of ways. She amazes me with her creativity." Samuel sat across from Zana with his back to the window so Zana and Brock could enjoy the view.

Katherine patted Samuel's hand. "She is good, isn't she, son? I don't know what I'd have done without her all these years."

"Yes, she is. I hope she's prepared my favorite dessert tonight. It's been awhile since I've joined you for dinner."

Zana laughed. "As old as these guys get, they're still little boys when it comes to sweets."

"Yes, indeed." Katherine looked at Samuel. "Yes, dear, we're having Black Forest cake tonight."

Her son rubbed his hands together in delight. "Brock, Edith makes the best desserts so save plenty of room. You'll want more than one slice of her cake."

Katherine hid her smile. Her son did love his sweets, just as he had as a boy. During dinner, Samuel and Brock discussed their business ventures. In the past she'd tried to counsel Samuel on some of his business investments. But when did her son ever listen to her? Never. He'd stopped considering her opinion after college. Education had taken him from under her control. She resented the loss.

After dessert they remained at the table to enjoy their coffee. Samuel and Brock had both eaten two pieces of cake and now paid for their splurge. She snickered as Samuel struggled to prevent a yawn.

"Katherine, where did you grow up?" Zana asked. Katherine almost choked on her coffee. It was a question she'd not expected.

She sat her cup down and dabbed at her mouth with her napkin. "I lived most of my life in Colombia."

Samuel looked taken aback. "How come I never knew that?"

"Well, I suppose because you never asked." She shrugged and glanced around at everyone. "You know how kids are. They think their parents didn't have a life before their birth. Plus, my life was hard. It wasn't an experience I wanted to advertise."

"But—"

"Zana." Katherine rushed ahead to change the subject. Now wasn't the time to discuss her past. "Tell us what your Katy was like."

Zana lips tilted and she chuckled. "You've met Shelia. Katy was like a younger Shelia only she had dark hair and hazel eyes flecked with gold. She peered closely at her. "Much like your eyes, Katherine."

Katherine did her best to stay still under Zana's scrutiny.

"Bright, she could out argue a lawyer." She shook her head. "But she was insecure. She thought I loved Jonathan more than her."

"Why would she think that?" Samuel saved Katherine from having to ask.

"My husband's grandmother lived with us." She smiled. "We called her Nana, Katherine, just like Daniel calls you Nana. After his death, when I had to leave home to run errands, I always took Jonathan with me and Katy had to stay home with Nana. She wasn't able to look after Jonathan because he was so active.

Katy wasn't a bother to her, actually helped her if needed. I'd have worried about leaving Nana by herself, yet she was able to supervise Katy. In a sense, they looked after each other."

"That makes sense to me," said Brock.

"Yes, but you don't have a child's perspective. She didn't understand my reasons and saw it as showing favoritism. If I had it to do over, I'd have figured something else out."

Katherine considered her remark. "How? What could you have done differently?"

"I truly don't have a clue. It was hard for people to leave their homes, but I could have tried to find someone willing to come and stay with Nana."

Brock clasped his wife's hand. "If that'd had been a possibility, I'm sure you'd have made arrangements. Face it, sweetheart, you did the best you could at the time."

"I do know my poor child must have gone through hell during the avalanche." Her voice cracked. "Nana died and there's no telling what horrors Katy experienced buried under the snow before rescuers found her frozen body two weeks later. She went through rebirth alone. If she'd been with us, at least she might be with me today."

Voice thick with sympathy, Samuel said, "You can't know that for sure. Seventy-five years is a long time. For a child, rebirth might not have been successful after such a length of time."

Her son might be right in that respect. Katherine hadn't thought about the time factor.

Samuel added, "Don't give up hope, Zana. You still might find her."

Zana smiled and spoke with conviction. "I'll never give up."

She's serious, but does she really understand what things will be like now? "If you do, she'll be an old woman. Are you prepared for that?"

"Of course I am. Roles will be reversed, but I'll care for her as I would my mother, as I did Nana, and every minute I'm with her will be precious."

Katherine mulled that information over. "She'll be, what, eighty-something years old?"

"If she's alive, she'll soon be eighty-four."

Had Katy misconstrued her mother's reason for leaving her with her Nana? Yes, children did have selfish ideas and often didn't understand their parents' reasoning, just that it was unfair to their way of thinking. It was something Katherine needed to think about.

~ * ~

Zana couldn't sleep. Memories from the past danced around in her head. Katy's leaping into David's arms when he returned from a job, her tenderness with her brother when teaching him to hold a spoon. Then there were the temper tantrums and pouting. They usually didn't last long, but her child made everyone in the house aware of her displeasure. Questions plagued her. Something buried in her head wanted to surface, but she couldn't pull it forth.

She lay propped up on two pillows gazing out at the ocean depths on view. Beside her Brock snored softly, one hand possessively lying on her leg. Solar lights must have been strategically placed to illuminate the area at night. Not bright enough to disturb guest sleep, they gave off just enough luminosity to make the outer area appear natural. The hotel was located on one of the upper levels so it was closer to the sea's surface. The scene should have been soothing, yet tonight it haunted Zana, its vastness emphasizing the depths of the mind and its many hidden places.

Bubbles rose in the water and hovered in front of the glass. Zana watched mesmerized as two changed from a thin, air-filled film into beautiful eyes—hazel eyes flecked with gold. Instead of continuing to rise, they drew nearer and stared through the window at Zana, teasing her, drawing upon recollections buried in her soul. She gaped, fascinated with the expressiveness of the orbs.

The musical notes of Katy's laughter echoed through Zana's head. She felt her warmth as she cuddled against her on nights she'd climbed into her bed after a nightmare. Zana's heart ached with love at her child's trust, knowing her mother a safe haven. Then eyes filled with accusation stared at her as they had the morning she'd left Katy with Nana to go grocery shopping. The orbs outside the window messed with her memories. Katy's eyes…Katherine's eyes…Katy…Katherine… Zana shot up in bed. Surely it wasn't so. They weren't the same, were they? No. No one could be so cruel as to keep the whereabouts of a mother's child from her. Could they?

~ * ~

"You're kidding, right?" Samuel's mouth hung open in shock, mirroring Brock's earlier reaction. In the early hours of morning, an unfamiliar noise woke him. Zana sat up in bed, her body shaking with unrestrained sobs. Dread filled him. She'd not forgiven him for the situation on the day they arrived—his inability to love.

His attempts to apologize had resulted in a screech of anger.

"It's not…not…about you, Brock Callahan."

Well, hell, that was good, wasn't it? He wasn't entirely sure.

"It's Katy." She'd stared at him, her mouth twisted with despair. "Katherine Whiteside is my daughter. How could she be so cruel?"

He'd tried to reassure her Katherine's eyes being like Katy's was coincidence, nothing more. Nothing he said could change her mind. She was adamant and wanted to confront Katherine right then, at three o'clock in the morning. Over a pot of coffee, he convinced her to wait until later.

"No, I'm not. Zana is adamant. She believes your mother is her daughter Katy and wants you to go with us to talk to her." Zana wasn't sure of the woman's health and didn't want to cause a heart attack if the confrontation grew strained.

"Based on what? The fact that Mother's eyes are similar to those of Zana's daughter?" asked Samuel. "It doesn't make sense. If Mother was Katy, don't you think she'd have said so back when Zana went through rebirth? We put out a notice broadcasting her name and seeking information. If not then, why not last night?" He shook his head. "No, it can't be true. Zana wants to find her daughter so bad, she's projecting—making too much of mother's hazel eyes."

Brock didn't know what to think either. Was Zana creating a make-believe dream world? Or was the old bat, Katherine, capable of being so cruel as to deceive her own mother? There was only one way to find out the truth and set Zana's mind at ease. "She won't be happy until she talks to Katherine so we might as well humor her and go see her."

Edith opened the door for them. "Come in. She's expecting you." Samuel had insisted he call ahead.

If Katherine suspected the nature of their visit, she didn't let on. Sitting in her favorite chair like a queen on her throne, she waved at the sofa. "What a pleasant surprise. Sit down and join me for a cup of coffee."

Zana opted for the chair Samuel had occupied last night. Before she sat down, she pulled the chair closer to Katherine and turned it to face the older woman. Katherine's brows rose in surprise. She pursed her lips but didn't comment. "No coffee for me, but thank you." They'd drunk two pots since rising early that morning. With all the caffeine she'd consumed, Zana's calm demeanor surprised him. Her bearing indicated serene resignation and determination. This morning she wouldn't be denied, wouldn't give up until she knew the truth. Samuel was the only one to pick up a cup and fill it with the hot brew. He still wore an expression of disbelief.

Katherine set her cup on the table beside her chair and looked between the three of them, waiting for one of them to speak. Silence and suspense hung in the air. Zana leaned forward to better study the older woman. Katherine leaned back in her chair, hands in her lap. She still wore her robe, an elaborate affair of quilted black satin trimmed in red, with slippers on her feet to match. This morning she was bare of jewelry but her hair was neatly coiffed.

"What's going on? Why are you here so early this morning?" When no one answered, she leaned forward in her chair, turned to Samuel and pounded the floor with her cane. "I demand an answer."

"We're here for answers, Katy."

Katherine's head whipped back to Zana. A frown deepened the wrinkles on her forehead. "What'd you call me?"

"I called you Katy. That is what you were called as a child, isn't it?"

She shook her head. "No, my mother and father never called me that." She sniffed and lifted her chin in defiance. "Why would you even think such a thing?"

"You're lying. I can see it in your eyes, just as I could when you lied to me as a child." Zana's voice caught and Brock knew she struggled not to cry. "Admit it. I can't bear not knowing any longer."

Samuel's jaw dropped and stopped his cup in mid-air on its path to his mouth. Brock doubted anyone had called his mother a liar before. He had to admit, the comment shocked even him, but he didn't interrupt and watched Katherine as her shrewd eyes narrowed in rebellion. The two women eyed each other waiting to see who backed down first. Brock saw strength of mind in the set of Zana's mouth.

After several seconds, Katherine looked away, and then back to Zana. She exhaled and her body sagged a fraction. The old lady wasn't about to show any vulnerability. "Oh, all right. I'm your daughter. How'd you know?"

"Your eyes, Katy. They're so like my own." Now that the hoax was over, Brock had to agree. There were other similarities in their features—their chins were identical. How had he missed it? Zana was known to raise her chin in defiance just as Katherine had done a moment before.

"Mother!" Samuel's mouth opened and closed like as fishes as he struggled to find the right words. Brock could just imagine the man's shock at learning of his mother deception. "Why?"

"Why what?" The old lady wasn't giving an inch. She intended to play this out to the hilt.

"You know what. Why didn't you tell me Zana was your mother while she was undergoing rebirth? You knew locating her family was a major priority. You could have been there, given her your support."

Her presence would have meant so much to Zana, eased her worries all these months. But if she'd known, would she have moved to Refuge? It was selfish on his part, but a sense of thankfulness overwhelmed him. He took a steadying breath. No, she'd probably have stayed here in Abyss and wouldn't be his wife today. Maybe he should thank Katherine. Zana wouldn't appreciate the response so he'd keep his mouth shut.

Katherine looked out the window, her face bleached of color. Brock worried this was too much for her. He certainly didn't want to see her have a heart attack, keel over or something. Zana would blame herself. He stood. "Maybe we better leave and finish this conversation later."

"No, I'm fine. Let's get things in the open." She turned to Zana. Brock sat back down. "I didn't want you to know I was alive because I wanted you to suffer like I had." Her frail hands clutched the arms of her chair. "All these years I've carried the anger and bitterness I felt when you left me that day. That hostility developed into hate, an emotion that allowed me to survive a hard life, one filled with abuse and pain."

Zana gasped and stuffed her fist in her mouth to stifle a sob. "Oh God, I'm sorry, Katy, so sorry."

As if Zana hadn't spoken, a faraway expression in her eyes, Katherine continued. "It was so dark and cold in that house—our coffin. Nana and I gathered every blanket we could find. We closed the doors to the den, folded out the sofa bed, piled the covers on top and crawled under them. For a while, the embers in the fire, though the smoke made us cough, kept the room relatively warm. We snuggled together under the covers and when I started crying for you, Nana tried to distract me with stories about the old days. It'd work for a while, but then the fear and panic would set in again. It grew colder. Nana's body was no longer warm. I couldn't wake her."

Katherine turned calm, cold eyes on Zana. "I screamed and cried for you until my voice was hoarse. Tired and weak, I fell asleep. When I woke, fear remained but the cold was replaced with periods of constant pain and blackness. You experienced rebirth, so you know some of what I went through, except I was a child and didn't have the understanding you did." She stopped to catch her breath. "I called for you every time I woke, but you never came. I couldn't understand why. A child needs her mother, you know, and you weren't there."

Zana was openly sobbing, her body shaking with the force of her despair. He wanted to go to her, fold her in his arms, but didn't dare move and break the flow of Katherine's confession.

"When my physical torment ended at last, my emotional ordeal began. I was shuttled from one foster home to another until I was adopted. Six months later we moved to Columbia. That's when my hell began. The only reason I'm alive today is because of my sister Leona."

She picked up her cup and studied the contents. "That's all I intend to say on the matter today. I'm tired." She took a sip of the now cold coffee and frowned. "Pour me another cup, would you, son?"

Like a robot, or a man who'd been cold-cocked, Samuel stood and did her bidding, but didn't return to his seat. "Mrs. Juarez is your sister?"

"Thank you, dear." She raised the coffee to her lips and sipped. "Yes, my sister and my best friend. Without her by my side all these years I'd have gone insane."

"Why did you keep that from me?"

She shrugged. "When your father and I married, it seemed best for no one to know. Afterward, I saw no reason to correct my withholding of information. It was easier that way."

"Easier for who?" asked Samuel. Face red, words dripping with anger, he bellowed, "Learning that I have a grandmother is hard enough, but to learn my aunt has been posing in my home as an employee and been treated like a servant for years instead of like a beloved relative is appalling. You've cheated me, Mother, of a close relationship with her."

Twenty-Three

Katherine regained some color in her face and bristled. "That was certainly not my intention."

Samuel snorted. "And hiding the truth from Zana? What was your intention in this situation? Keep my grandmother from me and from my son?"

"I was trying to protect myself from further hurt. Is that so hard to believe?"

"Mother, you went through a lot as a child, much of which you obviously aren't ready to share with us. I understand that, but as much as you want to blame it on Zana, it wasn't her fault. She didn't leave you at home because she wanted to. She didn't have a choice."

"And how do you know this? You weren't there."

Samuel sighed and waved his hands in agitation. "Zana has shared her feelings of guilt over leaving you that day and the reason why she did with several people, including me—and you for that matter. We discussed this last night, Mother. Zana relayed the information to you herself." He raked a hand through his hair. It stood up in disarray. "Your nana couldn't keep up with Jonathan and it was hard on your mother taking you both with her shopping."

She thumped her cane. "You don't know what you're talking about. You weren't there. You didn't live it."

"Maybe, but letting a child's perspective keep you

from making peace with your mother is childish."
Samuel clenched his fists and shook one at his mother.
"I've been given the gift of a grandmother. I don't
intend to throw it away so you better get used to the
idea."

She sputtered. "Are you threatening me? You'd
choose her over me?"

Zana had had enough. She wiped the tears from her
face and stood. "That's enough, Samuel. Your mother
has been hit with a lot this morning. I'm an emotional
wreck and I know she must be too."

Brock rose and moved to Zana's side. His arm
slipped around her waist and she leaned into his side
grateful for the rock solidity of his body. His lips found
her forehead and placed a kiss there. "Let's go back to
the room. You need to rest."

Samuel turned to Zana, his longing in his eyes. He
opened his arms and Zana walked into them. This was
her grandchild. A sense of joy and homecoming filled
her. Her throat closed with the need to cry. Love for
this man rose within her and she mourned the loss of
not having seen him as a baby and watching him grow
to manhood. She'd lost so much, but she wasn't about
to waste time bemoaning what couldn't be. Samuel
squeezed her tightly and with her arms around his
waist, she hugged back.

His voice was thick with emotion. "I have a
grandmother." He pulled back and laughed. "What shall
I call you?"

She choked on a giggle. "How about Zana for
now?"

He nodded. "Wait until I tell Daniel."

Realization hit. Oh my God, Daniel was her great-grandchild. She embraced the knowledge. Her heart swelled. How blessed could one woman be? To have lost everything and now have a grandson and great-grandson was almost more than her mind could grasp. If only Katy would forgive and accept her in her life, Zana's world would be perfect.

She searched his face. "How did I not see the resemblance? You reminded me of someone early on and it's your grandfather. You have my dark hair but his blue eyes and his smile." She cupped his face. "He'd have been so proud of you, as he was of Katy."

Brock chuckled. "Shelia is going to flip. Not only does she have a step-mother, but now she has a great-aunt, too." He nodded to Katherine, who wore an expression of horror.

She sniffed disdainfully. "Don't count on it."

Zana couldn't restrain her mirth. "And Katy has a step-father."

"Unlike the rest of you, I do not see the humor in this situation."

Katherine might want everyone to think she was a tough old broad, and she was, but Zana didn't doubt that part of the delightful, loving child was still somewhere hidden in the depths of Katherine's soul. She prayed Katherine would let her out.

It was time to go and let Katherine rest and be alone with her ghosts. Hopefully she'd put them to rest. Plus, Zana was tired herself. Confronting Katherine after a sleepless night had sapped her of energy. Both her body and spirits sagged from fatigue, but she couldn't leave just yet.

She knelt in front of Katherine and took her hands. "I love you, Katherine, just as much as I loved

Jonathan. If you'll view the situation through an adult's eyes, you'll see that and understand why I left you at home that day. Ideally, I would have gotten a sitter, but the weather was so bitter people didn't want to leave their homes except for necessities. I love the child you were, Katherine, and would like the opportunity to know the woman you've become. Life cast us a terrible blow in separating us all those years ago. Don't let that keep us apart."

~ * ~

Katherine sat rooted to her chair. The very idea of that son of hers, delivering an ultimatum—to her. He'd not give up his grandmother, even for her, his mother. How dare he? After all she'd done for him, all the sacrifices she'd made. Hadn't she paved the way for him to become Governor of Abyss? His lack of appreciation galled her.

She'd not had the benefit of grandparents. Oh, she'd had Nana for a while but she'd had to share her with Jonathan. She'd had Jonathan, her baby brother. He'd been so cute. Most of the time she'd loved him. He'd run to her if something frightened him and Mommy or Nana wasn't around. His little arms would clutch her around the waist and she'd hold him close. She'd felt powerful and needed.

The morning Samuel was born she'd gazed into his eyes and for the first time in years remembered Jonathan, her baby brother. Jonathan had been such a pretty child, as was Samuel. Both babies had blue eyes and blond hair, Jonathan's had been almost white. Her son's had darkened as he'd grown. If Jonathan had lived, would his hair have turned dark like Samuel's as Mother always said it would? She didn't want to think about Jonathan. It hurt too much to remember.

Katy favored Zana. She'd often looked at herself in the mirror as a young woman and seen her mother staring back at her. Her looks had drawn a lot of attention, some not wanted.

Why couldn't her mother have taken her with them that day? If so, she'd still be a child and wouldn't have had to suffer the pits of hell growing up. If she'd lived, that is. It was possible rebirth wouldn't have been achievable for her after being frozen for seventy-five years instead of two weeks. She'd only been on the medicine that kept her tissues alive for a year.

Though she'd loved her brother, she was glad he was gone. If she allowed her mother into her life, she wouldn't have to compete with him, but she would have to tolerate Brock's little redheaded brat.

Was she actually considering a relationship with Zana? How could it benefit her? Samuel would be pleased. Conceding didn't mean she'd forgiven her mother or forgotten, only that she'd put her animosity on hold to give her mother a chance. Yes, she'd bide her time and see how things went. She'd be a celebrity in the community when the news reached everyone's ears that she'd reunited with her long, lost mother. A smile stretched her lips. Yes, that was the ticket. She'd been out of the limelight since her husband, the governor, had died. It'd be nice to be a sought after guest again.

"Edith, call the hotel and ask to speak to the Callahans."

~ * ~

The communicator buzzed, the sound a soft pulsing that didn't wake Zana. Brock rolled over in the bed and reached to touch activate the communication receiver. Katherine's voice filled the room. "I'd like to talk to Zana."

"She's asleep right now, but I'll tell her when she wakes."

"You do that, young man."

Without a goodbye, she closed the connection. Brock grinned. The old biddy thought the world revolved around her. He wanted Zana to have a relationship with her daughter, but the old lady would not run over his wife. He'd see to it.

Truthfully, he didn't think Zana would allow Katherine to boss her around. Zana was the mother after all, and though they'd been apart all these years and Katherine was much older, Zana's mother- instinct would kick in. That Katherine was her daughter still flabbergasted him. He was happy for Zana. Finding Katy would allow her closure, to bond with her child and move on with her own life. The hate Katherine harbored against her mother was misplaced. It reminded him of Rafael's acts of revenge. Would the older woman be able to put her childish hatred aside and go forward? He hoped so as he didn't want to see Zana hurt further.

He lay back on the pillow and studied Zana's face as she slept. On her side, one hand under the pillow, the other on top, she slept without worries, her face relaxed, her rosy lips slightly open. His wife. She was so beautiful and his heart surged with joy. She'd finally found her child. Hopefully, Katherine would return Zana's love and they'd enjoy each other's company for the remainder of their lives. In Abyss it was common for people to live healthy lives for one hundred years and more. He wanted that for Zana. Hell, he'd even agree to have Katherine come live with them if it made his wife happy.

If only he could heal the rift her declaration of love had opened between them. As some wives might have done, she didn't give him the silent treatment or withhold sex. For that he was grateful. To outsiders they appeared happy but he saw the hurt in her eyes when she didn't know he was looking, the longing glances she sent his way. If only he could give her the words she needed to hear, but fear she'd be taken from him sealed his heart and his mouth.

Hopefully the tension between them would soon heal. He sighed and closed his eyes. He'd better get a little sleep before she woke and they learned what Katherine had on her mind.

~ * ~

"If you really loved me, you'd move to Abyss and take care of me." Zana shuddered at Katherine's petulant tone. The childish comment grated on Zana's nerves and sounded foreign coming from the elderly woman sitting in her maroon chair, feet propped on the matching footstool. For a second Zana wondered if her daughter was mentally disturbed, but then pushed the idea aside. She was spoiled, that was the explanation.

They'd spent several hours the past three days talking and getting reacquainted. Katy had steered clear of any mention of her adopted family other than to say her marriage to Mr. Whiteside saved her from having to continue living in Columbia. Though she'd admitted being abused as a child, she refused to confide in Zana, her own mother, a fact that nagged at Zana. How could she help Katy without the whole story? Perhaps Katy had received professional help years ago and she'd buried her demons. It'd be nice to know if all her daughter's emotional issues had been resolved. From her actions and attitude, Zana doubted it.

"Katy, would you listen to yourself? You know I can't leave my husband and our child." Plus, she didn't want to live in Abyss, could never adjust to their methods of controlling relationships. "Brock would never leave Refuge. He's my husband. My place is with him."

"You'd choose him and Shelia over me?" The stubborn tilt of her chin spoke volumes. "Shelia's not even your child."

"She is now." Shelia needed her and Zana loved the child. No way would she desert her. "How could you even suggest I leave her after what you experienced all those years ago? I'd think you'd show more empathy."

"What happened to your declaration of wanting to take care of me?"

"I still want to care for you. I want you to move to Refuge with us. You can live in the cottage and we'll get someone to live in with you full time. I'll be able to see you every day." It was the perfect solution for them all.

"You're joking, dear. Me…live in that God forsaken hell hole?" She laughed, the sound an ugly cackle. "Never." She shrugged. "My friends are here. I'd be lonesome in a new place. I'm too old to start over."

Zana understood her hesitancy to leave everything familiar. She sighed. "You're right, of course. Your life is here." There was no help for it. They'd have to live apart and she'd have to make the trip back to Abyss as often as possible. After finding her daughter, she'd do all she could to bridge the distance between them. Maybe she could convince Katy to at least come visit for a while. Her prejudices about Refuge could only be dissolved with a trip to see the place for herself.

"Would you at least visit us in Refuge? We'd do everything possible to make you comfortable. You might enjoy a change of scenery."

Katy cocked her head in thought. "Hmmm, maybe. I'll think about it."

The communicator hummed and they heard Edith talking to someone. She came into the room. "Mrs. Whiteside, Mrs. Nolan called to see if you might talk to the Ladies Club about being reunited with your mother."

Like a child, Katy clapped her hands in glee. "At last they want to include me again. Tell her I'd love to." Edith smiled and turned to leave. "Wait, wait a minute, Edith. On second thought, get the information and tell her I'll check my schedule and think about it."

Edith nodded. "Yes, ma'am."

Her petulant expression disappeared to be replaced with a sly smile. "They've excluded me since Mr. Whiteside passed on. I don't want to be too quick to accept the gossiping old women. Of course, many are my friends, but they've neglected me."

Zana hid her smile. "Just imagine how excited they'll be to hear about Refuge. The only way you can provide them with proper details is to visit and see the village firsthand."

~ * ~

"Are you okay?" Brock and Zana stood on the deck

of Retriever and watched the oilrig fade into the distance, now a mere speck on the horizon.

"Yes, I'm more than fine. I know Katy is alive. Though our reunion wasn't the joyous one I'd expected, at least I can see her. Hopefully our relationship will grow and improve."

Brock wasn't so sure. Katherine was a selfish old woman. She'd done her best to manipulate Zana. Thank goodness she hadn't caved in to her daughter's demands. He questioned whether Samuel would ever pardon his mother for keeping his aunt from him all these years. In his shoes, Brock would find forgiveness extremely difficult. Not revealing her identity to Zana was just another black mark against her. Knowing her daughter lived would have been such a comfort to Zana while she went through the pain of rebirth. And what about when she'd been poisoned? Katherine had known then Zana was her mother. What kind of person wouldn't come to offer a loved one comfort? He had his doubts about the woman but didn't want to put a damper on Zana's happiness and optimism.

"I wonder how she'd have turned out if we'd never been separated, if I could have raised her to womanhood." Zana's tone held soft regret.

"It's hard to know, hon." Katherine had suffered, yet Zana still had no clue the extent of abuse her child had undergone. Katherine refused to reveal details. In some ways he was glad as knowing would be an added burden for Zana, additional guilt for not having been there for her child. Many children faced hardships and it didn't warp their personalities for life. What was he thinking? Just because Katherine was a difficult, opinionated woman didn't mean she was evil. Yet, he never failed to feel uneasy around her. He wasn't afraid of her. His uneasiness had to do with expectations. He didn't trust the woman. "At least she agreed to visit us."

Brock wasn't sure he was looking forward to Katherine descending on their happy village. He wouldn't put it past her to cause havoc. She'd probably look down her prejudiced nose at them. If she offended any of their people he'd see to it she returned to Abyss on the first available boat.

"Of course," said Zana with a mischievous grin, "You know why she decided to come."

"No, why?" He'd wondered and figured it probably wasn't out of the goodness of her heart. It was too much to ask that she'd agreed for Zana's sake.

"So she'll have more fodder for her gossip sessions with her ladies group. Seems she's somewhat of a celebrity now, because of my rebirth and our relationship, and since they've neglected her over the past few years, she intends to keep her stardom alive with fresh details." Though Abyss had seen a number of rebirths, Zana's made superstar status because she was Katherine's mother. After all, Katherine had been the wife of the previous governor of Abyss. And Zana was not only Katherine's mother, she was Samuel's grandmother, Daniel's great-grandmother. What a story.

Leave it to Katherine to cash in on Zana's experience. The woman's machinations tickled Brock. He couldn't restrain the laughter that bubbled forth. He threw his head back and let loose a rip-roaring guffaw. Zana's rounded eyes and gaping mouth made him laugh harder. She giggled. The tinkling mirth grew until she howled with hilarity. They hugged the rail to hold themselves erect and swiped at the tears one handed.

It was so good to see her laugh with abandon. Was it possible she'd gotten past the gap that developed between them on the trip? Lord, he hoped so. He wanted his fun-loving wife back.

Zana slapped him on the arm. "You are bad, mister."

He grinned. "Couldn't help it. The picture of Katherine reigning over a bunch of old ladies, regaling them with the horrors of our poor society, set me off."

"Katy will be surprised at what she finds in Refuge. She's expecting a primitive village with outdoor toilets and half-dressed natives."

Brock knew people had no clue how advanced their community had become. It was a source of pride for him and the citizens of Refuge. Of course, progress had been slow, but they were pretty much self-sufficient. They traded for many commodities, but if necessary could manage without those items.

"Hey, Daddy." Footsteps pounded on the wooden deck as Shelia ran toward them. She wiggled her way between him and Zana. She looked up shyly at Zana. Zana put her arm around Shelia and hugged her to her side. Shelia was still a little unsure about Zana's affection. It made him happy to see Zana lavish his child with love. He didn't doubt Zana's sincerity. Soon Shelia would have no doubts, either.

Brock yanked on Shelia's shiny red French braid, a style she'd sported since he and Zana had married. Zana brushed and braided the child's hair every morning. He enjoyed listening to their chatter during those grooming sessions. His child was the image of health and happiness. She made him so proud. "What've you been up to?"

"Luke let me look through that thing that shows the fish and stuff in the water. We saw a sea turtle which Luke said was unusual in this cool water."

"Maybe the ocean is warming up some." Odd as winter weather was upon them, but in truth, the seasons were no longer predictable. "I bet you enjoyed seeing all the sea life while at Abyss."

"Yes, especially at Mrs. Whiteside's. She has that humongous window. One day we saw a shark eatin' a big tuna. It scared Daniel. He started cryin' and to distract him Mrs. Whiteside took us in her room to see her shiny jewelry."

"Did it work?" Brock asked. Seeing a shark attack would be frightening for a youngster Daniel's age.

"Sure did. For a minute leastways. Daniel got tired of looking at the trinkets and was interested in Mrs. Whiteside's pets instead. She calls them her babies. He tried to open the glass aquarium tank-like thing to pick one up." She rolled her eyes and grimaced. "I couldn't even see what was in there, just a bunch of leaves and some little bugs, so don't know why he was so fascinated. But his nana was upset and yelled, 'No,' real loud. She smacked him on the butt several times real hard. Then she hugged him close and said, 'We don't touch Nana's babies.'"

Zana glanced at Brock to catch his reaction. Surely he didn't approve of Daniel being smacked, especially over attempting to touch a pet reptile. His expression didn't give any indication of what he was thinking. Shelia turned and with a wave skipped to the stairs leading to the con deck. Without missing a beat, she ran up the set of steps with all the agility of youth.

Concern eating at her mind, she rounded on Brock. "Don't you think spanking a child for touching an aquarium is a bit extreme?"

He leaned, propped his forearms on the deck rail, and gazed out to sea. For a minute she thought he'd not heard her, or was ignoring the question. He scratched his chin. Finally he answered. "I don't know. It's hard to discern what's in a person's mind. My first response would be, no, I don't approve. It's possible she's afraid he'd pull the tank down on top of him causing a serious injury." He shrugged. "Or, the tank would break and he'd be cut by glass."

She'd not considered those possibilities. "That makes sense. I guess since we don't know the full details I shouldn't judge her method of discipline. Daniel loves her so she must be good to him."

He straightened and placed his hands on her shoulders kneading them gently. "It's only natural for you to be concerned about your great-grandchild, but I think Samuel trusts her with his son, so we must too." Brock was right. She shouldn't question when she didn't know all of the details. When the opportunity arose, she'd ask Samuel about the situation. Better yet, she'd ask Katy.

Zana had spanked Katy a few times when she was young, but only when she was blatantly disobedient or had done something that might cause her harm. Maybe Brock was right in his assessment of the situation. Broken glass was definitely dangerous as was something heavy landing on him. She shuddered at the thought.

"You're probably right. She dotes on Daniel." Who wouldn't? He was an adorable child and sharp as a tack.

He slipped an arm around her shoulders and turned her toward the expanse of ocean before them. With him behind her, his chin resting beside her ear, his arms cradling hers, her body relaxed and molded to his. Brock might deny he loved her, but he cared deeply. Though his lack of verbal commitment hurt deeply, she didn't intend to let the rift between them to widen. She could be satisfied with what they had and hopefully one day he'd be able to give more to their relationship.

She wove her fingers through his and focused on the beauty around them. It was soothing to watch the water below them twist into something resembling white-streaked green marble as the boat churned through the waves. Nature was a glorious artist, painting pictures only the most gifted of humans could replicate. She shifted her gaze past the stirring water to the swells that rose and fell, their darkness indicating what appeared to be a bottomless pit, depths that unnerved her with a fear of the unknown.

Twenty-Four

"Hurry up, you guys. It's almost nine o'clock and the boat will be docking anytime." Shelia bubbled with excitement. Katy was coming for a visit. Her friends were fascinated with the prospect of actually seeing this 'sister' who was old enough to be Shelia's great-great-grandmother. Zana couldn't wait to see how Katy reacted the first time Shelia introduced her as a sibling. She grinned at the thought and struggled to restrain a giggle. Now was not the time to get into Shelia keeping the sister fact low key.

Brock held the door for them. "We've got plenty of time. Remember we're taking the rover." Katy would need the small vehicle to get up the path. Brock would allow them to use it around the village so Katy wouldn't have to walk. Actually, Zana wasn't sure how mobile her daughter was. If she visited their home, Zana suspected Brock would have to carry her up the path. It would be tiring for a healthy older woman and Katy's health didn't appear to be that good.

Shelia rushed ahead. Brock stopped her before she could charge out the door. "Hold it, miss. Where's your jacket?"

"Ah, Daddy. It's not cold enough for a coat."

"We're not leaving until you're wearing one, or a sweater."

"Oh, all right." She stomped to her room and came

back with a light jacket. "I'm ready."

Brock waved his hand ushering her forward. "Lead the way." He bowed to Zana. "After you, my dear." She grinned and followed Shelia down the steps.

When they reached the bottom of the steps, Shelia hopped into the driver's seat. "Get into the back, brat."

"Oh, Daddy, let me drive. You know I can."

"I may know it but now is not the time. Don't argue with me on this." His expression brooked no argument.

Huffing, lips rolled into a pout, she hopped out, got into the back seat, and sat arms folded across her chest. He got into the driver's seat and Zana slid in beside him. Life would never be dull around these two. She loved their exchanges. Shelia's stubbornness equaled her daddy's. Zana hoped it didn't cause too much dissention between father and daughter when Shelia became a teenager.

"Wipe that frown off your face or you can go to school this morning while we fetch Katherine." Brock didn't turn around in the seat so he didn't see Shelia use her eyes to shoot daggers. "I'm waiting, Shelia." Zana, pleased with the way Brock handled the situation, bit her tongue to keep from laughing.

"Oh, all right. But, hurry up. We're gonna be late."

Brock grinned and turned the key. The rover's electric motor hummed to life, powered by a solar panel suspended above the small roof. The sides were open to the elements. The day wasn't very cold, so their jackets and sweaters served to keep them warm. Zana carried a couple of blankets in her lap for Katy and Edith. Living in an encapsulated environment she doubted the two women owned a coat and probably had no idea they'd need one in Refuge.

When they pulled to a stop, Abyss's boat was pulling into the dock. Katy and Edith stood on the deck draped in warm throws. Shelia hopped out and ran to the dock. She jumped up and down shouting, "Hi Mrs. Whiteside, Miss Edith. Welcome to Refuge."

Edith waved and the corners of Katy's mouth tilted upward. Zana liked Edith and was glad she'd come with Katy. Both Shelia and Daniel seemed to like the woman, a good recommendation in her opinion.

Shelia's voiced blared across the small distance separating them. "Can I call you Katy now that you're my sister?"

The smile on Katy's face wilted into a grimace.

Katherine feared she'd be deaf after spending time around the child. Edith chuckled at her side. Katherine poked her in the ribs and hissed, "The impudent little scamp."

"She is that. Cute as a bug, too."

Katherine wanted to smack the woman, but smiled and waved at Zana instead. Truth be told, she admired the little minx. She didn't mince words, said exactly what she thought. And yes, the child was cute, but Katherine would never let Edith know she thought so. She shivered. It was cold. No one had prepared her for the temperature difference. Samuel tried to get her to postpone this visit so she'd be more equipped, but the Ladies Club was eager for details on Refuge and she wanted to fulfill their curiosity and her own. From what she could see from the deck, it was sand and mountains with some green foliage. Not a tall building in sight though a few rooftops showed beyond the trees.

As soon as the crew rolled the ramp across to the

deck, Brock crossed to her side and took her arm. "Let me help you, Katherine. Zana is thrilled you've come and Shelia is beside herself. She'll probably want you to go to school and meet her friends." She pulled back at his comment and the man had the gall to laugh. He'd better be teasing. "Don't worry. I'll protect you."

The minute she stepped onto the pier, Shelia grabbed her around the waist and squeezed. "I'm so glad you're here, Katy."

Brock unwound the child's arms from around her. "Whoa, now, she's not said you could call her Katy. She might prefer Katherine or even Mrs. Whiteside." Katherine sucked in a lung full of air. Brock had that right. She didn't like the name Katy but suffered through letting her mother use the childhood name. But, no one else would, not this child.

"Well, Daddy, you can't expect me to call my sister Mrs. Whiteside. That sounds dumb."

"Shelia's right, Brock," said Zana.

Katherine threw up a hand. "Oh all right, child. Call me Katherine."

"Cool."

"Come along, Shelia. Let your daddy help Katherine to the vehicle." Zana approached Edith. "Hi Edith. I'm glad you were able to come also."

Edith smiled. "It's a delight to get away from Abyss for a change." She looked around. "It's been too long since I've been on dry land."

Katherine listened to their exchange. She hadn't missed the land one day. Odd that Edith did. They'd both been away for the same length of time. Off hand, she couldn't remember how many years it had been.

"Let's get you two settled," said Zana.

Members of the ship's crew set their bags in a compartment attached to the back of the little transport. Brock wrapped a blanket around each of them and helped her and then Edith into the back seat. Shelia sat between Brock and Zana in the front chattering nonstop.

"Everyone is excited about you coming. I bet they'll give a party." She turned around on the seat and announced. "I can drive this vehicle but Daddy wouldn't let me."

Well, thank you, Brock for that small favor.

Five minutes later a large fort-like structure came into view. The tall gates stood open and they passed through, down one block, and then turned onto a side road. They stopped in front of a small house.

"Why are we stopping? Surely you don't live here." She looked up and down the lane. With narrow, dirt streets, the small community reminded her of the one where she grew up in Columbia, only much cleaner and considerably nicer. "It's way too small. Surely you don't live here." It'd be very crowded with three people living in it much less house two guests.

Brock turned the motor off and got out. He took her arm and helped her out onto the dirt street. He nodded toward a tall rock hill evident above the wall of the fortress. "We live up there and were afraid all the steps to reach the top would be too much for you. Zana used to live here in the cottage. It's new and quite modern. You'll be very comfortable. She spent a lot of time getting it ready for you ladies."

"I don't see a house up there." Maybe it was her eyes. She blinked to clear her vision but it didn't help.

"Our home is in a cave." He bent down to her level

and with one hand on her shoulder, pointed. "If you follow the steps up, you'll see a large door set into the rock face."

Katherine strained to locate the steps and could barely make them out, but didn't see a door. She turned to him. "I can't believe my mother is living in a cavern. I insist on seeing it while I'm here." She sized up his wide shoulders and muscular arms. "I think you can carry me up there with ease."

"I'd be happy to, Katherine. We'd love for you to see our home."

She eyed him suspiciously. He appeared serious. How he could be proud of a cave home? Living like an animal didn't make sense to her. So far she'd been surprised to see the quality of the structures in the small community. The streets were dirt, most likely to prevent contributing to the heat during the summer months and to allow for water run-off when it rained.

Katherine let her eyes wander from the hillside to the blue atmosphere above. It was odd to see the sky again and the greenery of the forests. She saw the oceans depths every day, but not the surface of the water. Counting in her head, she figured it'd been forty years since she'd been out of Abyss. Before now she'd never been interested in being on the outside. Though the undersea beauty of Abyss was magnificent, this morning's sunrise had equaled her home city's splendor. But, watching the orange orb rise out of the ocean had been a shock, bringing memories she'd hidden away to the surface. Perhaps coming up from the depths hadn't been a good idea.

~ * ~

Brock deposited Katy in the cottage and unloaded

their luggage. From the expression on his face, he'd escape as soon as Zana didn't need him. She didn't blame him in the least. Her daughter's demanding attitude was a bit much to put up with. She walked him to the door. He pulled her close and started to kiss her. At Katy's snort of disgust, Brock placed a chaste kiss on her forehead. Since their trip to Abyss, his expressions of affections had been less flamboyant, as if he feared she might rebuff him. A month ago he'd have bent her back over his arm and kissed her passionately just to aggravate Katy. She missed his playfulness and it saddened her, but she didn't know how to change things.

Brock waved. "Goodbye, ladies. I'll see you at dinner."

Katy muttered. "Good riddance."

Zana struggled not to chuckle. It would never be dull when Brock and Katy were in the same room. She cleared her throat a couple of times. "Would you like to lie down for a while, Katy? We've got a busy afternoon."

"I suppose so. Edith, will you help me to the bed?"

"Yes, ma'am." Edith took the older woman's arm and led her toward the larger of the two bedrooms. Zana hurried ahead and turned down the covers.

Shelia popped her head in the door. "Would you like a cup of tea to help you relax? I can make some real quick."

Katy looked up from where she sat on the bed, apparently surprised at Shelia's thoughtfulness. "Why, yes child. That'd be very nice."

Zana mouthed a "thank you" when Shelia returned with the cup. The hot brew would tide Katherine over until lunch. Propped up on pillows in the bed, she sipped at her tea while Zana and Edith unpacked their luggage. When Zana glanced back at the bed, Katherine's eyes were closed and she appeared to be asleep. She quietly left the room and joined Shelia in the kitchen.

After a light lunch, Zana helped the two women, now dressed in jackets she and Shelia had retrieved from the cave, into the rover. Katy sat in front with her and Shelia in the back with Edith. They pulled out onto the main street to find it lined with people. Shouts of "Welcome, Mrs. Whiteside," echoed around them. Katy sat up taller, smiled and waved.

In front of the school, students held a banner that read, *Hi Shelia's Sister. Come visit us at school.* Katy pursed her lips, but when one of the children ran out with a bouquet of flowers, she put a hand on Zana's arm. "Stop the vehicle, dear."

Zana halted the rover and the child shyly approached the side where Katy sat. Katy held out her arms and like a queen accepted the flowers. She smiled down at the little girl. "Tell your friends and teachers I'd be happy to visit your school tomorrow." The child grinned from ear-to-ear and ran back to deliver the message to her teacher.

"Hold on a minute, Zana." Shelia hopped out before Zana could respond and ran to where her friends stood in a group.

"Does the child ever remain still?"

"When she's asleep." Zana chuckled. "She's much like you were at that age." She watched the children, as heads together they planned some escapade. "I wish you and Jonathan had had the opportunity to play outside with the freedom these children have."

Face immobile, attention on the children, Katy said, "Freedom can be overrated."

Shelia hurried back preventing Zana from asking Katy what she'd meant. Her comment must have to do with her childhood in Columbia.

"Can I spend the afternoon with them? They're going to watch a movie at Ruthy's house." She turned to Katy. "I promise I'll spend more time with you tomorrow."

Katy looked taken aback, but fortunately she didn't hurt the child's feeling and nodded graciously. "That will be fine, dear."

Shelia turned pleading eyes on Zana. "Can I? Please."

"All right, but meet us at the cottage by four o'clock. Do not walk home by yourself. Understand?"

She grinned and nodded. "I promise. See you later." With a wave she was off to join the girls waiting for her.

Edith leaned toward the front seat and spoke. "You don't trust her to be safe outside the wall?"

"No. Even before we were accosted on the hill, there were dangers lurking in the form of wild animals. We all carry a weapon and Shelia is expert in using her ray gun, but I don't want to take any chances. Shelia was attacked by wild hogs once and killed one before the guards on duty came to her aid." Brock's response to the near death situation mirrored Zana's own. She didn't intend to take any chances with the child's life.

Katy sniffed. "I knew this was a savage place." She pulled her bouquet of flowers to her nose and sniffed. "Though Refuge is a nice enough, I can't imagine choosing to live here rather than Abyss."

Zana bristled. "Did you participate in selective mating, Katy?"

"Why no. Why would I? I met my husband before moving to Abyss."

"Then I don't think you can be a fair judge. It's a despicable practice and I'd much rather face a little danger than have my personal life controlled by drugs."

"Well, that comment is proof of your antiquated way of thinking." She shrugged. "Of course, since you've been frozen for seventy-five years, you've not been able to change as society changed."

From the back seat, Edith leaned forward and stuck her head between them. "Ladies, you don't want to argue on this beautiful day."

"You're right. Let's just drop it."

After a turn through the village, they drove through part of the vineyard. Brock met them inside the winery and hosted a wine tasting for Katy and Edith. Several city representatives were in attendance and solicited their opinion on Refuge. Both were gracious in their responses but non-committal. From Edith's enthusiastic response earlier, Zana felt she might have been more vocal if Katy hadn't been within earshot. To the officials' joy, Katherine promised to attend one of their meetings. She thrived on the attention and Zana didn't fail to notice how much her daughter enjoyed interacting with other people. Hopefully when she returned to Abyss, her friends would continue to keep her busy.

By late afternoon, Katy's face was drawn with strain. "We better get you back to the cottage to rest." If she fell ill, she'd never want to return.

"Yes, I think I better have dinner in bed tonight and rest up for tomorrow. It wouldn't do to disappoint the school children." She shuffled toward the bedroom and sank into the padded chair Zana had placed in the corner. Edit knelt to remove Katy's shoes.

"While Edith helps you to bed, I'll prepare something."

"There's no need," said Edith. "I'll get her settled and fix us something light. You run on home."

"I hate to leave when she's not feeling well." What if she needed medical care?

"There is nothing you can do. She needs to recharge, that's all. We have days like this on occasion."

"Are you sure?"

"I'm positive. It's the way we do things many nights."

Biting her lip, Zana nodded in agreement. It stung to realize someone else could better take care of her daughter than she could.

When Edith had Katy tucked in bed, Zana went in to say goodnight. "I hope we haven't over tired you."

Though frail, her smile was sincere. "Oh no. I had a wonderful time. I'll be ready to go again tomorrow."

"I'm glad." Zana leaned over and kissed her cheek. "Brock left a communicator here in case you need us. I'll be here in the morning and go with you to the school. Thank you for agreeing to speak to the children."

Katy looked over at the slightly wilted flowers they'd put in a glass of water. "It's the least I can do for them. They need to know there are alternatives to living in Refuge."

Twenty-Five

The following morning, Brock accompanied Zana to the cottage to meet their guests. He wasn't about to let Katherine speak to the children of Refuge without talking to her first. The object of his interest came from the bedroom wearing a pantsuit of deep blue material. The swathe of pearls around her neck was the ones she'd worn the night they'd had dinner at her apartment in Abyss. It was hard to imagine how her skinny neck withstood their weight.

"You look nice, Katherine. A bit over dressed for school children, though. They'll have a hard time concentrating on your speech for eyeing your jewelry." He couldn't resist a little dig to spark the old lady's wrath. Heck if he wasn't growing fond of her.

She drew herself up. "Thank you, but I'm also speaking to the city council and the administrator before lunch. I'll be meeting the governor and want to make a good impression for Abyss. After all, my husband was a governor and now my son is one." She fiddled with the strands that lay against her shrunken chest. For a moment he felt empathy for her. It must be hard for a beautiful, powerful woman to lose her looks and her influence. "Will you be there, Brock?"

As if anyone could keep him away. "Yes, I will. I look forward to hearing what you have to say, but Katherine, I'm warning you, watch your comments when talking to the children at school." He didn't want them impressed by her expensive clothes and the glorious picture she'd paint of life under the sea.

Eyes narrowed, she bit out. "What do you mean? Don't you want me to tell them the truth about Abyss? You want me to lie to them?"

He sighed. "No, I don't want you to lie. I just don't want you to elaborate on selective mating. Our children know things are done differently there. We want them to be educated about those differences, but I don't want you to sing the praises of your drugging practices."

She frowned. "What kind of person do you think I am, anyway? They wouldn't understand the advantages of discriminatory pairing. I only want them to know how advanced Abyss is, what it has to offer."

"Fine, we're on the same page then." He offered his arm. "Shall we go?"

Like a queen she took his arm and called, "Come along, Edith, Zana." He winked at Zana as she rushed around them to open the door. She flushed and ducked her head to hide the blush. They'd made love early this morning and she'd jokingly fussed about having to wear makeup to cover the whisker burn on her face. Edith stepped onto the porch before them. He couldn't resist squeezing Zana's butt as he and Katherine walked past her. She hissed in embarrassment. He couldn't resist a chuckle. The woman made his blood sizzle.

The school gathering room was crowed. Katherine was delighted to see many parents had joined their children to hear what she had to say. It pleased her immensely to know the citizens of Refuge were interested in Abyss. Maybe they weren't as happy here as Brock thought. She glanced over prepared to send him a smug smile.

A round of applause and a cry of, "Hello Mr. Governor," froze her in mid smirk. Brock Callahan was the Governor of Refuge? She stifled a snort of disgust. The man could have informed her of his stature in the community, or her mother could have. He smiled and waved at those in the filled room, but he didn't step toward the podium to talk. He inclined his head toward the teacher who looked at him for guidance.

The woman clapped her hands and when she spoke the sound came out across the room, amplified just enough to be heard but wasn't overpowering. "Welcome students and parents." She turned and nodded toward Brock and Zana. "We're pleased to have Governor and Mrs. Callahan with us today along with our esteemed guest. To introduce her, we'd like Shelia Callahan to come forward and do the honors."

Shelia, hair in a French braid hanging down her back came up onto the stage. Without a shy bone in her body the child prissed forward, took Katherine's hand, and led her center stage where a chair had been set for her.

When she was settled, Shelia laid a hand on her shoulder. "This is Mrs. Whiteside. Her husband used to be Governor of Abyss. Now her son is. His name is Samuel and he's my uncle because he was married to my aunt Delia." She paused for breath. "Anyway, Mrs. Whiteside is my step-sister because her mama is Zana who is my step-mama because she married my daddy. Now, I 'spose you're wonderin' how someone as old as Mrs. Whiteside could be my sister and Zana's daughter." Her head bobbed up and down as she looked around the room for the other children to confirm their desire to know the answer to the mystery. Katherine looked out at the group and indeed the majority of the youngsters mimicked her actions. "She's going to explain it all and also tell us about Abyss. So, listen up and pay attention cause I bet we'll be havin' a test tomorrow."

Her last comment brought chuckles from the adults, groans from the kids. The teacher stepped in and put an arm around Shelia. "Thank you, Shelia. That was a wonderful introduction. Now, let's give Mrs. Whiteside a round of applause in welcome."

~ * ~

"Take a nap if you can. You're trying to do too much in this one trip. It's not like you can't come back again." Zana smoothed the covers around her. Katherine peeked through half closed lids at her mother. Zana was right. She was wearing herself out but for the first time in a long time she felt useful. Ever since news had gotten out that Zana, the newest rebirth, was her mother, her life had been given new meaning. Now, as she gazed at her mother's attractive, youthful face, Katherine wondered if she'd be able to forgive the woman's transgressions. Yes, she knew her feelings on the subject were skewed by childish conceptions, but they were *hers* and by God no one told her how to think and feel.

"Yes, you're right. All the questions of the children wore me out. They were cute though, weren't they?" It amazed her how intelligent children were today. She'd known Samuel was a gifted child but thought he was an exception because he was her son. His father was a talented scientist so Samuel came by his intelligence naturally. Daniel showed signs of being a bright child also. Today's experience brought to mind the idea of getting more involved with the children of Abyss. She didn't know what she could do, but would check in to the matter the minute they returned home.

Zana's face turned soft and dreamy. "Yes, they were. And they loved you. You were great with them."

She studied her mother carefully. Was she patronizing her? No, her expression indicated her sincerity. Of course, some people were good at fooling others. Was Zana one of them? No, Katherine didn't think so. It wasn't in her mother's nature to try to deceive.

"I want to be rested enough to go up the hill to see your house tonight. I can't imagine living in a cave. That little redheaded imp says I'm going to be so surprised I'll swallow my tongue. Harrumph. That'll be the day."

Zana laughed. "She's a mess, isn't she? But, she may be right. The cave is beautiful inside and I have no doubt you'll feel the same way."

"We'll see."

"Brock will be down at six this evening to bring you up. Wear something warm."

Katherine slept deeply and woke slowly, her mind clouded with sleep. Still drowsy, she looked around the room noting the dark shadows on the wall as the dim, filtered rays of the setting sun passed through the floral curtains. Images mingled and twisted and formed shapes she didn't want to remember, much less see. Shadowy shapes rushed together to form a visage, one that filled her with horror, pain, and hate. She gulped for air and clutched at her racing heart. *Breathe slowly. He's not here, he's dead. Your mind is playing tricks on you again.* She squeezed her eyes tightly shut and told herself to take slow breaths. *Focus, Katherine, think about something else. You're in control here, not the demons from the past. Don't let them destroy your peace.*

Being on the outside, above her safe ocean home, had opened a door in her mind, one she'd kept closed and locked for years. All those years ago, when she'd married and left Colombia, she'd buried the key to her pain and suffering, to memories she never wanted to visit again or share with anyone. Was it the fresh air and the beautiful blue skies that'd had jogged her psyche making her remember things no child should ever have to experience? Maybe it was the jungle greenery in the distance. She could feel the foliage slapping at her skinny limbs as she ran through the thickets fleeing from her demon. *Run, run, he's getting closer. Gasping for air, she stumbled, but righted herself and kept going. Tired, so tired she wanted to drop and crawl under a leaf. He'd find her. He always found her.*

Her body shook as though with the ague. She'd done too much in the last couple of days, seen too much, and allowed her heart to open and feel. It was too much. She didn't want to care for the mother who'd left her to suffer in a house covered in snow, or for the child who was so like Katherine had once been. Before all the darkness, the pain, the hate.

No more, she needed to get back to her safe place below the water. The demons couldn't find her there. She and Edith would go home tomorrow, but she needed to get through the night at Brock and Zana's. What would they think if they saw her shaking as she was now? It would never do for them to know of her flaw, her ailment.

"Edith," she called. She cringed at the weakness and fear infused in her voice. "I need my medicine."

~ * ~

"I'm sorry to have spoiled your planned dinner last night, but I fear the trip has been too much for me." Katherine dabbed at her nose with a fancy handkerchief. "Plus, these detestable pollens in the air are upsetting my sinuses."

Zana had to admit, the redness of Katy's nose and eyes proved her discomfort. She'd been let down and concerned when Edith called and said they'd have to skip dinner, and anxious to arrive at the cottage this morning. Katy was up and on the sofa with a blanket wrapped around her legs. "Don't you worry about dinner. I'm concerned about you. Don't you think we should call the doctor in to have a look at you? Dr. Boone is very capable. He could give you something to control your discomfort."

She patted Zana's hand. "I'm sure he is, but I'll see my regular doctor when I return to Abyss. Plus, my symptoms will likely disappear after I'm home a few days. I'm afraid we'll have to cut our visit short."

"When do you plan to leave?" Disappointment assailed her. She'd so enjoyed having Katy here, but her daughter's health was of major concern. Her allergy problems made sense. Why hadn't they considered the possibility and asked the doctor for something prior to her trip? Well, it was too late now but something they could remember for next time.

"I've called Samuel and the craft will be here in the morning for us." She took Zana's hand and squeezed before dropping it. "I'm so sorry. I know you're disappointed. I am too." She smiled. "I must say I've had a much better time than I expected." Laughing, she held up a hand. "Now, don't take offense. I truly didn't know what to expect to find here. It's a tad more civilized than I'd imagined."

"Thought we ran around naked wearing leaves and living in straw huts, huh?"

"Well, not that primitive, but close." She chuckled. "Though, I'd still be worried about the pirates and wild animals."

Zana wondered if everyone in Abyss thought of them as extremely backward. A little research would eliminate that misconception.

"That's understandable, but it rarely happens and we are prepared."

"I can see that and though we don't have wild animals in Abyss, I guess it's possible we could be attacked by pirates or other settlements. Of course, we do have a massive military system, one that Samuel trained with before becoming governor." She preened. "So, we're well prepared."

"Of course you are. Abyss is a major power in the world today." And, they were, but just not the ideal place for everyone.

"Do you think you'll feel up to dinner with us tonight? We can have it early if that will help."

"Yes, I'm looking forward to seeing your home and don't want to leave without visiting it."

~ * ~

Brock seemed to have no trouble carrying her up the steps. She could hear Katy chatting and the bass rumble of Brock's response. Zana waited for them with the door open.

When Brock set Katy on her feet, Zana placed a kiss on her cheek. "Welcome to our home, Katherine." She looked behind them. "Where's Edith?"

"She said she wanted to stay at the cottage and pack. I think she didn't want to impose on our little family dinner."

Zana was disappointed. She liked the woman. "That's a shame. I feel as though she's family."

Katherine studied her daughter. What an odd comment. Surely she didn't know Edith's true identity. No, if her mother suspected, she'd have given Katy the first degree.

Shelia bounced to a halt in front of her. "Hey, Katherine. Wanna see my room?" Tonight the child wore her hair down. It formed curls around her face accenting her beautiful eyes.

She couldn't resist a smile. "Maybe later, child."

Katherine stood for a minute in the entryway and looked around the room. It was spacious, larger than living areas in Abyss, and tastefully decorated. Though the walls and ceilings weren't straight, the room's interior looked nothing like a cave. The floor was smooth and polished. A beautiful rug in Earth tones covered the area in front of the sofa.

"Your home is very nice, Brock Callahan. Nothing like I expected."

He grinned, looking much like the wicked pirate she believed he was. "Thought we lived in a primitive cave, huh? One with a dirt floor, bats, and a fire pit to cook over."

"I did no such thing. Your daughter described her home to me. Of course, children tend to elaborate." But

Shelia hadn't fully captured the uniqueness of their home. Katherine looked forward to seeing the other rooms.

"I'm glad you approve."

Shelia took her arm and helped her to a stuffed chair while Brock and Zana returned to the kitchen. "Here you go." The chair was low and Katherine sank into its softness. She would need help getting out.

Shelia plopped down on the arm of the chair, legs stretched out in front of her crossed at the ankles, and flung her arm across the back totally at ease. It must be a favorite spot for her. If she feared Katherine resented her closeness, she didn't show it. The cheeky child was secure in her environment. Katherine admired the trait in her.

"Told you, didn't I?"

"Yes, child, you did indeed."

Zana called from the kitchen. "Dinner will be ready shortly. How about a glass of wine?"

"I'd love one."

Brock brought her a glass and she sipped appreciatively. It had a lovely flavor. She closed her eyes as the liquid slid down her throat.

"I wish I could have a little glass, but they won't let me have one."

Katherine's eyes popped open at Shelia's comment. She couldn't resist a chuckle. "I suspect they don't want you to be an alcoholic by the time you're thirteen."

She snorted sounding much like her father. "Pooh, one little glass isn't going to hurt me."

"So you say, but it's your parents' decision, not yours."

"Yeah, yeah, I hear that a lot."

"Shelia, help Katy to the table, please."

Katherine sat her wine on the side table and rocked in the chair trying to gain enough momentum to stand, but gave up and settled back. "Give me your hands, Shelia." With Shelia's help, she stood and walked with her to the table.

"This looks wonderful. You've outdone yourself."

"Zana made your favorite meal from when you were little—meatloaf with mashed potatoes. And the bread is homemade." Shelia beamed. "She let me knead it."

Katherine hadn't had meatloaf in seventy-five years. It wasn't a dish her adoptive family enjoyed and for some reason, she'd never prepared it for her own family. She'd never asked Leona or Edith to prepare it either. Odd. Maybe she'd not wanted to be reminded of the past. She glanced up to find Zana watching her, waiting for her response. If she waited for nostalgic tears, she had a long wait.

"Thank you, Zana. I'm surprised you remembered."

Voice choked, Zana retorted, "How could I ever forget, Katy?"

~ * ~

"Oh, Lord, what is wrong with me?" Zana swiped at her mouth with the wet washcloth she'd soaked with cold water. She pushed away from the toilet bowl and hadn't fully risen when the heaving began again. Clutching the cold porcelain, she endured the dry heaves that racked her body. What little she'd eaten earlier had long since been flushed away.

Ten minutes passed before she felt well enough to

get up and prepare for her day. She brushed her teeth and rinsed her mouth. Thank goodness Brock had taken Shelia down the hill with him when he'd left. That's all she needed—trying to explain to Shelia why she'd been throwing up again today. Yesterday had been hard enough. It was awkward to have a child standing over you while you puked, but to have to answer questions too made the experience worse. She remembered Katy behaving the same way when Zana had been pregnant with Jonathan. Yesterday she'd convinced Shelia something she'd eaten hadn't agreed with her. That story wouldn't fly two days in a row.

Zana smiled to herself as she gathered a towel and washcloth for her shower. She turned on the water, hung her robe on a hook on the wall, and stepped under the warm spray. The water soothed her tense muscles, the ones she'd used by bending over the toilet. As she lathered and rinsed the suds away, she thought about telling Brock their news. It was time to see Dr. Boone. She didn't need the doctor to tell her she was pregnant, but Brock would want reassurances she and the baby were in good health. She couldn't wait to tell Brock. He'd be pleased. When they told Shelia, she'd be thrilled.

For a moment, apprehension flitted through her mind. What would Katy think? A normal daughter under common circumstances would be happy, but Katy wasn't a typical daughter and the situation was anything but ordinary. Her child was a bitter, eighty-four year old woman. Proof was obvious from her behavior at dinner last week the night before she left for Abyss. Though she'd admitted to loving Jonathan, Katy hadn't seemed at all grieved he was dead. Of course, she'd had seventy-five years to get past his death. Her jealousy during childhood had been palatable.

Emotion clogged her throat and left an ache in her chest. Finding Katy had given her closure and eased her pain of loss somewhat. She loved Katy, but if she didn't welcome this child Zana would be disappointed in her.

Was having more children a means of trying to replace Jonathan or for that matter capturing what she'd lost with Katy? No, she didn't believe so. She wanted a family for Brock, Shelia, and for herself. And if Katy wanted to be a part of that family, Zana would be thrilled. If she didn't, she'd be very disappointed but would deal with it. The fact that she was a grandmother and a great-grandmother still amazed her. It was a thrill, a gift she cherished. Several times she'd noted Samuel reminded her of someone. Why she hadn't connected his likeness to herself, or for that matter, Daniel's, she didn't know. They both had David's blue eyes, though Daniel's were more gray in color, they had her skin and hair. She chuckled. Daniel was such a cutie, a precious child. Samuel was doing a great job parenting the little boy.

She'd better get a move on or she'd be late. After she picked up Shelia at school they'd go by the clinic so she could see Dr. Boone. Of course she'd have to stall Shelia's questions. The child was sharp as a tack but surely she didn't know the symptoms of pregnancy.

At the front door, she sealed the panel and waited for the men in the guard tower to signal her they were watching. Though there were no recent threats on her life, Brock insisted she remain under surveillance. Being observed gave her confidence as she made her way down the long steps. Just in case, she patted her pocket to make sure she had her weapon and felt the bulge. One of the guards waved and she started down the steps.

After her morning working at the winery, Zana met Shelia in front of the school.

Shelia was full of questions when Zana informed her they were going by the clinic. "Well, if you're not sick, why do you have to go?"

A slight wind blew making the air feel cooler. Zana pulled her jacket closed and zipped it up. "Because, sometimes women need to go for checkups and make sure they're healthy."

"Daddy doesn't go unless he's sick or gets a cut like when Rafael cut his belly."

Zana sighed. "Okay, look, you know how your friend's baby brother has his private parts on the outside of his body?"

Shelia cocked an eyebrow and gave an unenthused nod.

"Well, some of a woman's private parts are inside her body and she'd can't always tell if everything is okay or not. The doctor has to take a look. It's best if she has a checkup once a year."

Her eyes rounded and her mouth fell open. The child's expression of aversion made Zana want to laugh out loud, but she coughed into her hand to cover it up.

"You've got to be kidding me. That's the most disgusting thing I've ever heard." She shuddered. "Just thinking someday I'll have that monthly thing is bad enough... No way is a doctor lookin' at me down there." She stomped ahead down the road to the clinic. Zana hurried to catch up.

"Don't you want to get married and have children

some day?"

"Not if I have to go through that." She shook her head. "Uh-uh. No way." She rounded on Zana. "Does Daddy know girls have to go through that?"

"Yes. Beings he's been married and has a child, I'm sure he does."

"Why hasn't he told me? He doesn't keep things from me and the doctor's never tried to look at me there before."

"Your father hasn't told you because there hasn't been a need. You're not old enough to worry about it. The only reason I'm telling you today is because you asked me why we're going to the clinic."

Shelia visibly relaxed. "Whew! Thank goodness." As they walked, it appeared she was mulling the information over in her mind. "Do you reckon Janie knows about this?"

"I don't know, but it's not your place to tell her. Her mother will talk to her when she thinks it's necessary. Do you understand? You are not to mention it."

"Oh, okay. Gee, can't a girl share nothing with her friends?" She kicked at the dirt in the road.

"This discussion is just between you and me. Of course, you can tell your father if you want."

"What fun would that be? He already knows."

Yes, indeed he did.

When they entered the clinic, Shelia darted off to visit with some children she knew in the waiting room. It took only a minute for Zana to be taken back to an examination room. Some things hadn't changed in the past seventy-five years. She peed in a cup, undressed, and put on the examination robe. The routine reminded her of the one she'd gone through back when she'd been pregnant with Katy and Jonathan.

The nurse came back, big smile on her face, and made sure Zana was comfortable.

"Well, am I pregnant?"

"I'm afraid I'm not allowed to say. Dr. Boone will be in shortly." Before she closed the door, the little man bustled through in.

"Well, well, well, Mrs. Callahan. I see congratulations are in order. I'd say in approximately eight months you'll have an addition to the family."

Joy exploded inside her.

"Really, I'm pregnant?"

"Yes, indeedy, you are. Would you like to know the sex?"

"You can tell all that from a urine specimen?"

"Yes, it's amazing what bodily fluids can tell us today. We know your heart, lungs, kidneys, bladder, pancreas, spleen, liver, and gall bladder are healthy which considering what you've been through is phenomenal."

She sighed with relief. The health of her organs would play a major factor in her pregnancy. Dr. Boone had announced her fit and healthy when she'd seen him before marrying Brock, but having it reinforced added another ounce of happiness to her already joyful mood. Did she want to know the baby's sex? It didn't really matter, but yes, she wanted to know.

Dr. Boone waited, one eyebrow raised in question. Her wide grin must have given him his answer. "You're having a boy."

Tears filled Zana's eyes and she bit her lip to keep her lips from trembling and blubbering out loud.

"Now, now, none of that. Can't handle tears even if they're happy tears. Save them for Brock. Now lie back and let me check things inside and see if everything is as it should be."

In the waiting room, she collected Shelia and they headed for the front gate and home. Shelia kept shooting her sideways looks. "Why're you grinnin' like that?"

Zana stopped on a step leading up to the cave and tried to wipe the expression from her face but couldn't. She turned to Shelia, grabbed her in a tight hug.

Shelia squealed. "I can't breathe! What's wrong with you, Zana?"

"Something wonderful. As soon as your father gets home, I'll tell you."

Twenty-Six

"I need you to strip the sheets off the beds so we can wash them. Can you do that for me?"

Shelia mumbled, "I guess so."

"Thank you. I'll be fixing us something to eat in the meantime."

"Good, I'm starving." The child was always hungry. She needed new clothes as she had about outgrown her old ones.

"Change out of your school clothes first."

She could hear Shelia's grumbling from her bedroom as she opened and closed storage units. Zana keyed in a message to Brock. She struggled between telling him about the baby now and waiting until he came home for dinner. No, she couldn't wait. Her note was short and sweet. *We're pregnant.* Grinning, she went into the kitchen to make sandwiches and put the leftover soup from the day before on the instant burner to heat.

Zana heard the hum of the device called the laundry center. Good. Today Shelia wasn't dragging her feet on getting her chores done. The piece of equipment used a minimum of water, but items came out smelling fresh and spotless. It used energy waves to make soil release its hold on fabrics. During the wash cycle, the released dirt was swept away so it couldn't re-attach itself to the fibers. Within thirty minutes, the sheets would be ready to put back on the beds.

She had four sandwiches made and three bowls of soup on the table when the front door whooshed open and Brock's voice roared through the room. "Zana, Zana! Where are you?" His heavy boots pounded across the rock floor. She met him in the dining room. From the look of him, hair windblown and without his coat, he'd run all the way home. Winded, he took deep breaths. "Is it true? You weren't teasing me, were you?"

Shelia came into the room. "Is what true? What're you doing home, Daddy? Where's your coat?" She folded her arms across her chest. "You'd be fussin' at me something fierce for going out in the cold without one."

He looked down at his chest in confusion. "Must've forgotten it." He looked up and his eyes pleaded with Zana. "Tell me."

Grinning, she nodded. "Yes, it's true." She ran into his arms and clasped him around the neck. "Are you happy?"

He held her tight and voice thick, whispered against her neck, "Oh God, sweetheart. I'm the happiest man on Earth." He stepped back and grinned like a fool. "I can't believe it." Grabbing her face with both hands, he kissed her, and then lifted her into his arms and spun around in a circle.

"Stop it. You're making me dizzy. I'll be hugging the toilet bowl again."

"Oops, sorry, we don't want that." He set her on her feet.

Shelia propped her fists on her hips. "What's going on?"

Brock rushed to his daughter and scooped her into his arms. "You're going to have a brother or sister in about…" He looked to Zana.

"Eight months. And it's a brother."

"A boy, a little baby boy for you to help Zana take care of. What do you think about that, pumpkin?" Brock's entire face was a mask of joy. If he grinned any wider, his mouth would chip but she was thrilled to see him so happy.

Shelia narrowed her eyes and thought a second. "Well, I don't know. Janie's baby brother sure makes a mess in his diapers and it stinks something awful." She shook her head. "I think I'll pass on changing diapers unless they're just wet, but Janie says you have to watch for his little tee tee thing as it'll start squirting all of a sudden and get you wet everywhere."

Brock threw his head back and roared with laughter. "Janie's right. Zana and I'll take diaper duty. There'll be lots of other ways you can help." He hugged Shelia before setting her back on her feet. "Are you pleased a baby is coming into our family?"

She looked indignant that he'd ask such a stupid question. "Of course. Haven't I always told you I wanted a brother or sister?"

"Yes, but you're not acting too overjoyed right now."

"Well, gee Daddy, today has been trying. I've learned icky stuff about being a woman and before I can get used to all that, I find out I'm about to be a sister. Again! That's a lot for a girl to take in."

Brock looked from Shelia to her. She tried to swallow her chuckles, but a giggle escaped. "Let's sit down and eat before the soup gets cold."

When they were seated, Brock reached for her hand. "Are you feeling okay?"

"I've had some morning sickness, pretty bad the last couple of days, but it will pass."

Shelia blurted, "Ah ha, that's why you were pukin' in the bathroom yesterday."

"That's right, but it's normal to be sick in the mornings sometimes."

Shelia nodded and went back to her soup. "Yeah, Janie's mom was sick too." After a couple of sips, she looked at her daddy. "Dr. Boone had to look at Zana's inside privates today." Brock froze, spoon in midair.

She cocked her head at Zana. "Is that how he could tell you were gonna have a baby?"

"Partly. But, he did a test too. From them he could tell my organs were healthy."

Shelia quirked an eyebrow. "Daddy, how come you haven't told me all this woman stuff? You do know about it, don't you?"

Brock actually blushed. It was a good thing the big man had married, as he'd have had a difficult time explaining some things to his daughter. He cleared his throat. "There wasn't any need to tell you right now. I planned to tell you when you got a little older, say like forty."

Shelia's mouth fell open. "Forty? That's way too old."

"I'm teasing you, brat. It's a good thing we have Zana now so she can keep you informed on all the girl stuff."

"Yeah, I wanted to see if Janie knows about those inside parts but Zana said I couldn't mention them to her that it was her mother's place to tell her." She rolled her lips out and popped them back in. "I sure would like to discuss this with her though."

Brock cringed and Zana took pity on him. "When you're older you girls can sit around and discuss it, but now is not the time." Actually, since Janie's mother had a new baby, Janie might know all about a female's intricate reproductive system, but Zana didn't dare mention that fact to Shelia. The child would make a mad dash to her friend's house for a chat.

Shelia grinned and bounced in her chair. "What're we going to name the baby?"

Brock scratched his chin. "Let's see…how about Calhoon?" He snapped his finger. "No. How about Rufus?"

"Daddy, those names stink. As soon as I finish eating I'll start making a list."

He laughed. "You do that, but no sissy names, you hear."

~ * ~

Brock couldn't wait to tell his friends and crew about the baby, but before word got out, Zana needed to tell Katy and Samuel. Of course, if the two found out via the grapevine, it wouldn't be the end of the Earth, but his wife wanted to share the news with them personally. He understood her reasoning. They needed to hear the news from her. She'd notify them this afternoon while he was at work. He and the crew were performing routine maintenance checks on *Retriever*. It was hard to keep his mind on the task at hand. His imagination ran wild, wandered to Zana big with child, or Zana holding their child while she breast fed the infant. Oh, Lordy, why did his body harden with need at that picture?

Another imagine floated in front of him. Shelia changing the baby's diaper and him peeing in her face. He could hear Shelia's screech of panic. A loud hoot rumbled from his belly and out his mouth. It bounced off the wall in the service bay. Everyone stopped what they were doing and stared at him.

"What the heck's so funny?" asked Digger.

"Yeah," added Luke. "Share it with us. We could use a good laugh."

"Ah, sorry guys. Nothing's particularly funny. I'm just happy."

Brock didn't miss the looks that passed between the men or the smiles and nods they exchanged. It wouldn't surprise him if the whole community had it figured out by sunup.

After work, Shelia met him at the door with a two-page list of names. She waved it in front of his face.

"Let me shower and change clothes. We'll look at them over dinner."

"Well, hurry up."

Zana led her away from the bedroom door, their voices fading as they walked back toward the kitchen. "Honey, you know we have eight months to pick a name, don't you?"

"Well, yeah, but I want to get used to calling him by his name. You know, so it'll become familiar." She had a point.

"How'd you like the names Shelia came up with?" Shelia was in bed. He and Zana sat on the sofa enjoying a cup of hot cocoa. Wine would be out for the next year or so. He had no doubt Zana would want to breast feed their baby and not want alcohol in her system. Her head cradled on his shoulder, Brock stroked her arm marveling in its softness.

"I did, especially Brandon and Garth. What about you?"

"There were probably ten I could live with, including those two. I'm glad she's taking an interest and is excited about the baby. I expected she would be, but you never know about kids." She rolled to face him and he turned to tuck her closer, his hand caressing her hip.

"She's a good kid, Brock, kind, and loving. You've done a good job raising her."

"Thank you, sweetheart. I'm so glad you're here now to tell her about all about a woman's inside parts." He couldn't resist a chuckle.

"Glad to help."

"How did Samuel and Katy take the news?"

"Samuel was thrilled and raved on and on about how I should have the baby in Abyss where they had excellent medical care, yada, yada…."

Brock stiffened. "Abyss? Do you want to have him there?"

"No, Dr. Boone is perfectly capable of delivering our baby and providing all the care we need. This is home and where he'll be born."

Brock sighed with relief and snuggled her closer. "Good. As long as you're comfortable with the medical treatment you'll receive here, this is where I want us to be when he's born."

Yes, Abyss had state-of-the-art facilities, but the hospital here was capable of taking care of most all situations. No, they wouldn't do brain surgery or organ transplants, but their staff was well trained in pre-natal, delivery, and post-natal care. If Zana needed treatment not available here before or after delivery with the diagnoses equipment Dr. Boone had at his disposal, he'd see the need and move her to Abyss.

"What about Katy? Was she excited?"

Brock felt Zana's body tense, knew something was wrong before she spoke.

"I don't think so."

Damn the old woman. She was a self-centered individual. He'd thought possibly she'd changed, especially after her improved attitude while visiting, but evidently he was wrong. "Did she say why?"

"No, she mouthed all the platitudes. It was the tone, the lack of emotion that alerted me. I'm afraid Katy is a sick individual. You know, one of those amoral types who are only concerned with themselves, their own wants and needs."

~ * ~

"Are you sure you feel up to this trip, sweetheart?" Brock had been particularly solicitous since learning of her pregnancy as if afraid at any minute something would happen to her and the baby. His worry was misguided and related to his fear of losing those he loved. The man believed he was jinxed. No amount of reasoning seemed to sway him. Her big, strong warrior husband would stand toe-to-toe with his worst enemy and fight to the death, but the idea of losing another loved one unmanned him. Loved one? Hmm, he wouldn't admit to loving her, but he did care. Not for just the baby, but her too.

He stood beside Zana on the deck of *Retriever*. It was dark, the only light the moon reflecting off the water. Winter was upon them. Cold air blew in off the ocean. Zana wore a long water resistant, hooded coat. It kept her warm, but her face felt the bite of the icy sea spray.

They were on their way to Abyss to see Katy, Samuel, and Daniel. Katy had called back the morning after Zana told her about the baby and apologized if her lack of enthusiasm had dampened Zana's excitement. Katy had been so surprised by the news, she'd been practically speechless. Zana could understand. After all, she'd only been married two months and it must have been a shock for an adult to hear her parent was pregnant. She grinned. Lord knows, as a young woman, she'd have been horrified to learn her mother was going to have a baby.

"I feel fine." And, she did. It'd been four months since she'd learned about the baby. Her morning sickness was gone. Now she wanted to eat everything in sight and sleep half the day away. She knew that too would pass. Determined to stick with a routine, she continued to work a half-day at the winery. Due to the icy weather and fear she'd fall, Brock walked her to work every morning, and Shelia held her arm as they traversed the steps home at noon. She fussed about being coddled. Brock threatened to put handrails beside the stairway, which would be safer, but ruin the natural ambiance of the mountainside. Both helped her at home, so she got plenty of rest. Dr. Boone praised her progress.

She laid a hand on her slightly rounded belly. It was hard to tell by looking at her she was entering the sixth month of pregnancy. Because of her height, at nine months with Katy and Jonathan, she'd appeared to be only seven months along. Her body camouflaged her condition until later pregnancy. "This may be my only chance to visit them before Ethan is born."

They'd named their baby, Ethan James. Shelia deemed it a strong masculine name. They'd all agreed Ethan James Callahan sounded perfect. "Before long I'll not want to venture far from home." She patted the arms that surrounded her from behind. "I'm fine, so stop your fussing."

"Yes, ma'am, but promise me you won't overdo."

"I promise. Katy and Mrs. Joseph will keep Shelia busy while we're there. I can visit with Katy while you tend to any pressing trade business."

"Let's go to bed." Chuckles rising from his chest vibrated against her back. "Shelia's already asleep so you two won't be able to laugh at my expense."

~ * ~

"Come in, Zana," called Katy. She'd yet to call her Mother, but Zana tried to understand. If the situation were reversed, she might feel the same way. But the omission still hurt. Katy was in her chair, more cheerfully dressed than usual in an olive green pant suit. A large amber pin adorned the lapel of the jacket and emphasized her eyes.

Brock and Shelia followed her across the room. She bent and kissed Katy on the cheek. "You look lovely today. That color makes your eyes sparkle."

Her face lit with delight. "Why thank you, dear."

Shelia squeezed past Zana, leaned in, and enfolded Katy in an embrace. She squeezed. Her fondness for Katy touched Zana. The child loved easily. "Hey, Katherine? We're having a brother. Isn't that neat?"

"Lands, child. You're going to squeeze the stuffing out of me." She awkwardly patted Shelia on the back. "Yes, yes, I know all about Ethan James."

Shelia stood up and grinned. "I guess you're too old to change diapers and stuff. Because you're my sister, I'll do your share."

Katy stiffened and dropped her chin. "I've not forgotten how to change diapers, young lady. That big man over there, your uncle, messed up his share." She sniffed. "But, I suppose I won't be around much with ya'll so far away. I'll concede my share of dirty britches to you."

Shelia turned to Zana. "What does concede mean?"

"To acknowledge defeat, to give into."

Katy looked up at Brock. "I don't want a hug or kiss from you. A hello will suffice."

Brock grinned, his eyes lit with mischief. He leaned down. "I think I want to kiss you right on the mouth, Katherine."

Her daughter looked horrified and pushed back as far as the chair would allow. "Don't you dare." Zana couldn't contain her laughter. The banter between the two made her happy.

Inches from her face, he winked. "Hello, Katherine."

She tried to swallow her chuckle and sputtered. "Go sit down over there, you scoundrel. You, too, Zana. Shelia, pull that chair up beside me." Shelia did as told and emulated Katy's posture as she sat. Katy looked around the room. "Samuel, where's my kiss and my grandson?"

Samuel came through the kitchen door, his hand on Daniel's back. The child had found the cookies and his face was smeared with powdered sugar. "Hi, Nana. You make good cookies."

"Come here, precious." She kissed him on each

cheek. "Your daddy used to say the same thing." She winked at Samuel. "And back then I did indeed bake them myself."

Zana watched Katy in amazement. Her daughter appeared to have morphed into a likeable old woman, one with the ability to charm. Maybe it was the added attention she'd been getting of late. She'd stayed busy attending her ladies meetings. It's possible her bitterness had stemmed from loneliness.

"Leona, come in here, please," Katy called from her throne. A dark haired woman, probably as old as Katy came into the room. Edith came in behind her carrying a tray with coffee and snacks. She bustled around them setting out cups and plates. Leona placed her hand on Katy's chair back and waited. "Zana, I want you to meet Leona Juarez, my sister. Leona, this is my mother, Zana Forrester Callahan."

Zana stood, her eyes glued to the woman who stared back at her with an emotion she couldn't identify. She considered embracing her, but Zana's instinct told her the gesture wouldn't be welcome. Instead she extended her hand. "Hello, Leona. I'm pleased to meet you."

Leona took her hand in a firm grip. "Thank you, ma'am. It's good to meet you at last." Zana didn't know what else to say so returned to her seat. She wanted to ask if Katy ever talked about her when growing up but doubted her daughter would appreciate the intrusion into her past life.

"Samuel, pull up a couple more chairs for Edith and Leona."

He did as she bid and after pouring coffee and serving everyone cookies and sandwiches, Leona and

Edith sat down. Zana regard it as odd for Katy to have her sister working as a servant in her home. Maybe Leona needed the money and Katherine considered it a way to help her financially.

Curious, Zana asked, "Leona, are you younger or older than Katy?"

Leona exhaled and appeared to relax. "I'm older. When Katy came to live with us I was eleven years old. Edith, our baby sister, hadn't been born yet."

Stunned at Leona's comment, Zana looked at Samuel to see if he was aware Edith was his aunt. The color drained from his face. His jaw dropped, and then he snapped his mouth shut. The muscle in his jaw jumped as he gritted his teeth. Color rose from his neck and infused his face and ears. Zana leaned over and touched his arm. He physically shook himself, patted her hand, and set it aside.

"Mother, you astound me. What else have you kept from me all these years? Do I have brothers and sisters hidden away somewhere? Next I'll learn my entire life has been a lie." He stood up and hovered over her chair, his face in hers. "Am I even your son?"

Shelia for once apparently realized the seriousness of the adult's conversation and didn't interrupt. Her eyes were round as she looked from Samuel to Katherine. She moved from her chair beside Katherine's to sit cross-legged on the floor and pulled Daniel onto her lap. With a cookie in each hand he was content. Thank goodness for Shelia's intuitiveness.

Hand on her son's chest, Katherine pushed Samuel out of her face. "Of course you are. Don't you have your daddy's blue eyes? And that dimple of yours and your dark hair, you got from my side of the family."

She sneered. "And no, you do not have any brothers or sisters. You think I'd be that callous?"

"Why shouldn't I?" He pushed away from the chair and paced. "You're a piece of work, Mother. All these years I've had two aunts. I was lonely all my childhood, longed for relatives." He flung out his hands. "Don't tell me…I have a couple of cousins I never knew about, too."

Leona spoke. "No, Samuel, though Edith and I submitted to selective mating and married, unfortunately we were unable to have children."

"But why didn't I know about you and Edith? Hell, I even have uncles I've never met." He turned back to Katherine. "Why the hell did you keep all this from me, Mother?"

"Watch your language if you please. It's disrespectful to me and there are children present."

Sure enough, the anger in his father's voice caught Daniel's attention. He looked up, eyes round with alarm. "No fuss, Daddy. You loud."

Samuel picked up his son and patted his back. "I'm sorry, son." He carried him to the dining table and set him on his feet. "Let's find your art supplies. Shelia, you want to come and draw with Daniel?"

Shelia frowned. Obviously she'd prefer to stay to hear the outcome of the adult's conversation, but a nod from Brock had her rising to her feet. "Oh, all right. I'm coming."

When Samuel rejoined them, Katherine took another sip of her coffee and set it aside. She leaned back in the chair, her chin dropped to her chest. "I married above my social status. Your father had an image to uphold here. He was next in line for governor." Hand trembling, she raised it to fondle the broach on her jacket. "He let me bring Leona and Edith to Abyss as long as I never revealed they were related to me."

"Tell the boy the truth, Katherine," said Leona. "You were the one who needed the prestige and didn't want the society folks to know you were the daughter of a poor farmer from Columbia. You could never have passed us off as part of the upper class."

"We weren't that poor, Leona," said Edith. "We always had food, were given a basic education, but had none of the polish of the ruling class of Abyss. Not that Katherine did either, but under Mr. Whiteside's tutelage, she adapted quickly. Of course, over the years living here, some rubbed off on us, but Leona and I were never at ease socializing." She nodded at Katherine. "Katherine took to it like a natural. After several months you'd never have known she wasn't born wearing those fancy clothes. She enjoyed the parties, attending the ladies clubs, and such." She shook her head. "I was very young when we moved here. When Leona married, I lived with her and her husband until a mate was selected for me. Leona and I both preferred quiet activities and avoided the crowd of which Katherine became a part. Having a job, even if we worked hard every day, is what made us happy."

Leona nodded. "That's true. Of course we were grateful to get away from Columbia and have Katherine to thank for making that possible." She cleared her throat and shoulders hunched, glanced from Katherine to Edith. "Our life was far from pleasant there. Other circumstances made leaving Columbia necessary, especially for Katherine."

"You've said enough, sister," said Katherine, hazel eyes narrowed in command. Zana wished she'd allow Leona to continue. What had happened in Katherine's life to cause her to have to leave Columbia?"

"But—" Samuel shook his head and sat back down.

"No buts," added Edith. "Samuel, you might think your mother did us a disservice, but we were much better off here than we would have been at home."

Katherine interrupted. "Samuel, I was young but feel I did the best I could at the time. I can see I was wrong to keep you from knowing your aunts. For that I'm sorry."

"You can't know what kind of environment we all came from," said Edith. "And now's not the time to talk about it. But know this, Leona and I were always around and would have come to your aid if you'd needed us. We love you and Daniel very much."

Samuel's face twisted. "I missed out on so much." His eyes pierced his mother. "Why now, Mother? What's happened to make you reveal all your secrets? Lord, there's not more is there?"

Katherine's voice was strained. "No, this is everything. What's changed? My mother and I have been reunited and I felt it was time. Please forgive me, Samuel." Her eyes implored his.

He shook his head. "I don't know, Mother. I need time." He waved a hand between Leona and Edith. "What about your sisters? Shouldn't you be asking their forgiveness, too?"

"No. I've never lied to them or kept you from them. They're fully aware of all my sins."

Twenty-Seven

Brock didn't know what to think about Katherine's revelations. That'd she'd used her sisters as domestics was bad enough, but to have kept their relationship secret from Samuel was criminal. Children needed their family to help them through the trials of life. Samuel hadn't mentioned having close friends here in Abyss. How had he turned out as well as he had? Maybe his father had filled that emptiness. Until now, Shelia hadn't had family, but she'd had the love and support of all of his friends.

Zana stood up. "Let me clear these dishes and take them to the kitchen. I'm sure you're tired, Katy." Edith had left and they'd sat around, the conversation subdued. Shelia and Daniel still sat at the dining room table intent on their coloring. Their friendly chatter filled the background. Shelia's patience with the boy pleased him. She'd be a good sister.

"No need, dear. Leona will get them before we go to bed. She's staying here with me full time now." She pushed herself out of the chair. "Come into my bedroom with me. I want to show you some pieces of jewelry you might like."

Shelia's ears picked up on the word jewelry. "Can me and Daniel come too?"

"Yeah, Nana. Me too?"

"Not right now, children. I'll show you another

time." She took Zana's arm and they left the room. Zana had been in such a joyful mood earlier in the evening. After Katherine's confessions, she'd been subdued, her concern and disappointment evident. Maybe time alone with her daughter would cheer her.

He and Samuel sat, enjoying the chatter of the children.

"Nana's got lots of pretties, Sheda. I gets to wear 'um sometimes."

"Cool. You reckon she'll let me wear some?"

"Don't know."

Brock chuckled at the expression on Samuel's face. "Putting on a little jewelry isn't going to warp him."

Samuel grinned. "Yeah, I guess you're right."

"Nana's gots new pets."

The word 'pets' both startled Brock and reminded him he'd never talked to Samuel about the incident with the glass tank.

"Last time we were here Sheila mentioned your mother had an aquarium where she keeps her pets. What kind of pets does she have anyway?"

Brows furrowed, Samuel said, "You know, I don't have any idea. I've never seen them. She didn't have them when I was at home."

"Shelia said Daniel tried to pick one of them up and Katherine got real upset and spanked Daniel."

"What?" He looked over at the kids and lowered his voice. "Mother knows I don't approve of corporal punishment."

"I'm sorry. I should have gotten in touch and filled you in, but before we knew it Katherine was in Refuge and she kept us busy. Then we got the news about the baby." He shrugged. "Zana was really upset about the spanking. We discussed it and thought maybe Katherine was afraid Daniel would pull the tank over on him, or it would break and he'd be cut." Lord knows, he'd popped Shelia on the butt enough times when she'd gotten into something that could hurt her.

"Would you spank Daniel if you were afraid for him?"

Samuel thought for a minute. "Yeah, I probably would."

"Nana panked me," Daniel announced. He'd left the table and sidled up to Samuel, his lower lip trembled.

Samuel hugged the boy to his side. "Was Nana afraid you'd get hurt?"

He nodded.

"You know that tank is probably heavy. It could squash you if it fell on you. If it broke, the glass would cut. Nana loves you. I bet she was scared."

"He wasn't pullin' on it or nothing," said Shelia as she marched over to join them. "Just standing on that little trunk and went to open the top and reach in and pick up one."

Samuel lifted Daniel onto his lap. "Has Nana let you see her pets before?"

He nodded and shook his finger. "Nana say, 'no touch frogs. Po…sin.'"

Frogs? Posin? Brock couldn't imagine… "Do you mean poison?"

"Yeah, posin."

The hairs on the back of Brocks neck stood to attention. "What color are these frogs, Daniel?"

"Lella. They purty."

Realization hit Brock like a brick to the head.

Katherine Whiteside, Zana's own daughter wanted her mother dead. She'd attempted to kill Zana twice and come damn close the second time. Hell, no. She'd tried *three* times. Somehow she'd sent someone to Del Ara to hire Rafael to kill her. Katherine had known Zana was her mother all along and wanted her dead. The woman was crazy. His soul screamed, *Delia, the bitch killed Delia. And Pepe.* Rage consumed him to be replaced with fear for his wife.

"Holy Hell," groaned Samuel. "My mother, my own mother killed my wife." He stood with Daniel in his arms and rushed into Leona's bedroom. Brock followed ushering Shelia before him.

Startled, Leona cried out when they entered and rose from the chair in front of the small window. "What on Earth?"

"Watch the children. I'm afraid Mother is going to hurt Zana. They're in her room."

"Dear, God. Hurry. The frogs. She'll use the frogs." She wrapped her arms around the children burying their faces against her body.

They hurried to Katherine's bedroom. Brock grabbed Samuel's arm, held a finger to his lips, reached for the door panel and pushed the open button. Nothing happened. It was locked. *Damn it. They had to get inside. Adrenalin pumped through his body. He feared his heart would burst. The door would have to come down.* He took a couple of steps back and prepared to charge with his shoulder. Samuel stopped him, raised a finger to wait, and rushed back into Leona's room. He returned and keyed in a code. With a whoosh, the door slid into the pocket in the wall.

Brock's heart lodged in his throat. Both women

turned toward them. Zana stood with her hand outstretched, palm up. Katherine was seated in a straight-back chair. She held one of the two inch long Golden Dart Frogs, her hand directly above Zana's to drop it on her palm.

Brock's life, with all his insecurities and misconceptions, flashed before his eyes. He loved this woman, loved her more than he'd dreamed possible. If he lost her, admitting that love to himself or her wouldn't change the depth of his despair one iota, but not having told her would be a stab wound to his already broken heart.

"No," yelled Brock as he threw himself forward and pushed Zana out of Katherine's reach. She fell against the wall but caught herself before falling. The tiny frog hit the floor and bounced once before scurrying under the bed.

"What on Earth is wrong with you?" asked Zana as she rubbed the arm that had hit the wall. "Have you gone mad?"

Had he hurt her? He started toward her, but she evaded him.

"No, Zana." Samuel stood looking down on Katherine, his expression filled with revulsion. "My mother is the one who's mad. She tried to kill you, again. That frog has enough poison to kill ten healthy men."

Zana gasped. Her hand instinctively went to her belly.

Brock put his arm around her. "She killed Delia and Pepe, sweetheart. I'm sorry, but there is no telling how many people's lives she's taken."

"You're both wrong." She pointed at Katherine.

"She held that frog and she looks fine." She dropped to her knees in front of her daughter and would have moved closer but Brock held her back. "Tell them they're wrong, Katy."

Katherine laughed, the sound a wild rasping cackle. "You are so stupid," she screamed. "I hate you." She pounded her head with her fists. "Go away, go away." She glared at Zana, her hazel eyes distorted with hate and something else. Madness was the only way Brock could describe the transformation.

"Why couldn't you have died that day in your pod?" She cackled. "Set the medical team hopping when those alarms sounded. I couldn't get near you from then on."

She sneered. "Things were fine after you came here again, even after you learned my identity. I'd decided to give you a chance, maybe forgive you, but then you went and got yourself pregnant. Not only are you pregnant, but pregnant with a boy, another Jonathan. I was never enough, was I?" She started coughing and clutched her stomach.

Zana covered her mouth with her hands and sobbed. "Katy, my poor, Katy. Oh, God, what could I have done differently?"

Brock pulled Zana to her feet. "It's not your fault. You have to know that."

She brushed tears from her face. "Call the emergency team. There may be time to save her."

Katherine held a hand out to Samuel. "Son, I love you."

"Love me? You're kidding. You don't love anyone but yourself." He hit the wall several times with his fist. "You killed Delia, the love of my life. You took my only chance at happiness away." Face contorted with pain, he spat out, "I hate your guts. I hope your death is as painful as Delia's was."

"You don't mean that. Please, Samuel. It's the demons." She shook her fists at Zana and wailed, "They came back because of you." Her eyes pleaded with Samuel. Sobs wracking her body, she begged, "Tell me you forgive me."

"Never." He turned toward the door. The yellow frog hopped out from under the bed and stopped a short distance from Samuel's foot. He looked around for something to use to pick it up and saw a cloth napkin on a tea tray. He shook it out and bent to grab the frog.

Katherine groaned, "No!" and fell forward on top of the creature trapping it under her.

~ * ~

Katherine lay so still on the gurney. In death her features were relaxed and for just a second, Zana saw the beautiful laughing child she'd once been. Her dry eyes burned. No doubt they were swollen from the tears she'd shed all night long. Her stomach ached from the sobs that had racked her body and the retching that followed. The medicine Dr. Bartholomew prescribed helped ease her queasiness and the spasms of her stomach. If only he could relieve the pain in her heart.

She turned to Brock and buried her face against his chest. Hands warm on her back, he massaged the tense muscles. His touch gave her some comfort. Or her mind was so numb, she couldn't feel anymore.

"She's at peace, sweetheart. All those demons that haunted her, they can't hurt her anymore."

A heart-wrenching groan drew her eyes to Samuel, her grandson, as he stood on the opposite side of

Katherine's body. His face a mask of agony, deep sobs shook his body. Thrusting her own pain aside, she went to him and gathered him close. His arms surrounded her, his head dropped to her shoulder as he wept aloud. All she could do was hold him.

He pulled back and his voice cracked. "Maybe I should have forgiven her, let her die in peace." Zana understood his struggle. His pain for not forgiving his mother intensified his grief.

"Maybe you should have, Samuel. But you were hurt and weren't given the time to process your feelings. Don't beat yourself up. You did nothing but give her your love all your life." That her child could be capable of such cruelty, even commit murder without a twinge of guilt or remorse still appalled Zana. "She murdered your wife and tried to kill me, her own mother." Her chin trembled and she compressed her lips in to keep from crying again. "Katy was a monster. At one time she was a sweet little girl, spoiled perhaps, but she wasn't unkind. What could have happened to distort her mind? I know being buried under the snow and freezing must have been a terrible experience, but could it have demented her so?"

"We'll probably never know. And if we find out, I doubt it will change things one bit." Brock, always the voice of reason, placed an arm around each of them and ushered them toward the door. "She hurt you both. She's dead. Dammit, she tried to kill you four times, Zana. I know she was your daughter and your mother, Samuel, but she was an evil old woman and deserved to die. And she certainly didn't warrant your forgiveness, Samuel. If she weren't dead already, I'd take joy in strangling the life out of her."

They were already in the hall. Zana stopped. She wanted to smack Brock for his callousness. His comment caused hurt and grief rose again in her chest. She threw his arm off her shoulder and stalked down the hall. "That was an insensitive remark."

"Zana, honey, I didn't mean it to be, or to hurt you." He caught her and made her took into his face. "I'm sorry, but I can't lie to you about how I feel. She tried to kill you, not only you, but also our baby. Can you imagine how I felt when we realized she had those poisonous frogs and you were alone with her in that room?"

"He's right, Zana," said Samuel. "If we'd been thirty seconds later getting in that room, you and your child would be dead."

"I think you're exaggerating." *How could something so small be that deadly?*

Brock bellowed. "You think so?" He released her. His hand chopped up and down as he emphasized his comments. "Let me tell you exactly how deadly those little creatures are. The venom of one frog can kill ten healthy men. If a dog walks across a paper towel where a frog sat, the dog dies." He took a deep breath. "If she'd just wanted pets, she could have prevented the frogs from being deadly. But no, she fed them the little insects that made them poisonous. Her every action was premeditated."

Zana gaped at him. Was he serious? Yes, Katherine died quickly, before the emergency team arrived. She'd killed the loose frog when she fell on top of it. Zana had no doubt Katy fell on the creature to keep Samuel from picking it up. Using a napkin wouldn't have saved him. The horror of it rushed at her. She laid both hands on her belly offering what protection for her child she could at the moment. Dear, God. At least Katy did one decent thing before she died. Fatigue overwhelmed her and she sagged against Brock.

"I'm tired. Let's go. I want to see the children. They'll have questions."

His arm supported her as they walked toward the transport station. "The kids are fine, Zana. Mrs. Joseph is keeping them occupied. Leona and Edith have been in and out and I'm sure they've explained some of what's happened."

"I'm ready for them to enlighten us on some things about Katy's past." Zana was convinced they knew the basis for Katy's behavior, what demons drove her.

"Right now you need to concentrate on getting some rest. You've overdone it and this isn't good for either you or the baby." He helped her into a transporter. After several transfers, they arrived at their destination.

It was quiet at Samuel's when they stepped inside the living area. Mrs. Joseph rose, held a finger to her lips, and nodded toward the bedrooms. The poor little tykes were worn out. With all the activity at Katherine's last night, the emergency team and the community police in and out, it'd been hard for them to wind down.

Leona and Edith sat at the dining room table. Mrs. Joseph, Daniel's nanny, spoke softly. "We didn't know when you'd be back so prepared a cold lunch. Come sit down."

Zana could only nibble at the food, but the hot tea warmed her inside and eased the pounding in her head. She needed a nap but wanted to talk with Leona and Edith first. It was hard to ask, but she had to know.

"Please tell me why it was necessary for Katherine to leave Columbia."

Leona and Edith exchanged glances. Leona said, "I don't think this is the time for you to hear everything."

Brock clasped her hand. "She's right, Zana. I don't know what they have to say, but you're tired and more emotional upset isn't good for the baby."

Edith stood and came around to her chair. Hands on Zana's shoulders, she said, "Come along. Let's get you down for a nap before the kids wake up. After the service in the morning, we'll tell you everything. Okay?"

They were right. She couldn't handle another emotional revelation right now and suspected Katherine's story was filled with horrors. How else could her child be so mentally ill? "Okay. I suppose you're right. I am tired."

Tucked in bed in the guest room, she closed her eyes and tried to clear her thoughts. Images of Katy and Jonathan playing flitted through her mind. She could hear Katy's laughter and Jonathan's shrill squeal of delight as they played hide and seek in the house. They'd had so much fun. There were happy memories of little arms squeezing her neck when she tucked them in bed for naps and at night. The remembrance of Katy's, "I love you, Mommy," washed over her and tears sprang to Zana's eyes. *Oh, my babies. I love you so much. I'll never forget you.* She curled into a ball and drifted off.

Twenty-Eight

The funeral service was a spectacle. People turned out to get a look at Zana. How she managed to stand beside Samuel and accept condolences was beyond Brock's imagination. He stood at her back and occasionally she leaned against him. If it were up to him, he'd have forgone the public service for a private one. But, due to Katherine's status in the community, Samuel felt the citizens of Abyss should be able to attend.

Oddly, Leona and Edith didn't stand with the family. Samuel explained they wished to remain unidentified as Katherine's sisters until a later time. They didn't want to add to the notoriety of Katherine's death.

At last they were able to sit. After a short sermon, the choir sang and Katherine's ashes, in a jewel encrusted urn, slowly ascended in a transparent tube to be released in the ocean. Thankfully the congregation remained seated while the family left the chapel. Brock didn't think Zana could hold up much longer.

Katherine's ladies' club provided lunch for them. Several women wanted to stay and serve the food, but Samuel ushered them out the door with the excuse Zana needed to rest. Mrs. Joseph had fed the children earlier, so Brock settled Zana on the sofa with her feet up. He covered her with a light blanket and tucked it in around her. Samuel handed her a plate, and she balanced it on her belly. The rest of them gathered around in chairs and held their plates on their knees.

"The service was nice, Samuel. I guess you guys here in Abyss can do some things with class." Brock couldn't resist a little dig.

Samuel snorted. "So, we're back to running down Abyss, are we?"

"Nah, just trying to change the atmosphere around here, lighten the mood a little."

Zana chuckled. "I'm not sure that's the correct way, Brock. You and I are outnumbered here." She sat her plate on the coffee table. "Leona and Edith, I need to ask some questions."

Mrs. Joseph stood. "Let me take your plates. I'll be in the kitchen if you need me for anything, Mr. Whiteside."

Samuel nodded to the woman. "Thank you. We appreciate your help the past few days. I'll be sure and see you're paid for your time."

"Oh, no sir. I don't want to be paid for helping out." She smiled and disappeared into the kitchen with a handful of dishes.

"She'll be offended if you try to pay her," said Leona. "A thank you note will be enough. Let people do things for you. It makes them feel useful."

"Leona is right, Samuel," Zana added. She dropped her head back against the arm of the sofa and closed her eyes as if gathering her thoughts.

Brock leaned back in his chair and waited for her to begin. He knew she needed answers but dreaded what she might hear. Unable to remain apart from her, he moved to the sofa, lifted her feet, and sat with them in his lap.

She opened her eyes and looked between Leona and Edith. "Did you know about Katherine's attempt on my life?"

"No, we—"

Leona laid a hand on Edith's knee. "Let me, sister. We knew nothing about the first incident. In fact we didn't make the connection between you and Katherine until the second time you left for Refuge. She had one of her spells then and needed her medicine. The next day we learned the reason." She nodded to Zana. "That you were her mother and she planned to make you pay. Of course, we didn't realize pay meant you'd die. Now I realize her spell was a fit of rage. You were no longer accessible.

"When we heard about the candy incident, we wondered, but she professed to know nothing about it." Despite her dyed hair, today Leona looked every bit her eighty-six years and then some. Katherine's death and the revelation of her crimes had aged the woman. Brock felt sorry for her and for Edith. "We knew the frogs were poisonous, but never dreamed she'd use them to kill someone. She was always so careful, especially around Daniel."

Brock remembered Leona's shocked expression when he and Samuel visited Katherine. Had she been horrified at the possibility Katherine committed murder and might die by lethal injection? Or was it the news Delia had been murdered. At no time, however, did they mention the name of the poison or the fact that it came from the yellow tree frog. It's possible she fainted for some other reason.

Samuel, his face a death mask, asked, "What about

Delia?"

Leona slumped in her chair, her face pasty. The older woman needed to lie down. Edith stood and took both of her sister's hands. "Come, Leona, why don't you rest a while? I can finish filling in the details."

"Yes, Leona, you can rest in my room," offered Samuel.

Her smile wan, she said, "Thank you. I believe I will." Edith helped her stand. "I can manage. You stay here."

"No, I'll walk you to your room and get you comfortable. I'm afraid you're going to fall." Leona didn't argue further, but leaned on Edith's arm as they left the room.

They waited until Edith returned to her seat. "This has been particularly hard on Leona. She feels responsible for not realizing Katherine was dangerous." She sighed and turned to Samuel. "We knew Katherine objected to your marriage, disliked Delia, but after learning about the baby, she did a quick turn-around."

Samuel's elbows were propped on his knees, his hands clasped. He dropped his head and rubbed his temples. "Yes, she was thrilled about Delia's pregnancy. I thought she'd learned to love Delia, too. It was all a lie."

"I...I'm so sorry, Samuel." A tear leaked from her eye and she wiped it away with her hand. "Delia was such a dear young woman. Leona and I were fond of her. If we'd suspected Katherine intended to hurt her, we'd have told you."

"Why didn't you tell me about her spells, or whatever you call them? I could have seen that she got help?"

"She had medicine for them and made us promise not to tell you. Leona and I both visited with her doctor when she saw him. He never hinted to either of us she might need additional care."

Zana had listened quietly, but now spoke. "What happened in Columbia? Why was it necessary for Katy to leave?"

Edith studied her hands. She chewed her lips. Brock suspected she gathered courage to reveal something she'd rather keep buried. "Shortly after Katherine joined our family, our father raped her."

"Oh, dear God." Zana wailed and covered her mouth with her hand.

"He did so every opportunity he got. Katherine would run into the jungle and hide for days. Either father found her, or she'd get so hungry she came home. Prior to that, he'd abused Leona." She took a deep breath and gazed at Zana with pain-filled eyes. "I'm sorry, Zana. Leona tried to protect her, but he'd turn his attentions to her and then beat her."

"Wha…what about your…mother?" Zana shook. Brock feared she'd rattle to pieces if he touched her.

"He beat her senseless when she tried to intervene." Edith dropped her head. "When I turned nine, father decided it time to shower me with his attention."

Brock growled. "Is the man still alive?" Dumb question, Callahan. The man would be at least a hundred years old by now.

Edith shook her head. "Katherine killed our father, chopped him to pieces with a machete one night while he slept."

Epilogue

Zana lay on the sofa, her feet propped on the arm. The baby kicked her in the bladder and she rubbed her abdomen in hopes the little bugger would move to a more comfortable spot. Her pregnancy progressed smoothly and in another month Ethan would be born. Brock insisted she stay home now and rest. For once she didn't argue with him. She was as big as a horse and her ankles swollen to twice their size. They'd converted the guest room into a nursery. Shelia had insisted on an underwater scene so the walls were covered with colorful fish.

Counseling had helped her deal with the horrors Katy had suffered before leaving Columbia. Not only had her adoptive father sexually abused her, he'd terrorized her. He beat her senseless and left her in the wilderness to fend for herself. Katy's adoptive mother took the blame for killing the man, but for some reason, suspicion continued to surround Katherine. Zana felt a kinship with Leona and Edith's mother. She'd given the ultimate sacrifice for Katherine. That she loved Katy eased some of Zana's hurt. Had it soothed some of Katy's?

Zana's only consolation now was her daughter no longer suffered. As if to agree with her thinking, the baby thumped her in several places in her belly. Why, the little bugger was changing position. Now maybe she'd be more comfortable.

The front door opened. Shelia flew through the living area in a flurry of flying pigtails. She'd grown taller in the last few months. "Hey, Zana. What's for lunch?" Brock came in behind her. The door whooshed closed behind him.

"Hey, missy," said Brock. "Is that any way to greet Zana?"

Shelia stuck her head around the doorway of her room. She grinned. "Hi, Zana. How are you and Ethan today?"

"We're fine, sweetie. Thanks for asking. I've got sandwiches in the refrigerator."

Brock bent to kiss her. His big hand caressed her protruding belly. From behind his back, he brought out a package. "I got this in the mail today from Leona and Edith. They were going through Katherine's things and found this. They knew you'd want it."

Zana took the package. It was approximately ten inches square. The two older women had tried to get her to take at least some of Katy's jewelry, but Zana hadn't wanted any. They'd been close to Katy, and Zana preferred they divide it up between themselves. She had taken the Danish Modern dining room set and chartreuse dishes. Both women said their modest apartments wouldn't hold it and Samuel said he preferred what he and Delia had selected.

"Well, aren't you going to open it?" He lifted her bare feet from the sofa, sat down, and placed them in his lap.

She tore at the paper to reveal a box. She lifted the lid and moved tissue paper aside to uncover a framed photograph. Her heart stopped and for just a second she couldn't breathe. She took several deep breaths and her body calmed. The frame was sterling silver. She remembered it well. It was a family picture taken shortly before the landslide that killed her husband, Katy and Jonathan's father. Fingers shaking, she traced the features of the three smiling faces and the bow shaped mouth of the blonde baby.

Tears pricked her eyes, but they were tears of joy. Katy smiled out at her, face alight with happiness. Her child hadn't forgotten her first family and she'd cared enough to keep this picture for seventy-five years. Katy must have known how much her parents loved her. She held the likeness against her chest and smiled up at Brock.

"Katy did care." The knowledge was a soothing balm to her heart.

"Yes, she did, sweetheart."

Brock massaged one of her feet and she groaned with pleasure. She looked up to catch him looking at her, his eyes twisted with pain. Her heart jumped into her throat. "What is it, what's wrong?"

He cleared his throat. "Nothing is wrong. I'm just happy." He cradled her belly with his hands, bent over and kissed the burgeoning mass. "I love you."

She chuckled. "I think Ethan knows how you feel about him." He told him often enough and surely their unborn child could feel the love radiating around him.

Brock raised his eyes to hers. Passion blazed beneath their gray depths. "I mean you, Zana. I love you."

Her chest expanded with joy. Through his actions, she knew he cared, but hearing the words sealed her happiness. Tears blurred her vision. She reached out and cupped his cheek. "Thank you."

Voice hoarse, he whispered, "I've loved you a long time, but wouldn't admit my feelings to myself until the day Katy tried to kill you with the frog. I knew then if you died, next to losing you my greatest sorrow would be not having told you"

He took her hand and kissed her palm. "Please forgive my cowardice and tell me I haven't lost your love."

"There is nothing to forgive. You fought a battle with your soul and won. I got the prize. I'll never stop loving you, Brock Callahan."

Linda LaRoque

About the Author

Linda LaRoque is a Texas girl, but the first time she got on a horse, it tossed her in the road dislocating her right shoulder. Forty years passed before she got on another, but it was older, slower, and she was wiser. Plus, her students looked on and it was important to save face.

A retired teacher who loves West Texas, its flora and fauna, and its people, Linda's stories paint pictures of life, love, and learning set against the raw landscape of ranches and rural communities in Texas and the Midwest. She is a member of RWA, her local chapter of HOTRWA, NTRWA and Texas Mountain Trail Writers.

Linda writes contemporary western romances, time travel historical romances, women's fiction and futuristic romances.

~ * ~

Visit Linda at these locations:

www.lindalaroque.com
http://www.lindalaroqueauthor.blogspot.com
https://www.facebook.com/linda.laroque
http://www.goodreads.com/author/show/649259.Linda_LaRoque

Other Books by Linda LaRoque

Contemporary Westerns
Forever Faithful
Investment of the Heart
When the Ocotillo Bloom

Time Travel
The Way Back
My Heart Will Find Yours—The Turquoise Legacy
Book 1
Flames on the Sky—The Turquoise Legacy Book 2
Desires of the Heart—novella
A Law of Her Own—novella
A Marshal of Her Own—novella
A Love of His Own—novella
A Time of Their Own—an anthology containing A Law
of Her Own, A Marshal of Her Own, and A Love of His
Own
Birdie's Nest

Women's Fiction
Shattered Vows
Wounded Hearts—novella